DISNEY'S
PIRATES of the CARIBBEAN

Pirates of the Caribbean: The Curse of the Black Pearl
Screen Story by Ted Elliott & Terry Rossio and Stuart Beattie
and Jay Wolpert
Screenplay by Ted Elliott & Terry Rossio

Pirates of the Caribbean: Dead Man's Chest
Pirates of the Caribbean: At World's End
Based on characters created by Ted Elliott & Terry Rossio and
Stuart Beattie and Jay Wolpert
Written by Ted Elliott & Terry Rossio

Based on Walt Disney's Pirates of the Caribbean
Produced by Jerry Bruckheimer
Directed by Gore Verbinski

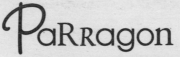

PaRRagon

Bath · New York · Singapore · Hong Kong · Cologne · Delhi · Melbourne

First published by Parragon in 2007
Parragon
Queen Street House
4 Queen Street
Bath BA1 1HE, UK

ISBN 978-1-4054-9157-0

Printed in UK

PIRATES of the CARIBBEAN

THE CURSE OF THE BLACK PEARL

Chapter 1

Young Elizabeth Swann stood at the bow of the HMS *Dauntless*, one hand resting on the rail as she sang an old pirate shanty. The *Dauntless* was one of the strongest ships in the Royal Navy. The ship was agile and fast and, for those reasons, she had been commandeered to carry Elizabeth and her father to Port Royal, where Elizabeth's father was governor.

The sailing had been smooth and clear for most of the journey. But now, a thick fog blanketed the unusually calm sea, obscuring the *Dauntless's* bowsprit and masts. As the wind whipped Elizabeth's light brown hair around her fair face, she continued to sing her shanty. She was unbothered, perhaps even entranced, by the eerie calm of the Caribbean Sea.

Suddenly, a hand clamped down on her shoulder. Startled, she quickly turned and found herself face-to-face with a member of the crew –

one Mr Joshamee Gibbs. He was an older man whose appearance seemed like a record of all the places he'd sailed to and the things he'd done and seen. His face was wrinkled and weather worn and his hair was as grey as a stormy sea. As he leaned close to Elizabeth, she could smell the strong scent of the sea on his skin and clothes. "Quiet, missy!" he snarled. Then lowering his own voice, he added, "Cursed pirates sail these waters. You want to call 'em down on us?"

Elizabeth opened her mouth to respond, but before she could, a commanding voice called out, "Mr Gibbs. That will do."

Striding over to Elizabeth and Mr Gibbs, Lieutenant Norrington came to a stop and glared down at the older seaman. Outfitted in the uniform of the Royal Navy with a wig of shocking white hair below his hat, Norrington cut a striking figure. He had been ordered to accompany Governor Swann and his daughter to Port Royal. And to Norrington, that duty included keeping old, superstitious sailors away from his young charge.

Following close behind Norrington was Governor Weatherby Swann – Elizabeth's father. He wore the white, curly wig of a political figure and while he looked uneasy aboard the swaying ship, he still carried himself as befit his high status. But, the presence of neither Norrington nor the governor was enough to stop Gibbs from speaking his mind.

"She was singing about pirates," he argued. "Bad luck to sing about pirates, with us mired in this unnatural fog – mark my words."

"Consider them marked," Norrington responded in his clipped British accent. "Now, on your way." He continued to glare at Gibbs, waiting for the sailor to leave.

Finally, Gibbs shrugged and turned to go, but not before muttering, "Bad luck to have a woman onboard. Even a miniature one."

Elizabeth didn't seem to notice the remark. Her mind was still reeling from what Gibbs had said earlier. Cursed pirates roamed these waters!

"I think it would be rather exciting to meet a pirate," she said dreamily.

"Think again, Miss Swann," Norrington replied pointedly. "Vile and dissolute creatures, the lot of them."

From his spot beside the lieutenant, Governor Swann sighed. How was Elizabeth to be a proper member of Port Royal society if she remained obsessed with pirates and legends of the sea? "Elizabeth," he said, "wouldn't it be wonderful if we comport ourselves as befits our class and station?"

"Yes, father," she replied dutifully. But as she turned back to gaze over the bow's rail and out to sea, she added, "But I *still* think it would be exciting to meet a pirate. . . ."

Her voice broke off as she imagined what it would be like. Would he be kind? Most undoubtedly not. In all likelihood, he would be mysterious, and threatening and . . .

Suddenly, Elizabeth was distracted by a movement through the fog. Something appeared to be floating out on the water. The shadow was faint and seemed to sway back and forth along the top of the waves – almost as if it were dancing on the swells. Slowly, it came closer. Elizabeth noticed a spot of colour and, as it finally broke free of the mist, she gasped. It was a parasol! Elizabeth watched as it slowly came closer and closer, drifting towards the *Dauntless* before gently bumping into the hull.

Elizabeth could not believe her eyes. A

parasol in the middle of the sea? It just did not seem right. As she gazed down at the fragile item, another, much larger, item floated into view. It looked like something heavy and lifeless lying on top of a large piece of flotsam. Elizabeth leaned over the rail and squinted to get a closer look. Then she realized just what it was.

"Look!" she cried. "There's a boy in the water!"

Elizabeth's cries brought Norrington, her father and most of the crew running to the rail. Murmurs and shouts rose up as they caught sight of the boy lying on his back on a small piece of wreckage. "Fetch a hook – haul him out of there," Norrington ordered.

The sailors, who had been looking overboard, leaped into action. Swinging one of the *Dauntless*'s hooks out over the rail, they lowered it down and quickly hauled the unconscious boy aboard. When he was safely on deck, Norrington leaned over to examine him. "He's still breathing," the captain declared.

"Where did he come from?" Governor Swann asked.

A gasp from Gibbs prevented Norrington

from responding. "Mother of all that's holy . . ." Gibbs muttered, staring into the fog.

All hands on deck, including young Elizabeth, turned and followed Gibbs' gaze out to the sea. It was no longer empty. Where moments before there had been nothing but rolling waves and endless fog, a burning hull now floated. As the *Dauntless* sailed past, they could make out the remains of the ship's cargo. Broken crates, splintered wood and wardrobes' worth of clothing littered the waves.

Gibbs spoke up again, his mind still on Elizabeth's ill-timed song. "Everyone's thinking it! Pirates!"

Norrington shot Gibbs a stern glare. Then, Norrington ordered the crew to search for survivors. If the boy had made it, there was a chance others had as well. While the sailors rushed about, Governor Swann stepped away from the rail and made his way to Elizabeth's side. His daughter was kneeling beside the boy, a concerned look creasing her brow.

"Elizabeth, the boy is in your charge now. You'll watch over him?" Governor Swann asked.

Elizabeth nodded and returned her attention to the boy. Since they had pulled him onto the *Dauntless*, he had not moved. His breathing was shallow and his skin pale and waterlogged. But it was the look in his eyes when they fluttered open that was the most haunting. He seemed so sad and lost. She brushed a lock of brown hair from his forehead, desperate to find out what had happened.

"My name is Elizabeth Swann," she said, placing his hand in hers.

With a cough, the boy tried to speak, and finally he managed, "Will Turner."

Will slipped back into unconsciousness, but before he did, his body shifted in such a way that the collar of his shirt opened. There, attached to a chain and resting on his bare neck, was a gold medallion. Curious, Elizabeth tugged it free. What she saw made her eyes grow wide. Staring back at her, engraved on the face of the medallion, was a skull. Elizabeth came to a quick conclusion. Will must be a pirate!

Hastily, Elizabeth hid the medallion under her coat. She couldn't let the lieutenant and her father see it. If they did, Will's life would most certainly be in danger.

Norrington then appeared at her side again. "Did he speak?"

"His name is Will Turner," Elizabeth replied. "That's all I found out."

Nodding in approval, Norrington moved on and Elizabeth let out a sigh of relief. When she was sure that the lieutenant was not coming back, Elizabeth pulled the medallion out of her coat. But before she could take a closer look, she caught movement out of the corner of her eye. Looking up, she nearly gasped. There, moving silently through the thick fog, was a tall ship with black sails. At the top of its highest mast flew a flag – a flag that had the same skull as on the medallion. A pirate ship!

Then, as silently as it had appeared, the ship slipped quickly back into the fog. On the deck of the *Dauntless*, Elizabeth watched until all she could see was the black-and-white flag billowing in the wind.

Chapter 2

Elizabeth Swann awoke with a start. The deck of the *Dauntless* was gone, replaced by the safety of her room in the governor's mansion. She had been dreaming again of Will and the pirate ship that she had seen eight years earlier on her way here, to Port Royal. And as always, the dream was so vivid and real to her. Her heart still racing, she reached over and turned up the oil lamp that rested beside her canopied bed. The room filled with dim light, gently illuminating the lavish furnishings and artwork that signified Elizabeth's status as the governor's daughter. Easing out of bed, Elizabeth picked up her oil lamp and made her way to her dressing table. She pulled open the top drawer and reached inside.

Her hand closed around a familiar object. Pulling her hand back out, she looked down into her open palm. There, lying faceup, was the gold medallion she had taken from Will's neck eight years ago. The grinning skull hauntingly stared at her.

A loud knock on the door caused Elizabeth to jump.

"Elizabeth," came her father's voice. "Is everything all right? Are you decent?"

"Yes . . . yes," Elizabeth stammered as the doorknob began to turn. She quickly placed the medallion around her neck and threw on a dressing gown, just as her father walked into the room carrying a large box. Estrella, Elizabeth's maid, followed and began to pull back the heavy curtains. Sunlight flooded the room. Outside, the town of Port Royal bustled alongside the blue waters of the Caribbean. Sitting out on a bluff was Fort Charles, its men, armed with cannons, keeping watch over the harbour.

Governor Swann smiled at his daughter. "I have a gift for you," he said proudly, holding the box out to her. Before she could respond, her father opened the box to reveal an elegant gown.

Elizabeth let out a pleased gasp. "May I inquire as to the occasion?" She asked taking the dress behind a screen as her father paced the room.

"I did think you could wear it to the ceremony today," he replied cautiously.

From behind the screen, Elizabeth silently groaned. The promotion ceremony! Of course! Since Norrington had accompanied Elizabeth and her father to Port Royal, he had only grown in standing with the Royal Navy. Now he was being made a commodore. Elizabeth knew her father would like nothing more than to see his only daughter wedded to such a noble man.

As if reading her mind, her father continued. "Captain Norrington, or, rather, Commodore Norrington . . . a fine gentleman. He fancies you, you know." Pausing, he added, "How's it coming?"

In reply, Elizabeth let out a gasp. Behind the screen, Estrella was pulling the laces on the corset as tight as they would go. Elizabeth felt the air being pushed out of her lungs as her ribs were bound tightly in the whalebone contraption. While the dress was beautiful – full of frill and lace – it was lacking in comfort.

"I'm told that dress is the very latest fashion in London," her father said.

"Women in London must have learned to not breathe," Elizabeth replied. She was not looking forward to being paraded around in front of the newly named Commodore Norrington in such a dress. Trying to take a deep breath, she winced. Deep breathing was clearly out of the question.

A moment later, the fitting was interrupted by a servant who announced a visitor.

Excusing himself, Governor Swann headed downstairs. Shortly after, Elizabeth followed, a frown on her face, as she tried to figure out a way to breathe in the tight corset and walk at the same time. At the top of the stairs she caught sight of the visitor and her frown disappeared, replaced by a beaming smile.

"Mr Turner!" the governor exclaimed from below.

Will Turner stood in the foyer of the governor's mansion, one hand clutching a long, rectangular case, the other behind his back. His black coat was worn and in need of darning, and his boots were scuffed. But Elizabeth did not mind. The frightened boy she had rescued eight years before was gone, replaced by a handsome young man. From the top of the stairs, out of sight of her father and Will, Elizabeth stared unabashedly at his sad eyes, strong jaw and thick brown hair, which was pulled back into a ponytail.

"Good day, sir," Will replied, unaware of Elizabeth's eavesdropping. "I have your order." Walking over to a table in the foyer, Will placed the case gently on top. Then, with the utmost reverence, he opened it to reveal a dress sword and scabbard. Will waited as Governor Swann pulled the sword from the case before continuing. "The blade is foiled steel. That's gold filigree laid into the handle. If I may . . ." Taking the sword back, he continued to point out its strengths.

"Very impressive," Governor Swann said when Will was done. "Do pass my compliments on to your master."

Sighing, Will nodded. The "master" was actually none other than Will himself. But the old blacksmith Will worked for tended to take all the credit for Will's skill.

"I shall," Will said politely. "A craftsman is always pleased to hear his work is appreciated . . ." His voice broke off.

Elizabeth was walking down the stairs, a smile on her lips. Her hair gleamed in the fractured sunlight and Will took an involuntary step forward.

"Elizabeth! You look stunning," her father said, voicing Will's thoughts.

But Elizabeth did not seem to notice her father or his compliments. Her eyes were riveted on the young swordsmith standing beside him.

"Will! It's so good to see you," she said warmly. "I dreamt about you last night. About the day we met. Do you remember?"

"I could never forget it, Miss Swann."

Oblivious to the effect she had on him, Elizabeth pressed on. "Will, how many times must I ask you to call me Elizabeth?"

"Once more, Miss Swann," he said. "As always."

Elizabeth's face fell. Will was just too proper and polite. Straightening her back and holding her head high, she descended the rest of the stairs. Right before she walked out the door, she turned. "Good day, *Mr* Turner," she said coolly.

Without another word, she walked out the door and into her carriage, leaving Will Turner behind.

Chapter 3

Inside the carriage, Elizabeth Swann sat in stormy silence. Will Turner was so aggravating! To act so proper and poised. How could he do it? Did he not want to smile? To joke with her as they once had?

The carriage made its way into Port Royal and towards Fort Charles, where Norrington's ceremony was to take place. But Elizabeth did not notice the beautiful sea or the bustling town. Her mind was still back in the foyer.

From his seat opposite hers in the carriage, Governor Swann spoke.

"Dear," he said, "I do hope you demonstrate a bit more decorum in front of Commodore Norrington. It is only through his efforts that Port Royal has become at all civilized."

Elizabeth did not reply. Instead, she turned and stared out at the sea. She wished she were free of this life and its "decorum". Free to sail away and not look back.

Meanwhile, at that moment, unseen by Elizabeth Swann or her father, a man who was already free sailed into Port Royal. Though perhaps "sailed" was not the most accurate of terms.

Standing atop the yardarm of a small fishing dory named the *Jolly Mon*, Captain Jack Sparrow surveyed the town of Port Royal. His tricornered hat sat jauntily atop his head, revealing the hint of a red bandanna beneath. When he smiled, the sun glinted off his several gold teeth. On almost every one of his fingers flashed a ring, and bits of silver and other trinkets hung from his brown, dreadlocked hair.

Looking down, Jack noticed that the *Jolly Mon* was no longer sailing on top of the water so much as through it. The boat was sinking.

Jack jumped from the yardarm to the deck and felt water soak into his knee-high boots. The deck was overrun with water. Quickly, he searched through the deck's clutter and found a bucket. Picking it up, he began to bail.

While Jack bailed, the *Jolly Mon* continued to sail into Port Royal's harbour. Quietly it slipped by a rocky outcropping from which five skeletons hung from nooses. One wore a sign that read: PIRATES – BE YE WARNED. Pausing, Jack Sparrow took off his hat and placed it above his heart – a moment of exaggerated respect for the doomed pirates.

The harbour of Port Royal was crowded with boats. There were fishing vessels of all sizes, but the most impressive was the HMS *Dauntless*, which lay at anchor in the tranquil waters. Her fifty cannons were quiet, but even at peace, she was an imposing vessel. Jack Sparrow took his time surveying the *Dauntless* before his eye was caught by a smaller vessel – the HMS *Interceptor*. The *Interceptor* was nowhere near the size of the *Dauntless*, but she was sleek and speedy. Glancing at the ship, Jack Sparrow's eyes sparked, but then he turned and focused on the task at hand – namely, docking.

Unfortunately, docking was going to be difficult, as the *Jolly Mon* was now almost completely underwater. Only the small portion of the mast and yardarm Jack had climbed back up on remained above water. With comic precision, Jack reached the dock just as the tip of the mast completely disappeared beneath the water. Stepping onto the dock, he came face to face with a very confused harbourmaster.

"Hold up there, ye!" the harbourmaster shouted. "It's a shilling to tie up your boat."

Jack glanced at him quizzically and then looked over his shoulder at the now fully submerged *Jolly Mon*. Not bothering to answer the harbourmaster, Jack shrugged and attempted to move on.

But the harbourmaster would not let him pass. "Rules are rules. And, I'll need to know your name."

A young boy who had been following the harbourmaster opened up a ledger. Looking at it, Jack pulled out a coin purse and threw a few coins onto the open book.

"What do you say to three shillings, and we *forget* the name?" Jack asked.

For a moment, the harbourmaster just stared at Jack, a mixture of disbelief and annoyance etched on his face. Then, thinking better of it, he closed the ledger. "Welcome to Port Royal . . . *Mr Smith*."

High above the harbour, inside the walls of Fort

Charles, Norrington stood at attention. He was dressed in the uniform of a commodore of the Royal Navy, and looked every bit the nautical hero he was. Standing before him was Governor Swann. With choreographed precision, Swann presented the sword and scabbard Will Turner had delivered earlier to the newly appointed commodore.

With a swish of the sword, Commodore Norrington saluted the governor before turning to his officers and the rest of the crowd that had assembled for the ceremony.

Meanwhile, Elizabeth Swann struggled to breathe. With every breath she took, the corset seemed to tighten around her ribs. The fan she held in her hand whipped back and forth as she tried to stay upright. In front of her, Norrington continued to preen, clearly enjoying his moment. As for Elizabeth? She did not know how much longer she could remain standing.

Back at the docks, Jack Sparrow was having no trouble breathing. In fact, everything seemed to be slipping into place perfectly. After disembarking from the *Jolly Mon*, he headed towards the navy dock. There, the *Interceptor* was anchored in all her beauty. Guarding her berth were two of the Royal Navy's dimmest marines – Murtogg and Mullroy. The two men wore the uniform of the navy, but instead of helping the duo command respect, their clothes somehow made them seem comical. Their bumbling personalities were not suited for such official attire. Murtogg's belly strained at his coat, and Mullroy's white pants seemed a bit too baggy for him. While the officers were up at Fort Charles watching Norrington's promotion to commodore, Murtogg and Mullroy had been assigned to guard the *Interceptor*.

As he swayed over to the marines, Jack Sparrow took in everything – from the *Interceptor*'s hull to the blank expression on the men's faces. Taking the *Interceptor* was going to be easier than he had hoped.

"This dock is off-limits to civilians," Murtogg said as soon as Jack walked up.

"Didn't know," Jack said, as the sound of drums and trumpets drifted down from the fort above. "Some sort of high-toned and fancy affair up at the fort? How could it be that your good selves did not rate an invitation?"

Murtogg glared at the poorly dressed stranger. "*Someone* has to make sure this dock stays off-limits to civilians," he explained.

Jack paused and looked past the guards at the *Interceptor*. Swaying slightly, he reached out to run his fingers along her sides. "This must be some important boat," he said casually. While he was well aware of nautical terminology, it behooved him to play dumb. And playing dumb with two nitwits was quite an enjoyable game.

At the word "boat", Mullroy rolled his eyes. Clearly they were dealing with a silly civilian who did not know the bow from the stern. "Ship," he pointed out. Then he proudly added, "Commodore Norrington's made it his flagship. He'll use it to hunt down the last dregs of piracy on the Spanish Main."

Jack reached up and played with the goatee that hung from his chin. It was a habit of his from long days at sea. Twisting it around, he waited a moment before responding.

"It seems to me a ship like that," Jack said, turning to motion towards the *Dauntless*, "makes this one here a wee superfluous."

"Oh, the *Dauntless* is the power in these

waters, true enough – but there's no ship as can match the *Interceptor* for speed," Murtogg pointed out, sounding pleased to know so much about his navy's ships.

"That so," Jack said, once again looking thoughtfully at the *Interceptor*. "I've heard of one, supposed to be fast, nigh uncatchable . . . the *Black Pearl*?"

Mullroy let out a laugh. The *Black Pearl* was a legend, an old ghost story told to young children to scare them. Even Mullroy knew not to be afraid of a ship that no one had ever seen – no less sailed on. This wobbling man with the bad teeth and a worn-out jacket was clearly not thinking straight. Mullroy pushed aside any thoughts that the man might be a threat and amended his original comment, "There's no *real* ship as can match the *Interceptor*."

"The *Black Pearl* is a real ship," argued Murtogg. "I've seen it."

Mullroy rolled his eyes. Now even his fellow marine was going loopy. The pair continued to argue back and forth, each one convinced the other was wrong. "You've seen a ship with black sails that's crewed by the damned and captained by a man so evil that hell itself spat him back out?" Mullroy asked as the argument continued to rage.

Murtogg looked down at his boots and shook his head no. Turning to tell Jack that he was right, there was no ship that could beat the *Interceptor*, Mullroy gasped. Jack was gone!

While the two had been arguing about the evidence for the existence – or lack thereof – of a ship with black sails, Jack had casually sauntered aboard the *Interceptor*. He now stood at the wheel of the ship, examining the compass and other instruments necessary for sailing the vessel. Hearing the marines approach, Jack glanced over at them, feigning surprise.

"Get away from there!" Mullroy shouted. "You don't have permission to be aboard."

"I'm sorry," Jack said innocently as the two ran up the gangplank and boarded the deck. "It's just such a pretty boat . . . ship."

Murtogg and Mullroy had had enough.

"What's your name?" Murtogg demanded.

"Smith. Or Smitty if you like," Jack answered.

"What's your business in Port Royal, Mr Smith?" Mullroy asked.

"And no lies!" Murtogg added.

Jack smiled. If it was truth this bumbling duo wanted, it was truth he would give them. "I confess: I intend to commandeer one of these ships, pick up a crew in Tortuga and do a little honest pirating."

Standing aboard the *Interceptor*, Murtogg and Mullroy exchanged confused glances. But they were prevented from any further discussion of Jack's plans for any ships by a commotion from above. Looking up, the three men watched as a young woman teetered on the edge of Fort Charles's imposing wall. For a moment, it appeared she would be fine. But suddenly, her arms flew up and she fell, hitting the water below with a mighty splash.

Chapter 4

Moments before Jack Sparrow and his dimwitted foes had witnessed the woman falling from the fort, Commodore Norrington's ceremony had come to an end. Norrington fought his way through the crowd that had gathered, making his way to Elizabeth Swann's side. In the afternoon light, she looked angelic. Her face was pale and her eyelashes fluttered as he gently guided her away from the crowd and came to a stop along the cliff wall.

"This promotion confirms that I have accomplished the goals I set for myself," Norrington began.

Elizabeth strained to pay attention as Norrington spoke, but she found it difficult. Standing in the hot sun throughout the ceremony had caused her to feel faint, and trying to breathe in her new dress and corset was impossible. Every breath she took felt too short, and her vision began to grow blurry.

Unaware of the distress Elizabeth was under, Norrington continued. "But the promotion also casts into sharp relief that which I have not achieved: marriage to a fine woman." He paused before adding, "You have become a fine woman, Elizabeth."

The tightness in Elizabeth's chest grew as Norrington's words sank in. Clutching at her chest, she exclaimed, "I can't breathe." Then, suddenly, she fainted, tumbling over the wall of the fort . . . and into thin air. Norrington watched in horror as she vanished into the water below. With a cry, he turned and ran, heading to the harbour. . . .

"Aren't you going to save her?" Jack asked the two marines.

"I can't swim," Mullroy replied while Murtogg shook his head. He couldn't swim either.

"Prides of the king's navy, you are," Jack said, lacing his voice with a heavy dose of sarcasm. Sighing, he began to take off his coat. It looked like he would have to wait to steal the *Interceptor* until after he saved the lassie. Next, he took off his pistol, followed by his bandolier, which jingled with trinkets, and finally he pulled off his hat. Ceremoniously, he handed them to Murtogg. "Don't lose those," he said, and without another word, he turned and dived into the water.

As Elizabeth drifted towards the sea floor, the medallion that she still wore around her neck floated up. Suddenly, a shaft of light slanted through the water, illuminating the medallion. Back on shore, Murtogg and Mullroy felt the dock beneath their feet pulse as if hit by a mighty wave. As the wind picked up and the sky clouded over, they moved closer together.

Meanwhile, underneath the water, Jack swam towards Elizabeth, unaware of the shock on shore or the odd change in the air. Reaching her, Jack wrapped his arm around her waist and began to head for the surface. He took several strokes before realizing he was not moving fast enough. The dress was pulling both of them down. Quickly, he reached around to the back of the flimsy material and ripped it off her. As it came free of her body, it caught in the current and slowly began to sink back to the floor. Jack quickly swam Elizabeth to the dock.

Murtogg and Mullroy, still slightly shaky, helped haul Elizabeth out of the water. When she was safe, Jack pulled himself up onto the dock.

More interested in getting his own breath back, Jack ignored the young woman who now lay before him. But Mullroy leaned over and put his cheek against her nose and mouth. "She's not breathing," he said.

Jack sighed. Did he have to do *everything*? Stepping forward, he deftly snatched a knife from Murtogg's belt and knelt down beside Elizabeth. In one quick and well-practiced move, he ran the knife down her corset, tearing it in two. For a moment, nothing happened. Then, Elizabeth, finally freed from the confines of the corset, began to cough and sputter. She was breathing!

"I never would have thought of that," Mullroy said in awe.

Jack smiled. "Clearly, you've never been to Singapore," he said mysteriously. But before he could elaborate, his attention was caught by the medallion around Elizabeth's neck. Reaching down, Jack picked it up and turned it over in his hand.

He was still kneeling at Elizabeth's side when a shadow fell across him, followed by the cold touch of steel against his neck.

"On your feet," a voice ordered.

Slowly, Jack stood. The scene did not bode well for him. The young woman lay across the deck, her corset ripped in half, and her dress gone. Meanwhile, he stood there without his sword, hat, or gun . . . defenseless against the man standing before him.

"Shoot that man!" Norrington cried out, pointing his sword at Jack.

Jack looked over at Elizabeth who was now being tended to by the very nervous governor.

"Father!" Elizabeth cried. "Commodore. Surely, you don't intend to kill my rescuer?"

Norrington looked down his sword at Jack. Then, ever so slowly, he pulled the sword away from Jack's neck and placed it back in its sheath. With a reluctant sigh, he held out his hand. "I believe thanks are in order," he said.

Gingerly, Jack reached out his hand and began to shake with Norrington. But in one quick move, the commodore tightened his grip and with his other hand yanked Jack's sleeve back. There, for all to see, was the letter *P* branded on Jack's arm.

"Had a brushup with the East India Trading Company – pirate?" Norrington asked. The men who had followed the commodore from Fort Charles drew their pistols.

As Norrington looked down on the pirate brand, his eyes caught sight of something else. There, right below the *P*, was a tattoo of a small bird flying across the ocean. It was faded and worn, but it told Norrington exactly what he needed to know. "Well, well . . . Jack Sparrow, isn't it?"

Jack grimaced. "*Captain* Jack Sparrow. If you please," he said, dropping into an elaborate bow.

"I don't see your ship – *Captain*," Norrington sneered.

Murtogg and Mullroy looked at each other. They had been keeping quiet to avoid any questions as to why they let a *pirate* save the governor's daughter. Murtogg finally spoke up. "He said he'd come to commandeer one."

"These are his, sir," added Mullroy, showing the pistol and bandolier.

Jack remained quiet as Norrington took the items from Mullroy and began to examine them. He peered into the gun and examined the belt, pulling trinkets off as he went – including a compass that dangled from the belt. When he had finished, he looked at Jack and smiled.

"No additional shot nor powder," Norrington began. Then, holding up Jack's Compass, he added, "It doesn't bear true." Lastly, he pulled the sword from its scabbard. Laughing at the pirate's obvious misfortune, he sheathed the sword. "You are, without a doubt, the worst pirate I have ever heard of," he stated in conclusion.

"Ah, but you *have* heard of me," Jack replied.

Norrington signaled one of his lieutenants to shackle Jack Sparrow. But before the man could get close, Elizabeth stepped forward. The jacket that had been covering her slipped off her shoulders, but she did not seem to care. Her attention was focused solely on the events unfolding in front of her.

"Commodore," she stated, "I must protest. Pirate or not, this man saved my life."

"One good deed is not enough to redeem a man for a lifetime of wickedness," Norrington replied evenly, trying to keep the frustration from his voice. Elizabeth seemed far too concerned with the safety of this *pirate*.

With another nod to the lieutenants, Jack was quickly shackled. The pirate safely captured, the rest of the men stood down, placing their weapons back in their belts. Only one marine continued to hold his pistol. That was just what Jack wanted to see. Before anyone knew what was happening, Jack snapped the corset that he still held in his hand around the wrist of the marine with the pistol. Flinging the man's hand into the air, Jack dislodged the pistol and sent it sailing smoothly out into the water.

As everyone turned to watch the gun fall, Jack sidestepped across the dock and grabbed Elizabeth. Throwing his manacled hands around her neck, he pulled her back against him.

Too late, the rest of Norrington's men drew their weapons. But now Jack had the perfect shield – Elizabeth. "Commodore Norrington . . . my pistol and belt, please," he said with a smug smile upon his lips. When Norrington hesitated, Jack pulled the manacles tighter against Elizabeth's neck, causing her to squirm. Norrington grabbed the pistol and belt from Murtogg and held them out. But Jack was not to be fooled. If he released Elizabeth to retrieve the items, his shield would be gone.

"Elizabeth – it is Elizabeth?" Jack whispered into his captive's ear.

Fuming, Elizabeth struggled against Jack's arms, trying to get as far from him as possible. But he simply pulled the manacles tighter and brought her closer. "Miss Swann," she replied.

"Miss Swann, if you'll be so kind?" Jack asked. Leaning forward, Elizabeth took the pistol and belt from Norrington. Before she knew what was happening, Jack had grabbed the pistol and now held it against her temple. With her firmly in his grasp, Jack pulled her around so that they were face-to-face. As he got her to slip his bandolier back on, he smiled deviously.

"You are despicable," she announced.

"I saved your life; now you've saved mine. We're square," he said. Then turning back to Norrington, the governor and the marines who had gathered, he smiled.

"Gentleman . . . milady . . . you will always remember this as the day you *almost* caught Captain Jack Sparrow."

Shoving Elizabeth away, he turned and grabbed a rope that hung from a nearby scaffold. With one quick movement, he pulled the pin that held the rope in place and shot up towards a higher dock. Below him, the marines opened fire but only Norrington's shot flew true. It hit the rope Jack was hanging on and he began to fall. But the manacles Jack was still wearing on his hands caught on yet another rope, and he quickly slid down it, landing safely on the deck of a docked ship. In an instant, Jack disappeared among the crowds of Port Royal.

As Norrington and the others took off after Captain Jack Sparrow, a breeze began to blow. Standing on the docks with her father, Elizabeth shivered and looked out to sea. On the edge of the harbour, a thick and eerie fog made its way towards the town. Drawing her jacket closer, Elizabeth turned and headed to the safety of her home.

Chapter 5

The fog crept along the streets and alleyways of Port Royal, draping everything in shadow. Combing the side streets and hidden corners, an armed party of marines searched for Captain Jack Sparrow.

Hearing their footsteps fade into the fog, the infamous pirate stepped out from his hiding place in the shadows. Once again, Jack Sparrow had slipped through the fingers of the enemy. Noticing a shop across the way, Jack walked over and tried the doors. They had been left unlocked. With one last look over his shoulder, Jack went in.

Inside, he found himself in a blacksmith's shop. The light was dim, and dust from the floor filtered through the air. Tools of the trade hung from the walls, and yoked to the bellows stood an old donkey that seemed unconcerned with the visitor. Jack smiled. Fortune was on his side today.

Surely among all these tools, there would be something strong enough to cut the manacles from his wrists.

Suddenly, a loud snort sounded throughout the forge and Jack jumped. He was not alone. Glancing around, his eyes came to rest on a bear of a man, slumped over in a chair, an empty bottle cradled in his arms. From the looks of him, Jack assumed this was the blacksmith himself. Given the man's condition, Jack did not think him a threat, and shrugging, he resumed his search for something he could use to take the manacles off. Walking over to the furnace, which was still glowing hot, Jack pulled a short-handled sledge from the wall and held it in his left hand. Then, Jack took a deep breath and reached out his right hand – directly over the furnace. Sweating, Jack waited as long as he could before pulling his hand away and wrapping the glowing chain around a nearby anvil. Then, with a mighty grunt, he brought the sledge down on the chain, shattering it.

One hand unmanacled, he placed it in a bucket of water, watching as the steam bubbled up. To be a pirate was dangerous work, he mused.

But at least he was that much closer to freedom. Hearing someone at the door, he ducked for cover and waited to see who it was.

Will Turner entered the blacksmith shop, still upset over his earlier encounter with Miss Swann. The shop, owned by his employer, Mr Brown, looked as it had when he left it. Mr Brown was slumped in a corner and the tools were all as they should be – all but one. The sledge that usually resided on the wall was now lying on the floor. Walking over, Will leaned down to pick it up when suddenly, the flat side of a sword slapped his hand. Looking up, he found himself face-to-face with a rather unusual-looking man.

Will stared with wide eyes at his attacker. The man's hat sat atop dirty dreads, and his teeth gleamed with gold. And while his clothes could have belonged to any poor sailor, the manacle dangling from his wrist gave him away. "You're the one they're hunting," he said. Then with a sneer, he added, "The *pirate*."

With a tip of his hat, Jack acknowledged Will's statement. From his vantage point, the boy did not seem a threat. He was of slim build, and while his hands appeared strong – most likely from working with hot metal and other tools of the blacksmith trade – his eyes were innocent. Jack very much doubted the boy had ever been in a real fight. But still, something nagged at Jack. "You seem somewhat familiar. Have I threatened you before?"

Will's glare grew darker. "I make it a point to avoid familiarity with pirates," he answered.

"Ah. Then it would be a shame to put a black mark on your record," Jack said, hoping that his escape from Port Royal would remain unhindered. "So, if you'll excuse me . . ." Slowly, he began to back away from Will, heading for the door.

But Will was not as unschooled in the world of fighting as he appeared. In one quick move, he reached over to a nearby grindstone and grabbed a sword resting on top of it. Jumping up and out of the way of Jack's blade, Will swished the sword in one well-practiced motion.

In response, Jack raised his own sword and settled into a fighting stance. If it was a fight this boy wanted, it was a fight he would give him. With a swish of swords, the two began parrying back and forth across the floor of the shop, Jack doing his best to stay one step ahead of the young blacksmith. But it was difficult.

"You know what you're doing," Jack said between thrusts, "I'll give you that."

In response, Will increased the speed of his swipes, matching every step Jack made. He was not going to allow the pirate to go without a fight. For another moment, the fighting remained intense as the pair dueled. But then, suddenly, Jack turned and fled towards the door. Seeing the pirate on the run, Will did the first thing that came to mind. With a grunt, he threw the sword – directly at the door through which Jack was hoping to escape. The sword buried deep into the wood, right above the latch. Reaching the door a moment later, Jack frantically lifted the latch up and down. But it did no good. The sword was stuck in deep and had effectively locked the door!

"That's a good trick," Jack admitted. "Except now, you have no weapon."

Will did not bother to answer. Instead, with a sly smile he simply picked up a sword whose tip had been resting in the furnace. In the bright glow of the sword, Jack's face paled. This boy would not give up, and it was growing tiresome.

Sighing, Jack once again began to parry with Will. As their swords continued to clash, Jack looked around, hoping for something to help him out of the current situation. Glancing down, he saw his manacled hand, the chain still dangling from his wrist. Swinging his arm, he attempted to hit Will, but the boy ducked. Jack swung again, and this time the chain made contact with Will's sword, hitting it and sending it flying.

Unfortunately for Jack, another sword lay at the ready and Will quickly grabbed it. Jack groaned. There were far too many weapons in this room. "Who makes all these?" Jack asked as they continued to duel.

"I do," Will answered. "And I practice with them at least three hours a day."

"You need to find yourself a girl," Jack teased. Noticing Will's jaw clench at the mention of "girl", he added, "Or maybe the reason you practice three hours a day is you've found one – but can't get her?"

With a groan of rage, Will kicked out, knocking a rack of swords to the ground. One of them fell into his left hand. He was now doubly armed against the pirate. Swinging wildly, the two continued to fight, their actions taking them onto a long, wooden platform. One end of the platform rested on the ground, while the other was balanced on a barrel. As the pair moved on to it, the wood began to tilt on the barrel like a see-saw. In the heat of the battle, Jack's chain wrapped around Will's sword. Seeing his chance, Will raised his sword up, bedding it deep in the rafter above, and he fastened Jack there, leaving him to dangle.

But Jack was not done fighting. In one swift move, he pulled himself free and swung up and onto the rafter beam. Will leaped up, too, and the fight continued. Back and forth across the beam they fought, each more determined than the other to conquer his opponent. Finally, they both jumped back to the floor, and as they did, Jack reached behind him into the ashes of the furnace. Grabbing a handful of soot, he turned and threw it right into Will Turner's face. Will stumbled back, temporarily blinded. Once he had cleared the ashes from his face, he looked up. Pointed directly between his eyes was Jack's pistol.

"You cheated," Will cried.

Smiling, Jack shrugged. He was a pirate.

What did the young blacksmith expect? Jack began to once again move to the door. But Will blocked his path, undeterred by the weapon in his face. Cocking the gun, Jack took a threatening step forward. "You're lucky boy – this shot's not meant for you."

Will was about to ask who the shot was meant for, when he saw a hand holding an empty bottle rise up over Jack's head. Then, with a thud, it came down, shattering. Jack crumpled to the ground. Mr Brown, the blacksmith, stood over Jack's body with a look of confusion on his face.

At that moment, the front and back doors of the shop flew open and the room filled with marines. Commodore Norrington strode forward and surveyed the shop. With a smile, he moved closer to Jack. "I believe you will always remember this as the day Captain Jack Sparrow *almost* escaped," he said with a laugh.

Norrington left the shop, followed by a group of marines dragging out one semiconscious, groaning and thoroughly *captured* Jack Sparrow.

Chapter 6

As night fell on Port Royal, the fog grew thicker, blanketing the streets, houses and harbour in an eerie mist. People rushed home to the warmth of their hearths while in the taverns that lined the streets, men sat at wooden tables, warming themselves with ale and idle chat. Sitting high atop the cliff, Fort Charles was left untouched by the fog. It stood watch over the shrouded and still town.

But out on the water, something moved.

The shape of a ship grew clearer as it cut through the fog and entered the harbour. From its masts flew tattered black sails, and the ship itself seemed to be made of shadow. No sound came from its decks as it grew ever closer to the town. Suddenly, the fog thinned, and from the topmast, a single black flag could be seen flying. As it snapped back and forth in the wind, a skull and crossbones became visible . . . a sinister smile on its bony face. . . .

Meanwhile, sitting in a jail cell in Fort Charles, Captain Jack Sparrow leaned against the prison's rock wall, his hat pulled low over his eyes. The fog that had covered the town below was of no consequence to the pirate. At the moment, he was too distracted by the thought of his hanging in the morning and the hapless prisoners in the cell beside him.

The prisoners were crouched down and pressed against the bars of their cell, intent on one thing – escape. One of them held an old bone through the bars, waving it in front of a mangy dog that held a ring of keys in its mouth, while another held out a rope to the mutt. If they could get the dog over to the cell, they would have the keys and a way out. Slowly, Jack lifted his head. "You can keep doing that forever," he said wisely. "That dog's never going to move."

"Excuse us if we ain't resigned ourselves to the gallows just yet," one of the men retorted.

Jack smiled, one corner of his mouth lifting to reveal his gold teeth. Then he lowered his head and once again slipped into silence. It looked like he and his fellow prisoners had but one fate – the gallows.

Back in the governor's mansion, Elizabeth Swann shivered in her bed. The eerie fog had crept into her chamber, making sleep impossible. Holding an unread book open in front of her, Elizabeth allowed Estrella to place a bed warmer at her feet.

"There you go, miss. It was a difficult day for you, I'm sure," the woman said gently, patting the sheets down and making sure the heat was not too much.

"I suspected Commodore Norrington would propose," Elizabeth said with a sigh. "But I was still not entirely prepared for it." Her thoughts drifted back to the moment at Fort Charles and Norrington's stammering request. Could he truly imagine they would make a good match? What of love? Surely the commodore could not be in love with her – they were very different types of people. "He's a fine man," Elizabeth continued. "The sort any woman *should* dream of marrying."

Estrella raised her eyebrows and leaned

closer, as if about to share an important secret. "That Will Turner . . . *he's* a fine man," she said softly.

From the bed, Elizabeth looked up sharply. Will Turner. Just the mention of his name sent colour rushing to her cheeks. The way he had treated her earlier in the day, and for Estrella to simply . . . it was too much. With a sharp word, she sent the maid from the room and picked up her book. To be lost in words would be a lovely distraction. But she could not focus. The words on the page blurred. Absently her hand went to her neck, toying with the medallion that still hung there.

Suddenly, the flame of the lamp beside her bed flickered and then lowered. Reaching over, Elizabeth tried to turn it back up. But it wouldn't work and the next moment, the light went out completely – pitching the room into darkness.

Inside the blacksmith's shop, Will Turner was hard at work, hammering out a piece of iron. With every hit, he tried to erase the events of the day. The morning at Governor Swann's, Elizabeth's fall, and then the run-in with that wily pirate. But it was no use. Pausing to catch his breath, Will walked over to one of the forge's windows and looked out. But he could not see far. Fog covered the streets, buildings and signs. Will felt a shiver down his spine and had a strange feeling, like he was being watched. Reaching up, he pulled an axe off the wall and walked outside. As he looked up and down the alley, he almost expected someone to walk out of the shadows. But other than a lone cat that ran past, he was alone. . . .

Commodore Norrington and Governor Swann walked along the parapet that surrounded Fort Charles. On one side was the Caribbean, and on the other a courtyard, from which the shadow of the gallows could be made out. The two men were lost in thought as they paced, their hands behind their backs.

"Has my daughter given you an answer yet?" the governor asked, breaking the silence.

"No," Norrington answered. "She hasn't."

Suddenly, the stillness of the night was shattered by a loud boom, and the dark sky lit up. "Cannon fire!" Norrington shouted as the two men were sent flying. When the dust settled, they glanced at each other in panic. Who was attacking them? Who had arrived in Port Royal?

Inside the prison, the explosions rocked the cells. Leaping up, Jack rushed to the small barred window and looked out into the dark. A smile formed at the corners of his mouth as explosions lit up the night sky.

"I know those guns!" he shouted happily. "It's the *Pearl*."

Beside him, the prisoners' faces grew pale. The *Black Pearl*? They had heard the stories of the dreaded ship. For over ten years she had sailed the waters of the Caribbean, preying on towns and vessels. Without warning, she would appear out of the night and attack, leaving nothing but chaos and destruction in her path. Walking over to the bars that separated their cell from Jack, the prisoners looked closely at the pirate. Jack stood with his face eagerly pressed against the window bars, a gleam in his eye.

"I've heard she never leaves any survivors," one of the other prisoners stammered.

"No survivors?" Jack said with a smile as another explosion rocked the prison. "Then where do the stories come from, I wonder?"

The *Black Pearl* moved steadily closer, its cannons blasting. Down at the docks, sailors ran for cover as the ground beneath their feet exploded, sending wood and dirt flying into the sky. Within moments, the *Black Pearl* had all but destroyed the docks of Port Royal. Even the fog seemed to be blasted away under the pirate ship's assault. Men, women and children ran screaming through the streets in search of safety.

With lightning speed, the crew of the *Black Pearl* dropped the longboats into the choppy water and rowed ashore. Carrying torches, swords and guns, they swarmed the beach. Their clothes were torn and faded, and their faces were creased with dirt. Two of the pirates stopped for a moment and looked around. They made an odd pair – Ragetti was tall and skinny with a mop of dirty blond hair, while Pintel was short and squat, his head bald except at the sides where patches of long, straggly grey hair hung down. As they took in the chaotic scene, they both smiled, revealing two sets of very dirty teeth. Holding out a wooden eye, Ragetti spit on it and then rubbed it clean before placing it in his empty eye socket. Then, with a nod, they took off, following the rest of the *Black Pearl*'s crew into Port Royal.

Inside the blacksmith's forge, Will Turner listened as the sound of the attack got closer. Glass shattered as pirates threw explosives into random windows and gunshots rang out from every direction. Will quickly began to gather weapons. His fingers closed around an axe which he placed in his belt before grabbing a sword from the table. Fully armed, he ran outside.

A young woman ran past, chased by a maniacal pirate. Her sharp screams cut the deafening noise of the attack. Acting quickly, Will reached for his belt, pulled the axe out and sent it sailing through the air – straight into the back of the pirate. The man fell where he was, his laugh silenced. Will retrieved his axe and ran off, the blade of his sword flashing.

Chapter 7

Elizabeth Swann stood on a balcony of the governor's mansion and stared at the terrible scene in front of her. Through the fog and smoke that filled the sky, she could make out the buildings in the town – or what was left of them. Fires raged all over the harbour and docks, illuminating the night with an unnatural glow. As Elizabeth watched, cannons continued to boom and, from Fort Charles, the sound of heavy gunfire could be heard.

Suddenly, the gate to the mansion was thrown open and pirates rushed into view. Elizabeth gasped. Turning, she ran inside and headed towards the top of the stairs. Reaching the landing that looked out over the foyer, she saw the butler approaching the front door.

"Don't," she started to shout. But it was too late. The butler opened the door to a mob of pirates, led by Pintel and Ragetti. Pintel aimed his gun directly at the butler.

"Hello chum," said Pintel, firing the gun.

As the butler crumpled to the ground, Elizabeth screamed. Pintel looked up and smiled, the gun still smoking in his hand. Glancing at Ragetti, the two dashed for the stairs in hot pursuit of Elizabeth.

Terrified, Elizabeth ran back up the stairs to her room, slamming the door and locking it. Estrella was right behind her, looking as terrified as Elizabeth felt.

"Miss Swann," she whispered. "They come to kidnap you?"

Elizabeth stared at Estrella in shock. The girl was right. She was the governor's daughter, after all, and would be very valuable in a trade if captured. The sound of a body slamming against the door snapped Elizabeth into action. As the door shook and the knob rattled, Elizabeth pushed Estrella back and out of sight. "They haven't seen you. Hide, and first chance, run for the fort," she ordered.

Suddenly, the door gave way and Pintel and Ragetti burst into the room just in time to see the flash of Elizabeth's white dress as she darted into the adjoining room. They raced after her.

Elizabeth, however, was not going to hide. She grabbed the closest thing to a weapon she had – the heavy pan filled with hot coals that served as a bed warmer. As Pintel entered the room, she swung, hitting him square in the face and knocking him to the ground. While he lay on the ground groaning, she swung again, this time aiming for Ragetti. But the tall pirate reached up and, with one hand, stopped Elizabeth in mid-swing. Laughing, he watched as she struggled to pull the pan away from him.

"Boo," he said with a laugh.

Glancing up at her raised hand, Elizabeth cocked an eyebrow. Ragetti followed her gaze, looking confused by the girl's lack of fear. Then, with one quick pull of her finger, she flipped the heated pan's latch and the lid flipped open, dropping ash and burning coals onto Ragetti's upturned face. Screaming, the pirate let go of Elizabeth.

Without a backward glance, Elizabeth ran out of the room and headed towards the foyer staircase. On the landing that overlooked the foyer, Elizabeth's eyes grew wide. All around her pirates raced back and forth. Some were chasing the governor's servants, while others dragged loot away. Elizabeth flew down the stairs, her white bedroom slippers a blur beneath her dressing gown. Pintel and Ragetti followed close behind.

Just as she reached the bottom of the stairs, Ragetti leaped over the balcony and landed in front of Elizabeth, a flaming torch in his hand. He let out a vicious growl, forcing Elizabeth to take a step back – closer to Pintel. Frantically, Elizabeth looked back and forth between the two pirates, unsure of what to do. She was trapped. Suddenly, a low whine filled the air, causing Elizabeth and the two men to glance curiously towards the mansion's front door. Moments later, the wall exploded as a cannonball ripped through the room, taking down a pirate as he struggled with an armful of gold and jewels.

With Pintel and Ragetti distracted, Elizabeth once again took off at a run, ducking into the dining room. Quickly, she placed a candelabrum over the doorknobs, temporarily locking out the pirates. As the pirates cursed and pulled at the door, Elizabeth frantically searched the room for a weapon. Her eyes landed on a pair of crossed swords hanging on a piece of carved wood above the fireplace. She reached up to grab one, but it was stuck in the wood. The swords were nothing more than decoration. The rattling at the door grew louder. Diving into the small linen closet, Elizabeth shut the door behind her and waited as quietly as she could.

Just as Elizabeth shut the closet door behind her, Pintel and Ragetti broke through the door to the room. But the room looked empty to the pirates. Elizabeth was nowhere to be seen. In the dim torchlight, they noticed that one of the windows was open, its curtain blowing in the gentle night breeze.

"We know you're here, poppet," Pintel said in a singsong tone. "Come out, and we promise we won't hurt you."

Inside the closet, Elizabeth whimpered.

Pintel continued to pace around the room, his eyes scanning the walls. "We will find you, poppet . . . you've got something of ours, and it calls to us," he said. Then, with a smile, he added, "The gold calls to us."

Shrinking back against the linen-lined shelves of the closet, Elizabeth reached for her neck. The medallion! Pulling it away from her neck, she held it in her fingertips, watching as a ray of light from outside caused it to spark and glow brighter. Suddenly, the light faded and the medallion returned to darkness. Looking up, Elizabeth gasped. Staring back at her through a crack in the door, mere inches from her face, was Pintel.

"Hello, poppet," he said. He flung the closet door open. Cocking his gun, Pintel took one step forward. But Elizabeth's next words stopped him cold.

"Parley," she said. "I invoke the right of parley! According to the Code of the Brethren, set down by the pirates Morgan and Bartholomew, you must take me to your captain!"

Pintel glared at Elizabeth. "I know the Code," he said slowly, his eyes flashing in anger. The girl was smart. To invoke parley guaranteed that she would remain safe – for a little while longer. As Ragetti took a threatening step forward, his knife drawn, Pintel put out a hand to stop him. "She wants to be taken to the captain," he said, "and we must honor the Code."

Chapter 8

While Elizabeth was busy invoking the right of parley, Will Turner found himself in the middle of a sword fight with a very large, very bald and very angry pirate. Suddenly, Will felt a chain wrap around his wrist and he was dragged up against his large adversary. Looking up into the bald man's eyes, Will grimaced. This was the end for sure. Closing his eyes, he waited for the death blow, but it never came. Instead, a bomb whizzed out of the melee, landing a direct hit on a nearby building. Fortunately for Will, the explosion also happened to unhook a hanging sign, which slammed the bald pirate square in the chest.

Freed from the pirate's grasp, Will turned and headed back into the streets of Port Royal. He had only managed to take a few steps, when a flash of white caught his attention. Looking over, he saw Elizabeth being dragged towards the harbour by two vile-looking pirates. Feeling his gaze on her, she turned, her eyes seeking him out across the street.

"Elizabeth," he said to himself.

Just then, another group of pirates passed. Reaching out, one of them brought a heavy candleholder down on Will's head. With a groan, Will collapsed to the ground.

Meanwhile, in his prison cell, Jack Sparrow stared out his window, watching as bombs continued to blow Port Royal to bits. The four men jailed next to Jack had long since given up their attempts to lure the dog with the keys closer, and now sat defeated. Glancing up into the sky, Jack saw the faint outline of the moon, barely visible behind the thick clouds of smoke.

Suddenly, a bomb burst clear through the prison wall into the cell next to Jack's, ripping a giant hole in the stone. Hazy moonlight poured into the now-open cell, illuminating the four prisoners as they leaped to their feet and headed for the hole. One of the convicts turned back to Jack.

"My sympathies, friend," he said. "You've

no manner of luck at all!" Then, along with the others, he slipped outside to freedom.

No luck at all? Jack was not so sure. Left alone, he walked over to examine what was left of his former neighbours' prison wall. The unfortunate nature of events had left both the bars of his own cell and the outside wall intact. The other prisoner had been right. He had no luck – there was no way for him to get out. Sighing, he walked over to the front of the cell just as the clouds parted, revealing a bright and full moon.

Reaching through the bars, his rings gleaming in the moonlight, Jack picked up the bone the other prisoners had dropped and began to wave it. "Come here, doggie," he called. "It's just you and me now. You and old Jack." From under a bench down the hall, the guard dog lifted his head. Slowly, he crawled out and began to make his way towards Jack, his tail wagging back and forth timidly. "That's it," Jack said, attempting to sound sincere. But he was a pirate, and the dog was not moving fast enough. He couldn't help but add, "You filthy, mangy, stinking cur." The dog let out one whimper, and then Jack watched in horror as it took off down the hall – with the keys.

Just then, a shout came from the top of the entranceway that led to the prison. With a mighty crash, a red-coated marine came flying down the stairs and, smashing into the stone wall, was knocked unconscious. Close behind the marine came two pirates – known to their crew as Koehler and Twigg. Both were tall and wore the grungy garb of men long at sea. Koehler had a head full of long, black dreadlocks, and Twigg wore a tight hat. As they drew closer to Jack's cell, he stood up and casually placed his hands through the bars of his cell.

"Well, well, well," said Koehler as he sheathed his sword. "Look what we have here, Twigg. It's Captain Jack Sparrow." He leaned forward and spit at Jack's feet.

His arms still through the cell bars, Jack looked first at Koehler and then down at his feet, a puzzled expression on his face. But he remained silent.

"Last time I saw you," said Twigg, "you were all alone on a godforsaken island, shrinking into the distance." Laughing, he turned to Koehler and added, "His fortunes haven't improved much."

Jack put his face right up against the bars.

"Worry about your own fortunes, gentlemen," he said with a smug smile. "The deepest circle of Davy Jones's locker is reserved for betrayers . . . and mutineers."

With a growl, Koehler reached through the bars of the cell. His fingers wrapping tightly around Jack's throat, forcing him to lean back – right into a shaft of moonlight. As Jack clutched the pirate's arm trying to free himself, his eyes widened. In the moonlight, Koehler's arm appeared to be nothing but the bones of a skeleton.

"So there *is* a curse," he said. "That is interesting."

Koehler's fingers tightened. "You know nothing of pain," he said with a snarl. Then, with one final squeeze, he released Jack.

As the pair walked off, Jack stepped back up to the bars. "That's *very* interesting," he said softly. And as the pirates' footsteps faded away, Jack smiled. The night had just taken a decidedly positive turn.

Chapter 9

For Elizabeth Swann, however, the night had taken a decidedly *negative* turn. She now found herself sitting at the prow of a longboat, being rowed towards the hull of a massive, black ship. Looking up, her gaze fell upon the bow of the ship, from which hung the ornately carved figure of a woman. In her outstretched hands, she held a bird. Elizabeth, shivering and afraid, couldn't help but see the irony in having such a peaceful figure for such a horrid ship. As the moon slipped behind thick clouds, the figurehead disappeared into the darkness.

From the ship's sides, cannons continued to fire, blasting more holes in Port Royal and filling the air around the ship with ash and powder. Elizabeth's eyes scanned her surroundings, taking in the tall masts from which heavy black sails hung. A few lights illuminated the deck, casting a pale glow over the rough wood and creating eerie shadows. And from onboard, she could hear the shouts of the pirates and the sound of metal, presumably loot, being thrown around.

All too soon, the longboat pulled up beside the ship and Pintel and Ragetti pushed Elizabeth unceremoniously onto the deck. As she stumbled on her long, white nightgown, her eyes caught sight of a man standing in the shadows – removed from the chaos onboard. But it was only a glimpse. Looking around, her heart began to pound faster and she struggled to breathe. There were pirates everywhere. She heard men shouting in different languages as bodies pushed by her, unbothered by her presence. But there was one member of the crew who was indeed bothered by Elizabeth. The Bo'sun, a tall, dark man with tattooed dots surrounding his eyes and mouth, approached.

"I didn't know we was taking captives," he said in a heavily accented voice.

Keeping a firm hold on Elizabeth's arm, Pintel explained. "She's invoked the right of parley," he said, "with Captain Barbossa."

Pulling free, Elizabeth strode forward. "I am here to . . ." she began. But she was silenced when the Bo'sun reached over and slapped her across the face – hard. Shocked, Elizabeth stepped back, a hand on her stinging cheek.

The Bo'sun raised his hand to strike again when another hand reached out and grabbed his wrist. "You'll not lay a hand on those under the protection of parley," said Captain Barbossa, his voice gravelly with age, but still powerful.

Elizabeth looked over at Barbossa, curious to see what type of man could captain such a crew. At first sight, he seemed more gentleman than pirate. Though his bearded face was lined and weathered, and the whites of his eyes were more yellow than white, he wore a fine feathered hat and long, black dress coat. A monkey wearing a white dress shirt perched on his shoulder.

"My apologies, miss," Barbossa said.

"Captain Barbossa," Elizabeth began boldly. "I am here to negotiate the cessation of hostilities against Port Royal."

Around her, several of the crew chuckled, while a smile played at the corner of Barbossa's mouth. Shaking his head and looking around, the captain answered. "There was a lot of long words in there, miss, and we're not but humble pirates," he said, laughing. "What is it that you want?"

Elizabeth paused. "I want you to leave and never come back," she replied proudly.

Now all of the crew laughed. A silly girl in a nightdress was asking their captain to just up and sail away. It was indeed a laughable request. And Barbossa seemed to agree. "I am disinclined to acquiesce to your request," he said, throwing Elizabeth's fancy words back in her face. Then, with a smile, he added, "Means no."

"Very well," Elizabeth replied, raising her chin proudly. Then she remembered something Pintel and Ragetti had said. They were looking for something she had. Something that was theirs. In one swift move she reached up and ripped the medallion from her neck. Storming over to the ship's rail, she threw her arm over the water, letting the medallion dangle from her fingertips. "I'll drop it," she said threateningly.

In the light from the cannon fire, the medallion lit up. For a moment, the captain's eyes grew wide and he shifted uneasily. Regaining his composure, he gestured around the ship. "My holds are bursting with swag," he pointed out. "That bit of shine matters to us? Why?"

Elizabeth felt herself grow even madder. Glaring at Barbossa, she shouted, "Because it's what you're searching for." Then she added, "I recognize this ship. I saw it eight years ago, when we made the crossing from England."

"Did you, now?" Barbossa replied.

Elizabeth's eyes jumped from Barbossa to his crew, looking for a sign that the captain was bluffing. All eyes were on her and the dangling medallion. "Fine," she said. "I suppose if it *is* worthless, there's no sense in me keeping it. . . ." As her voice trailed off, she opened her fingers, allowing the medallion's gold chain to slip through her fingers towards the water below.

Barbossa and his men leaped forward, shouting "No!" Her hand still grasping the chain, Elizabeth smiled and nodded. So she had been right. The medallion was what the pirates were looking for, after all.

With a throaty chuckle, Barbossa moved closer, and Elizabeth's smile began to fade. While she held the medallion, she had some element of control over the situation. She dared not lose it.

Pulling the gold closer to her, she steeled herself against the pirate.

"You have a name, missy?" he asked, giving her a long, hard look.

"Elizabeth," she began, before stopping herself. If she revealed her last name, Barbossa would surely figure out that she was the governor's daughter. She could not risk it. Looking down at the medallion, she had an idea. "Turner," she finished quickly. "I'm a maid in the governor's household."

Barbossa's eyes grew wide and he turned to face his men. "Miss *Turner*," he announced. At the mention of the name Turner, the men began to mumble, while Pintel uttered a single name. "Bootstrap."

"Very well," Barbossa said, once again focusing his attention on Elizabeth. "You hand that over, we'll put your town to our rudder and ne'er return." Holding out his hand, he waited as Elizabeth considered the exchange. Reluctantly, she dropped the medallion into his open palm. Barbossa's monkey, who up until that point had simply sat on the captain's shoulder looking bored, leaped down and grabbed the medallion.

Then, with a screech, it jumped onto a mast line and into the rigging. Elizabeth's bargaining chip was gone.

Without another word, Barbossa turned and started back towards the rear of the ship. Calling out orders to the crew, the Bo'sun prepared to leave Port Royal. But no one made a move to send Elizabeth back. "Wait!" she shouted, chasing after Barbossa. "You must return me to shore! According to the Code. . . "

Barbossa whipped around, cutting her off. "First, your return to shore was not part of our negotiations, nor our agreement and so I 'must' do nothing. And secondly, you must be a pirate for the Pirate's Code to apply. And you're not." He paused, a smile creasing his weather-beaten face. "And thirdly . . . the Code is more what you'd call *guidelines* than actual rules."

Elizabeth felt hands grab her arms as Pintel and Ragetti began to drag her away. But not before Barbossa got in his final word. "Welcome aboard the *Black Pearl* . . . Miss Turner."

Chapter 10

In Port Royal, Will Turner awoke with a headache. Reaching up, he winced as his fingers brushed the spot where he had been hit the night before. Blinking his dark brown eyes, he looked around. The smoke and fog that had covered the town only a few hours earlier were gone, replaced by blue skies and sun. But all around, signs of the pirate attack could be seen. Rising to his feet, Will looked out at the harbour. It was a disaster. Ships lay burning at anchor, and the docks were nothing more than splintered wood.

Suddenly, the image of Elizabeth being dragged by pirates towards the harbour returned to his mind. Without thinking, he took off at a run.

Moments later, he burst into the courtyard of Fort Charles. Men in red uniforms carried the wounded, while others attempted to clear away debris. But Will did not notice. His eyes landed on the man standing in a stone archway, his gaze riveted to a map in front of him. It was Commodore Norrington. Despite the night's events, the commodore looked remarkably well put together. His blue uniform was crisp and his white wig was pulled tightly and neatly against his scalp. On either side of him, armed marines stood watch, their sabers pointed high.

"They've taken her!" Will shouted, rushing up the steps and coming to a stop in front of the commodore. "They've taken Elizabeth."

"Mr Murtogg," Norrington replied, not even looking up from the map, "remove this man."

Will stared at the commodore in disbelief. He was not going to look for Elizabeth? It was beyond belief. "We have to save her!" Will exclaimed.

From behind the commodore, a figure turned and moved closer to Will. It was the governor. Where Norrington appeared calm and in control, the governor was clearly shaken. "And where do you propose we start?" he asked Will. "If you have any information that concerns my daughter, then please – share it. If anyone does, tell me!"

"That Jack Sparrow," Murtogg stammered. "He talked about the *Black Pearl*. . . ."

Will leaned forward eagerly. Jack Sparrow! The pirate! Of course he would know of the *Pearl*. "Ask him where it is!" he said aloud to Norrington.

"The pirates who invaded this fort left Sparrow locked up in his cell," Norrington retorted. "Ergo, they are not his allies."

A loud thud shook the table on which the map rested. Will's axe was now buried deep in the wood.

But Norrington had dealt with worse things than an angered blacksmith. Reaching over, he pulled the axe out of the wood and palmed it in his hand. "Mr Turner," he said, making his way around the table. "You have nothing of value to contribute here." Then, pausing, he reached out and grabbed Will's arm. In a whisper, he added, "Do not make the mistake of thinking you are the only man here who cares for Elizabeth." Without another word, he pushed him out of the archway.

The discussion with Norrington was over. But Will had one more person to visit. He headed towards the prison . . . and Jack Sparrow.

Chapter 11

Inside his cell, Captain Jack Sparrow was unaware of the kidnapping of Elizabeth Swann or of Will Turner's plan to get her back. Sunlight filtered through the cell as Jack tried in vain to pick the lock of his cell – with a bone. Suddenly, the door to the prison creaked open. Leaving the bone in the lock, he fell to the straw-covered ground and lay there, one arm behind his head in order to look inconspicuous.

It was Will Turner. He was still fuming over his run-in with Norrington. Noticing that only one cell in the prison had remained intact from the night before, he stormed over to it and saw the reclining pirate.

"You. Sparrow," Will said. "You familiar with that ship? The *Black Pearl*?"

"I've heard of it," Jack drawled, not bothering to lift his head from the floor. He recognized the lad from the blacksmith shop. It was he who had helped get him captured and placed in this horrid prison in the first place.

"Where does it make berth?" Will asked.

"Where does it make berth?" Jack repeated, once again raising his head and looking at Will in disbelief. He lowered his head back to the ground and began to wave one hand in the air absently.

"Have you not heard the stories? Captain Barbossa and his crew of miscreants sail from the dreaded *Isla de Muerta* . . . an island that cannot be found." He paused and looked up at Will, "Except by those who already know where it is."

Will gazed down at the pirate, struggling to control his temper. "The ship's real enough," he said through clenched teeth. "Where is it?"

"Why ask me?"

"They took Miss Swann," Will replied, tightly gripping the bars of the cell.

At the mention of "miss", Jack raised himself up onto his elbows, his interest piqued. "Ah, so it is that you found a girl," he said with a knowing smile. "Well, if you're intending to brave all, hasten to her rescue, and so win fair lady's heart, you'll have to do it alone, mate. I see no profit in it for me."

"I can get you out of here," Will answered. Quickly he pointed out that he had helped build the cells and knew how to break in. Grabbing a nearby bench, he jimmied it into the bars and paused, looking down at the pirate. He would do no more until Sparrow agreed to help him.

Still lying on the ground, Jack cocked his head and looked at Will suspiciously. "What is your name, boy?" he asked.

"Will Turner."

Upon hearing the name, Jack sat up. "Short for William, I imagine. No doubt named for your father?" Jumping to his feet, he walked over and smiled through the bars at Will. "I've changed my mind. You spring me from this cell, and I'll take you to the *Black Pearl* and your bonnie lass."

"Agreed," Will said.

Putting all his weight on the bench that was still wedged in the cell door, Will pushed. With a creak and groan, the door sprang off its hinges. Grabbing his hat, pistol, belt and Compass, Jack headed out of the prison. He was free!

The next morning, Will found himself underneath a bridge looking out at Port Royal's harbour. In front of him stood Jack Sparrow, his hat safely back on his head. Men in uniform were frantically running up and down the loading docks, filling the hold of a smaller ship docked nearby. Behind it, the HMS *Dauntless* loomed, a British flag flying from its stern. "We're going to steal that ship?" Will asked, gazing out to the *Dauntless*.

"Commandeer," Jack corrected. "We're going to commandeer *that* ship." He pointed towards the closer and much smaller ship that was being loaded.

Gesturing for Will to follow, Jack tiptoed to an overturned rowboat. He had a plan. But first, he had to get them to the *Dauntless*. Lifting up the rowboat, the pair quickly ducked underneath it and walked down to the water's edge, pulling the boat under the waves before anyone spotted them. Safely in the water, breathing the air trapped beneath the overturned rowboat, Will looked over at Jack. "This is either madness or brilliance," he said.

"Remarkable how often those two traits coincide," Jack replied.

Moments later, they sneaked aboard the *Dauntless* and moved towards the small crew that manned the decks. "Everybody stay calm!" Jack shouted, holding his pistol steady. "We're taking over the ship!"

The marines burst into laughter. "This ship cannot be crewed by two men. You'll never make it out of the bay," one of them said, chuckling.

Jack rolled his head back and smiled. He was Captain Jack Sparrow! He never resisted a challenge.

Moments later, from the dock beside the *Interceptor*, a shout rose up. Out on the water, rowing *away* from the *Dauntless* was the ship's crew. Reaching into his belt, Commodore Norrington pulled out a spyglass and lifted it to his eye. Beyond the longboat, the sails of the *Dauntless* were being lowered. Norrington could make out Sparrow on deck, his arms flailing in the air as he ordered Will Turner about. "That is, without doubt, the worst pirate I have ever seen," Norrington commented.

Back aboard the *Dauntless*, Jack turned and glanced over his shoulder. His plan was working! Norrington was dropping the sails on the *Interceptor* and preparing for pursuit. While the *Dauntless* was heavily armed, she was not swift.

The *Interceptor* quickly drew alongside the bigger ship and dropped a gangplank across the rail. Quickly the men boarded the *Dauntless*, prepared to capture the two thieves. But no one was aboard.

Too late, Norrington heard the sound of a splash and looked back just in time to see the *Interceptor* pulling away. Jack was at the wheel of the smaller boat. He tipped his hat to Norrington.

"Thank you, Commodore," he shouted, "for getting us ready to make way! We'd've had a hard time of it ourselves."

From his spot beside the commodore, a marine watched in admiration as the ship faded into the distance, fast becoming nothing more than a speck on the horizon. "That's got to be the best pirate I've ever seen," he said.

Chapter 12

Out at sea, the *Interceptor* cut through the water, her sails taut in the breeze. Standing at the rail, Captain Jack Sparrow checked the lines, while at a nearby barrel, Will Turner methodically sharpened the blade of his sword. High atop the main mast, the *Interceptor*'s flag waved in the wind and waves crashed against the bow of the ship as she made her way steadily onward under the bright blue sky. For a moment there was silence, as the two men busied themselves with their tasks. Both had much on their minds.

"When I was a lad in England," Will said, not looking up from his sword, "my mother raised me herself. After she died, I came out here . . . looking for my father." Pausing from his sword sharpening, he looked over at Jack, waiting for the captain's response.

Testing a line, Jack looked up into the

rigging and then headed for the ship's wheel. "Is that so?" he asked innocently as he passed by Will.

But Will suspected that the pirate knew more than he let on. Cocking his head, he watched the pirate continue to crew the ship – by himself. Will's brow furrowed. Jumping up, he approached Jack. "My father. Bill Turner?" he pressed. "At the jail – it was only *after* you learned my name that you agreed to help. I'm not a simpleton, Jack. You knew my father."

Jack did not bother to look at Will as he spoke, his attention apparently focused on keeping the ship sailing. But the captain heard every word. If he were to sail this ship, he would need the boy – and he would need him to stop being so chatty. Sighing, he stood up and turned towards Will, his tan and weathered face mere inches from the blacksmith's. "I knew him," he said. "Probably one of the few who knew him as William Turner. Most everyone just called him Bootstrap or Bootstrap Bill." Moving away from Will, Jack took his place at the wheel before adding, "Good man. Good pirate. I swear, you look just like him."

At the word "pirate", Will's head jerked up

and pain flashed across his face. His father? A pirate? All these years, he had dreamed of his father, thought of him as a merchant marine and a law-abiding civilian. If Jack was telling the truth, everything he had come to believe was a lie and his father was just another one of the group he hated most in the world – pirates. Before he could stop himself, he drew his sword.

Hearing the swish of metal, Jack sighed. "Put it away, son," he said calmly, his hands never leaving the wheel of the ship. Realizing that Will was not going to let up, Jack did what any self-respecting pirate would do – he cheated. With a mighty shove, he spun the wheel, causing the ship's heavy boom to whip over the deck. Will, unused to life on the sea, was caught unaware. A second later, he found himself dangling off the boom and over the water.

Having Will's complete and utter attention, Jack decided to clarify a few matters before they sailed any farther. Picking up Will's sword, he pointed it straight at him. "The only rules that really matter are these: what a man can do. And what a man can't do." Pausing, he moved back towards the wheel. "You can accept that your father was a pirate and a good man . . . or you can't. But, pirate's in your blood, boy, so you're going to have to square with that someday."

Still hanging dangerously over the sea, Will kicked his legs and struggled to keep hold of the boom. Jack's words were painful to hear, but the pirate had a point – a twisted one, but a point nevertheless. With another push of the wheel, Jack swung the boom back over the deck, and Will fell to the ground, his arms shaking.

Will assessed his situation. Jack had not killed him – and he had promised to help him rescue Elizabeth. Reluctantly, Will agreed to follow Jack and, pleased with Will's decision, Jack set the course. He needed a crew for his new ship and there was only one place he knew that would satisfy this need – the rough and tumble pirate town of Tortuga.

Ah, Tortuga. Walking through one of the many alleys that littered the port, Jack smiled. To be a pirate meant to love Tortuga, with its crowded taverns, feisty women and flowing ale.

Will Turner, on the other hand, was not yet convinced of Tortuga's charms. The town was dirty and smelly, and the streets echoed with the sound of fighting and gunfire. Everywhere he looked, men and women caroused about, shouting and laughing. Looking up, Will watched as a man leaned back and began to pour rum from two different mugs down his throat, spilling the amber liquid all over himself. Nearby, three heavy women, their ample chests spilling out above tight corsets, laughed loudly.

Seeing Will's dismay, Jack piped up. "I tell you, Will," he said, "if every town in the world was like this one, no man would ever feel unwanted." Just as he finished speaking, a woman in a bright red dress with equally red hair stalked over to them. "Scarlett!" Jack said, his shiny grin growing wider as he took in the woman's familiar figure. But Scarlett was not nearly as happy to see Jack. Bringing her hand back, she slapped him hard across the cheek and then stalked off.

A few minutes later, Will found himself standing behind one of Tortuga's many taverns – the Faithful Bride. In front of him, an old sailor lay in the mud, his head resting on the belly of a sleeping pig. It was Joshamee Gibbs – the very same seaman who had warned Elizabeth of pirates eight long years before. Time had not treated him well – his beard was now more grey than black, his clothes were tattered and he smelled of pig and ale. But that didn't appear to bother Jack. Gibbs was a mate. Grabbing a nearby water pail, Jack doused the man, causing him to sit up, his gun drawn.

"Ah, Jack," he said, when he shook the water from his eyes. "You know it's bad luck to wake a man when he's sleeping."

"Well, fortunately," Jack told his friend, "I know how to counter it. The man who did the waking buys the man who was sleeping a drink." Leaning down, he pulled Gibbs to his feet and together the three men made their way into the tavern.

Moments later, Gibbs and Jack sat at a table, tankards of ale in front of them. Will stood a little way off, eyeing the debauchery around him. Glancing around to make sure no one was listening, Jack lowered his voice and leaned close to Gibbs. "I'm going after the *Black Pearl*. I know where it's going to be, and I'm going to take it." Pausing, he added, "I need a crew."

"Jack, it's a fool's errand," sputtered Gibbs.

"What makes you think Barbossa will give up his ship to you?"

In the light from the candles that illuminated the tavern, Jack's eyes gleamed. "Let's just say, it's a matter of leverage." Tilting his head, he nodded in the direction of Will, who still stood watch, apparently unaware of what Jack was saying. Gibbs stared blankly at Jack. Again, the pirate nodded at Will.

"The kid?" Gibbs asked, confused.

Jack nodded. "That is the child of Bootstrap Bill Turner." Then, pausing for dramatic effect, he added, "His *only* child."

Gibbs looked once again at Will. The young blacksmith seemed out of place among the rough-and-tumble tavern crowd. But Gibbs just smiled. Bootstrap Bill's only child. This was indeed fortuitous. Looking back at Jack, his grin grew wider. "Leverage, says you," he said wisely. "I feel a change in the wind, says I. I'll find us a crew."

Leaning back in his chair, Captain Jack Sparrow smiled. He was one step closer to Barbossa . . . and the *Pearl*.

Chapter 13

Far from the port of Tortuga, the *Black Pearl* sailed under a moonlit sky. As she cut through the dark waves, her sails appeared to be nothing more than shadow, and the only light on deck came from the moon, which was filtered by the clouds. High above the stern, candlelit windows stretched across the boat's length, casting an eerie glow on the water below.

Locked inside the cabin, Elizabeth Swann stood in her dressing gown and wrap, staring absently at the flickering candles that filled the room. Only her eyes gave away her discomfort and fatigue. Suddenly, the cabin door burst open and the two pirates who had viciously dragged her away from her home – Pintel and Ragetti – entered. Pintel carried a deep red silk gown.

"You'll be dining with the captain," Pintel informed Elizabeth. Then, nodding to the gown in his arms, he added, "And he requests you wear this."

Sticking out her chin and giving the men her stormiest glare, Elizabeth retorted, "You can tell the captain that I am disinclined to acquiesce to his request."

But the pair just laughed, revealing their dirty and rotten teeth. Miss Swann had no choice. It was dining with the captain in his cabin – or with the crew. Huffing, Elizabeth reached out and grabbed the dress from Pintel. While the captain was horrid, dinner with the crew seemed even less appealing.

A short while later, Elizabeth sat at a table filled with food. The aroma of freshly cooked meat wafted through the cabin, causing her stomach to growl. Succulent goat, fresh seafood, hot bread and juicy pieces of fruit covered every inch of the large table. At the head of the table, Captain Barbossa watched as Elizabeth picked up a piece of chicken and took a small bite. Her hand shook as she brought the meat to her lips. She was famished, but pirate ship or not, she would remain a lady.

Barbossa seemed to disagree. "No need to

stand on ceremony," he said, not touching his own plate. "You must be hungry."

He was right. Dropping her fork, Elizabeth picked up the chicken and tore into it, grease and sauce covering her lips and cheeks. As she ate, Barbossa watched, his hungry eyes never leaving Elizabeth's mouth. But still, he did not eat. Pouring a glass of wine, he offered it to his guest and watched once more as she gulped it down. Unaware of the captain's intense stare, Elizabeth continued to devour the food.

"And the apples," Barbossa said, holding out a green apple towards her. "One of those next."

Looking up, Elizabeth paused midbite, suddenly wary of Barbossa's offer. There was something peculiar in the way he was looking at her. Even his monkey was staring at her. Suddenly, a thought crossed Elizabeth's mind.

"It's poisoned," she said aloud, her face growing pale.

Barbossa laughed. "There would be no sense in killing you, Miss Turner." Reaching into his jacket, he pulled out Elizabeth's medallion. "You don't know what this is, do you?" he asked, dangling it in front of her.

"A pirate medallion," Elizabeth answered, shrugging her shoulders.

"This is Aztec Gold," Barbossa went on, his voice growing deeper and more grave. "One of eight hundred and eighty-two identical pieces they delivered to Cortés himself. Blood money. But the greed of Cortés was insatiable . . . and so, the heathen gods placed upon the gold a terrible curse." He leaned in close to Elizabeth before adding, "Any mortal that removes but a piece from that chest shall be punished for all eternity."

Elizabeth raised her eyebrows. In Barbossa's hand, the medallion flickered as the light played off its skull. But despite the captain's ominous words, Elizabeth was not afraid. "I hardly believe in ghost stories any more, Captain Barbossa," she replied haughtily.

Barbossa chuckled knowingly. That was what he had thought when he first learned of the curse, he told Elizabeth. But ah, how quickly he had been proved wrong. He and his men found the chest on *Isla de Muerta* and plundered the gold, quickly spending it on food and drink. But slowly, something began to happen. Food no longer filled their bellies and drink did not quench their thirst. "We are cursed men, Miss Turner," he said, his voice a whisper in her ear. "Compelled by greed we were, but now we are consumed by it." Suddenly, as if the tale were too much for the monkey to bear, it began to shriek, drawing Barbossa's attention away from Elizabeth. While he was distracted, she slowly reached up and pulled a steak knife off the table and slipped it into the sleeve of her gown.

Unaware of Elizabeth's movements, Barbossa continued, "There is one way to end our curse. All the scattered pieces of gold must be restored and the blood repaid." Pausing, Barbossa placed the monkey on his shoulder and handed to it Elizabeth's piece of gold. "Thanks to ye," he said, once again drawing close to her, "we have the final piece."

Still seated in her chair, Elizabeth shivered. "And the blood to be repaid?" she asked. "What of it?"

"That's why there's no sense to be killing you," Barbossa replied calmly. "Yet."

Elizabeth's eyes widened as realization dawned. It was her blood that would end the curse! Jumping up, she pulled the knife out of her sleeve and slashed at Barbossa, who quickly side-stepped out of the way. Racing around the table, she looked to the cabin door. If she could only get outside. But Barbossa was there, blocking her way. With a scream, she brought the knife down – stabbing him in the chest.

Gasping, she pulled away, expecting Barbossa to fall to the ground. But he didn't. "I'm curious," he said instead. "After killing me, what is it you planned to do next?"

Turning in terror, Elizabeth burst through the door of the cabin onto the main deck – and screamed. There, in front of her, where human sailors *should* have been, a crew of skeletons was at work swabbing the decks and coiling the lines. In the light of the moon, their bones glowed a bluish-white, and they were draped in tattered pieces of clothing. Screeching, Elizabeth tried to turn and run, but she fell, landing on a blanket in the cargo hold. A moment later, she was flung high into the air as skeletons pulled the blanket from beneath her. She came down, only to be caught by another skeleton as he swung by on a mast line. Terrified, she screamed again as she fell to the deck. All the while, the skeletons kept working on the ship, seemingly unbothered by her antics.

Desperate to get away from the crew, Elizabeth ran over and hid under a stairway. Gasping for breath, she let out another scream when the monkey swung down, landing in front of her face. It was a skeleton, too!

Once more, she jumped up, this time heading for the safety of the captain's cabin. But Barbossa was waiting for her in the shadows and he grabbed her, pulling her close. "Look!" he shouted. "The moonlight shows us for what we really are! We cannot die!" Laughing, he pushed Elizabeth out into the moonlight. As he stepped forward, the light hit his arm, and Elizabeth watched in disbelief as his flesh was replaced by bone.

"You best start believing in ghost stories," he said, finally stepping fully into the moonlight, turning his face into a grinning skull. "You're in one."

Chapter 14

While Elizabeth Swann was busy facing a crew of cursed pirates, back in Tortuga Mr Gibbs had managed to gather a ragtag group of sailors to crew the *Interceptor*. They now stood on the docks, awaiting Captain Sparrow's approval. Jack walked down the line, stopping periodically to question the men. Behind him followed Will, an unimpressed look on his face.

Indeed, it was not the most stellar crew. One of the men, known to the others as Cotton, had lost his tongue and couldn't speak. Instead, a brightly coloured parrot who sat on his shoulder did all the talking for him. The other men looked weak and hungry, eager to take on work for the chance of a berth and a meal. However, there was one sailor who seemed saucier than the rest. His head tipped forward, a wide hat hiding his face, he shouted out a question to the captain, "What is the benefit for us?"

The *Interceptor* is the fastest ship in the Caribbean Sea and the pride of Port Royal.

Young Elizabeth Swann watches over Will Turner.

Commodore Norrington vows to rid the sea of pirates.

Elizabeth's father wants her to marry Norrington,
but she wants nothing to do with the rigid commodore.

Swashbuckler Jack Sparrow plots to get his ship, the *Black Pearl*, back from Captain Barbossa.

The evil pirate Barbossa finally finds the last piece of cursed gold.

Jack and Will Turner take possession of the *Interceptor* to save Elizabeth from Barbossa and his pirate crew.

Barbossa tells Elizabeth how he plans to lift the curse from his crew . . . with her blood!

The gold is returned – but Barbossa
and his crew are still cursed!

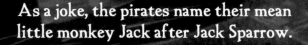

As a joke, the pirates name their mean little monkey Jack after Jack Sparrow.

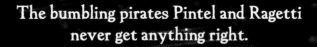

The bumbling pirates Pintel and Ragetti never get anything right.

Free of Barbossa and his crew, Will and Jack
take command of the *Black Pearl* once more.

Elizabeth and Will watch as Norrington
gives the order to hang Jack for piracy.

Everyone watches as Jack Sparrow
makes yet another daring escape.

Elizabeth and Will finally kiss ... and they
live happily ever after.

Walking over, Jack leaned down and lifted the brim of the sailor's hat. Just as he suspected – the he was really a she! More specifically, the she was Anamaria – the owner of one, now fully sunk, fishing dory named the *Jolly Mon*. In the bright Caribbean sun, her dark honey-coloured skin glowed. But it was her eyes that were the most striking – the dark brown orbs looked at Jack with a mixture of anger and frustration. Reaching out, Anamaria slapped him across the face, causing Will to smirk. Slapping seemed to be a recurring theme. But Jack deserved it. After all, he had "borrowed" her boat without permission.

Unfortunately for Jack, Anamaria was a good sailor, and he needed her on board. So, using his keen negotiation skills – and some help from Will, who promised Anamaria the *Interceptor* – he finally managed to convince her to join the crew. With a full crew, a stocked boat and his trusty Compass, they were now ready. It was time to sail for *Isla de Muerta* . . . and the *Black Pearl*.

Later that night, as storms rocked the *Interceptor*, Will Turner struggled to keep his footing. The ship pitched and dipped as waves buffeted her sides, while above, the sails flapped angrily in the wind. Standing at the wheel, Jack stared down at his Compass, oblivious to the rain that soaked his jacket and poured off the corners of his hat. Despite the poor conditions, the captain seemed sure of himself and his heading.

"How can we find an island no one can find – with a compass that doesn't work?" Will asked Gibbs, who was helping him cleat a rather large and very wet line.

"The Compass doesn't point north," Gibbs agreed. "But we're not trying to find north, are we?" he added cryptically.

Leaving Will to figure out the riddle, Gibbs headed towards Jack. The slippery deck and pounding rain made it slow going, and by the time he reached the captain's side, Gibbs was in a foul mood. Jack, on the other hand, looked oddly happy.

"What's in your head as puts you in such a fine mood?" Gibbs asked.

Jack looked over at his mate. Then, with a knowing grin, he answered, "We're catching up!"

While the *Interceptor* was drawing closer to *Isla de Muerta*, the *Black Pearl* had already arrived. She lay at anchor in one of the many rocky harbours that lined the island, a light mist rising up around her sides. Inside the captain's cabin, Elizabeth Swann stared out the window at the dark rocks that rose up into the sky. Suddenly, the door swung open and a group of pirates entered, led by Pintel.

"Time to go, poppet," the balding man said gravely.

Once outside, Elizabeth's hands were bound as Barbossa placed the medallion back around her neck. Despite the damp air and grey skies, Elizabeth did not shiver or cry out. Showing fear would do her no good. These were pirates – they did not care.

Moments later, she found herself sitting in the bow of a longboat being rowed towards a dark cave. In front of her, Barbossa stood in another boat, the cursed monkey on his shoulder and an eager gleam in his eye. They were almost there. Soon, the curse would be over, and he would be a free man once more.

Back aboard the *Interceptor*, an eerie quiet had settled over the crew as they lined up against the rail and stared out into a thick fog. As the ship glided slowly through the water, they could make out the shapes of half-sunken ships. Worn masts rotted in the air, the only sign of the vessels that lay below the waves. Elsewhere, upside-down hulls could be seen, holes worn away in the wood. It was a ship graveyard.

"Puts a chill in the bones," Gibbs said, breaking the silence.

From his spot beside him, Will nodded, his eyes straining for signs of life among the wreckage. Drawing his gaze from the destruction, he turned and looked up to where Jack stood, one hand on the wheel, the other holding his Compass. Cotton, the mute pirate, came up and stood behind him. Feeling the old man's eyes on him, Jack looked back and then snapped the Compass closed.

"How is it that Jack came by that Compass?" Will asked Gibbs as the sailor moved off.

Gibbs, never one to turn down the chance to tell a story, looked over towards his captain. "Not a lot's known about Jack Sparrow 'fore he showed up in Tortuga with a mind to go after the treasure of *Isla de Muerta*," he said. "That was back when he was captain of the *Black Pearl*."

"What?" said Will, turning so fast that his

own ponytail almost whipped him in the face. "He failed to mention that."

While Will was bothered by Jack's secrecy, Gibbs knew the man had a reason. When Jack had set out to find the treasure, Gibbs explained to Will, he promised his crew an equal share of the treasure. But they turned on him. As soon as he revealed the bearings, they mutinied, leaving Jack alone on an island . . . to die. But they weren't altogether cruel. They did leave him with a pistol and one bullet.

Gibbs sat down, gesturing for Will to come closer. "But, Jack," he said, when Will was eye level, "he escaped the island. And he still has that single shot. He won't use it though, save on his mutinous first mate."

"Barbossa," Will said, suddenly understanding Jack's eagerness to help him. He hadn't cared about Elizabeth. Jack wanted the *Pearl* . . . and revenge. But he still had one question. "How did Jack get off the island?" he asked.

Gibbs smiled. This was the best part of the story. Gesturing with his hands, he explained, "He roped himself a couple of sea turtles and lashed 'em together and made a raft."

"He roped a couple of sea turtles," Will said

flatly, looking at Gibbs in amusement.

"Aye. Sea turtles."

Leaning closer, Will stared into the older sailor's eyes, not sure who was crazier – Jack or Gibbs. Curious to see if Gibbs could further explain the mystery of Jack's escape, he asked one final question: "What did he use for rope?"

"Human hair," came Jack's voice. "From my back." While Gibbs had been telling Will the story, the captain had made his way over. He now stood glaring down at them, unimpressed. This was no time for storytelling. They had arrived. It was time to go ashore.

As a longboat was readied for Jack and Will. Gibbs jumped up and rushed over to the captain. "What if the worst should happen?" he asked just loud enough for Will to overhear.

"Keep to the Code," Jack ordered.

Without further discussion, Jack and Will slipped into the longboat and headed into the cave – towards Elizabeth and the treasure of *Isla de Muerta*.

Chapter 15

Stories told of *Isla de Muerta* spoke of hidden treasure beyond anyone's imagination. Gold and silver stolen from men and captains too bold to fear ghost stories and pirates. And all the stories were true. Deep inside the island that no man could find if he had not yet been there, a huge treasure lay – sparkling with untold wealth.

The large cavern in which the treasure lay was damp with age and smelled of the saltwater that surrounded it. In the dim light provided by a single hole in the top of the cave and the torch-light they carried, Barbossa's crew could see piles upon piles of gold and colourful treasure.

Sitting on the top of the highest pile of treasure was a single stone chest, its lid pushed aside. It was the chest of Cortés himself. The very same stone chest that had once carried the cursed blood money and which was now filled with eight hundred and eighty-one pieces of Aztec Gold – patiently waiting for the last piece.

Barbossa's crew entered and scattered around the cavern, their arms filled with more loot to add to the treasure. They barely even glanced at the large chest. It had long ago ceased to awe them – now it was simply a bane, the cause of their eternal suffering.

While Barbossa's crew was busy with the treasure, Jack and Will were slowly making their way closer. They sat in the longboat, the water illuminated in front of them by the light from the single torch that Jack held in his hand. Rowing the longboat, Will's mind drifted back to Gibbs' question on the *Black Pearl*. "What Code is Gibbs to keep to, if the worst should happen?" he asked Jack.

"Pirates' Code," Jack replied. "Any man who falls behind is left behind."

Suddenly, the cave began to grow brighter and Will could make out several other longboats moored to a stone shore. They had arrived. Rowing their boat up among the others, Jack and Will jumped out and followed the muffled sound of voices. Moments later, they found themselves looking through a hole into the treasure room. And there, standing behind the large Aztec chest, stood Elizabeth, her head held down by Barbossa's cruel hand.

"Elizabeth," Will said softly, stepping forward. But Jack put out a hand to stop him.

"Not yet," he said quietly. "Wait for the opportune moment."

Glaring at the pirate, Will shrugged off Jack's arm. While he did not often make sense, Jack *did* know these men and this cave. If he said wait, Will would. For now. Will looked through the hole and listened as Barbossa addressed his crew.

"Our torment is near an end!" Barbossa shouted, causing the crew to lift their hands and bellow in agreement. Nodding down at the chest in front of him, he continued. "Here 'tis the cursed treasure of Cortés himself! Every piece that went astray has found its way home – save for this!" Picking up a stone knife, he raised his hand and pointed to the medallion that lay around Elizabeth's neck. The pirates, sensing that the end of the curse was near, shouted even louder.

From his hiding spot, Will watched as Barbossa pointed the knife at Elizabeth's throat.

His heart pounding, he turned to Jack, only to see him slipping off. Will followed, unwilling to let the captain out of his sight. Sensing that he was being followed, Jack turned. "Listen, squire," he said to Will. "Have I ever given you any reason not to trust me?" Will didn't answer. "Please, stay here and try not to do anything stupid."

Jack walked away, disappearing into the darkness. Meanwhile, Will could hear the shouts of the pirates in the treasure room growing louder. Barbossa was working them into a frenzy. Will did not have much time. With one last look behind him, Will turned and followed Jack back towards the boats. As he passed an oar leaning against the stone wall, he picked it up, causing rocks to skitter down the stone path. Hearing the noise, Jack turned . . . just in time to see an oar swing out and hit him – right across the face. Soundlessly, Jack dropped to the floor. Will leaned over him, holding the oar. "Sorry, Jack," he said to the unconscious man, "but I'm not going to be your leverage."

He turned and ran towards the treasure room to save Elizabeth.

Chapter 16

Elizabeth Swann was beginning to think she might not get out of this particular situation alive. Ever since she had asked for parley and been kidnapped by a crew of cursed pirates, things had gone from bad to worse. Now she stood in a room full of treasure, surrounded by pirates who believed that she was capable of ending the curse and giving them back their lives. As she struggled against Barbossa, she felt his grip tighten around her neck. He shoved her further over the open chest of Aztec Gold. Indeed, things did not look good.

"You know the first thing I'm going to do after the curse is lifted?" Barbossa asked his crew with a grin. Then, answering himself, he said, "Eat a whole bushel of apples."

Grabbing Elizabeth's wrist in his cold hand, Barbossa held it out over the gold and raised his knife. Elizabeth turned her head away, closing her eyes as she prepared for the cut. She felt the blade on her palm and then a brief stab of pain. Opening her eyes, she looked down and watched as Barbossa placed the medallion over the small cut on her hand. Closing her fist, he waited, allowing her blood to touch the gold. "Begun by blood, by blood undone," he said. Then, forcing open her palm, he dropped the gold.

With bated breath, Barbossa, Elizabeth and the crew watched as it fell into the chest with the matching pieces. For a few moments, the room was silent as the pirates waited for something to happen.

"I don't feel no different," Ragetti said, speaking for the group.

"How do we tell?" Pintel asked.

From his spot by the chest, Barbossa frowned. It was true. Something did not feel right. While there was no guarantee that the curse's undoing would be dramatic, he had expected some sort of change. Drawing his pistol, he aimed it at Pintel and fired, hitting the stocky man in the centre of his chest.

Grabbing his chest in shock, Pintel looked

down, waiting for the blood that should follow. But no blood came. The curse had not been broken. Angry shouts and cries rose up, and the men's stormy glares fixed on Elizabeth.

"You," Barbossa snarled, grabbing up the medallion and shoving it in her face. "Your father. Was your father William Turner?"

"No," Elizabeth answered.

"Where's his child?" asked Barbossa. "The child in whose veins flows the blood of William Turner?"

When Elizabeth did not answer, Barbossa slapped her, sending her and the medallion flying down the pile of gold. She landed, unconscious, on a ledge of gems. To one side, a deep stream of seawater flowed, and as she fell, pieces of treasure slipped off the ledge and disappeared into the dark water.

With the girl out of the way, Barbossa turned back to his angry crew. The situation was getting dangerously out of control. "You two," shouted the Bo'sun, pointing at Pintel and Ragetti, "you brought us the wrong person!"

"She had the medallion!" argued Pintel.

"She said her name was Turner!" Ragetti added.

From his spot in the angry crowd, Twigg, the tall pirate who had had a run-in with Jack in the jail earlier, came forward. His expression was murderous as he stared at Barbossa. "You," he snarled. "It's you who brought us here in the first place."

As the accusations continued to fly, no one bothered to keep an eye on Elizabeth. Lying on the ledge, her eyes slowly opened and she tried to lift her head. Suddenly, a hand reached out and covered her mouth. It was Will! While the pirates had been busy attacking one another, he had slipped into the water and made his way to Elizabeth's side. Now, he gestured at the exit and started to pull her towards the water. Shaking her head, she nodded back at the medallion that lay close by. Silently, she crept over, picked it up and then slipped, unnoticed, into the water beside Will.

Barbossa, meanwhile, was trying to regain order over his crew. "Any more talk," he shouted, "and I'll chain ye all to a cannon and send ye to the watery depths!"

Suddenly, Barbossa's monkey began to jump up and down, screeching for all it was worth.

Barbossa turned, his eyes flying from the frantic monkey to the spot where Elizabeth was supposed to be – but wasn't. With a roar of rage, he looked over in time to see Elizabeth and Will's figures retreating to the safety of the longboats. "The medallion!" he shouted. "She's taken it!"

Scrambling into action, the pirates headed for the longboats. But when they arrived, they encountered a minor problem – all the oars were missing! Letting out a collective scream of rage, the crew scurried to find anything in the treasure room that could be used as an oar.

Close by, a dazed Jack Sparrow was coming to. In one hand, he held the oar with which Will had so unkindly smashed, while his other hand was pressed to his aching head.

"You!" said Ragetti, when his eyes landed on his old captain. "You're supposed to be dead!"

"I'm not?" Jack asked, utterly confused by the situation in which he now found himself. Last time he checked, he was sneaking away from Will, with a plan to get the *Black Pearl* back . . . sort of. Now he was surrounded by an angry mob of cursed pirates, and his head ached to high heaven.

Making matters worse, Pintel suddenly drew his pistol and aimed it at Jack's chest. He had to do something quickly, or, unlike the other pirates, he would be quite dead. "Par . . . Pas . . ." he stuttered, trying to say the one word he knew could help him. "Par . . . parsnip? No . . . parsley? Ah, parley. Yes, parley."

With a groan, the pirates lowered their weapons.

"Parley!" cried Pintel. "Curses to the depths whatever muttonhead thought up parley!"

As they led Jack away from the water and back to a waiting Barbossa, he leaned over to Pintel. "That would be the French," he said, a smile on his lips.

Chapter 17

Will Turner threw the last of the pirates' oars overboard and climbed onto the deck of the *Interceptor*. Streaming out behind him in a long line were the rest of the oars that he and Elizabeth had taken when they escaped the cave. Now, the two of them stood dripping in front of a crew of very confused-looking shipmates.

"Where be Jack?" asked Gibbs.

Elizabeth started at the mention of the notorious pirate. Had he been involved in her escape? The same man who had used her to get away from the Royal Navy had come to rescue her? It seemed very unlikely. But now this man that she quickly recognized as the grouchy sailor Gibbs, whom she had met eight years ago, was asking for his whereabouts.

"He fell behind," Will answered, not meeting the man's eye, as Anamaria gave the orders and the crew prepared to sail. The Code left them no options. They were to leave Jack.

Meanwhile, Jack Sparrow was attempting to negotiate his way out of a very sticky situation. Having no way to escape from *Isla de Muerta*, seeing as all the oars for the longboats had somehow upped and gone, he now found himself face-to-face with his old first mate and current enemy – Barbossa.

"How the blazes did you get off that island?" Barbossa asked upon seeing Jack.

Jack flashed his trademark grin, but his eyes remained cold and guarded. "When you marooned me on that spit of land," he said slowly, "you forgot one very important thing, mate. I'm Captain Jack Sparrow."

"Ah," said Barbossa. "Then I won't be making that mistake again. Gents – kill him."

The crew happily cocked their pistols.

But Jack held up a hand. "The girl's blood didn't work, did it?" he asked.

Barbossa snapped to attention. Leave it to Jack Sparrow to get the upper hand. "You know whose blood we need?" Barbossa asked.

Jack levelled his eyes with Barbossa's, a

knowing gleam flashing between them. "I know whose blood you need."

Meanwhile, back in a cabin on the *Interceptor*, Elizabeth Swann sat and attempted to bandage her wounded hand. It still stung from where the blade had sliced into her palm, but the bleeding had lessened.

Will Turner sat across from Elizabeth, his forehead etched with worry as he watched her fumble with the white gauze. Reaching out, he took her hand in his and slowly began to redo the wrapping. For a few moments, there was silence as the two gazed intently at their hands.

Finally, Will broke the silence. "You gave Barbossa my name as yours," he said. "Why?"

"I don't know," she answered, looking up and meeting his gaze. The searching look in her eyes caused Will to pull the gauze too tightly, and Elizabeth let out a little cry.

"I'm sorry – blacksmith's hands."

But that did not seem to bother Elizabeth. She began to lean forward, knowing that what she wanted to say would be done best without words.

Sensing what was about to happen, Will,

too, leaned forward. But instead of the kiss he had expected, he felt something cool pressed into his palm. Looking down, his eyes came to rest on a gold medallion.

"It's yours," Elizabeth explained.

Suddenly, Will remembered. "It was a gift . . . from my father. Why did you take it?" he asked.

"I was afraid you were a pirate," she said.

Understanding flooded through Will. It all made sense now. Elizabeth had told the pirates her name was Turner. Jack had mentioned that Will's father was Bootstrap Bill – a pirate. Therefore, the pirates had believed they held a pirate's child captive. "It wasn't your blood they needed," he said aloud. "It was my father's blood. My blood. The blood of a pirate."

Onboard the *Black Pearl*, Jack Sparrow found himself back where he belonged – in the captain's cabin attempting to reach an accord with Barbossa. Unfortunately, since he had last been in the room, the place had fallen into a sorry state of affairs. Sitting at the large dining table that filled most of the room, he glanced at the tattered fixtures. Pity, he thought, that such a fine ship should have become so neglected.

"You expect to leave me standing on some beach with nothing more than a name and your word it's the one we need," the cursed captain was saying, "and watch you sail away on my ship?"

Reaching over to pull a green apple from the bowl in front of him, Jack turned his attention back to Barbossa. "Oh, no," he said. "I expect to leave you standing on some beach with absolutely no name at all, watching me sail away on my ship – and then I'll shout the name back to you, savvy?" Smiling, he took a bite out of the juicy apple and watched as Barbossa squirmed.

As he jealously watched Jack chew the apple, Barbossa pointed out that the plan required trusting Jack's word – not something he was inclined to do given their history.

But, as Jack pointed out, of the two of them, only Barbossa had taken part in a mutiny. So, really, it was Jack's word that they should be trusting. Then, as an afterthought, he added, "Although I should be thanking you. If you hadn't betrayed me and left me to die, I'd have had an equal share in the curse."

They were interrupted by the Bo'sun, who

appeared at the door with news. The *Interceptor* was in sight. Without a word, the pair headed for the main deck. Pulling out a spyglass, Barbossa focused in on the *Interceptor*. She was making good speed, but she was no match for the *Black Pearl*. Suddenly, Jack's face blocked Barbossa's view.

"I'm having a thought here," he interjected. "We run up a flag of truce, I go over and negotiate the return of your medallion. What say you to that?"

Barbossa brought the spyglass down and glared at the wily pirate. He was always negotiating – and plotting. But Barbossa knew better.

"Now, Jack. That's exactly the attitude that lost you the *Pearl*. Bodies are easier to search when they're dead."

Turning, Barbossa ordered Jack to the brig. He would deal with him later. Now he needed to get to that ship . . . and the medallion.

Chapter 18

Aboard the *Interceptor*, Elizabeth Swann was just emerging onto the deck. She had left Will below, unsure of what to say to him now that she had given him the medallion. Looking around, she noticed that the crew was frantically running about as Gibbs and Anamaria shouted orders.

"What's happening?" she asked, running over to Gibbs. Following his gaze, Elizabeth gasped. There, on the horizon, surrounded by a thick fog, was the *Black Pearl* – and she was gaining. If they were to escape Barbossa's clutches, they would have to act fast.

Turning her attention back to Gibbs and Anamaria, Elizabeth said, "We've got a shallower draft, right?" At Anamaria's nod, she continued. "Then can't we lose them among the shoals?"

The three turned and looked to the horizon in front of them. Not far away, the indistinct shape of a rocky outcropping could be seen.

Apparently thinking that Elizabeth's idea was better than no idea, Anamaria turned to the crew and barked out new orders. "Lighten the ship! Stem to stern!"

Barbossa, however, had no intention of letting them get away. With Jack safely locked below, Barbossa watched as the crew of the *Interceptor* began to throw cargo overboard. He had them running scared!

"Raise the flag and run out the guns!" he ordered. "Haul on the mainsails and let go!" From the side of the *Black Pearl*, oars appeared and the crew began to row, adding to the ship's already increasing speed. And from the mainsail, a flag unfurled, revealing the black-and-white skull and crossbones of the Jolly Roger.

Walking onto the *Interceptor*'s deck, Will, too, took in the chaos and looked behind him just in time to see the Jolly Roger begin to snap in the air. Running over to the rail, he grabbed a line and watched as the *Pearl*'s oars appeared. All around him, the crew continued to throw whatever they could overboard. Just in time, he stopped two men from throwing a cannon into the water – that, they definitely were going to need.

But despite their efforts, the *Black Pearl* continued to gain on them. Acting quickly, Will ordered the crew to load the remaining guns with whatever they could find – silverware, nails, even glass. As long as it could be fired, it would do. Now, they just needed to find a way to get the *Pearl* along their port side – facing the cannons. Turning once again to Anamaria, Elizabeth shouted, "Drop the anchor starboard side!"

"You're daft, lady!" Anamaria shouted back, but she saw that the *Pearl* was now even closer and within moments would be in firing range. There was no time to argue. With a splash, the anchor dropped into the blue water and began to drag along the bottom. Hooking on a reef, the anchor line pulled taut and, with a loud groan, the *Interceptor* began to pivot, her bow almost pulled underwater by the motion. Belowdecks, anything not nailed down slid across the floor – including the gold medallion. Sliding across the table, it fell to the ground with a clank.

When the ship finally stopped pivoting,

there was a moment of odd silence as both crews evaluated the situation. The *Black Pearl* and the *Interceptor* now sat parallel to each other – at the ready for a fight.

At almost the exact same moment, "Fire!" rang out from both ships, and the air filled with the sound of cannons blasting. For several agonizing moments, the blue sky turned grey with smoke and screams could be heard across the water. When the smoke finally cleared and the guns were silenced, everyone took in the damage. Steaming holes gaped from the side of the *Interceptor*'s hull, while over on the *Pearl*, silverware and glass littered the deck and hull. Near one of the *Pearl*'s cannons, Pintel and Ragetti looked out at the other ship. Looking over at his friend, Pintel noticed that the man had a fork sticking out of his wooden eye. Yanking it out, the skinny one-eyed pirate shook his head. Blasted cannons!

Still locked in the *Black Pearl*'s brig, Jack peered through a hole in the ship and watched as the cannons fired. Suddenly a blast rang out and Jack ducked just as a huge hole was blown through his cell wall. "Stop blowing holes in my ship!" he cried out.

Then something caught his eye. Jack's luck had just taken another decidedly positive turn – the door to his cell had been blasted open. He was free. Skipping through the water, he pushed open the door further and made his way out. It was time to take back the *Pearl*.

As Barbossa continued to lay siege to the *Interceptor*, Elizabeth, Will, Gibbs and Anamaria desperately tried to think of a new plan.

"We need us a devil's dowry," Gibbs said hopelessly.

"We've got one!" shouted Anamaria, grabbing Elizabeth. "We'll give 'im her!"

But Will knew that Elizabeth was worth nothing to Barbossa. The cursed pirate would not stop the fight until he had something far smaller and of much more value – the Medallion.

Without another word, Will turned and headed belowdecks. If Barbossa wanted the medallion, he would get the medallion. Will had almost lost Elizabeth once – he would not lose her again.

Chapter 19

The fight was in full force as Will went belowdecks in search of the medallion. Back aboard the *Black Pearl*, Barbossa shouted orders to his men, eager to get what he was looking for and then head back to *Isla de Muerta*.

Suddenly, with a loud creak, the mast of the *Interceptor* snapped, sending it crashing down. Fallen, the long piece of wood created a bridge between the two ships. Seeing his chance, Barbossa ordered his men to board the *Interceptor*. "Find me that medallion," he shouted.

Jack, meanwhile, had snuck unnoticed onto the deck. As men hurried across the fallen mast and grabbed lines to swing over the water, Jack waited for his chance. One of the men, missing his landing, swung back over the water and dropped into the waves below. Grabbing the now free rope, Jack tipped his hat. "Thanks very much," he said to the man in the water below before he took hold and swung across. Upon landing, Jack scanned the deck. Spotting Elizabeth, he rushed over. "Where's the medallion?" he asked, grabbing her by the shoulders.

In response, she reached out to slap him. But Jack had learned his lesson on Tortuga. Grabbing her wrist, he noticed the bandaged hand and the look of fury in her eyes. "Ah," he sighed. "And where is dear William, then?"

The look of anger vanished as a realization dawned on Elizabeth. Will had gone belowdecks and not returned.

As water rose steadily below the decks of the damaged *Interceptor*, Will searched in vain for the medallion. Pieces of wood and debris floated past as his hands searched the water for any sign of the gold. Hearing a screech, he looked up to see the cursed monkey standing at a hole in the bulkhead. In the creature's hand was the medallion. With one last screech, it turned and leaped outside, leaving Will alone in the rising water.

Rushing over to the door to the bulkhead,

Will pushed against it, but it would not budge. It was blocked. Seeing the futility in trying to get out that way, he swam towards a grate that opened to the deck while the water continued to rise. On the other side, he heard Elizabeth call his name and then she was there, reaching her fingers towards him.

"Elizabeth," he said, desperation in his voice. Then, as he watched helplessly, two pirates grabbed her by the shoulders and dragged her away. A moment later, his fingers slipped down as he disappeared beneath the water.

As Will was claimed by the sea and Elizabeth was dragged away by the cursed pirates, Jack saw his last bargaining chip being carried back towards the *Black Pearl* in the hands of a monkey. The medallion glittered in the sunlight as the creature scampered over the mast. Taking off after it, Jack shimmied across the mast, using his hands to balance. On the other side, he reached out to grab the medallion, but it was too late. Another hand had reached out first.

Bringing his gaze up, Jack's eyes landed on Barbossa. "Why, thank you, Jack!" the man said.

"You're welcome," Jack replied.

"Not you. We named the monkey Jack." Turning, Barbossa raised the medallion and addressed his crew. "Gents," he shouted, "our hope is restored."

A short while later, the crew of the *Interceptor* found themselves tied to the *Black Pearl's* mast. Holding the medallion in his fingertips, Barbossa waited, while Pintel pointed his gun at the captives. "Any of you so much as thinks the word 'parley,' I'll have your guts for garters."

Tied up with the crew, Elizabeth stared over at the *Interceptor*. Fires burned over the hull and the remaining sails were ripped and torn. And somewhere onboard, Elizabeth believed, was her beloved Will.

Pushing the ropes up and over her head, she slipped free and moved forward. But before she had taken even two steps, the *Interceptor* exploded, sending debris high into the air. "Will!" Elizabeth shouted, rushing to the rail. With rage in her eyes, she attacked Barbossa.

Grabbing her by the wrists, Barbossa just laughed. "Welcome back, miss. You took advantage of our hospitality last time. It holds fair now you return the favour." With another laugh, he shoved her at a group of dirty pirates who began to hoot and jeer.

But they were interrupted by a shout. "Barbossa!"

Climbing up onto the rail, his clothes soaking wet, was Will Turner. At Elizabeth's excited shout, he gave her an almost imperceptible nod before jumping off the rail and grabbing Jack's pistol, which lay on a table of loot nearby. "She goes free," he demanded, walking to Barbossa and cocking the pistol.

"What's in your head, boy?" Barbossa asked, unbothered by Will's dramatic appearance. "You've only got one shot – and we can't die."

Jack Sparrow, standing off to one side, shook his head. "Don't do anything stupid," he muttered to Will.

But it was too late. Raising the pistol, Will stepped back onto the rail and pointed it at his own head. "You can't. I can."

Seeing that he would have to step in and defuse the situation – or at least try to keep Will from ruining his plans – Jack spoke up. "He's no one," he explained, dismissively. "A distant cousin of my aunt's nephew once removed."

Ignoring Jack, Will went on. "My name is Will Turner. My father was Bootstrap Bill Turner. His blood runs in my veins."

Murmurs of understanding began to ripple among the crew as Will's words sunk in.

"Name your terms, Mr *Turner*," Barbossa said.

Glancing over at Elizabeth, Will demanded that she and the crew go free. He neglected, however, to mention Jack Sparrow. From his spot on the deck, Jack sighed. Try and help a man out and what does he do? Stab you in the back. Young Mr Turner was turning into quite a pirate.

Elizabeth Swann, her dark dress billowing in the ocean breeze, stood on a plank over the blue Caribbean Sea. Behind her, Will struggled against the ropes that held him, his eyes flashing with anger as he tried to call out. But it was no use. He was bound and gagged, helpless, as he watched Elizabeth walk to her "freedom".

Barbossa had got what he needed – the medallion and the blood. As for his promises?

Well, they were open to interpretation. After giving Will his word that Elizabeth would go free, he had set course back to *Isla de Muerta* – with one stop on the way.

Now, the *Black Pearl* sat off the shore of a small island that was nothing more than a strip of beach and a few palm trees. Turning his attention back to Elizabeth, Barbossa ordered her off the plank. But not without first asking for his dress back. Scowling, she ripped it off and threw it at him. "Here!" she said, trying to sound braver as she stood shivering in her shift. "It goes well with your black heart!" With one last look at Will, she moved to the end of the plank and fell into the water below.

Jack Sparrow, his hands tied in front of him, was next. "I really hoped we were past all this," he said.

Walking over, Barbossa flung an arm around the man's shoulders and smiled, his teeth brown in the sun. "Jack, Jack . . . Now, didn't you notice," he said. "That's the same little island we made you governor of on our last little trip. Perhaps you'll be able to conjure up another miraculous escape." Pausing, he added, "But I doubt it."

Pulling out his sword, he urged Jack further out onto the plank. Time was wasting. There were curses to be *un*done and living to be done.

But Jack wasn't ready to jump quite yet. "Last time you left me a pistol, with one shot," he pointed out. When Barbossa produced Jack's pistol, the pirate tried his luck one more time. "Seeing as there's two of us, a gentlman would give us two pistols."

"It'll be one pistol, as before," Barbossa replied. "And you can be the gentlman an' shoot the lady and starve to death yourself." Taking Jack's effects, he threw them with a splash into the water. A moment later there was another splash as Jack dived in after them.

Stumbling onto the white sand that surrounded the tiny strip of an island, Elizabeth and Jack turned and watched as the *Black Pearl* faded into the horizon.

Loosening the rope around his hands, Jack squinted in the sun and sighed. "That's the second time I've had to watch that man sail away with my ship," he said. Then, turning, he strode off, leaving a hopeless Elizabeth in his wake.

Chapter 20

Watching Captain Jack Sparrow sashay away from the shore, Elizabeth Swann clenched her fists. She would not let him get away so easily. His pirating ways had landed them in this mess and now they would help get them out of it. With one last glance behind her, Elizabeth took off after him.

"But you were marooned on this same island before," she shouted as she caught up to Jack. "We can get off the same way you did then!"

The sound of Elizabeth's voice grated on Jack – as did her naïveté. Whirling around, he stood and glared at her, the red of his bandanna gleaming in the sunshine.

"To what point and purpose?" he asked. "The *Black Pearl* is gone. And unless you have a rudder and a lot of sails hidden in that bodice..." He paused and leaned back a bit as his eyes moved up and down Elizabeth. Then he added, "Young Mr Turner will be dead long before you reach him."

He began to stride away, his steps exaggerated as he counted under his breath. Undeterred by the pirate's erratic behaviour, Elizabeth continued to follow him, talking as she went. "But you're *Captain* Jack Sparrow! You vanished from under the noses of seven agents of the East India Trading Company!" Elizabeth reached out and grabbed Jack by the shoulders, turning him around so that she could stare directly into his brown eyes as she added, "Are you the pirate I've read about or not? How did you escape last time?"

For a moment, Jack seemed uncertain of what to say. The girl's interest and knowledge of him was quite flattering, but she did not have the whole story. Sighing, he confessed. "Last time," he said, stomping on the sandy ground, "I was here a grand total of three days." As he continued to speak, he pushed her backward and leaned down. Then, with a grunt, he leaned over and pushed aside sand, revealing a trapdoor. Pulling it up, he quickly descended the staircase and disappeared. His voice was muffled as he continued to speak. "Last time the rumrunners who used this island as a cache came by, and I bartered passage off."

Suddenly, from the hole, Jack's hand emerged, an old bottle of rum clenched tightly in his fingers. Elizabeth's eyes grew wide as the truth of Jack's so-called adventure sunk in. "So that's it?" she said in exasperation. "You spent three days lying on the beach drinking rum?"

Back above ground, Jack held out another bottle of rum to Elizabeth and shrugged. "Welcome to the Caribbean, love," he said, popping the cork of his own bottle and tilting his head back.

Beneath a starry sky, Elizabeth and Jack, arms linked, danced around a large fire with their rum bottles in hand. Their voices echoed off the empty sea as they sang a familiar pirate shanty. Dropping to the ground, Elizabeth dragged Jack down beside her. Her disappointment at learning Jack's true story had faded with the day – and now she was content to drink, sing and dance . . .

"When I get the *Pearl* back," Jack said, his

tone sounding quite serious, despite the bottle in his hand, "I'm going to teach that song to the whole crew, and we'll sing it all the time!"

"You'll be positively the most fearsome pirates to sail the Spanish Main," Elizabeth shouted.

For a moment, Jack considered the possibility. In the light from the fire, his brown eyes looked almost kind. "Not just the Spanish Main," he told Elizabeth. "The whole world . . . Wherever we want to go, we go. That's what a ship is, you know. Not just a keel and a hull and a deck and sails. That's what a ship needs. But what a ship is – what the *Black Pearl* really is – is freedom." With a sigh, Jack turned towards the sea, lost in thoughts of his ship.

Despite herself, Elizabeth momentarily felt her heart flutter. In his voice, Elizabeth could hear Jack's pain. While he swaggered about with a supreme air of confidence that Elizabeth often found infuriating, there was another side of him – a softer side. Leaning down, she rested her head on his shoulder and sighed. This new side of Jack was going to make what she did next a bit harder. "Jack," she said softly, "it must really be terrible for you to be trapped on this island."

However, at the moment, Jack was not at all opposed to being trapped. Unlike his last visit, he now had company. And, he realized, looking down at Elizabeth's porcelain skin and brown eyes, said company was quite easy on the eyes. Raising his arm slowly, he brought it around Elizabeth's back and rested a hand on her shoulder.

Shaking off his hand, Elizabeth raised her bottle. "To freedom," she said, pretending to take a swig.

"To the *Black Pearl*," added Jack, unaware of Elizabeth's ruse. Then, tilting his head back he began to swallow until, with one last gulp, he fell back into the sand, unconscious. Elizabeth had knocked Jack out cold.

The smell of fire filtered through Jack's nose, and with effort he opened one eye and tried to take in his surroundings. He was still on the beach near the remains of the bonfire, but the stars were gone, replaced by a brilliant blue, cloudless sky. But the smoke? It wasn't coming from the fire he had built the previous night. Suddenly, a loud explosion rocked the island. That was *definitely* not coming from the bonfire. Sitting up quickly,

Jack groaned and placed a hand on his aching head. What he saw when his blurry eyes focused made his head ache even more. Elizabeth Swann, her white dressing gown covered in soot, raced around a patch of palm trees, throwing barrels of rum into an already billowing fire. As they landed in the heat, the barrels exploded, sending splinters of wood flying high into the air.

"No!" shouted Jack, scrambling to his feet and placing his hands on either side of his head. "Not good! Stop! You've burned all the food, the shade – the rum!"

"Yes," Elizabeth shouted back as she continued to fuel the fire. "The rum is gone."

"But why is the rum gone?" Jack asked.

Turning her back on the flames, Elizabeth walked over to Jack. "That signal," she said, pointing to the fire, "goes up a thousand feet. The entire Royal Navy is out looking for me. Do you think there is even the slightest chance they won't see it?" At Jack's groan, Elizabeth raised her chin proudly and added, "Just wait, Captain Sparrow. In an hour, maybe two, there'll be white sails on that horizon."

Without another word, she plopped down

on the sand and wrapped her arms around her knees. Grabbing the pistol from his belt, Jack struggled to remain calm. The rum was gone. The shade was gone. And this little, aggravating fool thought she was so smart. Shaking with the effort to not use his last bullet on Elizabeth, Jack turned and stalked off, muttering under his breath.

A few minutes later, Jack crested a dune, still trying to put as much distance as he could between himself and Elizabeth. Looking out to sea, he did a double take. There, on the horizon, her white sails billowing, was the HMS *Dauntless*.

Sighing, Jack looked back to where Elizabeth sat. "There'll be no living with her after this," he murmured.

Chapter 21

Safely back aboard the HMS *Dauntless*, Elizabeth Swann found herself once again butting heads with a stubborn man. But this time, the man was not the infamous Captain Jack Sparrow. It was Commodore Norrington.

"We have to go back," she shouted at him. "We have to rescue Will!"

Governor Swann, who had chosen to accompany the commodore as he searched for Elizabeth, stepped forward. Unlike Elizabeth and Jack, who both wore a fine layer of dirt, gun powder and rum smoke on their skin, the governor looked dapper and clean. The curls of his white wig hung just so and there was only the smallest touch of worry in his eyes. After all, Elizabeth was now safe and the pirate Jack Sparrow stood captive between two marines, his ankles in chains. There was no need to complicate matters by worrying over the life of a young blacksmith. "The boy's fate is regrettable," he said, when Elizabeth accused him of condemning Will to death. "But so was his decision to engage in piracy."

The decision had been made. The *Dauntless* would return to Port Royal, Jack Sparrow would hang and the rest of them would continue on with their lives.

From his spot on the rail, Jack Sparrow listened quietly. An idea was forming in his head. Reaching up, he twirled his goatee in his fingers.

"If I may be so bold to interject my professional opinion," he said, stepping away from the two marines and shuffling towards the commodore and governor, the metal around his ankles clanking. Holding his hands up, he said, "The *Pearl* was listing near to scuppers after the battle. Very unlikely she'll make good time. Think about it, Commodore – the *Black Pearl* . . . the last real pirate threat in the Caribbean, mate. How can you pass that up?"

But apparently, Norrington could and would pass up the chance to capture the *Black Pearl*. Turning, he began to walk back towards the helm, only to be stopped by Elizabeth's voice.

"Commodore," she said. "I beg you – please do this . . . for me. As a wedding gift."

Slowly, Norrington turned and looked at Elizabeth, unable to speak. Governor Swann, on the other hand, was quite capable of speech. Rushing over to his daughter's side, he placed a hand on her shoulder. "My dear," he said with excitement, "are you accepting the commodore's proposal?"

"I am," she replied.

At Elizabeth's affirmation, Jack began to jump up and down. "A wedding!" he said. "I love weddings!"

Jack's outburst was just what Norrington needed to propel him back into action. With one last glance at Elizabeth, Norrington strode towards Jack, stopping mere inches from his face. "Mister Sparrow," he said in a clipped tone. "You will accompany these men to the helm and provide them with a bearing to *Isla de Muerta*. Do I make myself clear?"

"Inescapably," Jack replied, trying not to smile. He had got what he wanted, after all – they were going back for the *Black Pearl*.

* * *

While the HMS *Dauntless* changed course and began to head to *Isla de Muerta*, the *Black Pearl* was already well on her way. In the brig belowdecks, the surviving members of Jack's crew from the destroyed *Interceptor* stood and watched as Pintel and Ragetti mopped the floors.

Will Turner, in a separate cell, paced back and forth, his mind racing. Suddenly, he stopped and rested his arm on the cell bars. "You knew William Turner," he asked Pintel, the closer of the two pirates.

Pausing mid-mop, Pintel looked up and sighed. His bald head reflected the dim light from the lanterns along the walls and his eyes were cold. But still, he answered. "Ol' Bootstrap Bill? We knew him."

As Ragetti continued to mop, Pintel added, "It never sat well with Bootstrap what we did to Jack Sparrow – the mutiny and all. Said it wasn't right with the Code. That's why he sent off a piece of the treasure – said we deserved to remain cursed."

As Pintel continued to talk, Will lowered his head. His father was a man who knew right from wrong and who had made these pirates pay.

He was a good man. And a pirate. Will had spent all his life hating pirates. But now? Now everything had changed.

Pintel continued his tale of Bootstrap. "So what Captain Barbossa did, he strapped a cannon to Bootstrap's bootstraps and the last we saw, he was sinking to the crushing black oblivion of Davy Jones's Locker." At the mention of Davy Jones, there was a moment of silence. Then, Pintel added, "It was only after that we learned we needed his blood to lift the curse."

Suddenly, the sound of footsteps echoed through the brig and Barbossa appeared. "Bring him," he ordered, nodding in the direction of Will.

They had arrived at *Isla de Muerta*. It was time to end the curse once and for all.

Through the lens of his spyglass, Commodore Norrington stared out at the *Black Pearl*. Hidden among the rocks that lined *Isla de Muerta*, two of the *Dauntless*'s longboats floated gently in the water. Norrington sat at the head of the lead boat, his spyglass in hand, while behind him sat Jack, closely guarded by Murtogg and Mullroy –

the same two dimwitted marines the pirate had encountered back in Port Royal.

"I don't care for the situation," Norrington said, lowering his spyglass. The deck of the *Black Pearl* appeared empty. The only sign of life was a lantern or two rocking in the gentle ocean breeze. "Any attempt to storm the island could turn into an ambush."

"Not if you do the ambushing," Jack pointed out, moving closer to the commodore. While the pirate had successfully managed to get back to *Isla de Muerta*, there was still the matter of getting his ship back. And in order to do *that*, he would need to be in control of the situation – without anyone's knowledge of course. When Norrington did not immediately shut him up, Jack continued. "I'll go in and convince Barbossa to send his men out – leaving you to do nothing but blast them silly with your cannons."

Norrington paused to consider Jack's suggestion. While he hated to admit it, the pirate's plan was not entirely without merit. Nodding, he agreed. If Jack wanted to go in after the murderous Barbossa, Norrrington would not stand in his way.

At the commodore's nod, Jack smiled.

Things were working out perfectly. There was just one more thing he had to take care of – keeping Elizabeth quiet about the curse.

"Now, to be quite honest," he added, once more getting Norrington's attention by tapping him on the shoulder. "There's a risk to those aboard the *Dauntless*, which includes the future Mrs Commodore. . . "

Moments later, Elizabeth Swann found herself being dragged unceremoniously towards the captain's cabin – for her own "safety". Struggling against the men, she tried to explain that the pirates they were going after were cursed. But it was no use – the officers just laughed at her.

As the door shut behind her, she sighed in frustration. This was all Jack Sparrow's doing.

And out on the water, rowing swiftly away from the *Dauntless*, Jack Sparrow smiled. The *Black Pearl* was as good as his.

Chapter 22

Inside *Isla de Muerta*, the cave of treasure suddenly filled with light as Barbossa and his men entered with their torches. Will Turner was shoved into the room by Pintel and Ragetti, his hands tied behind his back and the gold medallion around his neck.

"No reason to fret," Pintel said with a laugh. "It's just a prick of the finger and a few drops of blood."

But the pirate Twigg had another idea. "There'll be no mistakes this time. We spill it all."

It appeared Will actually did have reason to worry. As he was shoved forward, Will felt his hope begin to slip away. It would take a miracle to get out of this situation – and he seemed to be right out of miracles.

A few moments later, the cave filled with the shouts of the pirates as the moment of truth drew nearer. Torchlight flickered off the cave walls and mixed with the moonlight filtering down from a hole above, adding an eerie ambience to the event. Hunched over the open chest of Aztec Gold, Will looked out at the frenzied pirates and groaned. Barbossa, standing close beside Will, held up a knife and listened as the shouts increased.

Suddenly, Barbossa caught a movement in the crowd and saw the flash of a familiar red bandanna.

"Excuse me. Pardon me . . . ah, begun by blood."

"Jack!" Will shouted when the pirate finally pushed and sashayed his way to the front of the crowd.

"Not possible," Barbossa hissed. He had left Jack to die on that island – again. And again, the rascally man had somehow managed to escape. It was clear that this man was more of a curse to Barbossa than the one caused by the Aztec Gold.

Jack lifted a finger. "Not probable," he pointed out.

"Where's Elizabeth?" Will asked, staring

Jack in the eye and shrugging off the hands that held him over the chest.

"She's safe, just like I promised," Jack assured, before adding that she had promised to marry Norrington and that, of course, Will had promised to die for her. So they were all good on their promises. When Jack finally finished his explanation, Barbossa threw up his hands. He didn't have time for this.

"Shut up!" he shouted, pointing his knife at Jack. "You're next."

As Jack recoiled, Barbossa turned and shoved Will back down over the chest. Holding his knife against the boy's throat, he prepared to cut.

But once again, Jack interrupted. "You don't want to be doing that," he said.

"No," Barbossa replied. "I really think I do."

Shrugging, Jack clasped his hands together and began to examine the slippery rocks around him. "All right," he said, appearing thoroughly intrigued by his surroundings. "It's your funeral." When Barbossa finally asked why, Jack looked up and began to take a step forward.

"Well," he explained, "because the HMS

Dauntless, pride of the Royal Navy, is floating just offshore . . . waiting for you."

As the pirates began to murmur and groan, Jack smiled. He had Barbossa and his men just where he wanted them.

Floating safely outside the cave was the crew of the *Dauntless*, but they were not aboard their ship. Instead, the majority of the crew sat floating in seven longboats, preparing for attack. Sitting among his men, Commodore Norrington kept a lookout for any sign of movement, while behind him Murtogg and Mullroy argued back and forth.

"What are we doing here?" whispered Murtogg.

Rolling his eyes at Murtogg's apparent stupidity, Mullroy replied, "The pirates come out, unprepared and unawares – we catch 'em in a crossfire and send 'em down to sea."

From his spot at the front of the longboat, Norrington smiled. Let Jack Sparrow think he was calling all the shots. It would only make victory all the sweeter when Jack, *along* with Barbossa and his crew, was caught in a trap of his own making.

* * *

Back in the cave, Captain Jack Sparrow was negotiating . . . yet again. Having caught Barbossa's attention with news of the looming attack, he was now hoping to put the last of his plan into action. But he needed to convince Barbossa to attack first. The other captain stood with his knife still in hand while Jack began to speak. Will, from his spot nearby listened closely, interested to see what Jack Sparrow had to say this time around.

"So you order your men to row out to the *Dauntless*, and they do what they do best," Jack began, "and there you are! With two ships. The makings of your very own fleet. Of course, you'll take the grandest as your flagship, but what of the *Pearl*?" Stopping, Jack waited and watched as Barbossa's eyes began to twinkle. When Jack was sure he had Barbossa dreaming of a fleet at his command, he made one more suggestion. "Name me captain. I sail under your colours, I give you ten per cent of my plunder and you get to introduce yourself as Commodore Barbossa, savvy?"

Commodore Barbossa. It had a nice ring to it. While he was more inclined to simply lock up Jack and continue on with killing young Mr Turner, there was something appealing about having his own fleet. But there had to be a catch.

"I suppose in exchange, you want me not to kill the whelp," he said, nodding at Will.

"Not at all. By all means, kill the whelp," Jack said casually, reaching down and picking up a handful of coins from the chest.

Will, helpless to do anything, glared at the pirate. He had been right not to trust Jack all along. But, as Will watched, Jack looked over at him and widened his eyes. Turning back to Barbossa, Jack added, "Wait to lift the curse until the opportune moment. For instance: after you've killed Norrington's men. Every . . . last . . . one of them." One by one he dropped the coins back into the chest, the clink of gold hitting gold emphasizing Jack's words. Only Will, curious after hearing the pirate use the familiar phrase, saw him slyly slip one coin up into the billowing sleeves of his shirt.

"You've been planning this all along," Will said, straining against his ropes and drawing the attention momentarily away from Jack. He was not sure what the pirate was up to, but he was willing to help – if only to save himself.

Ignoring Will, Barbossa brought the discussion back around to the subject of profit. "I want fifty per cent of your plunder," he told Jack.

"Twenty-five," countered Jack, "and I'll buy you the hat. The really big one . . . *Commodore*." Holding out his hand, he waited.

"Agreed," Barbossa finally said, as the room filled with the approving shouts of the crew. Turning his back on Jack and Will, Barbossa faced his men. It was time to procure himself the makings of a fleet.

"Gents," he shouted. "Take a walk."

From his spot right behind Barbossa, Jack cocked his head. A walk? But Norrington expected boats full of pirates.

Noticing Jack's confused expression, Barbossa smiled. Soon he would be a commodore, with Jack at his command, and not long after he would kill Will Turner and lift the curse. The night – and his future – was definitely growing brighter.

Chapter 23

Outside the cave, the clouds parted, revealing the bright face of a full moon. The *Dauntless*, resting at anchor, was silent. Only a small crew of men was left to stand guard. Underneath the water, shafts of moonlight pierced the murky blue, illuminating a school of fish. Suddenly, the fish scattered in all directions as out of the shadows of the cave marched Barbossa's cursed crew.

Once again, their flesh had disappeared and only their bones could be seen through their tattered clothing. In their hands they held swords and pistols as they made their way towards the unsuspecting *Dauntless*. When they were directly beneath her hull they began to climb.

As the cursed pirates climbed aboard the *Dauntless*, Norrington and his men sat in the longboats, unaware of the impending danger facing their fellow crew members. All eyes were trained on the cave entrance, when they heard a splash and into view rowed a longboat. Inside the boat, sat Pintel and Ragetti, dressed in women's clothing. As Pintel rowed, Ragetti twirled a parasol about. "This is just like what the Greeks did at Troy," Ragetti said, smiling. "'cept they wore a horse n'stead of dresses." Rolling his eyes, Pintel continued to row.

Back aboard the *Dauntless*, Governor Swann made his way towards the captain's cabin. The day's events weighed heavily on his mind – especially Elizabeth's decision to wed. Knocking on the door, he waited for an answer from Elizabeth. When none came, he began to speak anyway. "I just want you to know . . . I couldn't be more proud of you," he said.

Inside the cabin, Elizabeth turned at the sound of her father's voice, but made no move to answer him or open the door. Instead, she continued to button up the red marine jacket she now wore. Finishing, she moved towards the window and looked down into the water below. At the ship's stern, a single longboat floated in the water, a long line of knotted sheets serving as a ladder to the boat. She had no intention of staying inside. Will was somewhere out there. Grabbing ahold of the rope, she began to climb down.

As Elizabeth rowed away into the shadows, Governor Swann finally stopped speaking. He found it odd that his daughter had not yet replied. Knocking once more, he opened the door. There was no one there! Rushing over, he glanced out the open window and saw the sheet ladder. Sighing, he looked out at the empty water.

Meanwhile, Pintel and Ragetti, still dressed as ladies, were rowing ever closer to the *Dauntless*. For a few confused moments, all eyes on the *Dauntless* were focused on the longboat, allowing the rest of Barbossa's crew to finish boarding the navy ship. Just as the last of the skeletons dropped onto the deck, Pintel and Ragetti floated into the moonlight, revealing their true identities. On the *Dauntless*'s helm, the commanding officer gasped and turning, his eyes grew wide. Climbing up the steps to the helm was a crew of skeletons! The marines rushed forward, their guns blasting and swords drawn, while out on the water Norrington heard the guns and ordered his men back to the ship. The *Dauntless* was under attack!

Below the helm, Governor Swann heard the commotion and raced over to the door, just in time to see a skeleton stab a marine through the chest. Slamming the door shut, he sunk to the floor, terrified.

As the battle raged on, Captain Jack Sparrow busied himself looking through the massive amounts of treasure that littered the cave. Off to one side, Will Turner stood glaring at the wily captain, while behind him Barbossa sat thinking. Unconcerned by Will's stares or Barbossa's ponderings, Jack lifted a gold statue and held it up in the light.

"I must admit, Jack," Barbossa said thoughtfully. "You're a hard man to predict."

Turning to face Barbossa, the gold statue still in his hands, Jack raised his eyebrows.

"Me?" he asked, moving closer. "I'm dishonest. A dishonest man can always be trusted to be dishonest, honestly," he explained, tossing the statue over his head. Then, turning more towards Will, he added, "It's the honest ones you can't predict. You can never predict when they're going to do something incredibly . . . stupid."

As Jack explained himself, he moved closer and closer to Twigg, one of the few pirates who had not gone out to the *Dauntless*. Suddenly, he reached down and grabbed the sword out of Twigg's belt and, with a kick, sent him flying into a puddle of seawater. Throwing the extra sword to Will, Jack pulled his own sword from its sheath and rushed Barbossa.

The sound of clashing iron filled the cave as the men fought, ducking in and out of the moonlight. Turning quickly, Will held out his hands and Jack's sword slashed through the ropes that bound his wrists. Free, he turned to face his attackers. Seeing a skeleton where he expected a man, Will paused, but then quickly recovered and whipped his sword through the air.

Meanwhile, Jack and Barbossa parried across the cave, their swords flying furiously as each man tried to outdo the other. As their blades locked, Barbossa pulled Jack closer. "You're off the edge of the map, Jack," he said with a laugh. "Here there be monsters!"

With a cry, he pushed off, and the two men

continued fighting. Suddenly, Jack stepped to the side as Barbossa lunged forward and lost his balance. Taking advantage of the man's unguarded moment, Jack drove his sword through Barbossa's chest, pushing the captain back into a shaft of moonlight.

"You can't beat me, Jack," Barbossa said when he looked down and saw the hilt sticking out from his rib cage. In one swift move, he pulled the sword free and drove it back into Jack's chest.

For one long moment, there was silence as Jack looked down at his chest. Across the cave, Will paused mid-fight and looked over to see Jack stumble into the moonlight. As the light touched his skin, though, something happened. Instead of a body of flesh, Jack Sparrow was revealed to be a skeleton! He was cursed, too!

"Couldn't resist, mate," Jack said, pulling out the single gold coin he had taken from the chest and letting it clink over his skeletal fingers.

With a cry of rage, Barbossa lunged.

Chapter 24

Back out on the water, under the light of the full moon, Elizabeth rowed her boat up beside the *Black Pearl*. Pulling herself onto the empty deck, she pushed her long hair out of her face. She took a step forward and gasped as the skeleton monkey dropped down in front of her. A moment later, there was a clunk as the monkey fell overboard, landing on a cannon before it splashed into the water below.

On one of the decks below, two cursed pirates sat in front of a table covered in food. Looking from one treat to another, they tried to figure out what they would eat first when the curse was lifted. Hearing a splash, they looked out a cannon hole to the water below and then up to the deck just as Elizabeth looked down. With a cry, the pirates ducked back inside and headed up the stairs.

As the pirates went after Elizabeth, she

hurried down the stairs to the brig. There, still locked in a cell, was Jack's crew. Quickly, she raced over and let them out. If she was going to save Will, she would need all the help she could get.

Aboard the *Dauntless*, the fighting continued. Men and skeletons slashed at one another with swords, filling the air with the sounds of groans.

Governor Swann, meanwhile, was still hiding in the captain's cabin as the fighting outside raged. Suddenly, one of the skeleton pirates peered through the glass and caught sight of the cowering governor. Sticking his hand through the glass, he began to search for something to grab. Finally, his hand landed on the governor's wig, pulling it off. With a cry of rage, the governor grabbed the nearest thing he could find – a large candlestick – and brought it down on the pirate's arm. Looking down, he gasped. He was now holding the severed arm of a skeleton pirate – and it was still moving. Dropping it to the ground, the governor found himself being chased around the room by the disembodied hand. Finally he leaned down and, grabbing the arm, shoved it into a drawer. Shaking, he leaned against the drawers, overwhelmed.

*   *   *

Back aboard the *Black Pearl*, Elizabeth Swann was trying to convince the ship's crew to join her in rescuing Will. Standing beside a single longboat, she looked up and down the line of pirates.

"Please," she begged, "I need your help!"

But her plea fell on deaf ears. Jack had promised the crew a ship and now they had one. Plus, there was the Code, as Gibbs pointed out.

"Hang the Code! They're more like guidelines anyway," she shouted, quoting Barbossa.

Moments later, she rowed towards *Isla de Muerta* – alone. Behind her, the *Pearl* began to pull away. "Bloody pirates," Elizabeth fumed.

While Elizabeth rowed towards the cave – and Will – Commodore Norrington and his men finally reached the *Dauntless*. Swords drawn, they leaped onto the deck and joined the fight. As swords clashed, Norrington shook his head in disbelief. A crew of skeletons? No one in Port Royal would believe this!

Captain Jack Sparrow was in quite the predicament – immortal or not. Back inside the cave, he and Barbossa battled, ducking in and out of the moonlight. Leaping atop a pile of gold, Jack's body turned skeletal as the light from the moon fell on him. A moment later, he jumped back down, pushing Barbossa against another pile of treasure. His sword pointed directly at the other captain, Jack smiled.

"So what now, Jack Sparrow," Barbossa sneered. "Are we to be two immortals, locked in epic battle till Judgment Day and the trumpets sound?"

Jack hesitated, thinking over the idea, before answering. "Or," he suggested, "you could surrender."

With a growl, Barbossa leaped forward and resumed the fight. There would be no surrender . . . not yet.

Meanwhile, across the cave, Will Turner continued to fight. As his sword slashed through the air, he found himself face-to-face with a pirate who went by the name of Jacoby. Suddenly, Will lost his footing and fell to the ground. Advancing upon him, sword drawn, Jacoby sneered. He would finish Will Turner off yet.

"I'll teach you the meaning of pain," he snarled.

"You like pain?" came a voice from behind Will. Looking over, Jacoby had only a moment to recognize Elizabeth Swann before she swung a heavy gaff across his face, knocking him to the ground. With a sneer, she added, "Try wearing a corset."

Satisfied that Jacoby was done with – for the moment – Elizabeth turned towards Will and offered him the other end of the gaff. Grabbing it, she hauled him to his feet. For a moment, the sound of swords clashing faded as the two looked into each other's eyes. Taking a step forward, Will smiled. But Elizabeth's attention was quickly drawn back to the fight at hand. Looking over, she watched as Barbossa and Jack slashed at each other, nothing more than skeletons in the moonlight.

"Whose side is Jack on?" Elizabeth asked, not at all surprised to see that Jack had taken on his old crew's curse.

Shrugging his shoulders, Will sighed. "At the moment . . ." he replied.

Nodding, Elizabeth turned. There was no time to figure out Jack Sparrow now. Leaving him to fight his own battles, she and Will lunged at a recovered Jacoby and two other cursed pirates. Elizabeth swung her gaff, hitting one of them square across the chest and knocking him into Jacoby. Working as a team, Elizabeth and Will continued to fight, keeping the three clustered together. Suddenly, seeing a chance to get the upper hand, they grabbed ahold of one end of the gaff and charged, lancing all three pirates together. Stepping back, they watched as the three looked down at the bar running through their chests. Then, smiling, Will picked up a bomb Jacoby had dropped and lit the fuse. Stepping forward, he shoved it inside the man's chest and with a nod to Elizabeth, they pushed the three men out of the moonlight and into a shadow.

Clutching at his chest, Jacoby looked up, smoke beginning to pour from his mouth. "No fair," he said. A moment later, the bomb exploded, blowing the undead pirates to smithereens.

Meanwhile, Jack and Barbossa were momentarily distracted by the sound of the explosion. Looking over, Jack watched as Will recovered his footing and, grabbing the knife from atop the chest of Aztec Gold, he drew it across his palm. Quickly, Jack lashed out with his sword, catching the distracted Barbossa unaware. As the other captain struggled to stay upright, Jack threw his piece of the gold across the cave and watched as Will caught it in his hand.

At the same moment, Barbossa turned and pulled his pistol. Cocking it, he held out his arm and aimed – straight at the approaching Elizabeth. Seeing the gun pointed in her direction, she ground to a halt, almost losing her footing on the slippery rock beneath her feet. Across the cave, their eyes met as a shot rang out.

But it was not Barbossa's gun that had been fired. Perplexed, he turned and looked at Jack Sparrow, who stood, his smoking gun pointed directly at Barbossa's chest. "Ten years you carry that pistol, and now you waste your shot?" Barbossa said, a smile on his cracked lips.

"He didn't waste it," said Will.

Barbossa looked over to where Will stood, his left hand hovering above the Aztec chest. In his right hand Will held a knife, a strip of blood gleaming bright red in the moonlight. Barbossa watched in horror as Will opened his hand. Two pieces of gold – one the medallion that Elizabeth had carried for so long and the other, Jack's piece – fell with a clink into the filled chest.

From where she stood, Elizabeth smiled as she watched Barbossa turn back to Jack, a look of anguish on his face. Looking down, Barbossa pulled aside his jacket and revealed his white shirt. Suddenly, a spot of red appeared and began to grow larger. Jack, gun still in hand, waited and watched as Barbossa began to grow pale.

"I feel cold," Barbossa said softly, before he fell back to the ground and, finally, died.

Back aboard the *Dauntless*, at the very same moment that Barbossa drew his last breath, Norrington and his men continued to fight. With a cry of rage, Norrington lunged, piercing the chest of one of the cursed pirates.

Shocked, the pirate looked down. From the

wound in his chest, blood began to flow, and as he fell, the other pirates looked down at their own bodies. In the bright light of the moon, their flesh was visible. They were no longer skeletons! The curse had been lifted!

And that meant they no longer had the upper hand.

One by one, they began to drop their weapons until they stood, unarmed, in front of the marines.

"The ship is *ours*, gentlemen," Norrington announced, and with a cry of victory the marines thrust their swords into the air.

Back inside *Isla de Muerta*, Elizabeth stood in front of a pile of gold, her eyes filled with sorrow. They had won. Barbossa had been defeated, and she had helped save Will. But the price had been high. When she left this cave, she would return to the *Dauntless* and become Norrington's fiancée. Feeling as though her heart were breaking, Elizabeth forced back tears.

Hearing footsteps, she turned and found herself looking into the eyes of the man she truly loved and now could never have – Will Turner.

Smiling tentatively, she waited for him to speak.

Will, his own heart racing as he gazed down at Elizabeth's face, did not know what to say. The promise had been made. She was to be Commodore Norrington's wife, and there was nothing he could do. He was a blacksmith's apprentice – he had nothing to offer. Opening his mouth to explain, he was silenced by a loud crash.

Looking over, both Elizabeth and Will watched as Captain Jack Sparrow sifted through various pieces of treasure, randomly throwing them over his shoulder.

"We should return to the *Dauntless*," Elizabeth said sadly.

Will nodded and braced himself. "Your fiancé will want to know you're safe," he said, trying to keep the bitterness out of his voice.

Elizabeth's eyes filled with tears as she nodded. Then she headed out of the cave. Walking up behind Will, a crown of gold on his head and his arms piled high with jewels, Jack watched Elizabeth retreat.

"If you were waiting for the opportune moment," he said, raising a finger in the air thoughtfully, "that was it." Then, as he continued past the heartbroken Will, he added, "Now, if you'd be so kind. I'd be much obliged if you could drop me at my ship."

Moments later, Jack sat at the prow of a longboat, looking out at the empty spot of sea where his ship was *supposed* to be. On his head he still wore the gold crown, and around his neck was a string of pearls.

"I'm sorry, Jack," Elizabeth said.

For a moment, the captain said nothing, only his eyes betraying his sadness. Then, with a sigh, he spoke. "They did what's right by them. Can't expect more than that."

Captain Jack Sparrow, who had defeated a cursed crew and saved a governor's daughter, found himself in an all-too-familiar position. He was, once again, a captain without a ship.

Chapter 26

It was another beautiful day in the Caribbean. The sky was a brilliant shade of blue and there was a faint breeze in the air. Suddenly, from high atop the cliff that overlooked Port Royal, the sound of drums filled the air. Glorious day or not, there was to be a hanging.

Standing in front of a noose, his hands tied in front of him, stood Captain Jack Sparrow. As he listened, an officer of the Royal Navy listed Jack's crimes. Hearing himself being referred to as "Jack Sparrow," Jack sighed and muttered, "Captain. It's *Captain* Jack Sparrow." Looking out over the crowd of people who had come to witness his hanging, Jack's gaze fell on a trio of familiar faces.

Decked out in their finest, Commodore Norrington, Elizabeth Swann and Governor Swann stood on a platform a few steps above the crowd. Since they had arrived back in Port Royal,

Elizabeth had gone through the motions of being the commodore's fiancée. But that did not mean she agreed with his actions.

Staring at Jack Sparrow, she felt a horrible sense of loss. For better or worse, Jack had helped her and the man she truly loved. To see him die at the end of a noose seemed an affront.

"This is wrong," she said, speaking aloud.

Commodore Norrington heard the catch in her voice as she made her declaration. He was bound by law to hang pirates, and while he understood Elizabeth's sympathies – or at least allowed them – it did not change that. Jack Sparrow was to hang.

Suddenly, there was a shift in the crowd as someone began to make his way through. From their respective places, both Elizabeth and Jack strained to see who it was. A moment later, Will Turner appeared in front of Elizabeth. He wore a feathered cap, and resting on his shoulders was an elegant red cape. The combination was striking and when he spoke, his voice was bold.

"Elizabeth," he said, ignoring the glares of Norrington and the governor. "I should have told you – a long time ago. . . . I love you."

Elizabeth stood, shocked. She felt her heart begin to race. But before she could respond, Will nodded and disappeared into the crowd – just as the noose was placed around Jack's neck. Elizabeth glanced over and saw a familiar parrot land on a flagpole and caw. Smiling, she waited for what was to come . . .

As he made his way through the crowd, Will pushed back his cape and revealed two swords that hung on either side of his belt. Pulling one out, he rushed towards the gallows, while behind him Elizabeth pretended to faint, distracting her father and the commodore momentarily.

Unfortunately for Jack, Will was one step behind the executioner. With a growl, the hooded man pulled a lever, sending Jack falling through a hole in the wooden floor. The rope tightened around his neck, but then, his flailing feet found something to rest on. Will's sword! Just as Jack had fallen, Will had managed to throw his sword, imbedding it deep into the wood below the gallow's hole, buying Jack precious moments. Leaping onto the gallows himself, Will pulled out his other sword and began to fight the executioner while Norrington and his men charged.

Back and forth, Will and the executioner fought – Will armed with a sword and the executioner a mighty axe. Suddenly, Will's sword was knocked from his hand and, ducking, he narrowly avoided being beheaded by the metal axe. However, the axe did not fail to hit the rope from which Jack hung, and with a creak it was severed, cutting Jack free. Beneath the gallows, Jack quickly ran his ropes over the sword still stuck in the wood and took off. A moment later, Will sent the executioner flying into the crowd as he too took off.

Safely away from the gallows, Jack took the other end of the rope that he had only moments ago been hanging from and threw it to Will. Together, the pair headed for the parapet side of Fort Charles, using the rope as a weapon as they went. Marines fell as the odd pair ducked and weaved, pulling the rope taut and knocking the men unconscious against the stone pillars that lined the fort.

But as the duo somersaulted out onto the ledge that lined the cliff, they suddenly realized that there was nowhere left to go. A moment later, they were surrounded by more than a dozen marines, cutlasses drawn. Spinning around, they looked for a way out, but it was too late. As Jack blew Will's hat feather out of his face, the commodore approached, sword drawn.

"I thought we would have to endure some manner of ill-conceived escape attempt," he said as he glared at Will. "But not from you."

Joining Norrington, Governor Swann looked at Will with disappointment. "When we returned, I granted you clemency," he said. "And this is how you thank me? By throwing in your lot with him? A pirate?"

"And a good man," Will said simply as behind him Jack nodded and pointed a finger at himself, as if to emphasize the point.

"You forget your place, Turner," Norrington responded.

But Will had not forgotten anything. His place was beside the man who had helped rescue Elizabeth and who had told him the truth about his father. And apparently, Elizabeth's place was beside Will. Pushing her way through the marines, she came to stand beside him, her hand resting on his arm and her chin high in defiance.

At the governor's order, the marines lowered their weapons. Watching Elizabeth gaze up at Will lovingly, Norrington sighed. "This is where your heart truly lies, then?" he asked at last.

"It is," she replied.

A flash of colour drew Jack's attention away from the unfolding drama. Looking up, he grinned. Cotton's parrot! Sensing time was of the essence, Jack tiptoed around Will and Elizabeth and made his way over towards the commodore and the governor. "I'm actually feeling rather good about this," he said, bringing his face right up to the governor's. "I think we're all in a very special place – spiritually, ecumenically . . . grammatically." Sliding over to the commodore, he added, "I was rooting for you, mate. Know that."

Moving past a shocked and confused Elizabeth and Will, Jack jumped up onto the rim right below the fort's wall. Behind him, the cliff dropped steeply down into the crashing blue waves, while in front of him the marines stood at the ready, guns and swords drawn. Holding up a hand, Jack turned to the crowd. "Friends!" he said dramatically, "this is the day you will always remember as the day you *almost . . .*"

The rest of Jack's speech went unfinished as he tripped and fell back, plummeting head over feet into the water below.

Landing with a splash, Jack sputtered to the surface and gazed at the horizon. With a smile, his eyes landed on a familiar sight – the *Black Pearl*. Her black sails were no longer tattered and her sides gleamed in the bright sun. Grinning, Jack began to swim.

Back atop the cliff, Elizabeth and Will looked down at the water and then at each other. With a sigh, Will dragged his attention away from Elizabeth and looked over at Norrington. He had helped a pirate escape. Most likely, he now faced the hangman's noose.

But the commodore was not entirely without a heart. Drawing his sword, Norrington approached Will. "This is a beautiful sword," he said, holding up the same blade that had been given to him at his coronation ceremony not so long ago. "I expect the man who made it to show the same care and devotion to every aspect of his life."

Turning, he and the other officers moved off, but not before Norrington made it clear that

Jack Sparrow was not off the hook entirely – they would give him a day's head start.

Elizabeth and Will stood on the fort's parapet and gazed into each other's eyes. Governor Swann, seeing how happy his daughter was, sighed. It was not the life he had wanted for her, but she was headstrong and beyond his control. Just to be sure, he asked one last question, "So this is the path you've chosen? After all, he is a blacksmith."

Elizabeth looked over at her father and smiled. "No," she said proudly, turning back to Will and gently easing the hat off his head, "he's a pirate."

Leaning forward, Will pulled Elizabeth closer and there, high above the crystal blue waters, they melted into a long and lingering kiss.

Epilogue

Out at sea, Captain Jack Sparrow stood behind the wheel of the *Black Pearl*. On his head was the familiar tricornered hat and in his hand he held his Compass. As he looked out to sea and felt the *Black Pearl's* wood beneath his fingers, Jack smiled.

"Now bring me that horizon," he said. And setting a new course, Captain Jack Sparrow sailed his ship across the turquoise waves of the Caribbean.

PIRATES of the CARIBBEAN
DEAD MAN'S CHEST

Chapter 1

The moon rose high above a dark ocean. The quiet sounds of the sea – blowing wind, lapping waves and creaking lines – filled the night with an eerie symphony. On the walls of a stone prison that overlooked the scene, a flock of crows alighted. The moonlit night was made even eerier by the grunts, moans and rattling chains of captive prisoners.

A pair of guards dragged a prisoner in through the tower's stone doorway. The passage was clearly the way *into* the prison. The way *out* was very different indeed, as a number of unfortunate captives were about to learn.

More guards, carrying six wooden coffins, made their way to a wall on the prison's seaward side. With a quick condemnation, they shoved each of the coffins off the wall, allowing them to plummet down and splash into the hungry sea below. The coffins bobbed to the surface, and the tide began to carry them out like a fleet of haunted vessels. Two of the pine boxes sailed lower than the rest and began to sink slowly into the black sea.

One of the crows flew down from the prison wall, landing on a coffin. *Peck-peck, peck-peck.* He began to tap away at the wood. *Peck-peck-PECK.* The repetitive *peck-PECK-peck-PECK* was just another sound to fill the shadowy night. *Peck-PECK-peck.* It was also extremely annoying.

The person inside the coffin that the bird had chosen agreed. *Peck-peck-peck-PECK.* Suddenly, a gunshot was fired from inside the coffin that sent the bird blasting off in a cloud of feathers. An arm reached through the newly formed hole, found the latch that held the coffin closed and swung the lid open. Captain Jack Sparrow, the wiliest pirate ever to sail the high seas, quickly emerged and looked around. He was wearing his usual getup – well-worn clothing, knee-high boots and his signature red bandana. His gold tooth gleamed in the moonlight.

Jack didn't seem concerned with his situation – at first. Then his eyes grew wide and he began frantically searching the coffin. After a moment filled with high anxiety, he finally found what he thought he might have lost – his hat! With it placed firmly on his head at a smart angle, Jack was once again relaxed.

He bowed his head, crossed himself and reached down into the coffin one more time. "Sorry, mate," he said as he pulled and tugged until – *SNAP* – he plucked off the leg bone of his coffin mate. "Necessity is a mother," he noted with a grin. He used the bone for an oar and rowed toward the moonlit hull of his ship, the *Black Pearl*. She was patiently waiting for him out in the still water, covered by the dark of night.

Gibbs, an old salt and a fine pirate, was waiting on the *Pearl*'s deck for Jack's return. "Not quite according to plan?" Gibbs questioned, staring at Jack, who sat rowing a coffin with a leg bone in his hands. Gibbs helped his captain aboard.

"Complications arose," Jack said, tossing the leg bone overboard. "But I've found if you ask right, there's always someone willing to give a leg up."

Gibbs looked over the side of the ship at the one-legged skeleton. "Not in my experience,"

Gibbs said, shaking his head. "Can't go wrong expecting the worst from people."

Jack sighed. "It probably does save time," he said as he walked away from Gibbs. As he moved along the boat, Jack took a rolled piece of cloth from his sleeve. He began to examine it very carefully.

"Is that what you went in to find?" a toothless pirate named Leech asked anxiously. Every man on board was hungry for news of what treasure Jack had found.

"Aye, but I haven't had time to properly assess the prize," Jack answered with a sly smile. He did not seem willing to share just yet.

Suddenly, a small monkey swung out of the ship's rigging, landed in front of Jack and screeched as if he were the devil himself. Jack screamed back as the monkey snatched the roll of cloth and took it up into the sails.

Each time the monkey passed through a shaft of moonlight, it turned into a skeleton from head to tail – the result of a curse that had not been lifted. The monkey was the living dead. The horrible little beast's previous owner was the cursed Captain Barbossa, who had mutinied against Jack. Barbossa had named the monkey Jack, as a way to add insult to injury.

Jack hated the creature. He drew his pistol and aimed at the cursed monkey. Jack fired, but the gun only clicked. His shot had already been used on that blasted pecking crow. Jack grabbed a pistol from the belt of another pirate and fired again.

This time he hit his mark. The monkey was blown back and the cloth dropped from its grasp. But the monkey quickly jumped back up again, grinning.

Gibbs gave Jack a look. "You know that doesn't do any good," he told him, pointing to the gun.

Jack shrugged. "Keeps my aim sharp," he said as one of the pirates on deck scrambled to catch the falling piece of cloth. The monkey continued to screech.

"Why'd that eviscerated simian have to be the only thing to survive *Isla de Muerta*?" Jack grumbled. Then he saw the pirate who had caught the cloth examining it.

"It's a key," the pirate said, cocking his head to the side and squinting an eye.

"Even better," Jack added, raising a finger. "It's a *drawing* of a key."

The confused crew looked to Gibbs for an explanation.

"Captain," Gibbs said, clearing his throat, "I think we were expecting something a bit more . . . rewarding. What with *Isla de Muerta* going all pear shaped, reclaimed by the sea and all . . ."

"Unfortunate turn of circumstance," Jack agreed, remembering the island where the crew had had its most recent adventure, where Jack had finally defeated Barbossa *and* where he had reclaimed the *Black Pearl*.

". . . and then spending months fighting to get the British navy off our stern," Gibbs reminded him.

"Inevitable outcome of *le vie de boucanier*," Jack replied with a wave of his hand.

"We've been losing crew at every port, and it seems to us what's left that it's been a stretch since we've done even a speck of honest pirating," Gibbs continued.

Jack turned to his crew. "Is that how you're feeling?" he asked. "That I'm not serving your interests as captain?"

The crew shifted uncomfortably and then

suddenly a parrot squawked the only reply.

"ABANDON SHIP!"

The parrot belonged to the mute pirate Cotton and it spoke for him.

Jack drew his pistol again. "What did the bird say?"

"Cotton's parrot don't speak for the lot of us," Leech told Jack quickly. "*We* think you're doing a fine job."

"ABANDON SHIP," the parrot called out even louder. Jack was about to shoot the old bird, but lowered his gun instead. Cotton seemed relieved.

"At least there's one honest . . . man amongst you," Jack said, looking at Cotton's parrot. Jack shook his head and got down to the business at hand. He had questions to answer.

"Gentlemen, what do keys do?" Jack asked.

The anxious crew of rogues looked at each other. "They unlock things?" Leech asked, suddenly excited.

Jack made a face as if to say, "Yes, and . . ."

"And whatever this unlocks, inside is something valuable," Gibbs added, imagining chests of gold. "So, we're setting out to find whatever this unlocks!"

Jack shook his head. "No. If we don't have the key, we can't open whatever it unlocks, so what purpose would be served in finding whatever needs be unlocked without first having found the key that unlocks it? Honestly. Ninny."

The rowdy crew was very confused. They tried to follow along as best they could. "So, we're going to find this key?" Gibbs asked.

Jack looked into the crew members' blank faces and sighed. "What good is a key if we have nothing for the key to unlock? Please," Jack pleaded, "try and keep up!"

"So, do we have a heading?" another pirate asked.

"Aye! A heading!" Jack said. He turned away, took out his Compass and flipped it open. It was the very same Compass that had led him to *Isla de Muerta* and the caves of hidden treasure. But the readings on the Compass seemed to make Jack a bit uneasy now.

He snapped the Compass shut and waved his arm. "Set sail in a general . . . that way direction," he finally said, waving his hand dismissively out towards the sea.

"Captain?" Gibbs asked, confused. This was not typical Captain Jack Sparrow behaviour.

"I'll plot our course later. Now snap to and make sail!" he ordered as he marched off to his cabin. The crew stood and watched silently. "You know how it works!" Jack shouted impatiently and slammed his cabin door.

The crew unhappily began to get ready to sail. "Have you noticed lately, the captain seems to be acting a bit . . . strange?" a pirate whispered to Gibbs.

"Aye," Gibbs answered. "Something's got him setting a course without knowing his own heading. And I thought there was neither man nor beast alive could make him do that."

Chapter 2

While Jack's crew dealt with their captain's stranger-than-usual behaviour, a couple who should have been celebrating the happiest day of their lives was trying to avert disaster – a ruined wedding.

Outside a small seaside chapel in the Caribbean town of Port Royal, palm trees bent in the wind as rain drenched all the preparations for the nuptial celebration to be held that day. The bride, Elizabeth Swann, kneeled in her rain-soaked wedding dress, tears mixing with rain. Around her was an empty altar, overturned chairs . . . and no groom. Slowly, the young woman rose and entered the chapel to wait, her head in her hands.

The approaching sound of chains made Elizabeth look up. Through her tears she saw a man in uniform enter the chapel. He was followed by a company of marines who were dragging a prisoner. To her shock, it was her groom, Will Turner.

"Will!" Elizabeth called out. "What is happening?"

Will struggled toward her. "I don't know," he said sadly, taking in Elizabeth's ruined white satin dress.

Will had been taken prisoner earlier when marines battered down the door of his blacksmith shop and put him in irons. It didn't look like he'd be married today, after all. But waiting for his future wife, Elizabeth, was something Will was used to. He had loved her since Elizabeth and her father, the Governor of Port Royal, found Will drifting on the sea when he was ten years old. For years he had waited patiently, hoping she would finally love him back. And then she had. But it seemed that once again they would be kept apart.

Even now, standing there in chains, he couldn't help getting sentimental. "You look beautiful," Will said softly.

Elizabeth smiled. "You know it's bad luck for the groom to see the bride before the wedding."

"That explains the unexpected guests," he said, nodding at the company of red-coated marines surrounding them.

Their tender moment was interrupted by an authoritative voice. It was Elizabeth's father.

"You! Order your men to stand down and remove these shackles at once," the governor commanded.

The man in charge of the arrest made no move. "Governor Wetherby Swann," he answered. "My apologies for arriving without an invitation."

Governor Swann studied the man's face for a moment. "Cutler Beckett?" he finally asked.

"It's *Lord*, now, actually," Beckett replied.

"Lord or not, you have no reason and no authority to arrest this man."

"In fact, I do. Mr Mercer?" he said to an undistinguished-looking gentleman standing off to the side. Mercer opened a large dispatch case and handed Beckett several documents.

Beckett ceremoniously read off his newly appointed powers by the Royal Commission for Antilles Trade and Protection, then produced a warrant for the arrest of one William Turner.

Governor Swann looked at the warrant. But it wasn't for Will. "This is for Elizabeth Swann!" he exclaimed.

"Is it?" Beckett asked. "How odd . . . my mistake. Arrest her," he suddenly ordered.

The soldiers grabbed Elizabeth. "On what charges?" Elizabeth demanded.

Beckett ignored her as he shuffled through his papers. "Aha," he said, holding up another document. "Here's the warrant for William Turner. And I have another one for a James Norrington. Any idea where he is?"

"Commodore Norrington resigned his commission several months ago," Governor Swann answered quickly, "and we haven't seen him since."

Elizabeth gritted her teeth. She had once been betrothed to Norrington, though she never loved him. She suddenly found herself thinking about all she and Will – and Jack Sparrow – had been through.

Elizabeth was kidnapped by Barbossa and his men. To rescue her from the cursed pirate, Will had broken Jack Sparrow out of jail, only to be captured himself. In desperation, Elizabeth had agreed to marry Norrington in exchange for his help in saving Will. When the adventure had ended, Norrington had grudgingly agreed to give Jack Sparrow a day's head start before he would begin chasing him. It was only fair, as the pirate had saved Elizabeth. But even though it was the fair thing to do, Norrington had never forgiven himself for letting Sparrow slip away. He had lost his post and disappeared from Port Royal, disgraced.

"We are British subjects under jurisdiction of the King's Governor of Port Royal, and we demand to know the charges against us," Elizabeth said bravely, coming back to the present.

Beckett looked at his prisoners. When he finally spoke up, he sounded more than happy to make his announcement. "The charge is conspiring to secure the unlawful release of a convict condemned to death. For which, regrettably, the punishment is also death. You do remember a pirate named, I believe it is, Jack Sparrow?"

Will and Elizabeth exchanged a look. "*Captain* Jack Sparrow," they said in unison.

"Yes. I thought you might," Beckett answered, satisfied. He motioned to his men to haul the prisoners away.

Chapter 3

While Will and Elizabeth tried to sort out their current mess, Captain Jack Sparrow was dealing with problems of his own. Alone in his cabin aboard the *Black Pearl*, Jack held his Compass tightly in his hand. He sneaked a look at it once, snapped it shut, shook it and looked again. *Still* not to his liking. Jack reached for a bottle of rum. As the tattered cuff of his sleeve fell back, the branded letter *P* showed on his wrist.

Jack raised the bottle and sighed. It was empty. "Why is the rum always gone?" he asked himself. He lurched towards the cabin door and onto the main deck in search of another bottle.

"Heading, Captain?" Leech asked as Jack staggered past the wheel.

"Steady as she goes," Jack ordered, stumbling toward the ship's hold.

Below deck, pirates snored loudly as they

slept in their hammocks. A cage of chickens clucked as Jack entered. The captain raised his pistol and the chickens suddenly went quiet.

"That's what I thought," Jack said. Then he continued on.

Steadying himself on the ship's timbers, Jack made his way to the rum locker. He raised an eyebrow as he checked the racks. All were nearly empty.

Happily, Jack spied a bottle on a lower shelf and tugged it free. The bottle was encrusted with barnacles. Something was wrong. Jack uncorked it, looked inside and turned it over. Sand spilled out onto the deck.

"Time's run out, Jack," a voice suddenly said from the shadows. Jack turned. The face he saw was covered with starfish and barnacles. Crabs crawled up the man's arm as he stepped toward Jack.

"Bootstrap?" Jack asked, barely recognizing the voice. "Bill Turner?"

"Aye, Jack Sparrow. You look good."

Jack looked at the gruesome sailor. He wished he could say the same for him. He actually tried a few times, but couldn't bring himself to say it.

"Is this a dream?" Jack asked instead.

"No," Bootstrap Bill Turner, Will's father, answered flatly.

Jack shrugged. "I thought not. If it were, there'd be rum."

Bootstrap grinned and offered Jack a bottle. Jack pried the bottle from Bill's hand, uncorked it and sniffed it to be sure. Rum it was. Jack wiped the mouth of the bottle with his sleeve and took a long drink.

Bootstrap watched. "You got the *Pearl* back, I see." But Jack couldn't focus on his old shipmate's words. He was staring at the slithering, sliding sea life that lived on the man's skin.

The captain snapped himself out of it. "I had some help retrieving the *Pearl*. Your son," he said.

Bootstrap looked surprised. "William? He ended up a pirate, after all?"

Jack nodded, then added, "He's got an unhealthy streak of honesty to him."

"That's something, then," Bill told him. "Though no credit to me." The crustacean-crusted pirate fell silent.

"And to what do I owe the pleasure of your carbuncle?" Jack finally asked.

"Davy Jones," Bootstrap answered. "He sent me as an emissary."

Jack had been expecting this. "Ah, he shanghaied you into service, then."

"I chose it. I'm sorry for the part I played in mutinying against you," Bootstrap said sincerely. Jack waved it off and took another swig of rum. Bootstrap had been part of the *Black Pearl*'s crew when Barbossa mutinied. All the rest of the crew had decided to follow Barbossa and make him their captain. Jack had been left on an island to die.

"Everything went wrong after that," Bootstrap told him. "I ended up cursed, doomed to the depths of the ocean, unable to move, unable to die."

Jack shuddered.

"All I could do was think," Bootstrap continued. "And mostly I thought if I had even the tiniest hope of escaping this fate, I would take it. Trade anything for it."

"That is the kind of thinking bound to catch *his* attention," Jack said, knowing more than a bit about Jones's love for a good bargain.

"It did," Bootstrap said, nodding with regret.

"Davy Jones came. Made the offer. I could spend one hundred years before his mast, with the hope that after, I would go on to a peaceful rest."

Bootstrap stopped talking and looked his former captain in the eye. Then he added, "You made a deal with him, too, Jack. He raised the *Pearl* from the depths for you, and 13 years you've been her captain."

"Technically . . ." Jack said, about to object, but Bootstrap stopped him.

"You won't be able to talk your way out of this," Bootstrap warned as a crab crawled down his arm. The cursed pirate crushed it and shoved it into his mouth. "The terms what applied to me apply to you as well. One soul, bound to crew a lifetime aboard his ship."

But Jack wasn't about to let himself start looking like old Bootstrap any time soon. "The *Flying Dutchman* already has a captain," Jack argued, pointing out that Jones was the captain of the ghostly ship. "So there's no need of me."

Bootstrap expected as much from Jack. Captain Jack Sparrow never went down without a fight. Bootstrap sighed and nodded. "Then it's the locker for you, Jack. Jones's leviathan will find you and drag the *Pearl* back to the depths . . . and you along with it."

"Any idea when Jones will release said terrible beastie?" Jack asked, trying not to sound too worried.

Bootstrap raised an arm and pointed to Jack's hand. Jack took a step back, but it was too late. On his palm appeared the dreaded Black Spot. Jack stared at it. He was now a marked man.

"It's not a matter of how long till it comes after you," Bootstrap said as Jack looked down at the spot. "It's a matter of how long till you're found."

Jack looked up and Bootstrap Bill was gone. Jack let out a yclp and ran.

"On deck!" he yelled to his sleeping crew as he passed through the hold. "All hands! Lift the skin up. Scurry! Movement, I want movement!"

As the groggy pirates dragged themselves to their stations, Jack looked into the *Pearl*'s black sails. "Haul those sheets!" he ordered the men. "Haul 'em! Run, mates, run, as if the devil himself is on us!"

While the crew was distracted, Jack wrapped his hand in a rag to cover the Black Spot. He couldn't let anyone see that he was marked.

Gibbs looked for Jack and found him hiding behind the mast.

"Do we have a heading?" he asked.

"Land!" Jack yelled back.

"What port?" Gibbs asked.

"I said land! Any land!" Just then Jack the monkey jumped from the rigging, landed on Jack's shoulder and knocked the captain's hat overboard.

"Jack's hat!" Gibbs cried, knowing how fond of it the captain was. "Bring the ship about!"

"No!" Jack snapped. "Leave it."

Jack's crew stood stunned. They knew how much the hat meant to him. They could not believe he would actually *not* want to retrieve it. "Mind your stations, the lot of you!" Gibbs ordered, and then he turned to Jack. "For the love of mother and child, Jack, what's coming after us?"

Chapter 4

Captain Jack Sparrow's legendary three-cornered hat floated on the tide, turning slowly. By next morning, it had drifted far from the *Black Pearl*.

The hull of a small fishing vessel passed it and suddenly the hat was snatched up by a boat hook. A short, round sailor pulled it from the water and was pleased with the look of the hat. He quickly tried it on.

Just then, his mate yanked it off his head. The two were pulling on the hat when a shudder suddenly ran through the boat. The men stopped struggling.

From beneath the deck came a loud crunching. The sailors staggered as their little vessel rocked. They looked wildly around and then down at the hat. The strange turn of events must have something to do with the hat! The sailors fought to rid themselves of it.

But the fight ended quickly, as the deck splintered and the entire boat was pulled straight down. A giant geyser rose up from the sea, raining down wood and bits of canvas. And, in the blink of an eye, the water was still and the fishing boat was no more.

Not far away, in the headquarters of the East India Trading Company, Will Turner was escorted by two guards into the office of Lord Beckett. A large, unfinished map of the world took up one whole wall of the office.

"Those won't be necessary," Beckett said, pointing to the shackles on Will's wrists.

The guards released Will. "Do you intend to release Elizabeth, as well?" Will asked.

"That is entirely up to you," Beckett answered, and then quickly rephrased his response. "That is entirely *dependent* on you," he clarified. Beckett used his cane to stoke the room's fireplace. "We wish for you to act as our agent in a business transaction with our mutual friend, Captain Sparrow."

"More acquaintance than friend," Will said. "How do *you* know him?"

"We've had dealings in the past," Beckett said, displaying the letter *P* on the end of his glowing cane – the same *P* brand that was burned into Jack's arm. "We have each left our marks on the other."

"What mark did he leave on you?" Will asked, but Beckett did not respond. Instead he said, "By your efforts, Jack Sparrow was set free. I ask you to go to him and recover a certain property in his possession."

"Recover," Will said sceptically. "At the point of a sword?"

Beckett smiled. "Bargain," he suggested slyly. "To mutual benefit and for fair value."

He removed several large documents from his desk. They were signed by the King of England. "Letters of Marque," Beckett explained. "You will offer what amounts to a full pardon. Jack will be free, a privateer in the employ of England."

Will looked at the letters and shook his head. He knew that the Letters of Marque would give him the right to take Jack's possessions, but something didn't feel right. "For some reason, I doubt Jack will consider employment to be the same as freedom," Will pointed out.

"Jack Sparrow is a dying breed," Beckett snarled. He motioned to the map on the wall. "The world is shrinking, the blank edges of the map filled in. Jack will have to find a place in the New World, or perish.

"Not unlike you," Beckett continued, bringing the point home. "You and your fiancée face the hangman's noose. Certainly, that's motivation enough for you to convince Captain Sparrow to accept our offer. And for you to accept, as well, Mr Turner."

Will considered the proposal. "So you'll get both Jack and the *Black Pearl*?"

Beckett seemed surprised. "The *Black Pearl*? No, Mr Turner, the item in question is considerably smaller and far more valuable, something Sparrow keeps on his person at all times. A Compass."

Beckett noticed a look of recognition on Will's face.

"Ah, you know it," Beckett hissed. Then he added, "Bring back the Compass or there is no deal!"

Will Turner stormed out of Beckett's office and through the gates of the Port Royal prison. He pushed past the red-coated guard and moved down the stone corridor to Elizabeth's cell. Governor Swann followed closely behind.

"Here, now!" the guard called out. "You can't be here, Mr Swann!"

"*Governor* Swann," he said, correcting the guard. "I'm not wearing this wig to keep my head warm, you know." Swann looked into the guard's face. "Carruthers, isn't it? Enjoy your job, Mr Carruthers?"

The guard quickly changed his tone. "Yes, sir. Particularly when the folks come up to visit the prisoners."

"Very good," Swann said. He nodded toward the door and the guard quickly exited.

As the governor approached the dank cell, he heard Elizabeth say to Will, "Jack's Compass? Why would Beckett want that?"

Elizabeth was behind bars, still in her wedding dress. "Does it matter?" Will asked. "I'm to find Jack and convince him to return to Port Royal. In exchange, the charge against us will be dropped."

Will stepped as close to Elizabeth as possible with bars between them. "If I hadn't set Jack free . . ." he began, trailing off regretfully. "I never expected you would bear the consequences."

Elizabeth smiled. "I share the consequences gladly." She reached through the bars and took his hands. "How are you going to find him?" she asked anxiously.

Her confidence touched Will's heart. He suddenly felt he could do anything. "Tortuga. I'll start there and not stop searching until I find him, and then I will come back here and marry you."

"Properly?" Elizabeth asked.

"Eagerly," Will promised.

Chapter 5

Will Turner started his search immediately. He would check every island in the Caribbean if he had to – he was going to find Jack. He made his way to Tortuga, stopping at various island ports on the way. On one, he walked up the dock and asked the first man he saw of Jack's whereabouts.

"Captain Jack Sparrow?" the weathered sailor answered. "Owes me four doubloons. Heard he was dead."

Down a cobblestone alley on another island, Will made his way into a candlelit tavern. The innkeeper, a square, thickset man, told Will, "Ran off with a Creole woman to Madagascar." Then he added with a wink, "She was half his age and twice his height!"

On a beach a half-blind fisherman told his version. "Singapore is what I heard. Sure as the tide," he nodded with a toothless grin, "Jack Sparrow will turn up in Singapore!"

Will sighed. There were a thousand tales about Jack Sparrow's whereabouts. Will had one last chance to get the truth – ironically, in a place where truth was hard to come by – Tortuga!

Tortuga was a well-known haunt of Captain Jack Sparrow's. It was the dirtiest port in all the Caribbean; a place for drunken pirates on the lookout for fresh risks and high adventure. A place, Will remembered as the stench of Tortuga filled his nostrils, Jack held dear to his heart.

As soon as Will arrived, he saw a woman he had met the last time he had been to Tortuga with Jack. The woman had red hair and wore a red dress. Her name, if he remembered correctly, was Scarlett. He asked her if she'd seen Jack recently.

"I haven't seen him in a month," Scarlett snapped. "When you find him, give him a message." She raised her hand and struck Will across the face before stalking off.

Rubbing his cheek as he walked on, Will noticed a shrimper on the deck of a small boat.

"Can't say 'bout Jack Sparrow," the shrimper told Will as he pulled in his nets. "But there's an island just south of the straits where I trade spice for delicious long pork. No, can't say for Jack, but you'll find a ship there, a ship with black sails."

For a few coins, Will convinced the shrimper to sail him out to the island. As they came around the point, Will saw it for himself; the *Black Pearl* careened onto the sand! His spirits soared.

"My brother, he will row you to shore," the shrimper told Will. He gave a taller, round-faced man a nod as Will climbed into his tiny rowing boat. But halfway to the beach, the brother told Will, "No," and began to turn the boat around.

"What's wrong?" Will asked. "The beach is right there." But the man only rowed faster back toward the shrimp boat.

Will had no choice. He shook his head, dived in and swam to the shore.

Soaking wet, Will walked over the beach towards the *Black Pearl*. The huge ship rested, wedged into the sand. No noise came from her decks.

A bit further on, Will found the remains of a campfire. He felt the ashes. They were still warm. Jack must have been here. He had to be close!

"Jack!" Will called out. "Jack Sparrow! Mister Gibbs! Anyone . . ."

Will turned towards the dense jungle and saw a flutter in the branches. It was Cotton's parrot!

"Good to see a familiar face," Will said to the old bird, now even surer Jack and the crew were on the island.

"Don't eat me!" the parrot squawked.

"I'm not even hungry," Will said as he looked for a path through the jungle.

"DON'T EAT ME!" the parrot screamed even louder.

Will turned his attention back to the bird. "Look, you're nothing but feathers and bones and you probably taste like pigeon." The parrot went silent.

"Sorry," Will said, feeling guilty. "That was uncalled for. Listen . . . if anyone should ask, tell them Will Turner went into the jungle in search of Jack Sparrow. Understand?" Will sighed. "I'm talking to a parrot," he said to himself.

"Aye, aye, sir!" the parrot answered, bobbing his head.

Will grinned, drew his sword and began hacking into the jungle. He cut through the huge leaf of a palm and noticed a small, red flask on the jungle floor. "Gibbs . . ." Will said quietly, recognizing the old pirate's flask.

He crouched down to pick it up and noticed a trip wire was attached. Will smiled, thinking the pirates had set a trap. Holding on to the wire he followed it to a tree. Suddenly, two eyes appeared in the tree trunk as a perfectly camouflaged arm reached out and yanked the trip wire hard.

In an instant, Will was pulled off his feet and dangled upside down. As he hung by his leg, he saw a group of the island's warriors. They had bite marks all over their faces and bodies, and were wearing what looked like human bones! No wonder the shrimper had been so frightened. The warriors lunged at him with their spears raised. Will kicked off the tree and knocked several of them to the ground.

"Come on!" Will said, provoking one warrior. "I'm right here!"

The warrior raised a blowgun and fired a dart into Will's neck. Will went limp and the warrior cut him down.

Chapter 6

Meanwhile, in a dank cell in Port Royal, Elizabeth could do nothing but wait. Moonlight poured through the cell's small window and cast shadows on the wall. She was exhausted and had just closed her eyes when she heard the jangle of keys.

"Come quickly!" she heard a voice that sounded like her father's call out. Governor Swann stepped out from the shadows.

"What's happening?" Elizabeth asked. The guard swung open the door and Elizabeth hurried out of her cell. Governor Swann gave the guard a nod.

"I've arranged passage for you back to England," Governor Swann said as he and his daughter ran quickly down a torchlit corridor. "The captain is an old friend."

The governor led Elizabeth to a waiting

carriage, but Elizabeth refused to get in. She was waiting for Will.

"We cannot count on Will's help," the governor said desperately, drawing a pistol. "Beckett has offered only one pardon. One. And it has been promised to Sparrow. Do not ask me to endure the sight of my daughter walking to the gallows! Do not!" He pushed her inside and pressed the pistol into her hand. Then he shut the door and hastily drove the carriage to the waiting ship.

As they neared the dock, the governor slowed his horses to a stop. Two men stood huddled in the shadows. One of them wore a captain's hat.

"Stay inside," the governor said to Elizabeth as he leapt down. He hurried over to the two men. "Captain Hawkins!" the governor said, relieved to see a friend.

But Hawkins did not answer. The other man stepped away and the captain slumped forward, his tunic covered in blood. Governor Swann suddenly realized that the other man in the shadows had been holding the captain's body upright.

"Evening, Governor," the man said, slowly wiping the blood from his knife with a handkerchief. Swann gasped. He recognized the man. It was Mercer, Beckett's clerk.

"Shame, that," Mercer said as he motioned toward the body. Governor Swann bolted toward the carriage in a panic. "Elizabeth!" he cried out. But, with a whistle, Mercer had a company of troops assembled.

Mercer smiled and yanked the carriage door open himself. It was empty.

"Where is she?" Mercer demanded angrily.

"Who?" Swann asked.

Mercer slammed the governor against the carriage and snarled, "Elizabeth!"

"She was always a wilful child," the governor offered innocently. Mercer ordered the man to be put in irons and, with a violent jerk, led him away.

Chapter 7

Lord Beckett entered his dark office inside the East India Trading Company building. He lit a lamp on his large mahogany desk and noticed that the case that held the Letters of Marque was empty. He also sensed that he was not alone.

Elizabeth stepped from the shadows and raised the pistol her father had given her. "These Letters of Marque," Elizabeth said, slapping the documents on his desk. "They are signed by the king, but blank."

Beckett smiled, unafraid. "And not valid until they bear my signature and seal."

"I have information," Elizabeth said, the gun steady in her hand. "You sent Will to get you the Compass owned by Jack Sparrow. It will do you no good. I have been to *Isla de Muerta*. I have seen the treasure myself. There is something you need to know."

Beckett smiled smugly. "Ah, I see. You think the Compass points only to *Isla de Muerta*. I am afraid you are mistaken, Miss Swann. I care not for cursed Aztec Gold." He recalled the treasure trove in the cave where Jack defeated Barbossa. "My desires are not so provincial."

Lord Beckett motioned to a huge world map. "There is more than one chest of value in these waters," he said. "So perhaps you wish to enhance your offer . . ."

Elizabeth drew the hammer back on the pistol and levelled it at Lord Beckett's head. He suddenly stopped laughing.

"Consider into your calculations that you robbed me of my wedding night," Elizabeth said sternly.

At gunpoint, Beckett signed the papers, but he did not immediately hand them over.

"You are making great effort to ensure Sparrow's freedom," Beckett said, curious.

"These are not going to Jack," Elizabeth replied.

"Then to ensure Mr Turner's freedom. And what about me? I'll still want the Compass. Consider that in your calculations."

With that, Beckett released his hold on the Letters of Marque. Elizabeth now had what she had come for. She turned and disappeared into the dark.

The following morning, a merchant vessel, the *Edinburgh Trader*, sailed from Port Royal. As the ship moved into open water, a sailor on deck came upon something strange. He picked it up; it was a wedding dress.

Captain Bellamy heard the commotion and immediately came on deck. His bursar and quartermaster were trying to pull the dress from each other's grip.

"If both of you fancy the dress," Captain Bellamy shouted, "you'll just have to share, and wear it one after the other."

"It's not like that, sir," the bursar answered swiftly. "The ship is haunted!"

Bellamy looked at the dress. "Is it, now?"

"Aye," the quartermaster agreed. "There's a female presence here with us, sir . . . everyone feels it."

The crew began to grumble. "Ghost of a lady widowed before her marriage, I figure it," a sailor said and spat neatly, "searching for her husband lost at sea."

The bursar nodded. "We need to throw it overboard and hope the spirit follows, or this ship will taste the icy waters in a fortnight, mark my words!"

A sailor painting the rail listened closely to the argument.

"Enough!" Captain Bellamy ordered. He took the dress and examined it closely. "Men, this appears to me nothing more as we have a stowaway on board. A young woman, by the looks of it. To your duties. And if there is a stowaway and 'tis a woman, I don't see she's likely to escape without notice, aye?"

The crew considered this for a moment and then scattered, all searching for the lady. The sailor who was painting the rail turned to face the rest of the crew.

But it wasn't a sailor at all. It was Elizabeth, well disguised in sailor's clothes. She put down her paintbrush and joined the search for the lady, all but unnoticed by the rowdy gang.

Chapter 8

$\mathfrak{M}$eanwhile, in a distant jungle, Will Turner awoke to find himself tied up and being paraded through a small village filled with huts. The island's inhabitants watched the procession with curiosity. Finally, Will was set down before a huge throne.

He looked up . . . and smiled. Sitting on the throne, dressed in ornate ceremonial garb, was none other than Captain Jack Sparrow!

"Jack Sparrow," Will said. "I can honestly say I am glad to see you."

Jack didn't respond. He just stared blankly at Will. It was as though he had never seen Will before.

The warriors pushed Will forward. "Jack? Jack, it's me, Will Turner. Tell them to let me go."

Jack stepped down from his throne and gave Will's arm a pinch. He spoke in a language Will had never heard. The warriors nodded. Will suddenly noticed that the throne was no ordinary throne – it was made of human bones.

"Jack, listen," Will said desperately. "The Compass. That's all I need. Jack, Elizabeth is in danger. We were arrested for helping *you*. She faces the gallows!"

Motioning toward Will's leg, one of the warriors hungrily rubbed his belly, suggesting that Will would make a fine meal. Jack nodded and the tribe cheered.

"No!" Will shouted as the warriors grabbed him. "Jack, what did you tell them?" But Jack didn't answer. He climbed back on his throne and stared off into the distance.

As the warriors dragged Will past Jack to prepare him for dinner, Jack's eyes rolled wildly in his head, catching Will's attention. "Save me!" Jack whispered desperately out of the corner of his mouth.

The warriors dragged Will to a chasm where two cages made from bones hung from thick rope. Will noticed that some of the crew of the *Black Pearl* were trapped in the cages. Before Will could react, he was tossed into a cage.

"Ah, Will, you shouldn't have come!" Gibbs shouted in greeting.

Will struggled to his feet, then reached into his pocket. He handed Gibbs the flask he had found on the jungle floor. Gibbs raised it as Will asked about Jack's odd behaviour and leader status over the tribe.

"Why would he do this to you?" Will asked, looking around at the caged crew. "If Jack is the chief . . ."

"Aye," Gibbs answered dismally, "the Pelegostos made Jack their chief, but he stays chief for only so long as he *acts* like a chief . . . which means he cannot do anything they think a chief ought not do."

"He's a captive, then," Will said, "as much as any of us."

Gibbs frowned. "Worse, as it turns out. The Pelegostos believe that Jack is a god, trapped in human form. They intend to do Jack the honour of releasing him from his fleshy prison."

Out of the corner of his eye, Will noticed Cotton add his two cents. He mimed something about being cut up with a knife. Will frowned.

"They'll roast and eat him. It's a deeply

held religious belief," Gibbs mused. "Or, we figure, maybe they just get awful hungry."

Will could see most of the crew between the two cages, but a good many pirates were gone. "Where's the rest of the crew?" he asked.

"These cages we're in," Gibbs sighed, "wasn't built till after we got here."

Will looked at the cages of human bone and quickly removed his hand.

"The feast starts when the sun sets," Gibbs said gravely. "Jack's life will end . . . when the drums stop."

Chapter 9

In a small boat just offshore, two pirates in worn clothing, Pintel and Ragetti, rowed with their backs to the setting sun. The bumbling duo was all that remained of Barbossa's crew. Ragetti, the tall thin one, held a book in his lap. ". . . and I say it was divine providence what escaped us from jail," he said, adjusting his wooden eye.

"And I say it was me being clever," Pintel, the shorter one, replied. A dog with a ring of keys in its mouth suddenly raised its head at the bow. Pintel patted the dog on the head. "Ain't that right, poochie?"

"How do you know it wasn't Divine Providence what inspired you to be clever?" Ragetti argued. "Anyways, I ain't stealing no ship."

"It ain't stealing," Pintel said as they neared the point of the small island. "It's salvaging, and since when did you care?"

"Now that we're not immortal no more," Ragetti said nervously, "we need to take care of our immortal souls." He looked down at the book in his lap.

"You know you can't read!" Pintel shouted at him.

"It's the Bible," the wooden-eyed pirate Ragetti said, smiling, his teeth broken and brown. "You get credit for trying."

"Pretending to read the Bible is a lie, and that's a mark against ya," Pintel yelled, when the *Black Pearl* suddenly came into view. They'd been looking for it for what seemed like forever, and now . . .

"Look! There it is!" Pintel cried.

The dog suddenly jumped into the clear blue water and swam for shore. "What's got into him?" Pintel asked.

"Must have spotted a *cat*fish," Ragetti chuckled.

As they reached the shore, Pintel looked up at the ship's black sails. "It's ours for the taking!" he said greedily, as the sound of drums began to sound through the jungle and out to the sandy beach.

Chapter 10

The beat of the drums was building as the Pelegostos prepared for their grand feast. As they gathered wood for the fire pit, their guest of honour and main course, Captain Jack Sparrow, nodded his approval and tried to force a smile. "I notice women here, but very few children – why is that? Are the little ones most tasty?" he asked.

Jack didn't get an answer. The warriors were busy placing a large spit over the fire pit. Jack gulped and took a breath. "Not big enough!" he shouted, boldly striding towards the pit, pretending to act more like a chief in order to buy himself more time.

He frowned and shook his head as the Pelegostos stared. "Not big enough!" he said, widening his arms. *"I am the chief! I need more wood! Big fire!"* he said in the language of the Pelegostos. "MORE WOOD!"

The warriors dropped their spears and hurried away to find wood enough to satisfy their chief. Jack stood tall, his arms folded over his chest, and glowered until every warrior was gone. Then he took off like a shot.

Stumbling across a bridge of twisted vines, he ran past a group of huts. Suddenly finding himself at the edge of a steep cliff and about to fall right over, Jack began waving his arms in a panic. Righting himself, he ran to the nearest hut.

"Rope, long rope," he said, rummaging frantically through the uninhabited hut.

He found a box of spices with the East India Trading Company insignia on it. Jack was about to toss it aside when a huge warrior appeared in the hut's doorway. Jack stepped back and looked into the warrior's fearsome face.

"Not running away, nooo . . ." Jack said, opening the box of spices. He took a handful and rubbed it on his body. "See?"

Jack soon found himself dusted nicely with a coating of fresh spices and tied to the enormous spit, hanging over a huge pile of kindling wood set in a large pit. He sighed and looked down at the fire pit, which now, thanks to his own efforts, was huge. "Nice job," he said, nodding to the proud warriors. Too nice, he added silently to himself.

Meanwhile, inside their cages, the pirates waited helplessly. But Will Turner wasn't about to give up. Elizabeth's life was at stake – he had to get to Jack. "Swing your cage," he yelled to the men as he shifted his weight from side to side, causing the cage to rock. "Get to the wall!"

Leech and the pirates in the other cage got the idea. They rocked their cage to the side of the steep chasm wall and grabbed a vine. "Put your feet through," Will shouted. "Start to climb!"

Pulling with all their might and grabbing for footholds, the crew members slowly moved the two cages up the wall.

A guard passed and stared at the tilted cages. Every man instantly froze. But, after a moment, Leech's men tried to move up an inch. The guard noticed. With a loud scream he sent out the alarm. The drums stopped.

Inside the village, Jack, tied up like a turkey, heard the alarm just as a torch was about to light the pit. The guard suddenly burst into the village, screaming and pointing to the jungle. His meaning was clear – the prisoners were escaping!

"*After them!*" Jack ordered, still trying to appear in charge. He jerked his head toward the jungle. "*Don't let them get away!*"

The warriors hesitated, not knowing whether to light the fire or run. After all, it was their duty to release their god from his fleshy prison. But it was also their god who was commanding them to leave. They finally ran off, tossing the torch to the ground as they left.

Jack's eyes grew wide as the torch slowly rolled toward the pit beneath him. Suddenly, a twig at the edge of the pit caught fire. As the entire pit went up in flames with a giant *whoosh*, Jack tried to blow out the fire. But it was no use. Captain Jack Sparrow was as good as cooked!

Chapter 11

Meanwhile, back in the chasm, Will's cage reached the top first. In the other cage, Leech reached for a thick vine, but screamed as the vine came twisting *into* the cage. Leech had pulled on a giant snake, not a vine! The pirates quickly let go and the vine that had been holding them snapped from the weight of the jerking motion. The cage plummeted to the floor of the deep chasm with a crash!

Will heard the men's screams just as he rolled his cage up and out of the chasm. But he didn't have time to worry about Leech and the others. The warriors were racing straight toward his own cage.

With no way to escape, Will and the others pulled the cage up around their legs and began to run through the jungle with their feet sticking out of the bottom of the cage. They had to get to the *Pearl* – fast!

*　*　*

Back in the village, Jack was trying to move fast, too. He was desperately trying to bounce the spit up and down and completely away from the fire. A boy from the village watched as the bouncing pirate choked and sputtered over the flames.

Jack finally bounced high enough and fell away from the pit, gasping for air. He managed to stand upright and ran with the spit on his back as fast as his scorched feet would allow.

The boy who had witnessed Jack's escape ran into the jungle. He caught up with the warriors and told them that Jack had hopped away. The raging warriors howled and took off again. But now they weren't after Jack's crew – they were after Jack himself!

Not far away, Will and his portion of the crew had broken free from their cage and had arrived on the beach to find the *Pearl* already prepared. While the warriors had been busy chasing everyone around the island, Pintel and Ragetti had been getting ready to steal the ship. Luckily for Jack's crew, that made for a fast getaway!

Gibbs was the first aboard. "Excellent!" he called out, seeing the *Black Pearl* ready to make sail. "Our work's half done."

The crew barged past Pintel and Ragetti without a second look and took their positions on deck. "Boys, make ready to sail!" Gibbs shouted.

Will worked alongside Gibbs. "What about Jack? I won't leave without him."

Gibbs suddenly pointed to the beach in horror. Will looked up and saw Jack racing down the beach with a hoard of warriors at his heels.

"Jack! Hurry!" Gibbs shouted. Jack *was* hurrying. The wily captain had managed to get free of the spit. With his arms flailing about, he was trying to stay ahead of the warriors.

Gibbs turned to the crew. "Cast off! Cast off!"

On the beach, the Prison Dog, which had made it to dry land after abandoning Pintel and Ragetti, appeared and began growling at the warriors.

"Good doggy!" Jack shouted. He sloshed through the surf to the side of the *Pearl* and Gibbs quickly hauled him aboard.

The dog barked, holding the warriors at bay until the *Black Pearl* disappeared into the horizon. Suddenly, the dog seemed to sense it was in trouble. It stopped barking, wagged its tail a few times, looked at the warriors – the very hungry warriors – then turned and made a run for it.

Chapter 12

Jack Sparrow sat on the deck of the *Black Pearl*, catching his breath.

"Put as much distance between us and this island and make for open sea?" Gibbs asked him.

"Yes to the first and yes to the second, but only insofar as we keep to the shallows . . ." Jack replied, still panting.

Gibbs frowned. "That seems a bit contradictory, sir."

Jack nodded. "I have every faith in your reconciliatory navigational skills, Mr Gibbs," Jack said, matter of factly.

Then he moved to the rail, opened his Compass and stared at its face. He was so focused that he didn't notice he had company. Will Turner stood right beside him.

"Jack," Will said quietly.

"Not now," Jack answered, without looking up.

"Jack, I need . . ."

"Not *now*," Jack snapped, reaching for his pistol. Finally he looked up at Will. "Oh. You. Where's that monkey?" Jack asked, thinking that as long as he had his pistol handy, he might as well practise. High in the rigging, the monkey let out a teasing screech.

"Jack," Will said once again, trying to get the captain's attention. "I need that Compass."

"Why?" Jack asked, taking another look before snapping it shut.

"To rescue Elizabeth," Will said.

Jack shook his head and began to climb the rigging. "That has a familiar ring to it," he said. He was right. The last time Will had found himself in the company of Jack, it had been when he was trying to rescue Elizabeth. To drive the point home, Jack added, "Have you considered keeping a more watchful eye on her? Maybe just lock her up somewhere?"

"She *is* locked up. In prison. Bound to hang for helping you," Will snapped.

Jack paused for a moment as Will's words sunk in. Then he shrugged and continued to climb. "There comes a time when one must take responsibility for one's mistakes," Jack said as he settled into the ship's crow's nest.

Suddenly, Jack felt the cold touch of steel at his throat. It was Will's sword.

"You will hand it over. Now!" he said, leaning into the crow's nest. "In exchange, you will be granted full pardon and commissioned as a privateer in service to England."

Jack sighed. "I wonder, what will my crew think when they see you've skewered their beloved and duly chosen captain?"

"I think they will see it as an example," Will told him sternly.

"All right," Jack nodded. "You get the Compass, you rescue your bonnie lass. Where's my profit?"

"You get full pardon," Will explained. "Freedom. A commission."

Jack shook his head. "No, accepting those things is what *you* want from *me*. Don't you want to know what *I* want from *you*?"

Will lowered his sword and turned his head away. Nothing was stickier than negotiating with a blasted pirate. "What do you want from me, Jack?" Will said finally, giving in.

"It's quite dangerous . . ." Jack said, cautioning Will. "I will trade you the Compass, if you will recover for me . . ." he fumbled for the small piece of cloth in his pocket, ". . . this."

Will eyed the imprint of the key on the cloth. "So you get my favour *and* the Letters of Marque as well?" Leave it to Jack Sparrow to come away on the upside of a tricky bargain, Will thought.

Jack nodded. "And you save fair damsel."

"*This* is going to save Elizabeth?" Will said, looking at the cloth.

Jack leaned in towards Will as if the very air were listening. "How much do you know about Davy Jones?" he asked in a whisper.

"Nothing," Will said.

"Yep," Jack said, nodding firmly, "it's going to save Elizabeth."

Chapter 13

Elsewhere on the ocean, a figure slipped silently across the ratline of the *Edinburgh Trader*. It was Elizabeth Swann, still dressed in the clothes of a sailor. She moved towards the light of the captain's cabin, where she could hear voices raised in an argument.

"It's an outrage!" Captain Bellamy complained, looking at the ship's accounts. "Port tariffs, berthing fees and, heaven help me, *pilotage!*"

"I'm afraid, sir, Tortuga is the only free port left in these waters," the ship's quartermaster said, knowing the captain was bound to respond.

And respond he did. Bellamy was furious. "A *pirate* port is what you mean! Well, I'm sorry, but an honest sailor I am. I make my living square, and sleep well each night, thank you."

He didn't get to continue. "Sir!" the bursar interrupted, pointing to the cabin window.

"What?" Bellamy demanded angrily. But the bursar was shaking so hard he could only point. The captain turned to see a shadowy white dress float by the cabin window. He ran out onto the dimly lit deck.

"Tell me you do see that," the ship's cook asked, terrified.

"Aye, I do see that," Bellamy answered as he watched the white gown float to the bowsprit. High up in the rigging, Elizabeth secretly pulled the dress along by a fishing line. With a whisk of her arm, she pulled a line that raised the arm of the dress. It pointed to Captain Bellamy, then out to sea. His crew immediately shuffled away from him.

"She wants you to do something," the bursar said.

"Jump overboard?" the quartermaster asked quickly.

Bellamy tossed him a scowl. "She's trying to give a sign!"

Then, on the sea winds, a soft voice whispered, "Tor . . . tu . . . ga."

"Did you hear that?" the cook exclaimed.

"Ber-mu-da?" the bursar said.

"Tobago?" the quartermaster suggested.

Suddenly, the ghostly bride raced toward the rail and dropped over the side. As the crew was busy looking overboard, Elizabeth dropped down behind them.

"Look for a sign!" Bellamy shouted to his men.

"There!" the quartermaster said, pointing out to sea. "There it is! There's the sign!"

"That's seaweed," a sailor pointed out.

"Seaweed can be a sign," the quartermaster argued.

Elizabeth lost all patience. She grabbed the shoulder of the bursar and turned him around. "What's that over there?" she said in a low, deep voice.

On the deck, the word 'Tortuga' was burning in lamp oil.

"Is it telling us to go there?" the terrified quartermaster asked.

Elizabeth was about to burst with frustration, when Captain Bellamy spoke up. "Men," he said. "What say ye to a course change? Prudence suggests we make way for the island of Tortuga!"

As the crew shouted their approval, Elizabeth pulled her sailor's cap down lower over her face and smiled. Her plan had worked. Now, all she could do was wait.

Chapter 14

Elizabeth was heading to Tortuga to find Will, but Will was nowhere near Tortuga. He was with Jack Sparrow, heading inland.

Through a heavy mist, two longboats from the *Black Pearl* rowed to the mouth of the Pantano River. Will, Ragetti and Gibbs rode in the lead, followed by Jack, Pintel and Cotton. Next to Cotton was a cage covered with a length of canvas.

As they rowed past thick tangles of twisted roots and bark, Will quietly asked Gibbs the question the whole crew wanted to know. "What is it that has Jack so spooked?"

Gibbs heaved a sigh. "Jack has run afoul of none other than Davy Jones himself," he said gravely. "Thinks he is only safe on land. If he goes out to open water, he'll be taken."

"By Davy Jones?" Will asked in disbelief. Jack never seemed scared of anyone.

"Well, I'll tell ye. If you believe such things, there's a beast does the bidding of Davy Jones. A fearsome creature from the depths, with giant tentacles that'll suction your face clean off, and drag an entire ship down to the crushing darkness. The Kraken," Gibbs said, shuddering at the very name of the evil thing. "They say the stench of its breath . . ." Gibbs stopped, not wanting to go on, and Will could see real fear in the old pirate's eyes. "If you believe such things," he repeated with a tilt of his head, and kept rowing.

Will glanced back at Jack, who was nervously picking at a hangnail. "Never thought Jack the type to be afraid of dying."

"Aye, but with Jones, it ain't about the dying – it's about the punishment," Gibbs answered. "Think of the worst fate you can conjure for yourself, stretching on forever . . . and that's what awaits you in Davy Jones's locker."

For a moment, everyone on the longboat was silent as they pondered Gibbs's words.

"And the key will spare him that?" Will finally asked.

"Now, that's the very question Jack wants

answered," Gibbs whispered, looking over at the captain. "Bad enough, even, to go visit . . . *her*."

"Her?" Will said nervously.

"Aye," Gibbs nodded.

As the boats rowed into the still water of a steamy bayou, fireflies flickered in the heavy air. The longboats pulled up to a rope ladder that hung down from a sprawling wooden shack high up in a tree. A lantern hung at the door, casting a dim glow on the cautious pirate crew. They had arrived. Now the question was, where?

"No worries, mates," Jack said, trying to sound lighthearted. He grabbed the ladder. "I'll handle this. Tia Dalma and I go way back. Thick as thieves. Nigh inseparable, we were, er, have been . . . before."

"I'll watch your back," Gibbs volunteered.

"It's me front I'm worried about," Jack muttered.

With one last nervous glance around, Jack pushed his way into the shack, the rest of his crew sticking close behind. As their eyes adjusted to the low light, they saw all manner of strange creatures in jars and bottles. Some were stuffed and hanging from the rafters. Others moved around in jars of murky water. Overhead dangled an old, dusty crocodile. Ragetti noticed a jar of eyeballs in a corner and put a hand over his eye socket that was plugged with a wooden eyeball.

At a table, in the shadows, sat Tia Dalma, a mystic with an eye keener than any pirate's. She'd been hovering over crab claws when her head suddenly snapped up. She stood. "Jack Sparrow," she said. "I always knew the wind was going to blow you back to me one day."

Her eyes moved past Jack and landed on Will. She smiled as she looked at him. "You have a touch of destiny in you, William Turner," she said, moving closer.

"You know me?" Will asked, confused.

"You want to know me," she replied in riddle, staring into Will's eyes.

"There will be no knowing here," Jack announced, walking over to Tia Dalma and ushering her back towards the table. "We came here for help."

As the pirates gathered around the table, Tia Dalma pulled Will in close. "Asking for help does not sound like Jack Sparrow."

"It's not so much for me," Jack answered

244

coolly, "as for William, so he can earn a favour from me."

Tia Dalma nodded. "Now *that* sounds like Jack Sparrow. What service may I do you? You know I demand payment."

"I brought payment!" Jack said brightly, taking the cage from Pintel's hand. He raised the canvas, revealing Jack the monkey trapped inside. Jack raised his pistol and shot it. The angry little monkey barely blinked. He just glared back.

"See?" Jack exclaimed. He glanced up at the ceiling. "Perhaps you can give it the crocodile treatment?"

Tia Dalma stood and opened the cage.

Gibbs moaned as the monkey raced through the shack. "You don't know how long it took us to catch that," he said sadly.

"The payment is fair," she said, ignoring Gibbs. Her eyes wandered again to Will.

Jack produced the drawing of the key from his pocket and passed it to Will, who quickly showed it to Tia Dalma. "We're looking for this . . . and what it goes to," Will said.

"That Compass you bartered from me can't lead you to this?" Tia Dalma asked.

"No," Jack answered flatly.

Tia Dalma laughed and turned her attention back to Will as she spoke to Jack. "Your key goes to a chest . . . and it is what lies inside the chest you seek, isn't it?"

"What is inside?" Gibbs asked.

"Gold? Jewels? Unclaimed properties of a valuable nature?" Pintel said hopefully.

"Nothing bad, I hope," Ragetti said, still unnerved by it all.

Chapter 15

Tia Dalma smiled at the pirates that surrounded her, as if they were small children. Then she began to tell her tale. "You know of Davy Jones, yes? A man of the sea, a great sailor until he ran afoul of that which vexes all men."

"What vexes all men?" Will asked her.

Shc smiled. "What, indeed?"

"The sea," Gibbs said solemnly.

Tia Dalma shook her head.

"Sums," Pintel said.

The gypsy shook her head again.

"The dichotomy of good and evil," Ragetti suggested. Everyone in the room looked at the one-eyed pirate and shook their heads.

"A woman," Jack said, ending the game.

Tia Dalma smiled at the rough pirate. "A woman. He fell in love. It was a woman, as changing and harsh and untameable as the sea. He never stopped loving her, but the pain it caused him was too much to live with . . . but not enough to cause him to die."

They each nodded sadly, understanding the story all too well.

"Exactly *what* did he put into the chest?" Will asked.

Tia Dalma sighed. "It was not worth feeling what small, fleeting joy life brings, he decided, and so he carved out his heart, locked it away in a chest and hid the chest from the world. The key . . . he keeps with him at all times."

Will nodded, understanding. The key would open the chest that held Jones's heart.

"That was a roundabout way to get to the answer," Jack observed.

"Sauce for the gander, Jack," Tia Dalma replied with a wink.

"You knew this," Will said realizing that Jack had made a deal based on more information than he'd been willing to reveal.

"No, I didn't. I didn't know where the key was . . ." Jack stuttered, interrupting Will's thoughts.

Will rolled his eyes.

"But now we do," Jack said smoothly, "so all that is left is to slip aboard Jones's ship, the *Flying Dutchman*, take the key and then you can go back to Port Royal and save your bonnie lass."

Jack headed for the door but, before he could open it, Tia Dalma said, "Let me see your hand."

Jack hesitated. Slowly, he unwrapped his palm. Tia Dalma nodded respectfully at the sight of the Black Spot that made Jack a marked man.

Gibbs leaned in and saw the mark, too. Pintel and Ragetti watched the old pirate turn three times and spit for luck. Not knowing why, they did the same, just in case.

They watched Tia Dalma move across the room in her long, ragged dress and climb the stairs. At the top, she opened a great carved door. The sound of the ocean whispered from it. Tia Dalma slowly closed the door and descended the stairs. In her hands she carried a jar, which she handed to Jack. "Davy Jones cannot make port, cannot step on land, but once every ten years," she said to him. Leaning down, she scooped dirt into the jar. "Land is where you are safe, Jack Sparrow, and so you will carry land with you."

Jack looked into the jar. "This is a jar of dirt," Jack said, unimpressed.

"Yes."

"Is the jar of dirt going to help?" he asked sceptically.

Tia Dalma reached for the jar. "If you don't want it, give it back."

"No!" Jack cried, clutching it to his chest.

"Then it helps," she said, nodding.

Will faced Tia Dalma. "It seems we have a need to find the *Flying Dutchman*," he said. Tia Dalma smiled into his young face, then sat again at her table. Scooping up the crab claws, she tossed them down, casting a spell to reveal the direction. The claws did their job well. The crew was on its way to find Davy Jones.

Captain Jack is back for another adventure on the high seas.

Elizabeth Swann's wedding day is ruined.

Lord Beckett has put Elizabeth in jail, and Will
promises he will rescue her.

Will Turner sails off to find Captain Jack Sparrow.

Will is captured by warriors.

The warriors have a new leader – Captain Jack!

Elizabeth Swann disguises herself as a sailor.

Will listens while Tia Dalma tells them
the story of Davy Jones.

Jack sneaks away. He needs to leave
Tortuga and find Jones's chest.

Davy Jones captains the *Flying Dutchman*.

Will shows his father, Bootstrap Bill,
a picture of Davy Jones's key.

Pirates Pintel and Ragetti have stolen
Davy Jones's chest!

"Hoist the inner jib. Bring up with a round turn. Captain's orders," the man muttered.

"Sailor, there's no use," Will said. "You've run aground."

But the beaten man kept trying. "No . . . beneath us . . . foul breath . . . waves took Billy and Quentin . . . captain's orders!"

A wave suddenly shook the ship and out of the rigging dropped a dead sailor. Will jumped back as the body hit the deck. On the sailor's back, Will could see round suction marks. He turned the body over. The man's face was gone, completely suctioned off.

The Kraken! Gibbs's description of the sea monster came rushing back to Will.

Will quickly backed away from the body. He looked over the rail in a panic and saw nothing but the rolling blackness of the sea. An eerie calm suddenly settled on the waters. Then, almost as quickly, the wind picked up to a gale. The sea churned white and, rising from the foam like a great whale breaking the surface, came an awesome ship of great power. The *Flying Dutchman*.

Will had been tricked. In order to bait the real *Flying Dutchman*, Jack had sent Will aboard a wrecked vessel. But now the ship – and its captain, Davy Jones – had arrived.

It was unlike any ship Will had ever seen. It was made of pallid wood and bones, and completely covered in items from the sea – coral, shells and seaweed. With a splash, it slammed down into the ocean, the skeleton of a winged female attached to the bow. Will hid himself behind one of the wrecked ship's cannons, but it did him no good.

From the shadows, the *Dutchman's* crew boarded the ship. They were a hideous-looking bunch. Some had scales, while others were covered in barnacles. Will pulled his sword and broke cover. He ran for the longboat, but the *Dutchman's* first mate, a man with a coral-encrusted face, named Maccus, stopped him. The rest of the crew soon joined Maccus, surrounding Will.

"Down on your marrowbones and pray!" Greenbeard, the Bo'sun, snarled through the seaweed that covered his face.

For a moment, Will stood frozen by the sight of Jones's crew. But as soon as he regained his wits, he ran his sword through a vat of whale oil and thrust it into his lantern. His sword flamed wildly as he slashed away, searing the crewmen's watery flesh. Will spun around to attack the crew at his back when a pulley hit him squarely in the face and knocked him out cold. He was suddenly defenceless and at the mercy of the crew of the *Flying Dutchman*.

Chapter 17

When he came to, Will was still on the scuttled ship. He was part of a line of sailors, all of them on their knees. Will was the final sailor in this line. He looked off to the side and watched as someone strode on to the deck. It was Davy Jones himself – and he was as terrible as he'd been described.

The captain's dark eyes stared out from behind a long beard of octopus tentacles that moved and curled with a life of their own. He had a claw for a left hand and the fingers on his right extended out in rough tentacles, wrapping around an ivory cane. On his head he wore a black hat that resembled devil horns, and one of his legs was nothing but whalebone. With a dark glare, he looked down the line of sailors before him.

"Six men still alive," Maccus stated. "The rest have moved on."

Jones nodded and made his way down the line. "Do you fear death?" Jones asked the ship's helmsman, who appeared to be the most frightened. "I can offer you an escape," he taunted in a voice that echoed of waves crashing on a distant shore.

"Don't listen to him!" said the chaplain, who was also in the line, clutching his cross.

Jones turned and roared, "Do you not fear death?"

"I'll take my chances, sir."

"Good luck, mate," Jones said with a smirk. He nodded to Greenbeard, who tossed the man overboard.

Jones leaned close to the helmsman. His tentacled beard bristled and twisted. "You cling to the pain of life and fear death. I offer you the choice. Join my crew . . . and postpone judgment. One hundred years before the mast. Will you serve?"

The helmsman nodded quickly. "I will serve."

Jones smiled and moved down the line. At Will, he stopped and frowned. "You are neither dead nor dying. What is your purpose here?"

"Jack Sparrow sent me," Will replied, "to settle his debt."

Anger rose in Jones's face, the tentacles of his beard turning from pale pink to purple. "Did he, now?" He looked at Will for a long moment. "I am sorely tempted to accept that offer."

Jones turned his head and looked out into the darkness. It was time to take care of a little payment.

Chapter 18

Hidden in darkness on the deck of the *Black Pearl*, Jack Sparrow looked through his spyglass and gasped. Jones was staring straight at him.

As Jack slowly lowered his telescope, Davy Jones suddenly and jarringly appeared right in front of him. The crewmen of the *Flying Dutchman* were also transported to the *Pearl's* deck and they quickly surrounded Jack and his crew.

"You have a debt to pay," Jones said to Jack with a nasty growl. "You've been captain of the *Black Pearl* for 13 years. That was our agreement."

Jack nodded. "Technically, I was only captain for two years – then I was viciously mutinied upon."

"But a captain nonetheless," Jones replied. "Have you not introduced yourself all this time as Captain Jack Sparrow?"

"Not that I recall. Why do you ask? You have my payment. One soul, to serve on your ship. He's already over there," Jack said, referring to Will.

"You can't trade," Jones roared. "You can't substitute."

Jack raised a finger. "There is precedent regarding servitude, according to The Code of the Brethren . . ."

The tentacles on Jones's face twisted and curled. "One soul is not the same as another!"

"Ah, so we've established the proposal is sound in principle. Now we're just haggling over the price," Jack replied.

"As has been the case before, I am oddly compelled to listen to you," Jones confessed.

Jack saw his chance to bargain and pounced on it. "Just how many souls do you think my soul is worth?" he asked slyly.

Jones pondered. "One hundred souls. Three days," was the reply.

Jack flashed a sparkling grin. "You're a diamond, mate. Send me back the boy, I'll get started, right off."

"I keep the boy. A good-faith payment. That leaves you only 99 more to go."

"What?" Jack asked, astounded. "Have you

met Will Turner? He's noble and heroic, a terrific soprano – he's worth at least four. And did I mention he is in love? Due to be married. To a lovely young lady. You hate that malarkey."

Jones was not to be swayed by Jack's fancy words. "I keep the boy," he snapped. "You owe 99 souls. In three days. But I wonder, Sparrow . . . can you live with this?"

Jack considered the question briefly.

"Yep," he answered.

"You can condemn an innocent man – a friend – to a lifetime of servitude, in your name, while you roam free?" Jones asked.

"I'm good with it," Jack answered. "Shall we seal it in blood? I mean, ink?"

"Let's not, and say we did. Agreed?"

"Agreed," Jack said, still grinning. Jack looked down at his palm. The Black Spot was gone. When he looked back up, Davy Jones and his crew were gone, too.

Moments later, the *Flying Dutchman* sailed off into a distant storm with Will aboard. Jack watched silently as the ship faded from sight. He had three days to find 99 souls. There was only one place to go – Tortuga.

Chapter 19

In a corner of a crowded cantina in Tortuga, Jack sat, his feet up, Compass in hand. As Gibbs went about the business of recruiting Jack's much-needed 99 souls, Jack drank from a large mug and listened in. An unforgettable journey aboard the *Black Pearl* is what Gibbs promised a line of hopeful sailors. Of course, as it was Tortuga, every one of them was beaten and broken down.

"I've one arm and a bum leg," an old sailor told Gibbs.

"Crow's nest for you," Gibbs replied. After a few more interviews, Gibbs walked over to Jack.

"How are we doing?" Jack asked, looking up.

"Counting those four?" Gibbs sighed. "That gives us four." Gibbs worried over the number. "Nothing better happen to *me*," he added hastily.

"I make no promises," Jack said, raising an eyebrow. He was not fond of promises.

"You'd best be coming up with a new plan, Jack, and it better not be relying on that Compass. The whole crew knows it ain't worked since you was saved from the gallows."

Jack scowled as Gibbs moved back to the meagre line of recruits.

"What's your story?" Gibbs asked the next sailor. The man was drunk and unshaven, but his eyes were clear.

"My story," the man replied. "Same as your story, just one chapter behind. I became obsessed with capturing a notorious pirate . . . chased him across the seven seas. I lost all perspective, I was consumed. The pursuit cost me my crew, my commission, my life."

Gibbs took a closer look at the man. "Commodore?" he asked, suddenly recognizing him. It was Commodore Norrington – the very man who had chased Jack and the *Pearl* all the way to *Isla de Muerta*.

"Not any more," the former commodore answered. He slammed his bottle down. "So what is it? Do I make your crew or not?"

Gibbs didn't answer. He was stunned to see the fine commodore turned into a rough gentleman of fortune like himself.

The silence seemed to anger Norrington. "So, am I worthy to serve under Captain Jack Sparrow?" he roared. Then he turned and pulled his pistol. "Or should I just kill you now?" he said, aiming it across the room at Jack, who was trying to sneak away.

Jack froze and quickly forced a smile. "You're hired, mate!"

Norrington pulled the hammer back. "Sorry," he said, about to shoot anyway. "Old habits die and all that."

"Easy, soldier," a man said, grabbing Norrington's arm. "That's our captain you be threatening."

A wild shot went off and the man ducked, knocking over a table. Jack's new crew suddenly jumped up and began swinging. Pirates, out for a night of sport, joined in the brawl and swung back, tossing chairs and smashing bottles.

"Time to go," Jack said, nodding to Gibbs.

"Aye."

Jack danced through the brawl without even

a scratch. On his way out he stooped over a man who had been knocked out and tried on his hat. Too small, Jack decided, as he and Gibbs made their way to the cantina's back stairs. It was so hard to find a good hat these days, he thought to himself as the fight waged on.

As Jack and Gibbs slipped quietly away, Norrington was left with his back to a beam, slashing at the drunken hoard. "Come on, then. Do you want some British steel? You? You? You?" He was still shouting when a bottle was smashed over his head, taking him down.

Standing over him, dressed in her sailor's clothing, was Elizabeth. "I just wanted the pleasure of doing that myself," she shouted to the pirates. "Now, let's toss this mess out of here and have a drink!"

The pirates roared and tossed Norrington out to the pigs wallowing behind the cantina. Elizabeth suddenly recognized the man. And she couldn't believe her eyes.

Chapter 20

Moments later, Elizabeth rushed to the former commodore's side and knelt down. "James Norrington," she said, pitying the poor man. "What has the world done to you?"

"Nothing I didn't deserve," Norrington answered, as Elizabeth helped him to his feet.

Slowly, they made their way to the docks and stepped directly into Jack's path. "Captain Sparrow," Elizabeth said to him.

Jack looked at her. He didn't recognize her in her sailor disguise. "Come to join my crew, lad? Well enough, welcome aboard."

"I've come to find the man I love," Elizabeth declared.

Jack nodded, still not aware he was speaking to Elizabeth.

"I'm deeply flattered, son, but my first and only love is the sea," Jack replied.

"Meaning William Turner, Captain Sparrow," Elizabeth added stiffly.

"Elizabeth?" Jack said, eyeing her warily. "You know, those clothes do *not* flatter you at all."

"Jack," Elizabeth said, staying focused, "I know Will set out to find you. Where is he?"

"Darling, I am truly unhappy to have to tell you this but, through an unfortunate and entirely unforeseeable series of circumstances that have nothing whatsoever to do with me, poor Will was press-ganged into Davy Jones's crew."

"Davy Jones," Elizabeth repeated, not sure if she should believe the pirate.

"Oh, please," Norrington scoffed. "The captain of the *Flying Dutchman*? A ship that ferries those who died at sea from this world to the next . . ."

"Bang on!" Jack exclaimed. Then, recognizing Norrington, he added, "You look bloody awful, mate. What are you doing here?"

"You hired me," was his reply. "I can't help that your standards are lax."

"Jack," Elizabeth said, "all I want is to find Will."

Jack tugged at his beaded black beard for a moment before carefully replying, "Are you certain? Is that what you really want . . . most?"

"Of course," Elizabeth answered. She suddenly saw a gleam in Jack's eyes.

"I'd think you'd want to find a way to save Will . . . *most*," Jack replied.

"And you have a way to do that?"

"Well," Jack began, "there is a chest. A chest of unknown size and origin."

"What contains the still-beating heart of Davy Jones!" Pintel interjected as he passed, carrying a barrel onto the *Black Pearl*.

"Thump, THUMP!" Ragetti added, patting his hand against his chest with a grin.

Ignoring the scurvy pair, Jack quickly said, "And whoever possesses that chest possesses the leverage to command Jones to do whatever it is he – or she – wants. Including saving our brave William from his grim fate."

"How can we find it?" Elizabeth asked flatly. She didn't trust Jack, but she wanted to get to Will – soon.

Jack placed the Compass in her hand. "With this. This Compass is unique."

"Unique here having the meaning of 'broken'?" Norrington asked.

Jack tilted his head. "True enough, this Compass does not point north," he said. "It points to the thing you want most in this world."

Still sceptical, Elizabeth asked, "Jack, are you telling the truth?"

"Every word, love. What you want most in the world is to find the chest of Davy Jones, is it not?"

Elizabeth nodded. "To save Will."

Jack opened the Compass in her hand. "By finding the chest of Davy Jones," he said for emphasis. Looking at the Compass heading, he turned to Gibbs. "We have our heading!" he shouted. The *Pearl*'s crew was on its way . . . finally.

Chapter 21

Meanwhile, on the deck of the *Flying Dutchman*, Davy Jones sat playing an organ of coral that seemed to have grown from the organic moulding of the deck itself. The tune was sad and haunting and, as the notes drifted over the boat, Jones's eyes misted. His gaze was drawn to the image of a woman with flowing hair that was etched into the coral above the huge keyboard.

Elsewhere on the deck, the crew members were hard at work – including one of the newest additions, Will Turner. He was hauling a line when it suddenly slipped through his hands and a boom fell, crashing to the deck.

"Haul the weevil to his feet!" the Bo'sun shouted. In his hands he held a cat-o'-nine-tails. He slapped it against his palm. "Five from the lash'll remind you to stay on 'em!" he said, walking over to Will. But before he could take a swing,

Bootstrap Bill reached out and grabbed the crewman's wrist.

"Impeding me in my duties!" the Bo'sun snarled. "You'll share the punishment!"

"I'll take it all," Bootstrap told him.

"Will you, now?" Davy Jones asked. He had stopped playing the organ and was observing the situation carefully. "And what would prompt such an act of charity?"

Bootstrap lifted a barnacled hand, motioning toward Will. "My son. That's my son."

Jones smiled as he watched Will's eyes widen at the sight of his father. "What fortuitous circumstance be this!" Jones roared, slapping his knee. "You wish to spare your son the Bo'sun's discipline?"

"Aye," Bootstrap answered.

"Give your lash to Mr Turner. The elder," Jones ordered the Bo'sun.

Bootstrap Bill protested as the lash was placed in his hand. Being forced to lash his own son was the worst possible punishment.

"The cat's out of the bag, Mr Turner!" Jones roared. The crew cowered. "Your issue will taste its sting, be it by the Bo'sun's hand – or your own!"

The Bo'sun went to take back the lash, but Bootstrap pushed him away. He raised the lash to Will, his barnacled arm snapping forward.

Will half staggered to the hold later that night, Bootstrap following behind him. "The Bo'sun prides himself on cleaving flesh from bone with every swing," Bootstrap explained as he helped Will to a bench.

Will stared. He couldn't believe that after all these years, he was finally talking to his father.

"So I'm to understand what you did was an act of compassion?" Will asked his father.

Bootstrap nodded.

"Then I guess I am my father's son. For nearly a year, I've been telling myself that I killed you to save you," Will admitted.

"You killed me?" Bootstrap replied.

"I lifted the curse you were under, knowing it would mean your death. But at least you would no longer suffer the fate handed to you by Barbossa."

"Who is Barbossa?" Bootstrap asked blankly.

"Captain Barbossa," Will said, wondering how his father's mind could have dulled so as not to remember. "The man who led the mutiny aboard the *Black Pearl*? Who left you to live forever at the bottom of the ocean."

"Oh. Of course," Bootstrap said, nodding. His eyes misted. "It's the gift and the lie given by Jones," he told young Will. "You join the crew and think you've cheated the powers, but it's not reprieval you've found. It's oblivion. Losing what you were, bit by bit, till you end up like poor Wyvern here."

Will followed his father's eyes and noticed what looked like a carved image of an old sailor, his body part of the ship's hull.

Bootstrap sighed. "Once you've sworn an oath to the *Dutchman*, there's no leaving it. Not till your debt is paid. By then, you're not just on the ship, but of it. Why did you do it, Will?"

"I've sworn no oath," Will said truthfully.

Bootstrap's face brightened at the news. "Then you must get away."

"Not until I find this," Will said, showing his father the image of the key. "It's supposed to be on the ship. Jack wanted it; maybe it is a way out?"

Suddenly, old Wyvern moved, pulling himself free from the hold of the hull's wood. "The

Dead Man's Chest!" he moaned, his arms reaching for the cloth.

Will jumped back as the wooden creature, who had torn himself away from the body of the ship, opened his mouth and wailed. Will blanched. He knew that this was the fate for all who served Davy Jones. Old Bootstrap would soon fade into the hull, too. One more tormented soul to become part of the ship itself. But Wyvern's next words gave Will hope.

"Open the chest with the key and stab the heart," old Wyvern cried, then seemed to suddenly change his mind. "Don't stab the heart! The *Dutchman* must have a living heart or there is no captain! And if there is no captain, there's no one to have the key!"

"The captain has the key?" Will asked, confused by Wyvern's ravings.

"Hidden," was all Wyvern said. He withdrew, once again becoming one with the hull of the ship.

But Will had his answer – and that was half of what he needed.

The key was with Jones.

Will headed for the deck.

Chapter 22

Aboard the *Black Pearl*, Jack Sparrow found Elizabeth filling in the names on the Letters of Marque that she'd taken from Lord Beckett.

Jack immediately snatched them away. "These Letters of Marque are supposed to go to *me*, are they not?"

Jack spotted the signature on the papers. "Lord Cutler Beckett. *He's* the man wants my Compass?"

Elizabeth hesitated. "Not the Compass, a chest."

The word caught Gibbs's attention. "A chest? Not the chest of Davy Jones? If the East India Trading Company controls the chest, they'll control the sea," Gibbs grumbled.

Elizabeth's ears perked up – control of the sea. So *that* was why Beckett was so eager to get his hands on the chest! It had nothing to do with Jack. She turned her attention back to the captain.

"Aye, a discomforting notion," the captain agreed. "May I inquire as to how you came by these?"

"Persuasion," Elizabeth answered.

Jack raised an eyebrow. "Friendly?" he asked with a smile.

"Decidedly not," Elizabeth snapped. She didn't have time for Jack's games – or his flirting.

Jack scowled and looked again at the letters. "Full pardon," he huffed. "Commission as a privateer on behalf of England and the East India Trading Company. As if I could be bought." He shook his head and stuffed the letters in his jacket pocket. "Not for this low of a price. Fate worse than death, living a life like that . . ."

"Jack," Elizabeth said. "The letters. Give them back."

Jack looked at her. "Persuade me," he said with a grin.

Elizabeth hesitated, then turned her back on the infuriating pirate who was smugly patting the Letters in his jacket pocket. Norrington had been standing nearby, listening in. As she passed by him to leave, he couldn't help but notice a small smile playing on her face.

"It's a curious thing," Norrington said, falling into step with Elizabeth. "There was a time when I'd have given anything for you to look like that while thinking of me. Just once."

Elizabeth stiffened at the suggestion that she might have an interest in Captain Jack. "I don't know what you mean," Elizabeth said.

"I think you do," Norrington insisted.

"Don't be absurd. I trust him, that's all."

"Ah," Norrington nodded. He turned to walk away, but not without one final thought to leave with Elizabeth.

"Did you never wonder how your fiancé ended up on the *Flying Dutchman* in the first place?" Norrington asked.

Chapter 23

Back on the *Dutchman*, Will had made his way to the main deck. A game of Liar's Dice was being played by a few of the crew.

Standing back a bit, Will observed the game and tried to follow along.

"I wager ten years!" Maccus said hotly.

Another crewman matched the ten years and the game was on. Each man bid a number, then Maccus peeked at the dice under his cup. "Four fives," he said firmly.

"Liar!" another crewman in the game called. Maccus cursed as he revealed his dice. The barnacled sea man had only three fives.

"What are they playing for?" Will asked Bootstrap, who had followed his son.

"The only thing any of us has," Bootstrap sighed, "years of service."

"Any member of the crew can be challenged?"

Will asked his father thoughtfully.

"Aye," Bootstrap replied.

"I challenge Davy Jones," Will boldly announced.

The crew went silent and, as if by magic, Jones appeared instantly on the deck. "Accepted," he told Will, eyeing him carefully. "But I only bet for what's dearest to a man's heart."

"I wager a hundred years of service," was Will's reply.

"No!" Bootstrap cried.

"Against your freedom?" Jones asked.

"My father's freedom." Will thought he had no need to wager against his own freedom. He thought he was already free, having no idea Jack had been bargaining with his soul.

"Agreed," Jones answered and took a seat across from Will. Jones eagerly rolled first. "You are a desperate man," Jones remarked. "You are the one who hopes to get married. But your fate is to be married to this ship."

"I choose my own fate," Will replied.

"Then it wouldn't be fate, would it?" Jones answered. "Five threes."

Will took a breath. "Five sixes," he said.

Jones looked in his eyes. "Liar."

Will revealed his dice. To the crew's shock, he had five sixes! "Well done, Master Turner," Jones said, rising to leave. Will had won the first round. His father was free.

But Will wasn't satisfied. "Another game," he said suddenly.

The crew gasped. "You can't best the devil twice, son," Jones said, cautioning him.

Will smiled knowingly. "Then why are you walking away?"

Jones's beard curled wildly. He didn't like to be goaded.

"The stakes?" Jones asked, taking his seat again.

"I wager my soul," Will answered. "An eternity of servitude."

"Against?" Jones asked.

"What was it you said about that which is dearest to a man's heart?" Will asked, presenting the cloth. "I want this."

Jones heaved his huge head. "How do you know of the key?" he snarled.

"That's not part of the game, is it?" Will asked.

Jones scowled as one of his tentacles

reached into his shirt and pulled out the key. It hung from a chain Jones wore around his neck. That's what Will needed to see. He now knew where the key was hidden, and he tried not to show his satisfaction. He slammed his cup down along with Jones's, when another cup suddenly slammed down, too.

"I'm in," Bootstrap said looking at Jones. "Matching his wager, an eternity in service to you." Not waiting for permission, Bootstrap began a new game. "I bid three twos," he said, looking at his dice under the cup.

"Don't do this," Will begged.

Too much was at stake now that his father was playing. If Will lost, he would join Jones's crew, but at least his father would be free. But if Bootstrap lost, he would again be bound to the ship, even though Will would go free.

"The die's been cast, Will. Your bid, Captain," Bootstrap said, ignoring his son's pleas.

Davy Jones checked his dice. "Four threes."

"Five threes," Will said reluctantly.

"Seven fives," Jones told them.

Will couldn't go any higher. "Eight fives," he said, bluffing.

Jones smiled. He knew Will was lying. "Welcome to the crew, lad."

"Twelve fives," Bootstrap yelled suddenly. Jones glowered at him, but Bootstrap held steady. "Call me a liar, or up the bid."

Jones slipped the key back into his shirt. "Bootstrap Bill, you are a liar, and you will spend an eternity of service to me on this ship. William Turner, feel free to go ashore . . . the very next time we make port." Jones laughed and moved off.

Will was furious. "You fool! Why did you do that?"

Bootstrap dropped his tired head and said, "I couldn't let you lose."

"It was never about winning or losing," Will said, sighing. Bootstrap stared at him for a moment, then suddenly understood . . . it was about finding the key. And Will had, at least, done that.

Later that night, the merchant ship, the *Edinburgh Trader*, appeared on the horizon near the *Dutchman*. Grabbing Will, Bootstrap went to the railing and quietly pointed the *Trader* out to Will. "It's your chance," Bootstrap whispered.

Will nodded. But before he could get on the passing ship, he had something to take care of. He moved towards the captain's cabin and quietly slipped inside. Jones was asleep, sprawled across the organ. Will moved a step closer when Jones's finger suddenly hit a key. The noise echoed through the cabin, but the sleeping captain didn't move. Will held his breath and crept up to the organ. Pushing away Jones's tentacled beard, he reached for the key.

Just as Will had worked it off the chain, a single tentacle grabbed the key and tried to pull it back to Jones. Will looked down at the cloth that he still held in his hand. He rolled it up and quickly placed the cloth in the tentacle's grip. Satisfied to be holding something, the tentacle released the key and rested peacefully again with the cloth in its clutches.

Will retreated from the cabin and dashed back to Bootstrap. "Is she still there?" he asked, his eyes searching the dark sea for the *Trader*.

Bootstrap had readied a longboat for Will. "Aye, but the moment's slipping away."

Will's heart ached at leaving his father behind. He climbed over the side of the *Dutchman*. "Come with me," he pleaded.

"I can't. I'm part of the ship now, Will. I can't leave. Take this," he said, handing him a black knife from his belt. "Always meant for you to have it . . ."

Will smiled. "I will see you free of this prison. I promise you."

Will slipped into the longboat and disappeared on the dark waters of the night.

The next morning, a large crewman arrived to take Bootstrap's place on watch. He found the old pirate asleep and kicked him hard. "Show a leg, before the captain spots you."

Suddenly, the crewman's eyes fell on the white sails of the *Edinburgh Trader*. "All hands!" he bellowed. "Ship a quarter stern!"

Davy Jones came on deck and looked out to sea. "Who stood watch last night?"

The crew pushed Bootstrap forward. "How is it, Bootstrap, you let a ship pass by, unnoticed?" the tentacled captain asked.

"Beggin' your mercy, Capt'n, I fell sound asleep. Beggin' your mercy, it won't happen again."

"Bring the son," Jones ordered.

"He's not on board, sir," a crewman said. "One of the longboats is missing."

Jones immediately understood. He met Bootstrap's eye and watched the pirate's face grow pale. Jones pulled the chain from his shirt. The key was gone. There was only one person tricky enough to be behind this. "Jack Sparrow," he shouted. "Captain Jack Sparrow!"

Chapter 25

In the captain's cabin of the *Edinburgh Trader*, Will huddled underneath a blanket and clutched a warm drink in his hand. As he began to thaw out, Captain Bellamy tried to understand what was going on. "Strange thing, to come upon a longboat so far out in open waters," he said.

"Just put as many leagues behind us as you can, as fast as you can," Will replied. His eyes fell on Elizabeth's wedding dress, thrown casually across a chair.

"That dress. Where did you get it?" Will asked.

"Funny, that dress," Captain Bellamy said. "Found aboard the ship. Put quite a stir into the crew, thought it was a spirit, bringing an omen of ill fate. But it brought good fortune! The spirit told us, put in at Tortuga, and we made a nice bit of profit there – off the books."

Will ran his fingers over the white fabric and smiled. "I imagine some of your crew might have jumped ship there?"

"Bound to happen," Bellamy said with a wave of his hand.

A sailor on deck suddenly rushed to the cabin. "Captain! A ship's been spotted!"

"Colours?" Bellamy asked.

"She's not flying any, sir," the sailor replied.

"Pirates," Bellamy said, glancing warily at Will.

"Or worse," Will cried, rushing out on to the deck. He climbed the yard arm and looked out at the water.

"It's the *Dutchman*!" Will cried. "I've doomed us all."

Will had barely finished speaking when the *Edinburgh Trader* lurched to a sudden stop. "Mother Cary's chickens!" the bursar shouted in alarm. "What happened?"

"Must have hit a reef," the quartermaster answered. After all, large ships did not just stop of their own accord.

Captain Bellamy looked over the rail, trying to see what had halted them. The sea looked empty. "Free the rudder!" he commanded. "Hard to port, then starboard and back again!"

The sailors followed orders and turned for more instructions. But Bellamy was gone. The crew looked out toward the sea, where what appeared to be a tiny figure was wrapped in a huge tentacle. As the crew looked closer, it was clear to them that the figure was the captain! The tentacle rose high in the air and then slapped the screaming captain down upon the water.

"KRAKEN!" the crew shouted in terror.

Having taken out the captain, the Kraken came back for the ship. The arms of the huge creature swept over the deck and smashed the longboats.

In a spray of wood and sea foam, the Kraken broke the ship in two and pulled it under.

When it was over, six men kneeled on the deck of the *Flying Dutchman.* "Where is the son?" Jones asked, studying the line of terrified sailors. "And where is the key?"

"No sign," Maccus answered. "He must have been claimed by the sea."

"I *am* the sea!" Jones bellowed angrily.

"Overboard!" he shouted, motioning to the doomed sailors. They were of no use to him.

As his crewman tossed the last survivors of the merchant ship over the side, Jones paced the deck. "The chest is no longer safe," he growled, knowing that Bootstrap's son had the key. He also knew Will was working with Jack. "Crowd on sail and gather way. Chart a course to *Isla Cruces*."

"He won't find the chest," a crewman said.

"He knew about the key, didn't he?" Jones shouted impatiently. He would not risk Jack discovering the location of his heart. He needed to get to *Isla Cruces* before Will – or Jack – arrived. "Get me there first," Jones shouted. "Or there be the devil to pay!"

Holding fast to the stern of the *Dutchman* and able to hear every word on deck, the sole survivor of the *Edinburgh Trader*, Will Turner, now knew where the chest was hidden. Crouching down on the stern, he was suddenly filled with hope. He had a ride to the chest . . . and the key in his pocket!

Chapter 26

While Will was hitching a ride to *Isla Cruces* on the *Dutchman*, Jack was heading for the same island on the *Black Pearl*. Jack's Compass, in Elizabeth's hand, had finally given him proper direction.

But Elizabeth didn't seem very happy.

"Elizabeth, are you well? Everything ship-shape and Bristol fashion? My tremendous intuitive sense of the female creature informs me you are troubled," Jack gallantly said.

Elizabeth let out a sigh. "I just thought I'd be married by now," she said.

Jack smiled agreeably. "I like marriage! It's like a wager on who will fall out of love first."

Elizabeth moved away, but Jack pursued her. "You know, I am captain of a ship. I could perform a marriage right here on this deck, right now."

"No, thank you," Elizabeth said to his hasty proposal.

"Why not?" he asked her, smiling. "Admit it, we are so much alike, you and I. I and you."

"Except for, oh, a sense of decency and honour," Elizabeth said. "And a moral centre. And personal hygiene."

Jack looked himself over. "Trifles!" he said quickly. "You will come over to my side, in time. I know."

"You seem quite certain."

Jack nodded. "One word, love. Curiosity. You long for freedom. To do what you want because you want it. To act on selfish impulse. You want to see what it's like. Someday," he said, looking into her eyes, "you won't be able to resist."

Elizabeth's expression was stonelike. With a chill in her voice, she replied, "Because you and I are alike, there will come a moment when you have the chance to show it – to do the right thing."

Jack brightened. "I love those moments! I like to wave as they pass by!"

Elizabeth ignored him. "You will have a chance to do something brave," she told him. "And in that moment you will discover something."

Jack looked at her as if he couldn't imagine

what on earth that something might be. He looked puzzled, as if he were trying to figure it out.

"That you are a good man!" Elizabeth told him, finally.

"All evidence to the contrary," Jack pointed out.

"I have faith in you. Do you know why? Curiosity," she said confidently. "You're going to want it. A chance to be admired and gain the rewards that follow. You won't be able to resist."

Jack opened his mouth to retort but was stopped by a loud command, "Land, ho!"

Jack raced to the rail. He could see the tiny island of *Isla Cruces* on the horizon. He stared down into the suddenly still water. The island was too far away for Jack's taste. "I want my jar," he said meekly.

Chapter 27

Captain Jack Sparrow sat in a longboat, clutching his jar of dirt like a frightened child. Opposite him were Elizabeth and Norrington, both trying to take seriously what they saw as the captain's ridiculous behaviour. Pintel and Ragetti were rowing the longboat toward *Isla Cruces*.

"You're pulling too fast," Pintel complained to his one-eyed friend.

"You're pulling too slow," Ragetti answered. "We don't want the Kraken to catch us."

Jack cringed at the mention of the sea monster's name.

"I'm saving me strength for when it comes," Pintel said. "And I don't think it's 'Krack-en', anyways. I always heard it said 'Kray-ken'."

Jack cringed again. "What, with a long *a*? 'Krock-en' is how it is in the original

Scandinavian," Ragetti answered, leaning on the oars. "And 'Krack-en' is closer to that."

They heard a sudden splash in the water and the two took to rowing faster. They could debate later.

Reaching the shore, Jack gratefully hopped out. He took off his jacket, patted the pocket to make sure the Letters of Marque were still there, placed them and the jar in the longboat's bow and grabbed a shovel. "Guard the boat. Mind the tide," he ordered Pintel and Ragetti. Jack thrust the Compass into Elizabeth's hands and they made their way up the beach.

"I didn't expect anyone to be here," Norrington said, when they came upon an abandoned church.

"There's not," Elizabeth answered.

"You know this place?" he asked, surprised.

"Stories," Elizabeth said, moving on. "The Church came to the island and brought salvation, and disease and death. They say the priest had to bury everybody, one after the other. It drove him mad and he hung himself."

"Better mad with the rest of the world than sane alone," Norrington noted. Elizabeth stared at him. Norrington had changed so much since she first met him. This cynical man was not the commodore she had once known.

"No fraternizing with the help, love," Jack said, interrupting her thoughts. Elizabeth scowled, looked down at the Compass and continued to walk. Suddenly, the needle began to swing wildly – they had found the spot! Jack drew an X in the sand with the toe of his boot and handed the shovel to Norrington.

At the same time, on an outer reef of *Isla Cruces*, the *Flying Dutchman* came around the point. Through his spyglass, Davy Jones saw the longboat. "They're here," he scowled, stomping the deck. "And I cannot step foot on land again for near of a decade!"

"Ye'll trust us to act in yer stead?" Maccus asked him.

"I trust you to know what awaits should you fail!" Jones promised. "Down, then," he ordered his crew.

Maccus nodded and called out, "Down, down." The bow of the *Flying Dutchman* submerged into the blue sea, bubbles rushing over her deck. In a moment, the entire ship went under and moved beneath the waves as swiftly as if it were being pushed down by a huge, invisible hand. Fish darted by as the *Dutchman* headed, beneath the waves, for *Isla Cruces*, churning the sea above her to foam.

Sitting on the beach, Pintel and Ragetti stared out at the boiling sea and turned to each other in terror. Springing to their feet, they left the longboat and ran to warn the others.

Chapter 28

Time was running out for Jack. He and Elizabeth stood anxiously over the hole Norrington had dug. They gave a start when the shovel suddenly· clanked against something hard. They had hit the chest! Jack jumped into the hole and helped lift it out.

Jack quickly broke the lock with the shovel. He sank to his knees and opened the chest. Inside were the mementoes of a love lost; a strand of white pearls and a long white dress, dried flowers and faded love letters. Jack pushed the stuff aside and found a box. He lifted the box from the chest. It was bound in bands of iron and locked tightly, but the sound of a single deep beat could be heard coming from inside.

"It's real!" Elizabeth gasped.

Norrington was astounded. "You actually were telling the truth."

Jack raised an eyebrow. "I do that a lot, and yet people are still surprised."

"With good reason," came a voice.

The group turned to see Will Turner. He approached them, out of breath and soaked to the skin.

With a gasp of astonishment, Elizabeth rushed to him. "Will – you're all right!" She threw her arms around his neck.

Jack looked behind Will, worriedly. "How did you get here?" he asked.

"Sea turtles, mate. A pair of them, strapped to my feet," Will said, referencing a well-known legend that Jack Sparrow himself had escaped an island on the backs of turtles.

Jack grinned at Will's slight. "Not so easy, is it?"

"But I do owe you thanks, Jack," Will said. "After you tricked me onto that ship to square your debt to Jones—"

"What?" Elizabeth said, looking at Jack.

"—I was reunited with my father."

Jack gulped. "You're welcome."

"Everything you said to me – *every word* was a lie?" Elizabeth said, glaring at Jack.

"Yes. Time and tide, love," Jack nodded with no apology. Then the cocky expression left his face as he noticed Will kneeling beside the chest. Will had the key in one hand, the knife his father had given him in the other.

"What are you doing?" Jack asked.

"I'm going to kill Jones," Will answered.

In a flash, a cool blade was pressed against Will's throat. It was Jack's blade.

"I can't let you do that, William," Jack said. "If Jones is dead, then who's to call his beastie off the hunt? Now, if you please – the key."

Quick as lightning, Will slapped Jack's sword away, jumped back and grabbed the cutlass Elizabeth had been carrying since her trip to Tortuga. "I keep the promises I make," he said, facing off with Jack. "I intend to free my father."

But suddenly, Norrington drew his sword and turned it on Will. "I can't let you do that, either. Sorry."

Jack looked at the former commodore and grinned. "I knew you'd warm up to me eventually," he said, delighted with the sudden turn of events.

Norrington pointed his sword quickly toward Jack, and revealed his true intention. "Lord Beckett desires the contents of that chest. If I deliver it, I get my life back."

"Ah, the dark side of ambition," Jack sighed grimly.

The three men instantly sprung forward, their swords locked together in a clash of steel.

"Will," Jack said urgently, "we can't let him get the chest. You can trust me on this!" Will held his sword steady, his eyes wide with disbelief. "You can mistrust me less than you can mistrust him," Jack finally offered.

Will stopped to consider, then looked at Norrington. "You look awful," he said to the bedraggled commodore.

"Granted," Norrington replied. "But you're still naïve. Jack just wants Elizabeth for himself."

"Pot. Kettle. Black," Jack said, summing up the situation in three words.

The three men sprung back, clashing swords again.

"Guard the chest," Will told Elizabeth as he, Norrington and Jack swung wildly at each other.

"No! This is barbaric! This is not how grown men settle their affairs!" Elizabeth shouted. They paid her no attention.

From between the palms, Ragetti, who had made it safely off the beach, had been watching the scene. "Now, how'd this a-go all screwy?" Pintel asked, arriving beside him and crouching low. They both eyed the chest.

Ragetti sighed. "Each wants the chest for hisself. Mr Norrington, I think, is hopin' to regain a bit of honour, ol' Jack's looking to trade it to save his own skin and Turner there . . . he's tryin' to settle some unresolved business 'twixt him and his twice-cursed pirate father."

"Sad," Pintel commented. "That chest must be worth more'n a shiny penny. If we was any kind of decent, we'd remove temptation from their path." The two pirates gave each other a sideways glance and crept towards the chest.

Elizabeth was still trying to stop the wild sword fight, but nothing seemed to help. She fell to the sand, pretending to faint in the hope that the men would halt their battle and help her. She lay still as long as she could, then opened her eyes in time to catch Pintel and Ragetti making off into the jungle with the chest.

Jumping to her feet, she was torn for a moment between telling Will or chasing the chest. She narrowed her eyes as she saw the three men slashing away at each other in the distance, and decided to duck into the jungle and go after the pirates.

Chapter 29

The fight was in full swing and moving all over the island.

Norrington shoved Will back hard and the key was dropped.

"Hah-hah!" Jack howled, watching the key fly into the air before landing squarely in his hand. Norrington and Will stood stunned as Jack took off down the beach with the key, then quickly regained their composure and bolted after him.

Jack headed for the old church. Racing into the bell tower, key in hand, he climbed the wooden stairs. High above him, dangling from the timbers, was the skeleton of the legendary hanged priest. Jack gave the skeleton a quick nod and continued his climb.

Norrington and Will quickly caught up with Jack on the stairs. Norrington started swinging his sword at Jack. But Jack stepped aside just in time. The weapon whistled as it moved past his arm. With a grunt, Norrington slammed Jack with the hilt of his sword, grabbed the key and flung Jack from the stairway.

As Jack fell, he reached out and grabbed the bell-tower rope that held the priest's skeleton. Jack and the skeleton both dropped straight down. Will grabbed the second rope and was hoisted up just as Jack was making his way down. Will snatched the key from Norrington as he passed him near the top of the tower. When Will reached the top of the tower, the church bell began to toll.

Chapter 30

Down on the beach, a gentle ripple appeared in the water. Slowly and eerily, the heads of Jones's crew rose from the pale blue water and the fearsome gang stalked ashore. They gathered at the now-empty, recently dug hole.

Suddenly, the sound of the church bells drew the crew's attention to the tower. They watched as Will Turner stepped out onto the church's rooftop.

Will was trying to get away – from Jack, from Norrington and now from Jones's crew. He jumped across a break in the roof as Norrington slashed at him over the gaping void. Using the point of his sword, Norrington nimbly lifted the key from Will's grasp. The former commodore felt the sudden weight of the key as it dropped into his hand, then felt it disappear just as quickly as Jack snatched it away from him.

Norrington turned in a rage and knocked Jack's sword from his hand. He looked over his shoulder at Will. "Excuse me while I kill the man who ruined my life," he said, pardoning himself.

"Be my guest," Will answered, finally relaxing for a moment.

Jack raised a finger. "Let's examine that claim for a moment, shall we, former commodore?"

Will couldn't help but smile as Jack once again tried to turn the odds in his favour. "Who was the man who, at the moment you had a notorious pirate safely behind bars and a beautiful dolly belle bound for the bridal, saw fit to free said pirate and take your dearly beloved for himself?" Jack nodded toward Will.

Norrington didn't let Jack continue. "Enough!" he roared, slashing wildly at Jack. Unarmed, Jack threw up his hands and slid down the roof screaming. The key dropped to the ground.

"Good show!" Will said, clapping.

"Unfortunately, Mr Turner," Norrington said, turning his blade on Will, "he's right." Norrington hated Jack, but he wasn't fond of Will, either.

Below them, Jack took advantage of the

fight above, grabbing the key and running. "Still rooting for you, mate!" he called up to Will as swords clashed.

Jack slowed to a walk and put the key over his neck. Just when he thought he was safe, he stumbled into an open grave.

As Jack tried to get out of the hole, Will leapt onto a mill wheel that was attached to the side of the church. The old wheel creaked under his weight. Norrington jumped on as well and, with a huge crash, the wheel suddenly broke free. Will and Norrington steadied their legs to keep balanced.

Just as Jack finally pulled himself out from the grave, he was caught up by the rolling wheel. The key fell away from Jack's neck and was hooked on a splintered nail on the surface of the wheel. A moment later Jack was thrown off the wheel. He had lost the key – again! He sighed and then took off after the runaway wheel.

Chapter 31

Meanwhile, in the small island's jungle, Elizabeth had finally caught up with Pintel and Ragetti.

"'Ello, poppet," Pintel said, grinning, as Elizabeth confronted them. He and Ragetti set down the chest and drew their swords. Elizabeth reached for hers but suddenly remembered Will had taken it. Slowly, she began to back away.

The two pirates were about to attack when something came crashing through the jungle. The three turned to see the mill wheel roll past with Jack running at full speed behind it.

Pintel and Ragetti shrugged, focusing again on Elizabeth. Suddenly, a barnacle-encrusted axe hit a tree next to Ragetti's head with a twang. Jones's crew had arrived.

Pintel and Ragetti dropped their swords at Elizabeth's feet in horror. They grabbed the chest and made a run for it. Elizabeth took a sword in each hand, racing through the trees behind them.

Running as fast as they could, and still holding the chest, the pirates tried to pass on either side of a tree and slammed the chest smack into its trunk. Jones's crew suddenly burst through the jungle. Looking at the trunk, then at the imposing and terrifying crew, Ragetti, Pintel and Elizabeth made a quick decision: the three of them took off at lightning speed and left the chest behind.

On another part of the island, a chase was still going on. Jack was after the wheel, which held the key to what was *in* the chest. He picked up some speed and, for the first time, was running *next* to the wheel instead of *behind* it. Focusing on the key as it looped around, Jack timed his move perfectly and jumped back into the wheel.

From his spot on top, Will saw what Jack was doing. Will reached down, grabbed the key from the nail and swung himself back inside the wheel. Norrington was quick to follow. Slashing at Will, Jack grabbed the key, climbed up to the top and then jumped into a nearby palm tree.

Dangling from the palm, Jack noticed one of Jones's crew members coming – and he was carrying the chest! Jack reached for a coconut. Happy with the weight of it, he hurled it at the crewman's head.

Jack saw the undead crewman's head roll off as it was thwacked by his well-aimed coconut. He jumped down. No other crewmen were in sight. With the key in his hand and almost unable to believe his good fortune, he carefully approached the chest.

Jack took a breath. Kneeling beside the chest, he turned the key in the lock. His eyes widened as he finally saw what he'd been searching for: Jones's heart. Taking off his shirt, he reached into the chest and wrapped the heart safely up. Then he glanced around one more time, to make sure he hadn't been spotted, and took off.

Jack dashed directly to the longboat. He reached into the bow and grabbed his jar. Emptying some of the dirt onto the beach, he placed the covered heart inside and filled the jar back up with sand.

Jack looked up when he heard a sudden commotion. Bursting from the jungle came

Pintel, Ragetti and Elizabeth. They were once again hauling the chest and Jones's crewman were close behind them.

Elizabeth bravely slashed away at Jones's crew, but her efforts were increasingly futile. She was about to be overrun when the huge wheel came crashing out of the jungle.

The wheel rolled over several of Jones's crewmen, which allowed Elizabeth to catch up to Pintel and Ragetti as they dragged the chest through the sand towards the longboat.

Jack gritted his teeth, unhappy with how crowded the beach had become. He tucked his jar back into the bow and raised an oar, ready to shove off or fight.

The huge wheel finally lumbered to the waterline and tilted over with a splash. Will and Norrington dizzily climbed out. Norrington staggered over to the longboat and collapsed over the edge. He lifted his head and his eyes fell on Jack's jar. He reached into the bow.

Jack held his breath. He watched as Norrington's hand moved past the jar and reached for the Letters of Marque in his coat pocket. Jack didn't try to stop him. He had no need for those papers now, not when he had the heart that controlled Davy Jones and safe passage or peril for every ship that sailed the seven seas.

As Jack contemplated his good fortune, the fight on the beach raged on. It was now Sparrow's crew versus Jones's crew – and Jones seemed to have the advantage.

Suddenly, through the chaos, Will noticed the chest. The key was still in the lock. He leaned down to open it as Jack quickly spun around with an oar in his hand and whacked him in the head. Will dropped to the beach, unconscious. Rushing to his side, Elizabeth looked down at her fiancé.

"We're not getting out of this," Elizabeth said to Norrington, when she realized just how desperate the situation had become.

"Not with the chest," he replied, knowing what had to happen. He grabbed the chest and ordered her into the boat. "Don't wait for me," he called back and disappeared from the beach into the jungle. Jones's crew took off after him.

"I say we respect his final wish," Jack said quickly from his spot nearby.

"Aye!" Pintel agreed and began pushing the longboat into the surf. Jack hopped in and grabbed his jar. He had the heart, but didn't want to take any chances. Holding on to the heart, and Tia Dalma's dirt inside the jar, he'd be safe.

"We have to take Will," Elizabeth ordered. Jack rolled his eyes but nodded his head, and Pintel and Ragetti hauled Will into the longboat. Without another word, they pushed off ... leaving Norrington behind.

Chapter 32

Moments later, Jack's crew, minus Norrington, was back on the main deck of the *Black Pearl*. Will slowly opened his eyes. "What happened to the chest?" he asked groggily.

"Norrington took it – to draw them off," Elizabeth answered.

Gibbs appeared on deck and welcomed them all back. He was ready to make sail. "Jack!" he said. "We spied the *Dutchman* an hour past, rounding the point!"

"Is that so?" Jack replied with a confident look in his eye.

Gibbs gave his captain a funny look. He didn't have time to try to work out what was going on. There was a dangerous ship – the *most* dangerous ship to ever sail the seas – far too close. "All hands! Set sail! Run her full!" Gibbs shouted.

As the *Pearl*'s crew scrambled to get underway, Jack felt no need to rush. He sat down on a barrel, his legs dangling, and cradled his precious jar.

"Gibbs, is your throat tight?" he asked.

"Aye," Gibbs answered.

Jack nodded. "Your heart beats fast, your breath is short, you have an acute awareness of the vulnerability of your own skin?"

"Aye! Aye!"

"I fear you suffer from the malady of intense and overwhelming fear," Jack observed casually.

"What's got into you? We've got only half a chance at best – and that's if the wind holds!" Gibbs said, not understanding Jack's attitude. Only a few hours before, Jack had been a bundle of nerves himself.

Elizabeth walked to the rail. For once, she had to agree with Jack. "We are in no danger," she said to Gibbs. "I see empty horizon in all directions."

She had spoken too soon. As they watched in horror, the ocean began to bubble and foam. Suddenly, with a mighty splash, the *Flying Dutchman* shot up from below the sea. It settled down right next to the *Pearl*, sending a wave over her decks.

"Hard to port! Steal his wind! Full canvas!" Gibbs shouted with all his might.

As the crew worked furiously at their stations, Jack turned toward the *Dutchman*. Lifting the jar over his head, he pointed to it, nodded, smiled and gave a friendly wave.

At the helm of the *Flying Dutchman*, Davy Jones pulled back as if he'd been struck, realizing that Jack must have his heart.

"Ready the cannons," Jones said to Maccus.

Jack yelled out to the *Dutchman*, "Over here! Yoo-hoo! Parlay!"

Gibbs moved alongside. "What's your play, Jack?"

"Shhh!" Jack replied. He thumped the jar. "I have the heart. In here," Jack whispered.

"Bless me! How?" Gibbs asked.

Jack smiled. "I'm Captain Jack Sparrow, remember?"

Gibbs sighed as he watched the cannon ports on the *Dutchman* opening. Jack thought he was invincible, but Gibbs knew better – he had to protect the ship. "Hard a' port!" he shouted, turning his attention back to the ship. "Hurry, men!"

Jack's crew scrambled and the *Black Pearl* tacked hard, leaving the *Dutchman* at her stern.

A blast of cannon fire suddenly came from the *Dutchman's* forward guns. "Into the swells! Go square to the wind! Come on!" Gibbs yelled, adjusting course.

The *Dutchman* fired again, but the *Pearl* was pulling away. "She's falling behind!" Elizabeth cheered.

"Aye! With the wind, we've got her!" Gibbs nodded proudly.

"The *Black Pearl* can outrun the *Dutchman*?" Will asked him.

"That ain't a natural ship," Gibbs said, nodding at the *Flying Dutchman*. "It can sail direct against the wind, into a hurricane and not lose speed. That's how she takes her prey. But with the wind . . ."

"We rob her advantage," Will said, suddenly understanding.

"Aye," Gibbs said. "The *Pearl* is the only ship Davy Jones fears. With reason."

Chapter 33

Jack smiled as the *Pearl* sped farther and farther away from the *Dutchman*. He held his jar close.

"If we can outrun her, we can take her!" Will said, rushing to Jack on deck. "We should turn and fight!"

"Or flee like the cowardly weasels we are," Jack answered brightly.

"You've the only ship as can match the *Dutchman*! In a fair fight we've got half a chance."

"That's not much incentive for me to fight fair, is it?" Jack answered, drumming upon his jar.

Suddenly, the *Black Pearl* lurched. Sailors tumbled forwards. Jack's jar was knocked free from his hands and shattered, sending sand and dirt all over the deck. He dropped to his knees and pawed through it. There was nothing more than the dirt and sand.

Jack looked up at Gibbs and swallowed hard. "Um. I *don't* have the heart."

"Then who does?" Gibbs asked, as the *Pearl* groaned and shuddered to a stop. Jack went pale. He had neither Jones's heart nor Tia Dalma's dirt.

Elizabeth looked out over the rail as the *Pearl* ground to a halt.

"We must have hit a reef!" she called out.

Will frowned, he'd heard those same words aboard the *Edinburgh Trader*. "No! It's not a reef! Get away from the rail!"

"What is it?" Elizabeth asked, seeing the terror in Will's eyes.

"The Kraken," was all Gibbs said.

Chapter 34

The deck of the *Pearl* grew silent as Gibbs's words sunk in. The Kraken had finally found Jack.

On the floor of the ship, Jack had stopped sifting through the dirt and sand. It was no use. The heart was not there and the Black Spot had reappeared on his hand. He was marked, the situation was hopeless – he was doomed.

As quietly as possible, Jack headed towards the *Pearl*'s stern. None of the crew members noticed as he slipped into a longboat and rowed away from his ship.

The water around the *Pearl* began to churn and bubble, indicating the arrival of the Kraken. Then the terrible creature appeared from the depths, tentacles held high above the crew.

"To arms!" Will shouted. "Defend the masts! Don't let it get a grip." The pirates ran to their stations and prepared for the coming attack. Cannons were loaded and masts made ready.

Slowly, the Kraken's tentacles made their way over the railings. But Will had known that the Kraken would attack on the starboard side from his earlier encounter with the creature, and the cannons were ready. With a powerful command from Will, the cannons were fired. The Kraken was blown away – its body twisting in pain as it sank back away from the ship, smashing the longboats as it went down.

"It will be back!" Will yelled. Turning to Elizabeth he added, "Get off the ship."

"No boats," Elizabeth replied. The Kraken had destroyed every last one of them. Or *almost* every last one . . .

As the Kraken was getting ready to attack again, Jack was working on getting away in his longboat as quickly as possible. But there was something stopping him from making a clean break. He looked down at his Compass and watched the needle swing to its mark – the *Black Pearl* and his crew.

With a sigh, Jack began to row.

*   *   *

Back on the *Pearl*, it looked as if the Kraken was going to win this battle. Nothing the pirates did to stop the monster worked. They shot at it, stabbed at it, threw nets at it – but the beast kept coming.

Elizabeth stood in the captain's cabin, a rifle in her shaking hands. She knew Jack had disappeared and was furious. How could he leave at a time like this? He was the one the Kraken was looking for. He had got them into this mess. Then tentacles slowly moved through the windows and started towards her.

Stumbling, she dropped the rifle, headed towards the deck and ran straight into Jack. He was back.

"We've got some time. Abandon ship!" he ordered, ignoring Elizabeth's look of surprise.

"What chance do we have in a boat?" Will asked, coming over to Jack.

"Very little. But we can make for the island. We can get away as it takes down the *Pearl*!" As Jack said this, his eyes grew sad. There was no choice. The Kraken would return and the *Pearl* would go under. They had to get away.

Following orders, Will, Gibbs and the rest

of the crew headed toward the longboat. But Elizabeth lingered behind.

"Thank you, Jack," Elizabeth said softly. Moving closer towards him, she added, "You came back. I always knew you were a good man."

Leaning forward, Elizabeth kissed the pirate, then stepped back slowly.

CLICK.

Jack glanced down. Elizabeth had chained him to the mast of the boat while they kissed. "It's after you, not the ship – not us. It's the only way," she explained.

"Pirate," Jack said, with admiration.

Elizabeth took one last look at the pirate who had been the cause of so much trouble in her life and the cause of so much adventure. She rushed off the ship and left Jack . . . waiting.

Slowly, the tentacles of the Kraken snaked on board. With a mighty roar, the creature rose up in front of him, its mouth gaping and its breath deadly. And there before Jack, in the teeth of the mighty Kraken, was his lost, beloved hat. He plucked it out of the monster's mouth and placed it back on his head where it belonged.

"Hello, beastie," Jack said.

From the longboat, the crew of the *Black Pearl* watched as the Kraken and Jack battled. Slowly, the entire ship was covered by the terrible creature. With one mighty splash the ship, and Jack with it, was taken below the waves.

On board the *Flying Dutchman*, Davy Jones smiled. "Jack Sparrow," he said with satisfaction, "our debt is settled."

But Jones was not the only soul watching from the *Dutchman*. Bootstrap Bill was looking on as well. As Jack went down with the ship, Bootstrap's eyes grew wide with shock. What was left of his cursed heart wrenched.

With eyes full of sorrow, Bootstrap Bill looked out towards the still water where Jack and the *Pearl* had so recently been sailing. He remembered Jack Sparrow – *Captain* Jack Sparrow – with a heavy heart. Quietly and painfully, Bill whispered to the empty sea, "If any man could beat the devil, I'd have thought it would be you."

The *Black Pearl* was gone, along with her captain. And, already, the world seemed a bit less bright without them.

DISNEY

PIRATES of the CARIBBEAN

AT WORLD'S END

Chapter 1

*"**T**here be something on the seas that even the most staunch and bloodthirsty pirates have come to fear . . . "*

From his spot high in the crow's nest, a pirate trained his spyglass on the horizon.

Nothing. No sign of any ship besides his own and the two they travelled with. The Caribbean Sea was calm, the bright sun sparkling off the ocean waves. Everything was peaceful.

So why did he have such a strong sense of foreboding?

He lifted his spyglass again. This time he could see a smudge on the horizon. It might be a ship sailing towards them. Worse, it might be an East India Trading Company ship.

The pirate knew what would happen if they

were taken by Company agents. He'd heard stories of the recent executions . . . pirates hanged by the dozen, the *thunk* of the gallows' trapdoor the last sound they ever heard. And in the last few months, the executions were becoming more and more frequent. The East India Trading Company was intent on wiping out the pirates of the Caribbean – and beyond.

The pirate leaned over to call down to the captain. If it was an East India Trading Company ship, they would have to make a run for it. But, as he looked down, he saw a shape in the water beside them. A dark shape, rising up – and rising fast.

"CAPTAIN!" he shouted.

It was too late.

With an explosion of ocean spray, the shape burst through the surface of the water. First, pale masts rose into the air. Then came the rails and wooden hull, crusted with coral and shells. A carved, skeletal, winged female rode on the bow.

It was something out of the darkest of nightmares. It was something pirates spoke of in hushed and frightened tones.

It was the *Flying Dutchman*.

The ship opened her cannon ports as she surfaced. With a loud explosion, cannonballs blazed into the side of the pirate ship. The pirates on all three ships ran to their stations, trying to load and return fire, but the *Flying Dutchman* was too fast, too close, too powerful.

The attack was over in minutes.

Smoke curled over the burning wreckage. Bodies of dead pirates drifted past loose barrels and blackened wood.

The *Flying Dutchman* sailed through, regal, untouched. Unstoppable.

The doomed pirate in the crow's nest had been right. On the distant horizon, a ship appeared. It was an East India Trading Company ship, the *Endeavour*, carrying Lord Cutler Beckett, Admiral James Norrington and Governor Weatherby Swann.

In the captain's cabin of the *Dutchman*, Davy Jones sat at his pipe organ. His scaly skin glistened in the dim light while the octopus tentacles that hung from his face moved back and forth gently over the keys, filling the room with a melancholy sound. With a sigh, he lifted one of the tentacle fingers on his right hand to his eye and discovered a tear forming. Sadness and emotion . . . that could only mean one thing. He glanced up with a scowl.

Above the cabin, Admiral Norrington and Lord Beckett were coming aboard at that moment with a contingent of marines. The marines seemed afraid to be standing on the deck of the *Flying Dutchman*. And their fears were well founded. The crew of the *Dutchman* was covered in barnacles and scales – more monster than human.

"Steady, men," said Norrington, noting his crew's unease. "We stand aboard a seagoing vessel, no more and no less. You will compose yourselves as marines."

As he spoke, several of the men heaved a chest over the rail and onto the deck of the *Dutchman*. This was what they were here to guard: the Dead Man's Chest. Inside was the still-beating heart of Davy Jones.

From his spot on the deck, Lord Beckett smiled. He had waited and plotted for a great length of time to be standing where he was now, with Jones at his command.

Beckett knew that Davy Jones captained the fastest ship on the ocean. The crew of the

Dutchman were all bound to Davy Jones for 100 years, body and soul. Davy Jones himself was immortal. After his true love had broken his heart, he had cut out the offending organ and put it in the Dead Man's Chest, which he buried at *Isla Cruces*. Nobody could harm him unless they had his heart.

Which was precisely why Lord Beckett had spent so much energy searching for it.

To begin with, he'd arrested a blacksmith named Will Turner and the governor of Port Royal's daughter, Elizabeth Swann, on their wedding day. In exchange for their freedom, he'd sent Will to get a Compass belonging to the pesky pirate, Captain Jack Sparrow. This particular Compass pointed not north, but to whatever your heart desired most. Once Beckett had the Compass, he thought it would lead him straight to the Dead Man's Chest.

Things hadn't worked out quite as Beckett planned, but they still had worked out very much in his favour. Will, Elizabeth and Jack had found the way to *Isla Cruces* before Beckett. But Norrington, who had joined Sparrow's crew after losing his position within the Royal Navy for letting the pirate escape hanging, was able to slip in and steal Davy Jones's heart. He brought it back to Port Royal and relinquished it to Beckett. Immediately, Norrington was reinstated in the Navy and promoted to admiral.

So while Beckett hadn't got the Compass, he now had something of far greater value and with infinitely more power: the heart of Davy Jones . . . and complete control over the *Flying Dutchman*. With the power of this ship, Beckett – and the East India Trading Company – could rule the seas. Better yet, the *Black Pearl* – the only ship that could ever be a match for the *Dutchman* – had been pulled under by Jones's own pet monster, the Kraken.

"Go, the lot of you – and take that with you!" Jones bellowed, appearing from belowdecks. Shaking with anger, he strode up to Norrington but stayed a safe distance away from the chest. The closer the heart was to him, the more emotion he felt. Jones wouldn't feel safe until the heart was far away from him.

"I will not have that infernal thing on my ship!" Davy Jones shouted.

"Oh, I'm sorry to hear that," Lord Beckett

said coldly. "Because I will. Because it seems to be the only way to ensure that this ship does as directed by the Company."

Jones gripped the rail of the ship with the claw that formed his left hand. The long tentacles of his beard writhed with fury.

Beckett nodded at Norrington, who led the marines below with the chest.

"The *Dutchman* sails as its captain commands," Jones growled.

"And the captain is to sail it as commanded," Beckett responded. "This is no longer your world, Jones. The immaterial has become . . . immaterial. I would have thought you'd learned that when I ordered you to kill your pet."

Jones winced, remembering the Kraken. The powerful sea monster that had killed Jack Sparrow and dragged the *Pearl* under was now dead, one of the first casualties of Beckett's ruthless campaign against the 'uncivilized' seas.

At that moment, Governor Swann stepped forward. From aboard the *Endeavour*, he had watched the destruction of the pirate ships with horror. Not a soul had been left alive. The ships had been blasted to smithereens. His blood boiling, the Governor had followed Beckett and Norrington on to the *Dutchman*.

"Did you give these ships opportunity to surrender?" the Governor demanded of Davy Jones, his face pale beneath his white wig.

Jones smirked. "We let them see us. Methinks that opportunity enough."

Swann was outraged. "My daughter could have been aboard one of them!" he cried. "That alone is cause to exercise restraint!"

The Governor had been searching for Elizabeth for months, ever since he helped her escape her cell in Port Royal and saw her flee into the dark night. He knew she would have gone to find Will and Jack among the pirates. But since that night, he had not seen nor heard from her. By travelling with Beckett and Norrington, he had hoped to find her ... before she was caught and executed as a pirate.

But Beckett had different reasons to be displeased with Jones's disobedience.

"We need prisoners to interrogate," Beckett snapped at Jones. "Which works best when they are *alive*."

"I am exterminating pirates," Jones said, "as commanded by the Company." He gave a mocking bow, then turned to Swann. "And your daughter is dead. Pulled under with the *Black Pearl* – by my pet. Did Lord Beckett not tell you that?" Jones grinned mirthlessly.

Swann stood for a moment in shock. Lord Beckett had been lying to him all this time. Elizabeth was dead. He whirled around and ran for the cabin.

Lord Beckett gave Jones a dark look and followed him.

Norrington was just placing the key in the lock of the chest when Swann suddenly grabbed him and pulled him around.

"Did you know?" Swann yelled, shaking Norrington by his lapels. "Did you know?"

"Governor Swann!" barked Lord Beckett from the doorway. Swann shoved Norrington away. He seized a bayonet from the closest marine and brandished it. Norrington grabbed his arms, restraining him.

Beckett spoke sharply to the marines. "Out. Everyone."

The soldiers glanced at Norrington, who nodded. They filed out, leaving the chest alone with Swann, Beckett, Norrington, Jones and Beckett's aide, Mercer.

"Governor Swann," Beckett said soothingly, "believe me . . . I only sought to spare you from the pain–"

"You only sought to use my political connections to further your own cause!" Swann spat. "The worst pirate who ever sailed has more honour than you. Even Jack Sparrow had honour."

Beckett smiled thinly. "Jack Sparrow is no more. And was never more than selfish desire cloaked in romantic fictions. A legend we're well rid of."

Norrington was still confused. Why was Governor Swann so upset? "You knew Sparrow was dead," he said to Swann.

"Not him," Swann said. "Elizabeth!"

Admiral Norrington gasped. He felt numb with shock. While it was true Elizabeth had made her choice long ago – turning her back on their betrothal – Norrington still cared deeply for the headstrong woman. The news of her death struck him to the core. His grip loosened on the governor, and Swann was able to pull himself free and throw open the chest, revealing the beating heart of Davy Jones.

"No!" Jones shouted.

Swann raised his bayonet high.

But before he could strike, Jones's voice cut through his agony. "Are you prepared to take up my burden, then?" the immortal captain hissed. "If you slay the heart, then yours must take its place – and you must take mine. The *Dutchman* must always have a captain."

Governor Swann hesitated. He had not known about the dreadful consequences of stabbing Jones's heart. No one would willingly choose that kind of eternal captivity. But if it would stop Lord Beckett . . . Swann glanced at the aristocrat. Beckett spread his hands in a gesture that indicated the choice was Swann's. Swann turned back to the chest, but Norrington caught his arm and yanked the bayonet away from him.

"Let me!" Swann implored.

Norrington shook his head. "Elizabeth would not have wanted this," he said firmly.

The governor's shoulders slumped. Norrington was right. His anger drained away, replaced by deep grief. He had failed his own flesh and blood.

"Elizabeth . . ." he said sadly.

Norrington placed an arm over his shoulders and steered the governor gently out of the door. Beckett, Jones and Mercer watched them leave.

"You're dismissed, Captain," Beckett said.

Jones paused, still wanting to fight but knowing he was beaten, then turned and followed the others out. Beckett and Mercer looked at each other for a long moment. Beckett crossed to the chest and closed it softly, turning the key with a contemplative look.

"They know," said Mercer.

"I can order Admiral Norrington's silence," Beckett said. "He'll obey; it's what he does."

"And the Governor?" Mercer asked.

"Yes, well," Lord Beckett mused. "Every man should have a secret."

And as he smiled knowingly, the *Dutchman* sailed on, across the bright blue Caribbean seas, ready to bring more dark death and bloody destruction to the next pirate ship it found.

As long as Lord Beckett and the East India Trading Company controlled the heart of Davy Jones, no pirate was safe. It was only a matter of time before every pirate in the Caribbean was exterminated.

Chapter 2

Lord Cutler Beckett was wrong about one thing.

Elizabeth Swann was still very much alive.

She had seen the *Black Pearl* dragged to the depths of Davy Jones's Locker with Jack Sparrow on board. And she knew that no matter what stories were told, it was *her* fault he was dead. After fleeing *Isla Cruces*, the *Pearl* had come under attack by the Kraken. Why? Because Jack had been marked by the Black Spot. Its presence on his hand meant there was nowhere on the sea he could hide. And so the Kraken had found him.

At first, Jack fled – taking a longboat and heading back to shore . . . alone. But then he had a change of heart. He had returned to his ship to help Will, Elizabeth and his crew. But Elizabeth knew that if Jack were with them, the Kraken would not stop hunting them – and they would all die. So she distracted Jack with a kiss and then chained him to the mast of the *Black Pearl*, leaving him there to die.

In the aftermath, Elizabeth had been racked by guilt. She was determined to make amends. Along with Will and Jack's crew, she had gone to see a powerful mystic named Tia Dalma, who had helped Jack in the past.

The woman lived far up the Pantano River in a bayou that smelled of mystery and magic. The air was never quite clear and, as they had made their way slowly towards Tia Dalma's shack, it had been hard not to feel watched.

It was in the dim twilight that Elizabeth, Will and the remaining members of Jack's crew had rowed their way slowly up to Tia Dalma's rickety front porch. With a great deal of effort and an even greater amount of fear, they had made their way inside, where Tia Dalma waited.

There, the mystic had told them that there was indeed a way to bring Jack Sparrow back to the world of the living. But they would need the help of an old enemy . . . Captain Barbossa, the man who had stolen the *Pearl* from Sparrow many years before. Before their run-in with Jones, Will and Elizabeth had helped Jack reclaim the *Pearl*, and Jack had killed Barbossa on *Isla de Muerta*. But now Tia Dalma had brought Barbossa back from the dead. And she knew he could help them bring back Jack as well.

Singapore's harbour was a dark and shadowy place, full of secrets, unkempt pirates and flashing knives. Tall ships and smaller junks crowded together around ramshackle docks. Wooden boards creaked in the wind and hanging lamps cast flickering shadows over the faces that darted through narrow, winding streets.

A small boat drifted through the gloomy byways. In the bow, a cloaked figure used a long pole to manoeuvre the boat through a maze of pylons below the docks. The figure's voice drifted eerily through the darkness, singing an old pirate song.

"*The bell has been raised from its watery grave . . . do you hear its sepulchral tone?*" she sang. "*A call to all, pay heed the squall and turn your sails toward home!*"

Suddenly, the boat was illuminated by a lantern, revealing the figure. It was Elizabeth Swann. While she appeared calm, her large brown eyes darted back and forth, taking in the city. It had nothing like the manicured streets and stately mansions of her youth or her time in Port Royal. The corseted dresses she had once worn had no place here – the brown, shapeless cloak she had on was far more appropriate.

As her longboat floated under the docks, Elizabeth passed an old woman crouching over a mess of fish remains. Nearby, a man was blowing glass at a coal fire, the glowing orange-red light reflecting off the round glass shape. An explosion to her right made her jump; she saw a dazzling pinwheel spin out of a fireworks shed, sparks flying. A boy chased it, stamping down the sparks.

With a shiver, Elizabeth saw the shadow of a monkey race by. She moved forward, still singing, until she reached a dock where she tied up the boat and climbed out.

"*Yo ho, haul together,*" she sang as she tied up the line. Suddenly she stopped and ducked her head. A troop of East India Trading Company agents was passing by, led by Beckett's aide, Mercer. They were exactly who she *didn't* want to hear her song. She wanted the song to identify her as a pirate – but only to *fellow* pirates.

A few moments later, the march of their

boots faded away. Elizabeth resumed her song.

"*Raise the colours high! Heave ho . . .*"

". . . *thieves and beggars,*" a new voice joined in. "*Never say we die.*"

Elizabeth rose to her feet as a man stepped out of the darkness of a large sewer pipe. Two armed guards flanked him. He was tall and imposing, his sinewy muscles rippling under his dark robes. He had a menacing look in his eyes and a wicked sword at his side.

Despite the man's formidable presence, Elizabeth sighed in relief. This was Tai Huang, the man she was looking for. Or at least, the man who could take her to the man she was looking for. Tai Huang was second in command to Sao Feng, the fearsome Pirate Lord of Singapore.

Tai Huang narrowed his eyes, looking her up and down.

"A dangerous song to be singing," he said ominously, "for any who are ignorant of its meaning." He stepped closer. "Particularly a woman. Particularly a woman alone."

"What makes you think she's alone?"

Tai Huang and his guards turned at the sound of the new voice. Barbossa was standing behind them, a smile on his weather-beaten face.

"You protect her?" Tai Huang asked.

"What makes you think I need protection?" Elizabeth replied with a hiss. Tai Huang froze. Elizabeth's voice was in his ear, her knife pressed to his throat.

Barbossa tsk-tsked.

"Your master is expecting us," he said to Tai Huang. He added, pointedly, to Elizabeth, "And an unexpected death would cast a slight pall on our meeting." He eyed her knife, and slowly she lowered it but did not sheath it.

Tai Huang rubbed his neck and studied the old pirate. "You're Captain Barbossa," he said.

"Aye," Barbossa agreed. "And she be Elizabeth Swann. And Sao Feng has promised us safe passage."

Huang nodded thoughtfully. "For as long as it suits him," he said in a dark voice. He turned in a whirl of robes to lead them away, then abruptly held up his hand. Everyone stopped short.

The sound of boots heralded the passage of more East India Trading Company men. Tai Huang waited until the agents turned a corner, and then he signalled the others to follow him into the mouth of the large sewer pipe.

As Elizabeth and Barbossa vanished into the darkness, something peculiar was happening not too far away.

On one of the many dilapidated bridges that crossed over the canals and waterways of Singapore, a pair of East India Trading Company agents was standing guard. Had they looked over the edge into the water, they might have seen a line of coconuts floating by.

And below the coconuts was something that would have interested the agents very much indeed. Underneath each coconut was a member of the nefarious Captain Jack Sparrow's crew.

As the coconuts floated into the darkness under the bridge, one rose out of the water, revealing the top of the pirate Ragetti's head. He was wearing the coconut shell as a helmet, hiding him from sight up above. His one good eye darted back and forth, while his wooden one stared blankly ahead. Following behind him were Pintel, Gibbs, Cotton and Marty.

When they were safely hidden in the

shadows below the bridge, they took off their coconut helmets and swam over to a metal grate. From the oilskin bundles they carried, they produced large rasps which could be used to file through the bars of the grate.

Then they waited.

Squeak, squeeeeak. The East India Trading Company agents snapped to attention and peered into the gloom. What was that sound?

A moment later, a woman trundled out of the darkness, pushing a cart with squeaky wheels. The cart carried several birdcages holding twittering canaries, clanking bottles filled with mystery potions, and bags of flour. On top of the cages was a colourful parrot, and riding alongside the bird was a monkey turning the crank of an organ.

This was what Jack's crew had been waiting for. The organ's music, the squeaking wheels and the clattering sounds of the cart were all loud enough to hide any noise from below. It was time to act. The pirates set to work on filing through the bars of the grate.

The cart rolled closer and closer. The agents exchanged a suspicious glance. They stepped forward to stop the cart.

The music stopped. Down below, the pirates froze.

One of the agents pulled out his sword.

"You can't be here," the agent said gruffly to the woman.

She lifted her face. Although they did not know it, the woman was Tia Dalma. She leaned towards the agent who had spoken to her and whispered in an eerie voice, "Your mother always knew it be you who threw the linens down the well."

The agent jumped back, spooked. He stared at the old woman in fear.

"How did you know that?" he demanded.

She grinned, revealing a mouthful of blackened teeth. "The canaries," she hissed.

Both agents backed away. They didn't know what witchcraft was at work here, but they wanted nothing to do with it. 'Jack' the monkey picked up the organ again and went back to grinding, the music whirling brightly as the pirates resumed their sawing down below.

Not too far away, Tai Huang was leading Barbossa and Elizabeth towards a decrepit bathhouse. The bathhouse served as Sao Feng's hideout and was well protected. Elizabeth glanced about her, all her senses on high alert. Anyone they passed could be a pirate . . . or worse, an employee of the East India Trading Company.

She tugged on Barbossa's sleeve. "Have we heard anything from Will?" she whispered.

Barbossa shook his head. "The whelp is more than capable of taking care of himself," he pointed out. "But you – in the presence of Sao Feng, you'll be wanting to show a bit more diffidence than is your custom." He winked.

"He's that terrifying, is he?" Elizabeth asked.

"He's much like myself," Barbossa answered, "absent my merciful nature and sense of fair play." He grinned, and Elizabeth shivered.

Tai Huang stepped in front of a door, rapping a series of sharp knocks in a coded signal. A slit in the door slid open and a pair of eyes appeared. The eyes studied them. After a minute, the slit closed and, with the sound of bolts moving and hinges creaking, the door opened.

As Elizabeth and Barbossa stepped inside a small entry room, Tai Huang swung around, blocking their path.

"No weapons," he said. "Remove them, please."

Elizabeth could tell from his tone that the 'please' did not make his sentence any more of a request. It was an order.

"Of course," Barbossa said cheerfully. He handed over his pistol and his sword, and Elizabeth followed suit. But as they stepped forward, Tai Huang held up his hand and eyed Elizabeth.

"Did you think because she is a woman, we would not suspect her of treachery?" he asked. "Remove, please."

Elizabeth sighed and pulled off her coat, revealing two more hidden swords in scabbards tucked into the lining.

She started forward again – but Tai Huang stopped her. "Remove. Please," he repeated.

Elizabeth tried to protest, but it was no use. She was forced to turn over each of her hidden weapons, one by one. To add insult to injury, she was also ordered to change into a robe that would allow no weapons to remain hidden. Glaring at the men around her, Elizabeth pulled the belt on her blue silk robe tighter and tugged it down, hoping to cover her legs a bit more. Finally, scowling and completely unarmed, she followed Barbossa and Tai Huang deeper into the bathhouse.

As they walked through the maze of leaky, rusted pipes, past algae-crusted tubs and half-naked pirates, Elizabeth studied her surroundings. The pirates here all worked for Sao Feng. And they each bore his symbol: a dragon tattoo.

At last they reached a room that was cleaner and warmer than the rest. The Pirate Lord of Singapore was just stepping out of his bath. Silently, two attractive female attendants dressed him in all the glory of his pirate regalia.

Elizabeth stared at the man's scarred and weathered face, looking for a sign of weakness. But the powerful Lord's eyes were dark and cold, revealing nothing. From the corners of his eyes ran a pair of old scars that heightened his dangerous demeanour.

A long moment passed. Sao Feng did not seem to have noticed their presence . . . or else he was deliberately ignoring them. Finally, Barbossa realized it was up to him to speak first.

"Captain Sao Feng," he said smoothly.

"Thank you for granting me this audience."

Sao Feng looked up as if he'd just spotted them. "Captain Barbossa!" he said. "Welcome to Singapore." With a gesture, he turned to the nearest guard and said, "More steam."

The guard banged on the wall twice, and a burst of steam billowed out of the pipes.

"I understand that you have a request to make of me . . . ?" he said to Barbossa.

"And a proposal to make to you," Barbossa replied. "I've a venture under way, and I find myself in need of a ship and a crew."

Sao Feng straightened and looked at Barbossa with a sly smile. "And you consider me worthy of such an honour? A ship and a crew . . ." He chuckled. "That's an odd coincidence."

"Because you happen to have a ship and a crew you don't need?" Elizabeth said saucily. Barbossa gave her a warning glance, but Sao Feng only smiled wider, the scars at the corners of his eyes almost disappearing.

"No," he said. "Because earlier this day, not far from here, a thief broke into my most revered uncle's temple, and tried to make off with these."

Sao Feng strode across the room to a wizened old man in long robes who was clutching a set of ancient charts to his chest. The Pirate Lord reached for the charts but had to tug on them several times with a stern expression before the old man would relinquish them.

"Navigational charts," Sao Feng continued, turning back to Barbossa and Elizabeth and holding the charts aloft with a flourish. "The route to the Farthest Gate," he said softly, watching their faces for a reaction. "Wouldn't it be amazing if this venture of yours took you to the world beyond this one?"

Barbossa swallowed. "It would strain credulity, at that," he blustered.

Sao Feng gazed at him levelly. Then with a nod, he signalled to two guards near one of the baths. The guards leaned over and hauled a figure out from under the water.

The prisoner was none other than Will Turner.

Chapter 3

Will Turner was very unhappy.

There was something Elizabeth did not know.

Will had seen her kissing Jack on the *Pearl*.

Of course, he didn't know that she had done it to trick Jack. He didn't know that she had chained Jack to the mast. He thought Jack had *chosen* to go down with his own ship. He also thought that Elizabeth must no longer love him. Will was convinced she was now in love with Jack.

So Will did not particularly care that Jack Sparrow was dead. In fact, he probably would have left him that way, if it were up to him. But Will had his own mission, and unfortunately, it involved helping Jack.

After Beckett had ordered Will to hunt down Jack and his Compass, Will had ended up on the *Flying Dutchman* – no thanks to Jack's scheming. Will had been Davy Jones's prisoner for a short while. In that time, he had discovered something terrible. His own father, the pirate known as 'Bootstrap Bill' Turner, was enslaved aboard the *Dutchman*. Bootstrap Bill had once been a member of the *Black Pearl*'s crew, but he had ended up in the depths of the ocean after trying to get out of taking part in Barbossa's mutiny against Jack. Cursed by the Aztec Gold and doomed to be trapped there forever, he had been more than willing to bargain with Jones when he had been found by the tentacled man. But the price had been terrible: 100 years of servitude.

Bootstrap Bill was like the rest of the *Dutchman* crew now – covered in barnacles and crustaceans, a slave to Davy Jones. As time went by, he was gradually losing himself and becoming a part of the ship – literally. Long before the 100 years were up, he'd be lost forever, just another tortured soul swallowed up by the ship.

After reuniting, Will had sworn to rescue his father. He had made Bill a solemn promise: he would return to the *Dutchman* and free him, no matter what it took.

But in order to do that, he needed a ship – the fastest ship on the seas, the only one that could catch the *Flying Dutchman*. Which meant, he needed the *Black Pearl*. And that was why he was on this quest to save Jack. Wherever Jack was ... the *Pearl* would be there, too.

Now, soaking wet and defenceless, Will found himself in the middle of Sao Feng's hideout. The Pirate Lord grabbed Will by the hair and dragged him to Barbossa and Elizabeth.

"This is the thief," he snarled. "Is his face familiar to you?"

Elizabeth managed not to react. She and Barbossa both steeled their faces to look impassive, as if they had never seen Will before in their lives.

Sao Feng studied them and then shrugged. "No?" He picked up a large metal spike on a nearby table. This was a fid, a sharp tool used for winding ropes together. Sao Feng brushed the sharp end of the fid along the edge of Will's face. "Then I guess he has no further need for it."

He moved the fid sharply towards Will, and

Elizabeth tensed. She couldn't stop herself. The man Sao Feng was threatening was her true love and fiancé.

Sao Feng saw her reaction and frowned darkly. His suspicions were confirmed. Now he was sure they were working together. The two of them had come to beg from him, while their friend sneaked around to stab him in the back.

"You come into my city," Sao Feng growled, "you seek my indulgence and largesse, and you betray my hospitality?" His voice rose. "You betray *me*?"

Barbossa bowed and spread his hands. "Sao Feng," he tried, "I assure you, I had no idea—"

"—that he would get caught," Sao Feng interrupted.

Barbossa winced. The Pirate Lord had a point.

Sao Feng narrowed his eyes, tapping the charts against his chest. He was putting the pieces of the puzzle together. "You intend to attempt a voyage to Davy Jones's Locker," he said. "And I cannot help but wonder: why?"

Barbossa sighed. It was time to be completely honest – not something that came naturally to pirates. The ex-Captain of the *Pearl* drew a silver piece of eight out of his pocket and tossed it to Sao Feng, who caught it in mid-air and examined it.

A new, troubled look crossed the Pirate Lord's face. "A piece of eight," he murmured. He looked up at Barbossa. "It's true, then?"

"Aye," Barbossa answered. "The time is upon us. The Brethren Court has been called."

Sao Feng banged on the wall. "More steam!" he bellowed.

Below the floorboards, the boiler and bellow system was normally worked by two attendants. But the attendants were now tied up. They had been overpowered by Jack's crew of pirates, who had crept in through the steam tunnels. At Sao Feng's cry, Cotton hurried over to the boiler mechanism and quickly figured out how it worked. Soon, steam was billowing up through the vents.

The other pirates once again unrolled their oilskin bundles, revealing swords, pistols and grenades. They began placing the grenades in the floor joists, preparing to set off a massive explosion.

Gibbs, Jack Sparrow's first mate, and Ragetti

exchanged glances. They were underneath the room where their friends were confronting Sao Feng. If things didn't go the way they were supposed to . . . then this hidden group of pirates was the only chance Will, Elizabeth and Barbossa had to make it out . . . alive.

Sao Feng breathed in the steam. "The Court has not met in my lifetime," he said.

"Nor mine," Barbossa said.

Sao Feng's hand reached up and caressed the rope pendant he wore around his neck. "And when last it did, my father told me, it ended . . . badly."

"But the time before that, it produced the Code," Barbossa pointed out, "which has served us well . . . and it was the very first meeting that gave us no less than rule of the sea herself, didn't it?"

Barbossa was referring to the legend of Calypso, an ancient sea goddess. Made up of nine Pirate Lords, the first Court had captured Calypso and bound her in human form. With her no longer able to send storms to destroy them, their own rule over the sea had become absolute. It had been the turning point for pirates everywhere. The imprisonment of Calypso meant that they could be the lords of the sea.

Barbossa's voice turned darker and more serious. "And now that rule is being challenged."

"The East India Trading Company," Sao Feng hissed. He, too, had seen the devastation wrought by the agents of the Company. He had heard of the mass executions, and he had lost some of his own men to their terrible slaughter. He knew that pirates were in grave danger of losing not only their lives, but their reign over the seas . . . forever.

"Lord Cutler Beckett is a pox on us all," Barbossa said, nodding.

Sao Feng began pacing back and forth. "There is a price on all our heads, it is true," he said. "It seems the only way a pirate can turn a profit any more . . . is by betraying other pirates." He gave Will a significant look, then turned back to Barbossa. "But pirates are either captain or crew, and nine squabbling captains trying to chart a course is eight captains too many."

He shook his head and then continued, "Against the Company, what value is the Brethren Court? What can any of us do?"

Elizabeth couldn't keep quiet any longer. "You can fight," she cried.

Everyone turned to stare at her. Her frustration was boiling over. What was wrong with these pirates? Couldn't they see what was happening out there? Didn't they believe in the Pirate Code? Didn't they want to take back the sea – *their* sea?

"You are Sao Feng, the Pirate Lord of Singapore," she said boldly, stepping forward. "You command in the Age of Piracy, where bold captains sail free waters, where waves are not measured in feet but increments of fear, and those who pass the test become legend."

A large pirate with a dragon tattoo tried to pull her back, but she shook him off and stepped even closer to Sao Feng.

With passion in her voice, she added, "Would you have that era come to an end on your watch?"

Sao Feng regarded her with an impassive expression.

"But here you are," Elizabeth continued scornfully. "Your ships crowd the harbour, rotting on their lines, while you cower in your bath water!"

The Pirate Lord's eyebrows twitched, and Elizabeth grew silent. Had she gone too far? She held her breath as he circled her slowly, eyeing her like a predator might study an interesting bit of prey.

"Elizabeth Swann," he said, "there is more to you than meets the eye, isn't there? And the eye does not go wanting."

He gave her a charming smile, and she was shocked when she found herself smiling back.

Sao Feng turned back to Barbossa. "But I can't help but notice you have failed to answer my question." If the talk of the Brethren Court and Elizabeth's call to arms had been intended to distract Sao Feng, it had failed. He pressed once again: "What is it you seek in Davy Jones's Locker?"

"Jack Sparrow," said a voice from across the room. Will Turner shook the wet hair out of his face and stood up straighter. His gaze was level and unafraid as he stared at the Lord.

Sao Feng froze. Silence fell. Barbossa looked pained.

"He's one of the Pirate Lords," Will said.

One of Sao Feng's attendants, a girl named

Park, giggled, but hid her smile when Sao Feng glared at her. The other, Lian, seemed to be hiding a pleased expression as well. Both of them had clearly encountered the legendary Jack Sparrow before.

Will and Elizabeth could both see how angry Sao Feng was to hear the name Jack Sparrow. A vein throbbed in his temple as he fought to keep his voice calm.

"The only reason I would want Jack Sparrow returned from the realm of the dead," the Pirate Lord hissed, "is so I can send him back myself."

Barbossa rolled his eyes and glared at Will. "Exactly why we preferred his name go unmentioned," he said pointedly.

"So you admit you have deceived me," Sao Feng said. His eyes scanned the room, and suddenly he spotted something suspicious. In the billowing waves of steam and heat, the dragon tattoo on one of his men was melting. It was a fake! There was another spy here – one who had gone so far as to infiltrate his organization. The man went by the name Steng, and he had joined Sao Feng's pirates some time earlier. Through narrowed eyes, Sao Feng now glared at the man. Was he part of Barbossa's group as well? The layers of deception appeared to be growing deeper.

Barbossa hadn't noticed Sao Feng's preoccupation, and he was still trying to convince him that they were doing the right thing.

"Jack Sparrow holds one of the nine Pieces of Eight!" Barbossa said. "He failed to pass it along to a successor before he died."

As Barbossa spoke, Sao Feng caught the eye of Tai Huang. With a subtle gesture, he indicated Steng.

Barbossa kept speaking: "And so we must go and fetch him back–"

"WEAPONS!" Sao Feng bellowed suddenly.

All at once, the Singapore pirates sprang into action. Before Will, Elizabeth or Barbossa could move, the dragon-tattooed guards around them had seized swords and pistols from under the water in the bath. Within moments, the three were surrounded by a ring of weaponry, all pointed at them.

Barbossa held up his empty hands. "I assure you, our intentions are strictly honourable–" he began. But he was interrupted by the sound of swords sliding up through the floorboards. The pirates below had realized that things were going wrong and had acted quickly, to arm their crew up above. Within seconds, Elizabeth had seized two of the swords and thrown one across the room to Will. Barbossa found himself with two swords in his hands, and suddenly his claims of honourable intentions seemed much less believable.

Sao Feng grabbed Steng and held a blade up to the pirate's face.

"Drop your weapons, or I kill your man!" he shouted.

There was a confused pause. Barbossa and Elizabeth exchanged bewildered glances. They had never seen this man before.

"Kill him," Barbossa said with a shrug. "He's not our man."

Sao Feng could see that they were telling the truth this time. But then . . .

"If he's not with you," Will said, as though reading Sao Feng's thoughts, "and not us . . . who is he with?"

CRASH!

The answer came smashing through the windows.

East India Trading Company agents had arrived!

Chapter 4

Chaos exploded in the bathhouse. The pirates all turned to fight the East India Trading Company agents together. Whatever danger the pirates posed to each other, they knew that the agents were a much, *much* worse threat.

Below the room, Pintel and Ragetti lit the fuses on the grenades. A moment later, an enormous explosion rocked the building, and half the floorboards collapsed, forming a ramp to the lower floor. The pirates rushed up the ramp and joined the fight.

Sao Feng shoved Steng aside and leaped into battle, leading his pirates forward. The dust from the collapsing building shrouded the fight in shadowy smoke. The clang and crash of swords and pistols rang through the darkness.

Glancing up, Elizabeth saw Beckett's aide, Mercer, striding into the bathhouse with a phalanx of soldiers behind him.

As the walls continued to tremble and collapse around them, the pirates clambered over the rubble and escaped into the street outside. Pistol shots rang out as pirates leaped from dock to dock, swung on ropes and swarmed up ladders. They fled in all directions, fighting for their lives.

Amidst the fighting, Pintel spotted Steng, and, seeing his dragon tattoo, thought that he was a fellow pirate. Suddenly, a stack of crates started to fall and Pintel quickly leaped forward to push Steng out of the way.

Steng turned and slashed at Pintel with his knife. Pintel jumped back.

"Hey!" he protested, "you're a pirate!"

But Pintel was well versed in the Code, and he knew that a true pirate would fight the East India Trading Company before his own kind – even if they were *usually* on opposite sides. This man was no pirate!

Steng grinned and slashed at Pintel again. Pintel fell backwards over a rail and landed with a splash in the river below. He burst to the surface, spluttering and coughing but otherwise unharmed.

A few of the agents, running through the streets, came across the cart that Tia Dalma had been pushing. The mystic was nowhere in sight. Seeing a group of pirates turn to fire at them, the agents ducked behind the cart, using it as cover. But suddenly there was a great fluttering of wings, and all the canaries burst out through the doors of their cages, which had been left open. Something was wrong. Realizing it was a trap, the agents jumped up to run – just as the cart exploded in a giant fireball.

Nearby, a wall collapsed, and Mercer, who had been eagerly partaking in the action, was knocked into a shadowy corner. Slightly dazed, he stood to rejoin the fight and then froze.

He had happened upon an interesting scene.

Sao Feng had a knife to Will Turner's throat. In the background, the sound of fighting continued. But in this dark corner, Will and Sao Feng were alone – or so they thought.

"Odd coincidence, isn't it?" Sao Feng hissed. "The East India Trading Company finds me the day you show up in Singapore."

"It is coincidence only," Will replied.

With a twist he broke free from Sao Feng's grasp. He pulled his own knife and stood facing the Pirate Lord. Unseen in the shadows, Mercer grinned and drew his pistol. Here was the perfect opportunity to kill Will Turner *and* the Pirate Lord of Singapore. He aimed carefully.

"You want to cut a deal with Beckett?" Will asked Sao Feng. "You need what I offer."

Mercer paused.

"You crossed Barbossa," Sao Feng said. "You're willing to cross Jack Sparrow – why should I expect any better?"

"They are in the way of what I want," Will said. "You're helping me get it."

Sao Feng nodded. This was logic he understood. And he stood to gain much from this underhanded deal.

"You betray me," he said in a low voice to Will, "and I will slit your throat."

"Then we have an understanding," said Will.

They lowered their knives, and Sao Feng handed Will the navigational charts to the world of the dead. With a nod, Will disappeared into the darkness, Mercer close behind.

Having escaped the battle, Elizabeth and Barbossa ran up to the docks and found Will standing on one of the platforms. Barbossa spotted the charts in his hand.

"You have the charts!" he cried, delighted.

"And better," Will said. He indicated Tai Huang behind him. "A ship and a crew."

"Where's Sao Feng?" Elizabeth asked.

"He will cover our escape, then meet us at Shipwreck Cove," Will answered.

Elizabeth was puzzled. Why had Sao Feng given in, after arguing against them so strongly? Perhaps the attack by the East India Trading Company had made him realize what a grave threat they were. Regardless, they had what they had come for, so Elizabeth decided to accept it without any further questions.

"This way," Tai Huang said. "Be quick."

Tia Dalma, Pintel, Ragetti and Cotton appeared out of the smoke and together they ran after Tai Huang.

From his spot in the shadows, Mercer smiled to himself. He hardly had to do anything. The pirates were turning on each other, and as long as they were divided, they were no match for the East India Trading Company. Soon, they would be wiped out.

* * *

On board the *Hai Peng*, Will Turner stood at the rail, watching Singapore burn. The fire that had started in the bathhouse was now spreading quickly through the wooden shacks and platforms that made up the city. While his eyes were on the flames, his thoughts were far away. Over and over, he thought about the deal he had made with Sao Feng. If only he could tell Elizabeth . . . but that was impossible. They both had secrets now. And she would never understand his motivations, just as he could not, *would* not, ever understand her feelings for Jack.

As the ship continued to sail out of the harbour, Barbossa stomped up to Will. "You weren't supposed to get caught," he snarled.

Will regarded him evenly. "It worked out the way I wanted," he said, and moved away. Barbossa could never know that Will had *deliberately* let himself be captured so he could speak privately with Sao Feng and offer a deal. It had been a risky venture, but the risk would be worth it if it meant he could rescue his father. He slipped down into the depths of the ship.

Elizabeth Swann stood at the rail, too, watching as the fires consumed the harbour.

"There's no place left for him to cower," she said softly. "Do you think Sao Feng will honour the call?"

Tia Dalma stepped out of the darkness. "I cannot say," the powerful mystic murmured, her eyes seeming to see beyond the burning ships and docks. "There be something on the seas that even the most staunch and bloodthirsty pirates have come to fear . . . "

Elizabeth shivered, knowing that Tia Dalma was speaking of the *Flying Dutchman*. Although it was halfway around the world, she felt as if she could sense the dreaded ship lurking in the depths of the ocean.

They had to rescue Jack Sparrow. For there was only one hope for the pirates: to stand together against Davy Jones and the East India Trading Company. If they could not do that . . . they were all doomed.

Chapter 5

§now was falling.

Will reached out and caught a snowflake on his hand. Curious, he looked up at the sky and took in the dark, grey clouds that were massed above them. A cold wind whistled through the sails and made all the pirates shiver.

The *Hai Peng* was sailing through a frozen landscape. They were close to the edge of the earth – in the Ice Passage between worlds. Sharp blue-and-white glaciers jutted out of the water around them, reflecting glints of pale light. The water was dark and stormy, and the snow was coming down thick and fast. At the helm, Gibbs peered into the murky greyness and steered carefully through the floating blocks of ice.

Will moved to join Tai Huang, who was leaning over the navigational charts Sao Feng had provided. They were unlike any charts Will had ever seen. Strange circles within circles moved and rotated constantly. Peculiar riddles were inscribed around the edges.

"Nothing here is set," Will said to Tai Huang, puzzled. "They can't be as accurate as modern charts."

"No," Tai Huang said enigmatically. "But they lead to more places." He walked away without explaining himself.

Will watched him go, frowning. He glanced down and reread one of the inscribed poems under his breath. *"Over the edge, back, over again, sunrise sets, flash of green."*

"Barbossa," he called out loud. Perhaps the old pirate could help. "Do you care to interpret?"

Barbossa smiled, unworried. Not bothering to answer Will, he turned towards the helm. "Ever gazed upon the green flash, Mister Gibbs?" he asked the pirate.

Gibbs nodded his head while one hand stroked his grey-flecked beard. "I reckon I've seen my share," he said. To Will, he added, "Happens on rare occasions, at the last glimpse of sunset, a green flash shoots up into the sky." He gestured into the air, keeping one hand firmly on the wheel. "Some go their whole lives and never see it. Some claim to have seen it who ain't. Some say–"

Pintel jumped in: "–it signals when a soul comes back to this world from the dead!"

Gibbs glared at him.

"Sorry," Pintel said. He slunk off to join Ragetti by the rail.

"Don't they get it?" the wooden-eyed pirate said when his friend appeared at his side. "It's a *riddle*. Riddles are fun! *'Over the edge, back, over again–'*"

"Riddles are not fun!" Pintel spluttered. "The way it always goes is some poor bloke ends up dead, but just beforehand he realizes no, I wasn't supposed to listen to the sirens, I wasn't supposed to take the pot o' gold, but by then it's too late, and he dies in a horrible and oft-times ironical manner, and in this case, you and I be the poor blokes!"

His voice had grown louder and louder as he spoke, and Will couldn't help but overhear. He turned to Barbossa with a concerned expression. Dying in a horrible and ironical manner was not part of Will's plan.

Seeing Will's expression, Barbossa laughed. "Do not fret, Mister Turner," he said jovially. "We will find the way. It's not getting to the Land of the Dead is the problem – it's getting back!"

Will did not feel much better.

Later that night, Elizabeth once again found herself on the deck. The icy landscape was gone, the glaciers far behind them. The sea was now a dark mirror full of stars. She leaned on the rail, staring out at the water as her mind raced with unanswered questions. Would they find Jack in the Land of the Dead? Was there a way to bring him home? And . . . would he forgive her for leaving him to his death?

Jack Sparrow was a pirate through and through, Elizabeth thought. He knew that one often had to use underhand means to get to desirable ends. He knew that she had been saving everyone else by chaining him to the mast, and he had even seemed proud of her pirate-like actions. But that didn't mean he was going to be thrilled about dying. He would blame her, and she wasn't sure how he would react to seeing her again.

There was a movement behind her in the dark, and she sensed Will before she saw him. He came up and stood beside her. Leaning on the rail as well, he appeared completely wrapped up in his own thoughts, far away from Elizabeth. He seemed almost like a stranger to her. She still loved him, but she couldn't tell him about how she felt or about the guilt she was struggling with over Jack's death.

Will shifted, as if about to say something to her, but then he paused and turned away again. Elizabeth turned towards him, but he didn't look at her. After a moment, she stepped back from the rail and then walked away.

Will gazed out at the mirror of stars surrounding them, but his thoughts were not on the sight before him.

Suddenly a strange sound caught his attention. He leaned forward to listen. It sounded like . . . roaring.

"Barbossa!" he called, spinning around. "Do you hear that?"

Barbossa, standing up by the helm, cupped his hand around his ear. With a grin he said, "Aye, these be the waters I know. We're good and lost now."

"Lost?" Elizabeth repeated, alarmed.

"For certain you have to be lost, to find a place as can't be found." He winked. "Elseways everyone would know where it was, aye?" He started laughing.

Will noticed that the ship was turning on its own. It was being pulled towards the roaring sound! But Barbossa still seemed more amused than concerned.

"To stations!" Will yelled, waking the crew. "All hands! To stations!"

As pirates raced onto the deck, he ran to the rigging and clambered up, trying to get a better view of what was ahead. The sound of the roaring water was getting louder and louder, and the ship seemed to be going faster.

From the rigging, Will could see a line of white foam in the distance ahead of them. The line of spray seemed to reach from one end of the horizon to the other; it stretched for miles in every direction. There was no way to get around it; they had to go back. But was it too late for that? The ship was heading straight towards the white line, picking up speed while being dragged closer and closer.

"Rudder full!" Will shouted at the top of his lungs. "Hard a-port! Gather way and keep her trim!" If they used every sailing trick in the book, they might just escape the terrible danger ahead of them.

But as the pirates ran to obey his orders, Barbossa stepped forward and spoke in an even louder, more booming voice.

"Belay that!" he barked. "Let her run straight and true!"

He seized the wheel, but Will pushed him aside and began turning it as hard and as fast as he could. The *Hai Peng* began to swing . . . but not far enough. It was impossible to fight the current pulling them towards the edge.

At the rail, Elizabeth realized with terror what was ahead of them: a waterfall. A waterfall that dropped off the edge of the world, plummeting straight down into nothingness.

Tia Dalma came up from below, an island of serenity in the chaos of panicking pirates. She tossed a set of crab claws onto the top of a barrel and leaned over them, murmuring a magical incantation.

"*Malfaiteur en Tombeau, Crochir l'Esplanade, Dans l'Fond d'l'eau!*" She said it again, faster, and then again, slower. As she spoke, she turned the claws in an intricate pattern, weaving them about on the top of the barrel, casting her spell. The roar of the waves was now deafening, drowning out the sound of her voice, but Tia Dalma did not stop. She didn't even look up. Intent on the crab claws, she seemed not to care that the ship was about to plummet over the edge of the world.

Meanwhile, Will was still wrestling with the wheel, while Barbossa stood behind him, laughing. Rushing over, Elizabeth grabbed the old pirate and shook him, the spray of the water cascading around her.

"You've doomed us all," she cried.

"Don't be so unkind!" Barbossa protested. "Ye might not survive the trip . . . and these be the last friendly words ye hear . . . " He shook his head reprovingly.

Will leaned into the wheel with all his strength. The *Hai Peng* turned, turned . . . the bow tilted away from the waterfall, but the back was dragged forward, so the ship paused for a moment, parallel to the edge. The pirates looked over the rail, down into the endless black nothingness below.

Then, with a sickening screech of timbers, the ship tilted sideways – and over the edge.

All the pirates, except Barbossa, howled with fear as the ship crashed down, down, down . . . into the inky darkness.

Chapter 6

Captain Jack Sparrow stood on the *Black Pearl*, his eyes scanning the decks. His familiar red bandana appeared even brighter in the glare of the blue sky, and the small charm that hung from his headpiece gave off a bright spark with each turn of his head.

Tilting back his tricorn hat, Jack studied the distant horizon. There was no hope of reaching it today.

In fact, there was no hope of reaching it – ever.

The sails of the *Black Pearl* hung limp. The ship's hull was half buried in the sand of a vast, empty desert. Nothing moved in any direction. The sun beat down in a hot and merciless sky.

Jack was all alone, trapped with his ship in Davy Jones's Locker.

He was dead, and he did not care for it at all.

Flapping his hands at the nearest sail, Jack blew air from his mouth. Unsurprisingly, this had no effect.

"My soul I do swear, for a breeze," Jack muttered, his gold tooth sparkling in the glare from the hot sun. "A gust. A whisper. A kiss . . ."

But there was no wind, and there hadn't been for many days. Jack had no idea how long he had been dead. He only knew that it was a most unpleasant experience.

He hoisted himself over the rail and swung down to the ground. His well-worn, knee-high boots sunk into the sand, and with effort Jack floundered over to a rope tied to the bow of the *Pearl*. He picked up the rope and leaned against it with all his strength. He strained and pulled, trying to drag the ship along the sand himself.

Of course, it was no use. The ship refused to budge.

Jack slumped down into the sand. "No wind," he said woefully.

He spotted a pile of smooth, round stones scattered on the sand near him. Picking one up, he flung it away so it skipped across the surface of the sand.

Much to his surprise, the stone stopped in mid-skip and came rolling back to Jack.

It paused beside his boot. Then it began rocking – back and forth, back and forth, its movements becoming faster and faster. Suddenly, cracks appeared on the surface of the rock. Then, like an egg hatching, the stone split open and transformed into a small crab.

Jack stared at the crab. With an amused shake, the crab clicked its claws. Jack could have sworn it was laughing at him.

"Perfect," Jack said. "What would my torment be without unusual crabs here to mock me?"

He seized a handful of sand and threw it at the crab, which scuttled backwards. With a heavy sigh, Jack collapsed on his back, closed his eyes and lay there.

His eyes closed, Jack did not see the crab inch forward. Nor did he seem to sense the crustacean's eyes focused on him. And when, after a moment, the crab scuttled sideways to study the ship before hurrying over to the pile of stones, Jack did not notice that, either.

Time passed. Jack continued baking in the sun and drowning in despair.

Suddenly, a shadow crossed his face. With a small frown, Jack opened his eyes, blinking quickly to clear his vision.

Something was moving above him.

And that something was – the *Black Pearl*! It appeared to be floating across the sand!

Bewildered, Jack scrambled to his feet and looked his ship up and down. He bent over and peered underneath it. Then his kohl-lined eyes widened.

The *Pearl* was not actually floating. Instead, thousands of crabs were supporting the ship on their backs. As they scuttled across the sand, they carried the *Black Pearl* along above them.

"Interesting," said Jack.

Not too far away, a different ship had met a dismal end.

Broken wreckage was scattered along the shoreline and floating in the ocean – all that was left of the *Hai Peng*.

Pintel and Ragetti floundered out of the sea first, pulling themselves onto the shore. Despite the rather desperate situation, Ragetti was grinning madly.

"What has got into you?" Pintel demanded as they collapsed on the beach.

"I thought it was fun," Ragetti said.

"It wasn't fun!" Pintel said, outraged. He scowled at Ragetti's beaming face, and then, relenting, he added, "Maybe a little, the tilting-over part—"

"And the big splash at the end!" Ragetti said with glee.

Meanwhile, other figures were beginning to appear from out of the waves. Elizabeth and Will swam to shore and scrambled out of the water. Gibbs and Tia Dalma were not far behind, with Cotton, Marty, Tai Huang and the rest of his crew immediately after them. Last to emerge from the water was Barbossa, with 'Jack' the monkey clinging to his hat.

Gibbs stood on the shore and gazed up and down the shoreline. He took in the vast desert before them and the unforgiving stretch of sea behind them.

"This be truly a godforsaken place," he said.

Elizabeth wrung out her sleeves and pushed her wet hair out of her face. She looked worried, too. "I don't see Jack," she said. "I don't see anyone."

"He is here," Barbossa said confidently. "Davy Jones never once gave up that which he got from the sea."

"And does it matter?" Will cried. He was furious to see all his plans going to waste. "We are trapped here, by your doing. No different than Jack."

If he was now stuck in Davy Jones's Locker, there would be no way for him to rescue his father from the *Dutchman*. All of his scheming and plotting would have been for naught.

Unaware of Will's inner turmoil, Tia Dalma clucked her tongue, a mysterious smile playing at her lips. "Witty Jack be closer than you think," she said.

The others turned to look at her. Tia Dalma stared off at the desert horizon. A dozen crabs appeared from beneath the sand, scurrying up to her. She reached down to them, and they clambered up, balancing along her arms. The mystic cooed to them as if they were her pets.

Elizabeth's eyes shifted to the horizon beyond Tia Dalma. Something was moving over the dunes. She squinted, shading her eyes to see better. It looked like a sail.

It *was* a sail! More specifically, it was the *Black Pearl's* sail!

"Slap me thrice and hand me to my momma!" Gibbs exclaimed, his eyes sparkling beneath his bushy grey eyebrows as he, too, took in the sight. "It's Jack!"

The ship rose majestically over the dunes, with Captain Jack Sparrow proudly standing at the bow, looking every inch the pirate captain again. Thousands of crabs carried the ship closer and closer to them, finally scuttling past to bring it into the water. With a splash, the *Pearl* came down, at long last back in the sea.

Will, Elizabeth and Gibbs grinned as Jack jumped down and splashed through the water towards them. Even Barbossa cracked a smile. Jack waved to his crew, wading onto the beach.

"Will! Gibbs! Pintel and, uh, you with the one eye . . . where have you been?" he cried. "Were you killed by the Kraken? Or something else? Something painful, I hope–"

Jack assumed they must be dead, like him, which would explain why they were all in Davy Jones's Locker.

Ignoring his sarcastic welcome, Elizabeth

ran up to Jack and threw her arms around him, hugging him hard.

"I'm so sorry," Elizabeth said in a low voice to Jack. "So glad you're all right—"

"Contrition!" said Jack, not returning her embrace or accepting her apology. "Very becoming on you. Are you an aspect of my sun-addled brain?" He picked her up and shook her. "No." Then, seeing Tia Dalma, he dropped a stunned Elizabeth and stepped forward. "Tia Dalma, out and about!" He knew that the mystic rarely left her home hidden in the swamp. "How nice of you to come! You add an agreeable sense of the macabre to any delirium—"

"How ye be, Jack Sparrow?" Barbossa's voice came from the back of the group.

Jack froze. He turned, and the crew members stepped aside to reveal Jack's old enemy, the pirate who had stolen his ship and crew, who had betrayed him and left him for dead on a deserted island. The pirate Jack had killed to regain his beloved *Pearl*.

Jack quickly forced a smile onto his face. "Barbossa!" he cried enthusiastically.

"Jack, Jack, get over here!" Barbossa

responded with equal vigour.

"You old scoundrel!" Jack said, not coming any closer. "I haven't seen you in too long. Not since–"

"*Isla de Muerta*, remember?" Barbossa prompted. "You shot me!" He opened his shirt and pointed to a scar on his chest. "Right here! Lodged in my heart, it did."

Jack nodded, hiding his nervousness. "I remember," he said. "I wouldn't forget that!"

"We came to rescue you," Barbossa said. His eyes flicked to the *Black Pearl*. Noticing Barbossa's glance, Jack's expression shifted. He kept smiling, but his mind was working fast. He did not want to be indebted to this particular pirate. In fact, he did not want to be indebted to *any* of these would-be rescuers. He glanced at the ocean beside them, empty but for the *Pearl* and the wreckage of the *Hai Peng*.

"Did you now?" Jack said brightly. "How kind. But it would seem as I possess a ship and you don't, *you're* the ones in need of rescuing." He flipped his hands casually. "Not sure if I'm in the mood."

Barbossa pointed at the *Pearl*. "I see my ship right there," he said aggressively.

Jack squinted out to sea. He stood up on his toes and leaned from side to side as if searching for another ship.

"Can't spot it," he said. "Must be hiding somewhere behind the *Pearl*."

Barbossa's face turned red with anger. He could play along with Jack's games for only so long.

He stepped towards Jack as if he meant to attack him, but Will quickly intervened. It would do nobody any good for the two pirates to start fighting here.

"Jack, listen," Will said urgently. "Cutler Beckett has the heart of Davy Jones. He controls the *Flying Dutchman*."

"He's taking over the seas," Elizabeth added.

"The song has been sung," Tia Dalma intoned. "The Brethren Court is called."

Jack snorted. "I leave you folk alone for a moment, and look what happens."

"Aye, Jack," Gibbs said softly. "The world needs you back something fierce."

"And you need a crew," Will said, indicating the pirates around them.

Jack studied them with narrowed eyes. He strolled past Will, Barbossa, Pintel, Elizabeth and Tia Dalma, eyeing them one by one. "Why should I sail with any of you?" Jack asked. "Four of you have tried to kill me in the past." He stopped in front of Elizabeth and looked her straight in the eye. "One of you succeeded."

Will started. What was Jack saying? *Elizabeth* had killed him? Jack saw Will's reaction and smiled.

"She hasn't told you?" Jack asked, amused. "Then you'll have lots to talk about while you're here." He turned to Tia Dalma and paused.

"All right, you're in." He continued down the crew. "Gibbs, you can come. Marty. Cotton, all right. And Cotton's parrot, I'm a little iffy, but all right, you're a team–" He did not bother to include Barbossa, Will or Elizabeth.

He arrived at Tai Huang. "And you are?"

"Tai Huang," said the tall pirate with calm authority. He nodded towards the Singapore pirates who had sailed with him. "These are my men."

"Where do your allegiances lie?" Jack asked.

"With the highest bidder," Tai Huang answered.

"I have a ship," Jack offered.

"Sold," Tai Huang stated.

With a satisfied nod, Jack waved to Tai Huang's men, indicating that they could board the *Black Pearl*. Pirates began splashing into the water, swimming out to the ship and swarming up the ropes to the deck.

Jack pulled out his Compass with a flourish and glanced down at it. Jack had had some trouble with the Compass in the past, when it couldn't work out what his true desires were. But now Jack knew exactly what his desire was – he wanted nothing more than to escape Davy Jones's Locker. He'd been wishing for an escape with all his heart for days, perhaps even weeks or months – a very long time, in any case. With his greatest desire so clear in his head, surely the Compass would point the way.

But the needle was spinning wildly. The strange realm of the dead was too mysterious for this magical object. The Compass would be no help in leading them out. Displeased, Jack snapped it closed.

"Oh, Jaaaa-ack," said a voice behind him.

Jack turned around. Barbossa held up the

ancient charts they had got from Sao Feng. He waggled them with a toothy grin.

"Which way are you going, Jack?" he teased.

Jack scowled. He had no choice. Those maps were the only chance any of them had of finding a way back to the world of the living. He would have to allow Barbossa and the others to join him on the *Pearl*.

And then they would all have to pray that the maps worked and that they wouldn't end up sailing the dark seas together . . . for the rest of eternity.

Chapter 7

The *Black Pearl*'s sails billowed in the wind. Sun sparkled off the blue ocean, making the waves glisten. But underneath the waves, strange, dark shapes flickered, and no land could be seen in any direction. This was not the ordinary sea the pirates were used to sailing. This was the sea in Davy Jones's Locker – an endless stretch of water, where anything could happen, and the usual navigational instruments were rendered useless.

Barbossa strode about on the deck, an enormous grin on his face. At long last, he was back on the *Pearl*!

"Trim that sail!" he bellowed. "Slack windward brace and sheet! Haul that pennant line!"

"Trim that sail!" bellowed another voice behind him, a half-second later. Barbossa turned and frowned at Jack, who was following close on Barbossa's heels. "Slack windward brace and sheet!" Jack hollered. "Haul that pennant line!" He puffed out his chest in an imitation of Barbossa's swagger.

"What are you doing?" Barbossa asked.

"The captain gives orders on a ship," Jack explained.

"The captain *is* giving orders," Barbossa said. He looked down his nose at Jack.

"*My* ship," Jack said. "That makes *me* captain."

"They be my charts!" Barbossa shouted. The two captains were now nose to nose.

"Stow it, the both of you, and that's an order!" said another voice. "Understand?"

Barbossa and Jack turned slowly to see Pintel standing behind them, looking stern. They each gave him an incredulous stare, until Pintel's expression faltered, and then he put up his hands and backed away apologetically.

As Barbossa and Jack continued to bluster and argue, Will Turner stepped across the deck, searching the faces around him. He was looking for Elizabeth.

Will paced the deck, then climbed down into the cabins below. Finally he found her, sitting alone in a dark corner. Her hair was loose and her face was wet, as if she had been crying.

Will stepped into the room and stood over Elizabeth. He had not spoken to her since Jack's rescue.

"You left Jack to the Kraken," he said, his heart heavy. Elizabeth's secrets went deeper than he had suspected.

Pushing back her hair, Elizabeth looked up at him. She knew he was angry and disappointed in her. But she could not feel anything but relief. They had found Jack. They were taking him back to the world of the living. The terrible thing she had done would now be erased, and she could eventually move past the guilt, whether Jack forgave her or not. By coming here and risking everything, she had done what she had promised herself she would do.

"He's rescued now," she said wearily. "It's done with."

Will's expression remained troubled and grim. His eyes searched hers for a moment before he looked away.

Elizabeth scrambled to her feet. "Will, I had no choice!" she said.

"You chose not to tell me," Will snapped.

"I couldn't," Elizabeth said. "It wasn't your burden to bear." She started to push past him, but he pulled her around to face him.

"But I did bear it," he said, anguish in his voice. "Didn't I? I just didn't know what it was. I thought . . ."

Elizabeth looked up at him. "You thought I loved him."

She started to pull away again, but he blocked her, pushing her back against the wall of the cabin.

"If you make your choices alone," he said with quiet intensity, "how can I trust you?"

Elizabeth stopped pushing against him. She looked up into his eyes – the eyes of the man she loved, the man she had once promised to marry.

"You can't," she said softly. Will would never have been able to do what she had done to Jack. Perhaps he was too good. Perhaps she was too dark. Perhaps they were too wrong for each other after all.

Will once again looked away from her, pain written across his face, the same thoughts echoing in his eyes.

There was nothing more to say. Without another word, Elizabeth ducked under his arm and disappeared from the room.

Night had fallen. It was the *Pearl's* first night sailing the darkness between worlds. Stars glittered above and below them, and pirates moved uneasily about the deck, wondering where, exactly, the ship was going.

In the captain's cabin, two captains stood in the centre of the once-pristine room. When the Kraken had attacked the ship, it had ripped apart the cabin, leaving torn papers, glass and splinters of wood scattered around the floor. One wall was in ruins, and holes gaped out into the open air.

Barbossa kicked a pile of glass shards. "I see you neglected to care for my ship," he said.

"What, this?" Jack said. "Just ventilating. Clear out the stench of the previous owner, you know. Thinking of putting in French doors, actually. Feel the cross breeze?" He waved his hand in the air blithely, as if feeling the wind sail through.

Gibbs stuck his head through the space where the door had once been.

"Heading, Captain?" he asked.

At the word 'Captain', both Barbossa and Jack spun around.

"Two degrees starboard–" Jack began.

"*I'm* Captain of the starboard side!" Barbossa objected. "Two degrees starboard. The Captain will now take the helm." He bolted for the door, Jack close behind.

"Aye, sirs," Gibbs said. He stood aside as Jack and Barbossa raced down the hall, up the stairs and along either side of the ship to the wheel, where a nervous Cotton was presiding over the steering. Cotton glanced from one former captain to the other. Jack adjusted the wheel minutely. Barbossa adjusted it back. They eyed one another, both determined to prevail.

Meanwhile, Pintel was watching Ragetti. At the stern of the ship, Ragetti had been getting a fishing pole ready. Now he dropped the line over the side, peered into the dark water and waited.

But to his horror, instead of the silvery, flickering shapes of fish, the first thing Ragetti saw in the water was the all-too-still body of a man. The body floated past, its pale face turned towards the sky, eyes closed. It was an odd sight to come across in the ocean – especially where one had been hoping to fish.

With a startled yelp, Ragetti leaped back from the railing. Curious about his friend's odder-than-usual behaviour, Pintel came over to see what was going on.

There was more than one dead body.

In fact, there was a stream of bodies. Old men, young women, vigorous sailors, small children . . . the water was filled with the bodies of the dead. The two pirates strained to peer into the ghostly depths. Some of the bodies seemed closer to the surface; others floated farther down. They moved at different speeds, but all in one direction – the opposite direction from the *Pearl*.

"Downright macabre," Pintel observed.

Ragetti rubbed his chin thoughtfully. "I wonder what would happen if you dropped a cannonball on one of 'em," he mused.

They exchanged a glance. Would the flow of bodies be disrupted? Would any of them open their eyes and react? Would it sink any of the bodies it fell on?

Smiling slyly, Pintel hurried over and grabbed a cannonball. But as he turned back, the heavy ball in his arms, he found Tia Dalma glaring sternly at him. With a start, Pintel dropped the cannonball.

"Be disrespectful, it would," he stammered.

Tia Dalma raised an eyebrow. Then she strolled to the rail and looked out at the sea, sadly watching the bodies. Even Pintel and Ragetti could tell that there was some deeper meaning here for her.

"They should be in the care of Davy Jones," Tia Dalma murmured softly, almost as if she had forgotten the two pirates were there. She sighed. "That was the duty he was charged with by the goddess Calypso: to ferry those who died at sea to the other side. And every ten years, he could come ashore to be with she who loved him truly." Tia Dalma shook her head. "But he has become a monster."

"He wasn't always all tentacley?" Ragetti asked.

"No, he was a man once," Tia Dalma said. She leaned on the rail, her faraway gaze fixed on the deep heart of the ocean. "Poor, unfortunate souls . . . now they must find their own way."

Chapter 8

Daybreak came, and the sun passed slowly through the sky. It felt as if the *Pearl* had been sailing for years on this vast and empty sea. Yet they had got nowhere, and there was nothing in sight in any direction.

Even the wind had fallen still. The ship drifted, the sails drooping. Worse yet, there was no water on the ship and nowhere to refill the barrels. The crew was desperately thirsty, and everyone was losing hope. Was there no way to escape these cursed waters?

Will stood at the rail, watching the sun creep down towards the horizon. Soon it would be night once again.

He saw Pintel lift a water barrel and tilt it over his head. Pintel waited, his cracked lips parted, but not a drop fell from the empty barrel.

"No water," Pintel moaned, casting the

barrel aside. "Why is all but the rum gone?"

Gibbs held up the last, empty rum bottle. "Rum's gone, too," he said.

Tia Dalma came up behind him, her eyes studying the setting sun as well. "If we cannot escape these doldrums before nightfall," the powerful mystic said, "I fear that we will sail on trackless seas, under starless skies, doomed to roam the reach between worlds . . . forever."

"With no water, forever looks to be arriving a mite soon," Gibbs added gloomily.

Will said nothing. Moving away from the rail, he went to where Sao Feng's charts were laid out on a big table near the helm. He bent over the charts once again, trying to puzzle a way out of this strange landscape. Jack was already there, studying the mysterious circles and inscriptions. In the middle, Ragetti's wooden eye rolled back and forth, an odd instrument on an even odder map.

Barbossa, meanwhile, was up by the helm, rocking on his heels. He still did not seem concerned.

"Why doesn't he do something?" Will wondered. He read the riddle once more: *"Over the edge, back, over again, sunrise sets, flash of green."*

"There's no sense to it," Gibbs said. "Sunrises don't set."

"And the green flash happens at sunset, not sunrise," Will agreed.

"Over the edge," Gibbs muttered. "Driving me bloody well over the edge."

Jack idly twisted some of the rings on the charts. As he moved them, he suddenly spotted something. When they were positioned a certain way, Chinese characters on each ring lined up to read: 'UP IS DOWN'.

"Up is down," Jack repeated. "That's maddeningly unhelpful. Why are these things never clear?"

He tapped the map, watching a small drawing of a ship spin upside down. As it turned, rays spiralled out behind the ship like a sun setting.

Inspiration struck.

"Not sun set," Jack said. "Sun-down. And rise . . . up!" He had it! He understood the riddle!

Jack leaped to his feet. He pointed into the distance off the port side of the ship.

"Over there!" he shouted. Pirates all across the deck jumped, startled by the burst of energy. "What's that?" Jack yelled. "I don't know! What do you think?"

Gibbs rubbed his eyes. "Where?" he asked.

There was nothing to see out there – just as there had been nothing to see ever since leaving the beach where they had found Jack.

Jack ran over to the railing and everybody followed him, crowding around to stare in the same direction.

Suddenly, Jack turned and raced across to the starboard side.

"There, it moved!" he called as he ran. "It's very fast!"

The others chased after him, and the ship tilted as their weight shifted to the other side.

Meanwhile, Elizabeth had been lost in thought. Huddled by the rail, she was unaware of Jack's odd behaviour. But as the ship started to tilt further over, her attention was finally captured. She looked up in time to see Jack whirl around again.

"Thar! Over thar!" Jack shouted, running back to port with everyone running after him. Now even Elizabeth stood up and followed. The ship tilted even further back to the port side.

"What is it?" Elizabeth asked.

"It's not here!" cried Jack.

Once more he ran to the starboard side, and once more all the pirates ran after him, and once more the ship tilted even more.

Curious, Barbossa approached the table with the charts. He saw the message reading UP IS DOWN. He saw the drawing of the upside-down ship and the rays of the sunset.

"He's rocking the ship," Pintel observed, bewildered.

"We're rocking the ship!" Gibbs agreed, running with all the others.

All at once, Barbossa understood what Jack was up to.

"Aye, he's on to it!" Barbossa cried. "All hands together! Time it with the swell!"

The former captain of the *Pearl* ran over to the hold and cupped his hands to bellow down to the men belowdecks.

"Loose the cannon!" he called. "Unstow the cargo! Let it shift!"

Pirates ran to follow his orders. Crates were cut loose from their moorings. Barrels and bottles rolled freely across the floor, clattering from side to side as the ship continued to tilt more and more.

Cotton spun the wheel to turn the ship sideways to the swell. The waves helped the swing of the ship's tilt.

"He's rocking the ship!" Pintel exclaimed again, only this time he understood why. As the pieces fell into place, Ragetti ran up to him with a long rope.

"We tie each other to the mast," Ragetti explained, "upside down, so we'll be right side up when the boat flips!"

Pintel couldn't completely follow this logic, but it sounded all right to him. He quickly lashed Ragetti to the mast.

Meanwhile, Will raced to the rail with the others, gazing out across the empty ocean at the horizon, where the sun was sinking rapidly into the sea. The last rays began to disappear below the waves . . . the *Black Pearl* tilted back in the other direction . . . and Jack shouted: "And now, up is down!"

With an enormous heave, the ship overturned completely, sending everyone under the water.

The sails billowed as water filled them. Chains, cannons, cannonballs and anything not tied down plummeted into the depths. Pirates clung to the rails; Jack, Barbossa, Will and Elizabeth held on tightly to the ship. Gibbs lost his grip and began to float away, but Marty caught him and pulled him back. Pintel and Ragetti, tied to the mast, held their breath.

Will saw the charts begin to float away, and he reached out with one hand to grab them.

Then suddenly . . .

A flash of green on the horizon!

And *THWUMP*!

Water cascaded away from the *Black Pearl* with a giant splash. Everything came crashing back down onto the deck: pirates, cannons, parrot and all.

The *Pearl* was floating on the surface of the sea once again. But this was not the cold and empty sea of the underworld. Here, it was sunrise. Daylight was spreading across the sky, and an island beckoned from the near distance.

They had escaped Davy Jones's Locker. They were back in the real world at last.

Chapter 9

Jack immediately checked his hand. No Black Spot – did that mean his debt to Davy Jones was paid? Was Jack finally free of the Kraken's chase? He took a deep breath, savouring the fresh air of the world of the living.

"Blessed sweet westerlies!" Gibbs exclaimed, staring about them. "We're back!"

Pintel and Ragetti opened their eyes. They were still tied to the mast – upside down.

"This was your idea," Pintel said. "And the fact that I went along does not make you any less stupid."

"Well, it don't make you no more smart, neither," Ragetti retorted.

Will ignored the quarreling duo and turned, his eyes searching the deck. He found Elizabeth standing by the rail, gazing at the horizon. Cautiously, he made his way over.

"It's a sunrise," she said, grinning. They weren't safe yet – Davy Jones and Lord Beckett were still out there. But they had rescued Jack Sparrow and escaped the world of the dead. Reason enough to stop and celebrate.

Barbossa and Jack were grinning, too. A ripple of pleased relaxation spread across the deck, and then . . .

Quick as a wink, everyone drew their pistols and pointed them at each other.

Barbossa's pistol was pointed at Jack, and so was Elizabeth's. Will and Gibbs had their pistols trained on Barbossa. Jack aimed his pistol at Will; he quickly drew another and aimed it at Barbossa. Barbossa, too, pulled out a second pistol, which he pointed at Gibbs, while Elizabeth pointed her second pistol at Barbossa.

In the midst of everything, Pintel and Ragetti worked frantically to get themselves free.

Despite the unnerving fact that he had four pistols aimed in his direction, Barbossa did not seem particularly worried. Glancing from weapon to weapon, he smiled.

"All right, then," he said, taking a deep breath. He had been prepared for this moment.

He knew getting Jack out of Davy Jones's Locker was going to be the easier of his tasks. Now he had to set about the harder task – convincing Jack to attend the meeting of the Brethren Court. The wily captain would not be eager to go – many of the Pirate Lords would not be pleased to see him again. But it was the only way to make the sea safe for all pirates once more. Captain Jack Sparrow simply had to attend.

And *that* meant everyone had to work together. Barbossa continued, "The Brethren Court is a-gathering at Shipwreck Cove. Jack, you and I be going there, and there's no arguing the point."

"I *is* arguing the point," Jack objected. "If there's pirates a-gathering, I'm a-pointing my ship the other a-way."

"The pirates are gathering to fight Beckett," Elizabeth said, jumping into the conversation. "And you're a pirate." She took her second pistol off Barbossa and pointed it at Jack. In return, Jack stopped aiming at Will and aimed at her instead. But Elizabeth stared him down. She was not about to give up. Lord Beckett was a menace and a murderer. The East India Trading Company was

Can Captain Jack Sparrow survive Davy Jones's Locker?

Elizabeth Swann and Barbossa arrive in Singapore.

Will Turner has been caught stealing.

Sao Feng does not want to help save Jack Sparrow.

Davy Jones and his encrusted crew are killing
pirates everywhere!

Lord Cutler Beckett is pleased. He possesses
Davy Jones's heart . . . and soon the whole Seven Seas.

Barbossa must convince Jack to travel to Shipwreck Island.

Tia Dalma tells Will they must return to the
land of the living by sunset.

Jack's crew wants to help their captain.

Elizabeth Swann is worried about Will and
the fate of pirates everywhere.

Will Turner and Lord Beckett arrive for Parlay.

Can the two sides agree or will there be war?

a scourge to the seas. They had to be stopped.

From his spot on the deck, Will pulled out a second pistol, so he now could aim at Jack *and* Barbossa.

"Fight or not, you're not running," said Will.

"If we don't stand together, they'll hunt us down, one by one, 'til there's none left but you," Barbossa said.

They all knew it was true. Lord Cutler Beckett would be happy with nothing less than the complete annihilation of *all* pirates.

Jack grinned. "Then I'll be the last. I like the sound of that. Captain Jack Sparrow, the last pirate."

"Then you'll be fighting Jones alone," Barbossa said. "How does that figure into your plans?"

"Still working on it," Jack admitted. "But I'm not going back to the Locker, Barbossa. Count on that."

He cocked the pistol that was pointed at Barbossa. Then he fired.

Click.

Barbossa, Will and Elizabeth all fired as well.

Click. Click. Click.

Nothing happened. No gunshot, no puff of smoke. They studied their pistols, puzzled. Gibbs shook his and checked the barrel.

"Wet powder," he explained.

Will sighed and tossed his useless pistol aside. "So for now we're in this together," he said. "Right now, we need water. The charts show an island nearby." He pointed to a spot on the map, and then off at the small piece of land in the distance. "There. With a freshwater spring. We can resupply, and then get on with shooting each other."

It was a sensible plan. They could all agree about needing water more than anything else.

Jack eyed Barbossa suspiciously. "You lead the shore party," he said. "I'll stay with the ship."

"I'll not be leaving *my* ship in your command," Barbossa scoffed.

"And he'll not be leaving his ship in your command," Will interrupted. "Here's an idea. You both go, and leave the ship in *my* command."

Barbossa and Jack looked horrified and indignant at the very thought of Will captaining their ship.

"*Temporarily*," Will added. "All right?"

Uneasily, the two men agreed. Everyone else let out a relieved sigh. They had a plan – and a temporary peace.

A short time later, several longboats neared the deserted shore, while back on the *Black Pearl*, Elizabeth, Will, Tai Huang and a small contingent of pirates waited uneasily. From his spot at the front of one of the boats, Jack made out something large lying on the beach. While his eyes grew wide, his mouth remained shut.

The landing party leaped into the surf and pulled the boats up on the beach. Pintel and Ragetti, who had finally managed to free themselves of the mast, floundered through the waves. Suddenly, Pintel noticed the thing Jack had seen.

"Criminy!" he exclaimed.

Jack and Barbossa climbed out of the boats, and together, all the pirates walked cautiously along the sand towards the object. It looked like a giant whale.

A few steps closer, and all the men knew exactly what it was.

It was the Kraken!

The gigantic sea monster lay dead on the beach. Its tentacles were splayed out, its enormous eyes staring at nothing.

Jack Sparrow's most feared nightmare, the creature that had chased him across the Seven Seas and finally killed him, was now dead, while *he* had returned to the living.

Unsure of how to react, Jack moved even closer, approaching the creature with something like awe.

Pintel found a stick of driftwood lying nearby. Picking it up, he poked the Kraken, jumping back quickly just in case.

"Careful!" Ragetti said.

"Ahh, not so tough now, are you?" Pintel jeered. "Stupid fish! Serves you right!"

"Hello! I bet folk would pay a shilling to see this!" said Ragetti. "And a second shilling for a sketch of 'em sitting atop!"

"Kraken slayers!" Pintel said with glee. "We could carve mini'ture Krakens out of coconut and sell those, too! We could give 'em a slice as a souvenir!"

Ignoring the pirates' inane banter, Jack stepped closer to the Kraken. If he hadn't seen it with his own two eyes, he would not have believed it. It was almost . . . sad. As far as he knew, the Kraken had been the last of its kind. And here it lay, alone, nothing but a pile of rubbery tentacles where there had once been an awesome monster.

"Still thinking of running, Jack?" Barbossa said softly from behind him. "Think you can outrun the world? The problem of being the last of anything: by and by, there be none left at all."

"Sometimes things come back," Jack said. "We're living proof, mate."

"Aye, but that's a gamble with long odds, ain't it?" Barbossa answered. "There's no guarantee of coming back. But passing on – that's dead certain."

Jack considered that for a long moment. He didn't want to think about his own death right now, so soon after having escaped the last one.

"The world used to be a bigger place," Barbossa said.

"It's still the same size," Jack answered softly. "There's just less in it." He sighed heavily. It seemed he had no choice. "Summoning the Brethren Court, is it?"

"Our only hope."

"That's sad commentary, in and of itself," Jack said softly.

Moments later, the landing party climbed up to the freshwater spring, ducking through undergrowth and weaving around palm trees. The spring bubbled up from the ground into a clear pool surrounded by sharp rocks and black sand.

Despite his short stature, Marty was the first to reach the well. As he eagerly stooped down to drink, he noticed something floating in the pool. He leaned forward to take a closer look – and then jumped back with a horrified cry.

There was a dead body in the water.

Barbossa brought a handful of the water to his mouth, tasted it and spat it right back out.

"Poisoned," he stated. "Fouled by the body."

Two of the pirates crouched down and turned the body face up. Barbossa was shocked to realize that he recognized it. It was Steng – the man who had posed as one of Sao Feng's pirates back in Singapore! A wooden fid, like the spike Sao Feng had threatened Will with, was driven through one eye.

A terrible suspicion gripped Barbossa.

Almost immediately, as if in answer to his fears, a shout came from the direction of the beach. The pirates all rushed back to the shore to find Ragetti pointing frantically out to sea.

The *Black Pearl* was no longer alone in the water. Another ship was floating beside her. Barbossa quickly recognized the Chinese fighting ship. It was Sao Feng's *Empress*.

An ominous click sounded from behind them. Jack and Barbossa turned to find Tai Huang and his men training pistols on them. Unlike their own waterlogged weapons, they knew that these pistols would actually work when fired. And Tai Huang's pirates would not hesitate to use them.

Both men let out a heavy sigh. Luck was not on their side.

They had been betrayed.

Chapter 10

As the landing party was escorted back on board the *Pearl*, Barbossa and Jack could see that the pirates loyal to them had been shackled and stripped of their weapons. A swarm of Chinese pirates had taken over the ship, far too many to fight.

But at least someone had tried to resist. Elizabeth Swann stood chained between two guards who showed the unfortunate after-effects of trying to fight her. One had a bloody lip; the other had an eye that was swelling up. Neither looked pleased.

At almost the exact same moment, Barbossa and Jack spotted Sao Feng. Still dressed in the dark robe he had donned in Singapore, the Pirate Lord cut a striking figure against the blue sky. His eyes calm and his expression smug, he now strolled across the deck towards them.

"Sao Feng," Barbossa said, narrowing his eyes. "You showing up here, 'tis truly a remarkable coincidence."

"Fortune smiles upon those prepared to meet its gaze," Sao Feng answered wisely. He moved closer to Jack, who had quietly slid behind Barbossa and was now trying – rather unsuccessfully – to be as inconspicuous as possible. "Jack Sparrow. You paid me great insult, once."

Without warning, he punched Jack in the face, sending the pirate's hat flying. Jack staggered back and nearly fell, but, flailing his arms, he managed to stay on his feet. He bent and picked up his hat, putting it back on his head.

"So now we can call it square," Jack said, his eyebrows rising in hope.

"Hardly," Sao Feng spat.

At that moment, Will appeared from belowdecks, looking anxious. He quickly took in Jack's bruised jaw and Barbossa's angry glare. Then he saw Elizabeth in chains and hurried over to Sao Feng.

"She's not part of the bargain," Will said. "Release her."

"And what bargain be that?" Barbossa said sharply.

"You heard Captain Turner," Sao Feng said to his men, a hint of mockery in his voice. "Release her."

"*Captain* Turner?" Jack cried indignantly. How could this upstart whelp be a captain on Jack's own ship?

"Aye," Gibbs said with a gloomy air. "The perfidious rotter led a mutiny against us."

The weathered first mate was right. With the help of Sao Feng's pirates, Will had overthrown Jack's crew and taken over the *Pearl*. Now he planned to take the ship to find the *Dutchman* and rescue his father.

Jack shook his head. "It's always the quiet ones," he muttered.

As the chains dropped away, Elizabeth rubbed her wrists and stared at Will, her expression pained. She would never have guessed that he could betray them all like that.

"Why didn't you tell me you were planning this?" she asked.

"It was my burden to bear," said Will, echoing her own words back at her.

Elizabeth frowned and stood up straighter. If Will had confided in her, perhaps she could have helped him find another way. As it was, he was playing a very dangerous game, trusting all their lives to Sao Feng and his men.

"The only way a pirate can make a profit, these days, is by betraying other pirates," Barbossa said, repeating the words Sao Feng had said back in Singapore. Unfortunately for Barbossa, they had taken on a darker meaning, as *he* was now the one betrayed.

"I can live with that," Sao Feng replied.

"But you've no acrimony toward mutineers?" asked Jack. Jack himself had plenty of acrimony, now that he'd been mutinied against . . . twice.

"He did not mutiny against *me*, did he?" Sao Feng pointed out. No one had ever dared mutiny against the powerful Pirate Lord of Singapore.

"I need the *Pearl*," Will said. "That's the only reason I came on this voyage."

Listening to Will's weak attempt at an explanation for his unfriendly behaviour, a thought suddenly sprang into Jack's mind. "He needs the *Pearl*," Jack said, pointing at Will. Then he turned to Elizabeth. "And you felt guilty." He pointed at Barbossa. "And you and your Brethren Court . . . didn't anyone come to save me just because they missed me?"

Gibbs, Marty and Cotton raised their hands. A moment later, Pintel and Ragetti raised their hands as well. So did 'Jack' the monkey.

Jack moved towards his loyal crew. "I'm standing over there with them."

But before he could get very far, Sao Feng grabbed his arm. "I'm sorry, Jack," he said, not sounding very sorry at all. "But there's an old friend who wants to see you first."

"I'm not certain I can survive any more visits from old friends," Jack said nervously, rubbing his jaw where Sao Feng had punched him.

"Here is our chance to find out," Sao Feng said slyly.

He pointed over Jack's shoulder, and Jack turned to see a very unwelcome sight rounding the island. It was Lord Cutler Beckett's ship, the *Endeavour*. Jack stifled a groan. He had managed to elude the East India Trading Company for a long time . . . but no longer. He was trapped.

Chapter 11

Jack Sparrow had found himself in his fair share of sticky situations. Now it appeared he was in yet another one.

After being unceremoniously dragged away by Sao Feng's guards, he found himself thrown into the captain's cabin of the *Endeavour*. Lord Cutler Beckett, his white wig perfectly coiffed, stood at the window, staring out at the sea.

The guards dropped all of Jack's things on the table, including his Compass. With a brief nod, Lord Beckett dismissed the guards, leaving him alone with Jack. He remained at the window, his eyes now trained on the *Pearl*, as Jack glanced around the room.

"Remarkable," Beckett mused. "When last I saw that ship, it was on fire and sinking beneath the waves. I fully expected that to be the last I saw of it."

As he spoke, Jack began to tiptoe around the room, peering into cabinets and boxes.

"Close your eyes and pretend it's all a bad dream," Jack said flippantly. "That's how I get by."

"You can stop searching, Jack," Beckett said, still without turning around. "It's not here."

Jack froze, then carefully replaced the lid on the jar he'd been peering into.

"'It' being what?" he asked casually.

Beckett turned around then, fixing Jack with a knowing look. "Understand what it is a man wants," he said, "and no amount of knavery and machination makes him any less predictable." Jack still looked confused. "The heart of Davy Jones," Beckett explained. "It's not here. It's safely ensconced aboard the *Flying Dutchman* and therefore unavailable for use as leverage to satisfy your debt to the good Captain."

Jack paused to consider Beckett's news. So the heart wasn't here – but at least he now knew where it was. That, in and of itself, was far more than he had hoped to learn when dragged on to the *Endeavour*. But as for the debt . . . "By my reckoning, that account's been settled," Jack said.

"By your death," Beckett agreed. "And yet, here you are."

Jack considered this and then shrugged. "Yes, here I am," he said. "Painfully aware I am, in fact. Why am I?"

Beckett stepped over to the table and picked up Jack's Compass. He hefted the weight of it in his hands for a moment, then held it up for Jack to see.

"You've brought me this," he said. "I owe you a pardon and a commission." Beckett smiled thinly. He remembered all too clearly the bargain he had struck with Will Turner, although it seemed like a lifetime ago. When he had released Will from prison to search for Jack, he had offered a pardon for Jack in exchange for his Compass. And Beckett was always a man of his word . . .

"So I am offering you a job," Beckett said to Jack. "In the employ of the East India Trading Company. Working for me." His smile grew wider. He loved the idea of having Jack Sparrow under his boot. Forced to work for the very company he hated – the company that aimed to destroy everything that pirates stood for! It was quite the brilliant revenge.

But Jack was not so eager to bargain. He tilted his head and made a tsk-tsking noise. "We've been down that road before, haven't we?" he said. "And we both know how you get when your advances are spurned." He held up his wrist, where the burn of a branding iron had left its mark.

Beckett's face went cold with anger. Sparrow was impossible. "I had contracted you to deliver cargo on my behalf," he said, trying to keep the anger out of his voice. "You chose to liberate it."

"People aren't cargo, mate," Jack said.

Beckett shook his head. "You haven't changed," he said. "Our business is concluded. Enjoy the gallows."

"I've been," Jack said flippantly. "Once you've taken in the view, there's not much else to it." His voice shifted, becoming more serious. "But the fact is, I *have* changed. If you'll entertain for a moment a counter-proposal." He produced a piece of eight from a hidden pocket and rolled it meaningfully between his fingers. "The Brethren Court."

Beckett pulled out his own piece of eight and imitated Jack's gesture, scoffing.

"I am already aware of the Brethren Court and that it is meeting," he sneered.

"But you don't know where, do you?" said Jack. "I do." He flipped the coin onto the table, where it spun in a circle for a moment. Beckett watched the coin, as if hypnotized.

"That's the offer on the table," Jack said. "You square things with Jones on my behalf, assure me of my freedom, and in exchange . . ." Jack Sparrow smiled. "I will lead you to Shipwreck Cove and deliver up all the Pirate Lords on a silver platter."

Back aboard the *Black Pearl*, things were not going quite the way Will had expected. The ship was already full of Sao Feng's pirates, and as he watched, a crew of sailors from the *Endeavour* came aboard as well. They were led by Beckett's aide, Mercer. It was he who had arranged a deal between Sao Feng and the East India Trading Company after overhearing the Lord's secret conversation with Will back in Singapore. The very same deal that was now due to be completed.

Quickly, Mercer's men began to spread out across the ship, taking positions and preparing to sail. As Sao Feng and Will watched, one of the men took the wheel from Tai Huang. Will glanced at Sao Feng in confusion. This was not part of *their* deal.

"My men are crew enough," Sao Feng objected, apparently confused as well.

"Company ship, company crew," Mercer said with an oily smile.

"You agreed," Will said, turning to Sao Feng. "The *Black Pearl* was to be mine."

"And so it was," Sao Feng said. He gestured to one of his crew, who punched Will from behind, knocking the wind out of him. Will collapsed to the deck, gasping, as two other men shackled his arms.

Sao Feng turned to Mercer, his betrayal of Will neatly taken care of. "Lord Beckett agreed," he said, "the *Black Pearl* was to be *mine*."

Mercer smiled again. "And so it was," he echoed. Sao Feng stiffened. He could see now that he was going to be betrayed in turn. Shaking his head, Mercer added, "Lord Beckett wouldn't give up the one ship as might prove a match for the *Dutchman*, would he?"

The Pirate Lord looked around at the East India Trading Company men, all of them armed. They outnumbered his own men and looked ready to fight. If he started a battle here, there was every chance he could lose – and then he'd lose his deal with Lord Beckett as well. He'd be back to being another pirate in their sights . . . a pirate they would hunt down and kill without mercy.

With a sharp nod, he stepped back, and so did his man at the wheel, turning control over to Mercer. It pained Sao Feng to give up so easily, but he didn't see any other choice. Mercer gave Sao Feng a mocking half-salute and strolled away.

As Sao Feng stood fuming, Barbossa sidled up beside him.

"Shame they're not bound to honour the Code of the Brethren," Barbossa murmured. "Isn't it? Of course, honour's a hard thing to come by, nowadays."

"There is no honour to remaining with the losing side," Sao Feng responded sharply. "Leaving it for the winning side . . . that's just good business."

"The losing side, says *you*," Barbossa observed.

"They have the *Dutchman*," Sao Feng said. "And what do the Brethren have?" Nothing that could fight such a powerful ship, he was sure. And yet . . . if they did . . .

Barbossa leaned in closer. "We have . . . Calypso."

Sao Feng's eyes widened in surprise. Every pirate worth his salt had heard of the ancient sea goddess. Everyone knew the stories of how she had once ruled the ocean with her powerful magic. And every Pirate Lord could tell the tale of the very first Brethren Court, when the nine original Pirate Lords had captured and bound Calypso in human form. They had used a magic even more ancient than her own, taming her wild fury and bringing the sea under their command.

But surely those were just stories. Surely there wasn't a real Calypso – an actual goddess, trapped as a human. Or was there? Sao Feng's eyes darted across the ship towards the one woman on board – Elizabeth. Barbossa did not fail to notice.

"Calypso," Sao Feng said hesitantly. "An old legend."

"No," said Barbossa, his voice growing thick. "The goddess herself, bound in human form . . . fury or favour, you not be knowing . . . but when the mood strikes her, and its her favour she bestows upon a lucky sailor . . . well, you've heard – legendary."

Sao Feng had heard the tales. In the old days, when she was still powerful, if Calypso took a liking to a man of the sea, everything would go his way. The lucky captain who won her love would find only fair weather and smooth seas. He could easily be master of the ocean with the help of a goddess like her.

"There was a time when the seas be untamed, the world a rougher place, and a sailor made his own fate," Barbossa continued. He paused, letting his words sink in. Then he leaned towards Sao Feng again. "I aim to bring it back," he said. "And for that, I need the Brethren Court." With a significant look, he added, "All the Court."

"What are you proposing?" Sao Feng said quietly.

"What be you accepting?" Barbossa asked, suspecting he knew the answer already.

Sao Feng nodded across the ship. "The girl," he said.

Barbossa smiled. His fellow Pirate Lord had fallen for his plan.

From where she stood, Elizabeth had not

been following the conversation. But now, feeling the men's eyes on her, she looked over.

The conversation had caught Will's attention as well. "We give you Elizabeth in exchange for helping us escape?" he asked, horrified.

Sao Feng nodded.

"No," Barbossa said, pretending to care for Elizabeth's safety. "No. Out of the question."

"It was not a question," Sao Feng said.

"Done," said Elizabeth.

The others gaped.

"What?" Will cried out. "Not done!"

"You've put us in these straits," Elizabeth said to him, her anger finally spilling over. "If this frees us, then . . . done." She lifted her chin and stared bravely at Sao Feng.

"No," Will protested, his heart breaking. He had lost the *Pearl* and his one chance to rescue his father. Did he now have to lose his one true love as well?

"My choice," Elizabeth insisted. "My choice alone."

"Elizabeth, they are pirates," Will said.

She gave him a scathing look. "I've had more than enough experience dealing with pirates," she said. Her meaning was clear . . . pirates like *you*. She couldn't trust him any more than any other pirate . . . probably less so than many in fact.

Sao Feng smiled broadly. "I am pleased–" he began, reaching out to take her arm. Elizabeth yanked it away. She had agreed to go with him, but nothing else. To her surprise, he held up his hands and bowed respectfully. "My apologies," he said. "I know I must earn your favour."

Elizabeth didn't know what he meant by that, but she squared her shoulders and tried to look regal. "That's right," she said. "You do."

"Then we have an accord?" Barbossa asked.

"Agreed," Sao Feng said, shaking Barbossa's hand. He would tell his men to fight the East India Trading Company sailors and steal the *Pearl* back for Barbossa and for Jack's men. He would help them to convene the Brethren Court.

In exchange, Elizabeth would sail away with him on the *Empress*.

Chapter 12

Meanwhile, in the captain's cabin of the *Endeavour*, Jack Sparrow paced back and forth, his hands gesturing wildly. He was outlining the terms of an agreement between himself and Lord Beckett.

Through narrow and guarded eyes, Beckett took in the scene. He had learned from past experience to be wary of any plans that came from the peculiar and often devious mind of Jack Sparrow.

"You can have Barbossa," Jack said, counting on his fingers. "The belligerent homunculus and his friend with the wooden eye, both. And Turner. Especially Turner."

Beckett tapped his fingers together, noticing a particular person Jack did *not* mention. "And what becomes of Miss Swann?" he asked.

"The rest go with me aboard the *Pearl*," Jack answered, "and I will lead you to Shipwreck

Cove. Do we have an accord?"

Lord Beckett smiled at Jack's outstretched hand. But he did not shake it. Instead, he ran his fingers over the objects on the table and picked up the Compass again. "Jack," he said, "remember, I have this wonderful Compass that points to whatever I want."

"Points to what you want *most*," Jack noted. "And that's not the Brethren Court, is it?"

"No?" Beckett asked. "Then what is, Jack?"

"Me," said Jack. "Dead."

Beckett stared at him. Jack waved towards the Compass and gave a small bow, as if to say 'try it'. Beckett flipped open the Compass and looked down at the needle. Sure enough, it was pointing directly at Jack. Beckett scowled.

Jack did a small sideways dance and the needle followed him across the cabin.

Curse Jack Sparrow! He was right. What Beckett wanted most in the world was to see Sparrow dead.

Which meant the Compass was utterly useless to him. He threw it back at Jack, who caught it neatly in his hands. Beckett could wait. Jack could be useful for a short while, and then he could be just as dead later on, after the Pirate Lords were all captured.

Or . . . there was another option. Beckett raised his head. "It occurs: if I got what I wanted most, then wouldn't what I wanted second most become the thing I wanted most?" He took an ominous step toward Jack. "With you dead, I can find . . . Shipwreck Cove, was it? On my own." He took another step, his face dark. "Cut out the middleman, as it were . . . literally."

Jack stepped back, talking quickly. "Then you'll arrive at the cove, find it's a stronghold, nigh impregnable, able to withstand blockade for years, and you'll be wishing, wishing, if only there was someone *inside* to ensure the pirates come *outside*."

Beckett paused and thought for a moment. "And you can accomplish this?"

"I'm Captain Jack Sparrow, mate," Jack said, puffing up his chest. "Do we have an accord?" He stuck out his hand again. Beckett hesitated.

Suddenly, the ship was rocked by a huge explosion. Beckett stumbled forward, and Jack grabbed his hand, shaking it vigorously.

"Done!" Jack cried. He grabbed the rest of his things off the table and ran for the door as cannon fire continued to shake the *Endeavour*, blasting the wooden sides with fierce volleys. Beckett followed close behind.

Up on deck, Jack and Beckett found themselves staring at chaos. Bodies were littered across the deck, and smoke rose from the cannon ports below.

On the horizon, they could see the *Empress* sailing away, while gunshots and blasts of cannon fire still came from the nearby *Pearl*.

Jack was not going to watch his ship sail away – again. He glanced around, looking for a way to get himself over to the *Pearl*. His eyes widened, and he ran over to one of the cannons. Shoving the gunner away, he quickly flipped the cannon over so it was facing towards the *Pearl*. Before Beckett could even react, Jack had wrapped a rope around the cannon wheel, a burning fuse lighter in his hand.

"You're mad!" Beckett exclaimed.

"Thank goodness for that," Jack said. "Or else this would never work." He leaned back and lit the cannon.

Beckett and his crew dived out of the way as the cannon fired, sending an enormous cannonball hurtling seawards, the force causing it to glance off the *Endeavour*'s mast. Dragging behind came Jack, hanging on to the rope for dear life.

On board the *Pearl*, Barbossa saw Jack come flying through the air towards them. He couldn't believe it. Typical Jack. True, he was escaping, but he was doing it in the most dangerous and foolhardy way possible.

Barbossa winced as a series of horrible crashing sounds signalled Jack's arrival. He peeked his eyes open again to see a path of destruction across the deck: a splintered barrel, a ripped sail, scattered gunpowder. And then, standing on the rail, looking completely relaxed and unhurt – Jack Sparrow himself.

"Tell me you didn't miss me!" Jack cried, grinning.

Hopping down from the rail, he spotted Will among the crew. "Send this traitor to the brig," he commanded. Jack's crew set upon Will at once, shackling him and dragging him down to be imprisoned in the depths of the ship.

Jack beamed. All was as it should be. He was back on *his* ship. Just how he liked it.

* * *

Meanwhile, back on the *Endeavour*, Lord Beckett was standing amidst the wreckage, fuming. This was decidedly how he *did not* like it. An officer by the name of Groves came up to him, looking for orders.

"Which ship do we follow?" he asked, his face pale and ashen.

"Signal the *Dutchman*," Beckett said. "We follow the *Pearl*." He glanced up at the mast, which had cracked from the impact of Jack's cannonball. "How soon can we have the ship ready to pursue?"

As if in answer, the mast cracked a bit more and then snapped in two, crashing down with the sails billowing out behind it. Beckett knew the *Endeavour* would not be ready to sail again for quite some time. Jack Sparrow had seen to that.

Groves stared after the *Pearl* in admiration, shaking his head. "Do you think he plans it all out," he asked, "or just makes it up as he goes along?"

Chapter 13

Elizabeth Swann was not unused to privilege. After all, she was the daughter of a governor. But what she was not used to was luxury *among pirates*.

Having arrived aboard the *Empress*, Elizabeth now found herself surrounded by opulence and beauty. It was a strange combination in the heart of a pirate's world, and one that caught Elizabeth unawares – neatly putting her at Sao Feng's mercy.

The Pirate Lord's cabin was lit by flickering candlelight, which cast a glow over the shimmering hanging silks and the soft pillows scattered around the floor and on couches. Deep reds and golds added a level of exotic warmth to the cabin.

The room was not the only thing to be decorated. When she had first stepped on the ship, three Chinese maidens had attended to her every need. They had bathed her and dressed her in a traditional Chinese gown made of soft, shining silk.

Now she stood in the middle of the beautiful room waiting for Sao Feng . . . waiting to find out what he wanted from her.

The Pirate Lord entered the room quietly and for a moment stood still, amazed by the vision before him. Elizabeth's eyes sparkled with fire, and her skin glowed in the dim candlelight. The simple Chinese gown she wore made her appear both utterly female and utterly powerful. She looked like . . . a goddess.

Stepping forward, Sao Feng began to recite a verse from the poem 'To Zhang's Dancing': *"Young willow shoots. Touching, brushing, the water. Of the garden pool,"* he said.

He picked up a decanter from a low table and offered Elizabeth a glass of wine. She accepted it uncertainly.

"I admit," she said, "this is not how I expected to be treated."

She had thought she would be a prisoner, perhaps punished for her role in stealing Sao Feng's charts or for getting him into such a mess with the East India Trading Company.

Sao Feng smiled over the rim of his glass.

"No other treatment would be worthy of you . . . Calypso."

Elizabeth froze with the glass at her lips. What was he talking about? "Excuse me?" she said. Was he treating her so well due to some kind of mistaken identity? If so, it probably wouldn't be in her favour to let him know he was wrong.

"Not the name you fancy, I imagine," Sao Feng said, "out of the many that you have . . . but it is what we call you."

"We being who?" Elizabeth asked.

"Whom," Sao Feng corrected her.

"Who," Elizabeth insisted.

He considered the correction for a moment, and then shrugged, moving on. "We of the Brethren Court and our predecessors, who concealed you in this form. Your forgiveness. I lied. Who *imprisoned* you – oh. 'Who'. You were right."

He looked impressed, but Elizabeth was more concerned with the story than her grammatical win.

"Goddess?" she asked.

"You confirm it?" Sao Feng said quickly.

"Confirm what?" Elizabeth asked. "You've told me nothing." She moved to sit on the low red

444

couch, trying to conceal just how little she understood of the situation. Sao Feng followed her.

"The Brethren Court – not I, the first Brethren Court, who . . . whom . . . *whose* decision I would have opposed," stammered Sao Feng. "They bound you in human form, so that the rule of the seas would belong to men, and not . . ."

"Me," Elizabeth said, beginning to understand.

"But one such as you should never be anything less than what you are," Sao Feng said charmingly.

"Pretty speech from a captor," Elizabeth said, tossing her head and causing the extravagant headpiece she wore to slip a bit. She leaned back on the crimson silk and attempted to appear calm. "But words whispered through prison bars lose their charm."

"Can I be blamed for my efforts?" Sao Feng asked, leaning forward. "All men are drawn to the sea. Perilous though it may be." He gazed into her eyes, and she knew he wasn't talking only about the sea.

"Some men offer desire as justification for their crimes," she said softly.

"I offer simply my desire," he answered.

A small smile crossed her lips. "An item of such small value," she teased. "And in return?"

"I would have your gifts, should you choose to give them."

Yes, it was very clear now. Sao Feng had been sorely mistaken. She was not who he thought, nor did she have the powers he needed.

"And if I choose not?" she said, lifting her chin.

"Then I will take your fury," Sao Feng said. He took her shoulders and kissed her.

Surprised, Elizabeth pushed him away. But before she could do or say more, she heard a muffled explosion in the distance.

They both looked up, just as a cannonball blasted into the hull with an enormous crash, sending splinters of wood flying everywhere. Up on deck, there were shouts and screams and the sounds of pirates running to battle stations, pistols blazing. Elizabeth took cover behind a couch as more lead balls slammed into the room. Outside the porthole, the night was dark, and all she could see was fire and flashes of explosions. She had no way of knowing *who* was attacking.

Another explosion rocked the ship. Elizabeth

crawled to her feet and spotted Sao Feng through the smoke. He was lying on the floor, a long, sharp shard of wood buried in his chest.

"Sao Feng?" she cried.

"Here," he gasped. "Please."

He fumbled at his neck, pulling off the rope-knot pendant he always wore. "The Captain's Knot," he murmured. "Take it. So you'll be free! Take it! I must pass it on to the next Brethren Lord."

"Me?" Elizabeth exclaimed, astonished.

"Go in my place to Shipwreck Cove," he said.

"Captain!" a new voice yelled from the hallway. Tai Huang burst through the door, the sound of fighting close behind him. "The ship is taken!" Tai Huang cried. "We cannot–" He stopped short, seeing Elizabeth leaning over Sao Feng.

"Calypso," Sao Feng whispered, his eyes closing as he blacked out in pain and agony. Elizabeth paused, unsure of what to do or say next. Finally, she stood up and turned to Tai Huang, her expression grave.

"What did he tell you?" the Pirate Lord's lieutenant asked.

She held up the rope-knot pendant.

"He made me captain," she said.

Chapter 14

The new Captain of the *Empress* stepped out onto the deck, where bodies lay motionless and cannon smoke drifted through the air along with the moans of wounded pirates. Following close behind her came Tai Huang.

Elizabeth frowned as she finally caught sight of the ship that had attacked them.

It was the *Flying Dutchman*.

The barnacle-encrusted crewmen were swarming up onto the *Empress*, rounding up terrified sailors and shackling them. Elizabeth did not see Davy Jones among them, but suddenly the smoke parted, and she saw someone else she knew striding through it.

It was Admiral James Norrington – a man she had once been betrothed to, but whom she had never wanted to marry. She knew it was he who had stolen the heart of Davy Jones and handed it over to Lord Beckett. In exchange, he had regained his place in the Royal Navy and was a respectable officer once more. In her eyes, however, he had become less respectable for doing so.

"James?" she said, cautiously.

Norrington's eyes widened when he saw her. Of all the people he had expected to find on the ship of the Pirate Lord of Singapore, Elizabeth was certainly not among them.

"Elizabeth!" he cried. Joyfully, he embraced her.

"I heard you were dead!" he said, taking her shoulders and looking her up and down. He didn't dare believe his eyes. But there was no denying it. This was definitely Elizabeth Swann, alive and well despite what Davy Jones had told Governor Swann.

At that very moment, Davy Jones himself arrived on deck and began to inspect a line of trembling sailors. His tentacles twitched and writhed as he eyed the men.

"Who among you do you name as captain?" he barked.

Tai Huang pointed at Elizabeth. Norrington could not have been more surprised if *he* had been named captain. Elizabeth Swann, captain of a Chinese warship? Was it possible?

Despite the evil presence of Jones, Elizabeth stood straight and tall. Her eyes were cold and betrayed not a hint of the emotion Norrington knew she must be feeling. There was no question about it; the woman standing in front of him was no longer a refined governor's daughter – she was a pirate captain through and through.

"Tow the ship," Norrington said, turning his attention back to his own crew. "Take the sailors to the brig."

"You heard the Admiral!" Davy Jones called.

"The Captain may have my quarters," Norrington added, with a low bow to Elizabeth.

"No, thank you, sir," Elizabeth said proudly. "I prefer to remain with my crew."

She moved to follow her fellow pirates, who were being led away to the brig on the *Dutchman*. Norrington stopped her, his eyes pleading.

"Elizabeth, I did not know," he said.

"Know what?" she replied, her voice laced with scorn. "Which side you chose? Now you do."

In the depths of the *Dutchman*, crew members from the *Empress* were locked in different cells.

Elizabeth stepped through into the cold space and flinched as the door clanged shut behind her. She turned to look at the sailor who had escorted her in – a strange-looking man with a rough complexion like coral.

Suddenly, she remembered something. Will's father, Bootstrap Bill, was a crewman on the *Dutchman*. If she could find him, maybe he could help them escape.

"Bootstrap?" she asked the sailor who had locked her in.

The man just cackled and walked away. Either it wasn't him, or he wasn't going to help. A short way down the passage, a barnacle-covered seaman was mopping the floor. Elizabeth pressed her face to the bars and called softly: "Bootstrap? Bill Turner?"

She got nothing but a grunt in response. With a sigh, Elizabeth slumped down with her back against the wall. It was no use. She couldn't go searching for Will's father – she was trapped in this cell. She'd have to wait and try the next crewman who went past.

Suddenly, a pair of eyes opened in the hull next to her.

"You know my name!" croaked a voice.

Elizabeth jumped and scrambled away. She stared at the hull in shock. There was a man embedded in the wood of the ship! He was barely human any more. Only his face seemed capable of movement.

But this must be Bill Turner, Will's father. She felt a pang of sadness for Will, that his father had been reduced to such an existence.

"I know your son," she said gently. "Will Turner."

Bootstrap's face lit up. "William! He's all right?" he asked. Elizabeth nodded. She thought it kindest to leave out the fact that, at that very moment, his son was probably locked up in the *Pearl*'s brig.

"He made it!" Bootstrap said in a wondering voice. "He's alive. Hah! And now he's sent you to tell me that he's coming to get me. He promised. God's wounds, he's on his way!"

Elizabeth's heart ached for the poor man, and for Will. She knew that Will had only tried to steal the *Pearl* because he was desperate to save his father. But now, looking at what had become of Bootstrap, she knew it had all been for naught.

There was no way to save the man. He was but wood and sea life.

"Yes," she said aloud, trying to sound encouraging. "Will is alive, and – he wants to help you." That much was true. She couldn't exactly say that he was on his way, but if he could be, she knew he would.

But it was too late. The hope was fading from Bootstrap's eyes. A look of despair crept across his face instead. "No," Bootstrap muttered. "He can't come. He won't come."

"I don't know how," Elizabeth admitted, "but he will try, I am sure. You're . . . his father."

Bootstrap studied her with sad eyes. "I know you," the old pirate said. "He spoke of you. Elizabeth."

"Yes," Elizabeth said, a little surprised that he remembered her name.

"He can't save me," Bootstrap said. "He won't. Because of you."

"Me?"

"You're Elizabeth," he said.

There was a long pause before Bootstrap snapped back to attention. "If Jones be slain," he said, "he who slays him takes his place. Captain.

Forever." Seeing the look of horror on her face, he added, "Every man before the mast knows that, Elizabeth! The *Dutchman* must have a captain."

"I see–" Elizabeth said, finally understanding.

"If he saves me . . . he loses you."

"Yes," she said quietly.

"He won't pick me," Bootstrap said shrewdly. "*I* wouldn't pick me. The *Dutchman* must have a captain."

"You said that," Elizabeth pointed out. His words were starting to blur together, as if he were losing his train of thought.

Bootstrap nodded, and his features began to fade back into the hull of the ship. His voice grew fainter as he said, "Tell him – don't come! Tell him – stay away! Can you tell him? It's too late. I'm part of the ship. The crew."

His eyes closed, and he went still. Now he looked merely like a carving, a wooden extension of the ship. The man Will knew as his father was no more – and now Elizabeth would have to bear the news in silence.

Chapter 15

In another part of the ocean, not too far away, the *Endeavour*'s repairs were finally done and the ship was in pursuit of the *Black Pearl*. Lord Beckett stood on deck, staring out to sea, as Greitzer, one of his lieutenants, scanned the horizon with a spyglass.

Suddenly Beckett spotted movement in the far distance. He squinted and then turned to the lieutenant.

"Glass," he demanded curtly.

Greitzer handed over the spyglass and Beckett peered through it.

Strangely, the movement seemed to consist of a flock of birds congregating around something floating on the water.

Beckett ordered the ship to head in that direction.

As the *Endeavour* drew closer, the birds' cries

grew louder and louder. The tower of birds stretched up into the sky, and their wings flapped as they circled and dived towards the floating object.

It was a dead body. Beckett's lip curled when he saw that it was one of his own men. The bloated, pale shape had been lashed to two barrels to ensure that it floated. This was no accident. This man had not merely been tossed overboard; he had been left floating . . . as a sign.

Beckett ordered the body hauled onto the deck, although he daintily stayed out of the way of the corpse. Further investigation revealed a rum bottle on the man with a note inside.

It bore the symbol of the East India Trading Company.

Beckett smiled.

"Sir," interrupted Greitzer, pointing at the distant horizon. Nearly out of sight, but still visible, there was another tower of circling birds. Someone was most definitely leaving a trail for them . . . a path leading straight to the *Black Pearl*.

"Like bread crumbs," Beckett mused. "Ghastly." He indicated the note. "And we are meant to follow. Adjust course, Lieutenant."

* * *

Night had fallen. On board the *Pearl*, a shadowy figure crouched by the rail, tying another dead body to a barrel. With a heave, he began to lift it up to push it overboard.

But then a voice spoke up from behind him, stilling his actions.

"I knew the brig wouldn't hold you," said Jack.

Will Turner dropped the body and whirled around. He reached for his sword, but Jack flapped his hands casually.

"Hold on, William," he said. "Do you notice anything? Or, rather, do you not notice anything? Or, rather, do you notice something that is not there to be noticed?"

Will blinked, sorting through the rather jumbled and incoherent series of questions. "You haven't raised an alarm," he said.

"That's odd, isn't it?" Jack said. He studied the body and the barrel that Will had been lashing together. "But not so odd as this."

"I'm leaving a trail," Will admitted. "For Beckett."

"And you came up with this plan yourself?" Jack asked.

Will nodded uncertainly.

Jack was impressed, despite himself. It was a high-quality plan, full of piratey backstabbing and skulduggery. Not the typical style for young Mr Turner.

"Hmm," Jack said. "What do you intend to do, once you've given up the location of the Brethren?"

"Ask Beckett to free my father."

Jack snorted. "Now, *that* sounds like a plan you'd come up with. You couldn't trust Beckett to keep that bargain even if you shook on it; he certainly won't if you've already given him what he wants." He scrutinized Will. "You know what it will take."

"Killing Jones," Will admitted with a sigh.

"And you know the cost," Jack said. "Conveying the spirits of those that died at sea, not stepping foot on land but once every ten years . . ."

Will slumped. He knew it was all true. He knew that saving his father meant condemning himself to an immortal lifetime as the *Dutchman's* captain. He knew that it meant he could never be with Elizabeth.

"I'm losing her, Jack," Will said unhappily. "Every step I make for my father . . . is a step away from Elizabeth."

For so long, all he had wanted was her affection. For ten years he waited for a sign that she could care for him. And then Jack had arrived, and despite the rather dramatic adventure that followed, it had been worth it. Elizabeth had opened her heart. And now all of that felt so terribly far away. Then he remembered the man standing beside him. In a low voice, he added, "She was willing to do anything to save you."

"From the fate she consigned me," Jack pointed out.

"She felt terrible about killing you," Will countered.

"Yes, she's a prize, that one," Jack said, rolling his eyes. Studying Will, a thought came to mind. Perhaps he could make all of this work to *his* advantage. "What if there was a way to avoid making the choice at all?" he asked, his eyes gleaming. "Were someone else to dispatch Jones . . . that would free your father, just as sure as if you had done it yourself."

"Who?" Will asked, confused.

Jack cocked his head. Seeing Will's confused expression, Jack spread his arms and made a 'tada!' gesture.

"You?" Will said with immense surprise. "Last I knew, you were desperate to *avoid* service aboard the *Dutchman*."

Jack shrugged. "Death has a way of reshuffling one's priorities," he observed. "I know what awaits me in the world beyond this one. It is not a place I intend to revisit – ever." And plus, being captain on the *Dutchman* would be quite a different story from serving *under* Davy Jones.

Jack Sparrow leaned forward, his excitement growing as his plan took shape. "I get aboard the *Dutchman*," he outlined eagerly, "I find the chest, I stab the beating thing. Your father goes free from his debt, you are free to be with your charming murderess and I am free to sail the seas forever." He grinned. It really was a rather fantastic plan.

"You'll have to perform Jones's duty," Will pointed out, not quite as taken by the idea.

"So not quite free, then . . . but immortal has to count for something."

Will rubbed his head, debating. Sparrow

was far from the most reliable of allies. Still . . .

"How can I trust you, Jack?" he asked.

"Trust is an elusive thing," Jack said, "but he needs must go when the devil drives, eh?" He pushed something into Will's hands. Will glanced down and saw Jack's famous Compass. Jack continued, "Here. Be sure to give Davy Jones my regards."

Will looked up again, puzzled, but his expression turned quickly to surprise as Jack shoved him over the side of the ship.

With a huge splash, Will landed in the water. A moment later, the barrel and the body lashed to it splashed down right beside him. Will paddled over and clung to the barrel.

From above, Jack leaned over the rail with a broad smile. He waved cheerfully and disappeared.

Will sighed. As usual, Jack was following his own plan, and Will had no choice but to go along with it. Around him, the dark water slapped the barrel and his body, while above, a pale moon barely cut through the clouds.

It was going to be a very long night.

Chapter 16

On another part of the ocean, Elizabeth Swann found herself in darkness, too. Hers, however, was quite a bit drier. She was curled in a corner of a cell in the *Dutchman*'s brig. The barnacled ship sailed smoothly through calm seas, towing the *Empress* behind it.

Suddenly she heard the scrape of metal against metal. Her eyes flew open, and she saw her jail door slowly opening. Was it one of the *Dutchman*'s crew? She shuddered at the thought of one of the part-ocean-creature sailors creeping into her cell in the dark.

But then a lantern flickered in the darkness, and Elizabeth recognized the voice of James Norrington.

"Be quiet," he whispered. "This way. Hurry." He beckoned urgently.

Elizabeth scrambled to her feet and saw

that her crew members had been freed as well. They looked to her for guidance, and she nodded. Silently, they continued to creep past, scurrying towards the deck on catlike feet.

"What are you doing?" Elizabeth whispered to Norrington.

He met her eyes. "Choosing a side," he answered.

She gazed back at him, then nodded. He led the way along the passage, Elizabeth following closely. Behind them, the cell door hung open.

And inside the cell . . . a pair of eyes opened in the hull of the ship. Bootstrap Bill saw the open door and the now empty cell. With great effort, he detached himself from the wood, stepping forward. His mind cloudy, he shuffled out and along the passage to the deck.

Up on the stern balcony, Norrington led the way to the towrope that connected the *Dutchman* to the *Empress*. Elizabeth's crew immediately knew what they had to do. One by one, they slung themselves over the edge and began to crawl along the line. Hand over hand, they pulled themselves back to their own ship.

"Quickly now," Norrington whispered. He

turned to Elizabeth. "Do not go to Shipwreck Cove," he urged. "Beckett knows of the meeting of the Brethren. I fear there is a traitor among them."

Elizabeth shook her head, her eyes sad. "It is too late to earn my forgiveness," she said.

"I do not ask it," Norrington said. He knew there was no way to absolve himself of his mistakes, even though he had only been trying to be a good soldier. He only wished he could make Elizabeth understand – through it all his love for her had never wavered, despite her rather unfortunate inclination towards the pirate life.

Staring at the man before her, Elizabeth saw the regret and emotion in his eyes. Finally, she believed him. She saw that he meant what he said; that he knew what he had done, and that he was sorry for it.

"Come with us," she said.

Norrington hesitated.

"James. Come with me," Elizabeth said, taking his hand. Norrington was torn. He wanted very much to go with her, although it went against his nature as a member of the Royal Navy . . . but so did letting them escape in the first place. He was sure to be in grave trouble once his treachery was discovered. And he had chosen Elizabeth's side . . . the pirates' side . . . perhaps he *should* go with her . . .

He glanced at the line of Chinese sailors swinging across to their ship. Nearly all of them had made it now.

"Who goes there?" a voice said from the darkness. A figure shuffled towards them.

Norrington whirled and drew his sword. The moment was broken. He knew where he had to stand; where he would always stand.

"Go!" he cried to her. "I will follow."

"You're lying," Elizabeth said. She knew him well enough to know that.

Norrington looked into her eyes. "Our destinies have been entwined, Elizabeth," he said. "But never joined."

Impulsively, he took her in his arms and kissed her. Only for a moment – and then he pushed her back towards the rope.

"Go! Now!" he shouted.

Unwillingly, Elizabeth stepped over the rail and took the rope. She was the Captain of the *Empress* now. Her crew needed her. But James might need her, too. With one last look over her shoulder, Elizabeth began to shimmy out across the open water. She could only hope that Norrington would follow shortly.

Meanwhile, on the *Dutchman*, the shuffling figure had stepped into the circle of light cast by the lantern. It was Bootstrap Bill.

The old pirate wasn't sure what was going on. His mind was fuzzy and dim, with vague thoughts and memories flitting through it. Through the fog of confusion, his eyes made out a recognizable figure – Elizabeth, his son's beloved. She was crawling away along a towrope. A small part of his brain nagged at him. He knew that wasn't right. The crew of the *Dutchman* stayed with the *Dutchman* forever.

"No one leaves the ship," Bootstrap said.

"Stand down," Norrington said. "That's an order."

"Part of the crew," Bootstrap mumbled. "Part of the ship."

Norrington began to realize that this wasn't an ordinary sailor. This one was much further gone than the others; he'd become so much a part of the ship that he'd begun to lose his true self. That made him unpredictable.

"Steady, man," Norrington said, trying to make his voice sound soothing and calm.

But it was too late. "All hands!" Bootstrap bellowed in a surprisingly loud voice. "All hands! Prisoner escape, all hands!"

Crewmen quickly appeared from all directions, racing across the deck.

Elizabeth was halfway across the rope, but she heard the commotion and looked back. She saw the *Dutchman*'s sailors descending on Norrington.

"James!" she cried. She couldn't leave him in such a dire situation. She started to crawl back to the *Dutchman*.

But Norrington saw what she was doing, drew his pistol and fired through the towline. It snapped apart, sending the free rope swinging back to the *Empress* and splashing Elizabeth into the water.

Spluttering, she drew herself up along the rope, pulling herself hand over hand up to the deck of her ship. The *Empress* was already speeding away into the dark, leaving the *Dutchman* in her wake.

Chapter 17

While the *Empress* was pulling further away from danger, the *Black Pearl* was drawing closer to it.

In the middle of a vast, empty sea floated a strangely shaped island: Shipwreck Island. It was hollow, with a round water cove in the centre. It was here the Brethren Court would meet.

The *Black Pearl* was fast approaching the island. Gibbs stood behind Cotton at the wheel, intently watching the seas.

"Look alive, and keep a careful eye!" he instructed Cotton. "Not for nothing it's called Shipwreck Island, where lies Shipwreck Cove and Shipwreck City!"

Jack tilted back his hat and looked over at them. "You know," he said, "for all that pirates are clever clogs capable of the most underhand and duplicitous thinking . . . we are an unimaginative lot when it comes to naming things."

"Aye," Gibbs agreed.

"Step out, Mister Cotton," said Jack, moving to take the wheel himself. "There's some dangerous cross tides ahead that will prove a trick to navigate."

Dusk was falling as the *Pearl* sailed straight towards a towering cliff face. Pirates gathered along the rail, looking worried. Surely Jack was sailing them right into the rocks.

But at the last moment, they came around a giant rock formation and spied a hidden sea tunnel in the rocks ahead of them. The crew breathed a sigh of relief.

Slowly the ship manoeuvred through the tunnel, towards a light burning in the distance. At long last, they emerged from the rocky channel into a wide cove, surrounded on all sides by towering cliff walls. In the centre was Shipwreck City, a town constructed entirely of broken, derelict ships all loosely connected to each other. From a distance, it looked to be naught but flotsam, jetsam and debris. It seemed impossible that amidst the wreckage, there could be a meeting place worthy of the Brethren Court. However, there was something rather majestic about the island – as though it, like pirates themselves, was far more powerful than appearances would have one believe.

Moored around the island were a host of various pirate ships from all over the world. The other Pirate Lords had already arrived.

Pintel and Ragetti stared out, astonished.

"Look at them all!" Pintel exclaimed.

"There's not been a gathering like this in our lifetime," Barbossa said, looking pleased with himself.

Jack sighed. "And I owe all of them money."

Meanwhile, some distance away, Will had been found and dragged aboard the *Endeavour*. He now stood soaking wet and manacled, unsure of what would happen next. Lord Beckett's ship and the *Dutchman* were moored alongside each other as Beckett planned his next move. Davy Jones had been summoned to the deck of the *Endeavour*, much to his extreme displeasure.

"I believe you know each other," Beckett said to Davy Jones.

Jones smirked. "Come to risk your luck against me again, have you?" the man asked, referring to their previous encounter, when Will bested him at a game of Liar's Dice.

"No," Will said. "To join you. Well, him." He nodded at Beckett.

"Tell him what you told me," Lord Beckett said.

Will took a deep breath. The manacles weighed heavily on his hands, and he was tired from a long night drifting at sea and fighting off birds who had found him as tempting as the dead body beside him. But he had a mission, and he would see it through. "Barbossa has summoned the Brethren Court for a purpose. To free someone named Calypso."

Jones stiffened, a new look twisting his features – fear. Lord Beckett nodded, as if he had expected that.

"Calypso," Beckett repeated significantly.

"No," Jones said. "They can't. The Heathen Gods care for nothing and no one but themselves, and she is the worst of them. The Brethren were to keep her imprisoned forever; that was the agreement."

Will gave him a scrutinizing look, some of the pieces of the puzzle coming together. *"You* told the first court how to bind her," he realized. "And that's why you cut out your heart—"

Jones slammed his claw down on the table. "*Do not* venture there." He turned to Beckett. "We must stop them," he said urgently. "She will destroy us all."

Lord Beckett nodded slowly, looking thoughtful. "It is more imperative than ever that we find the Brethren Court," he said. "Which presents a problem." He turned to Will. "With you here, *if* it was indeed you who left us the trail—"

"It was," Will insisted.

"—then how will we find them now?" Beckett finished.

"I want your assurances," Will said, trying not to let his anxiety show in his voice. He needed to sound calm and in control of the situation. "Elizabeth will not be harmed."

"Ah," Beckett said. "Elizabeth. Of course." He paused before answering. "The last I knew of Miss Swann, she was Captain of the *Empress*."

"Captive," Will corrected him automatically.

"No, Captain," Beckett repeated.

Will thought about that for a moment, puzzled. "Nonetheless," Will said, shaking off his confusion, "she will not be harmed." He turned to Davy Jones. "And my father goes free."

"You ask much," Jones said, his tentacles writhing.

"I offer much," Will pointed out. He knew that this was his only chance to bargain with them.

"Where is Shipwreck Cove?" Lord Beckett hissed.

"I don't know," Will said.

Jones darted forward, pressing the tip of his claw into Will's chest, and snarling into his face as the tentacles of his beard snaked around Will's neck.

"Then you have nothing we want!" he growled viciously.

But Jones was wrong.

Will looked at Beckett and held up . . . Jack's Compass.

"What is it you want most?" he asked with a smile.

Chapter 18

BOOM! BOOM! BOOM!

The loud sound rang through the chamber of the Brethren Court as Barbossa hammered on the tabletop with a cannonball.

Jack glanced nervously around the room. He had a lot of enemies in here.

The chamber was hidden in the abandoned hull of a derelict ship, with curved spars rising up on either side of them like the ribs of a long-dead prehistoric beast. In the centre of the candlelit room was a large oval table. Eight Pirate Lords were assembled around it, some alone, others guarded by attendants.

Eight swords, one for each Pirate Lord who had arrived, were stabbed into a globe nearby, where the pirates had left them before taking their seats. In theory, this was supposed to be a peaceful gathering . . . in practice, it would be astonishing for Jack Sparrow to escape this room alive.

Lining the walls behind the Lords were their crews, packing the room full of fierce – and fully armed – pirates. While all of them had felt the threat from the East India Trading Company, they'd all had skirmishes with each other in the past, too. Feelings of trust were not running high.

Barbossa continued to bang on the table until silence finally descended upon the room. He gestured to a wooden bowl lined with a red scarf, in the centre of the table. "Your Pieces of Eight, my fellow captains."

Grudgingly, each Pirate Lord stood and dropped an item into the wooden bowl. Pintel, perched on a ledge and peering over the heads of the assembled pirates, noticed that the objects weren't actually silver pieces of eight – they were odds and ends of things one might find on any pirate ship – or busy harbour.

"Those aren't pieces of eight," Pintel objected to Gibbs. "Those are just pieces of junk."

Gibbs nodded. "The original plan was to use coins," he explained, "but when it came time, the first Pirate Lords didn't have a pence between them. But everyone liked 'Nine Pieces of Eight', so the name kind of stuck."

This didn't make a lot of sense to Pintel, but then again, he wasn't a Pirate Lord, so what did he know?

Apart from Barbossa, Jack and the missing Pirate Lord, there were six pirates gathered around the table. Ammand the Corsair was a tall, black-haired pirate who was known as the scourge of the Barbary Coast. Beside him sat Villanueva, a taciturn Spaniard with a bad temper. Captain Chevalle was next, an aristocratic Frenchman with a sneering expression, elegantly attired in brocade with lace cuffs. Fourth was Gentleman Jocard, a former slave turned pirate, whose gleaming black skin and fearsome muscles attracted many stares.

Then there was Mistress Ching, a female Chinese pirate. She was the only woman . . . but she was also one of the most dangerous people in the chamber.

Finally there was Sri Sumbhajee, a serene pirate who had travelled from the Indian Ocean for this meeting. He looked like an innocent, benevolent priest, but he was flanked by two hulking, nasty-looking bodyguards named Akshay and Pusan. He was not a man to upset.

As the Pieces of Eight clattered into the bowl, Mistress Ching lifted her head. "We're missing two," she said alertly.

Villanueva turned and glowered at Jack. "Sparrow," he growled.

Jack cocked his head, considering. If he handed over his Piece of Eight, there would be no more need for him here. Who knew what the others might do to him once they had it. Pirates, were, after all, quite the vengeful lot.

"We're still short one Pirate Lord," Jack pointed out. "I'm content to wait until Sao Feng joins us."

"Sao Feng is not coming," said a voice from the doorway.

Everyone turned to see Elizabeth Swann in full pirate garb, and Tai Huang and another Chinese crewman standing behind her. Jack's mouth dropped open in surprise.

"He named me Captain of the *Empress*," Elizabeth explained, "and passed his lordship on to me."

She started forward, but Tai Huang touched her shoulder to stop her and pointed towards the globe. Elizabeth drew her sword and stabbed it in alongside those of the other Pirate Lords.

"Captain?" Jack squawked indignantly. "*Captain*? They're just *giving* the title away now!"

"What happened to Sao Feng?" demanded Ammand the Corsair.

"She probably killed him," Jack muttered.

"Will you never forgive me?" Elizabeth said to him. Then she turned to answer the Pirate Lords. "We were attacked by the *Flying Dutchman*."

The room erupted in chaos at the mention of the terrible ship.

Jack and Elizabeth could see alarm spreading on the faces of the Pirate Lords.

"*Le monster des profondeures!*" Chevalle cried in dismay. The pirates along the edge were shouting in horror, demanding that they take to the seas and escape before the *Dutchman* found them.

"Listen!" Elizabeth yelled. "Listen to me! Our location has been betrayed! Jones, under the command of Lord Beckett – they are on their way here!"

This news, of course, only led to further uproar.

"And who is this betrayer?" Gentleman Jocard snarled, as if he were ready to strangle the traitor with his bare hands.

"Not likely anyone among us," Barbossa said.

Elizabeth looked around, and something occurred to her. "Where's Will?" she asked Jack.

"Not *among us*," Jack said pointedly.

Barbossa hammered on the table again, calling for quiet. "It does not matter how they found us!" he cried. "The question is, what will we do now that they have?"

"We fight," Elizabeth said in a voice that sounded stronger and braver than she felt.

Pirates all around the room began laughing. Fight the *Flying Dutchman*? Was she crazy? Did she think they were all fools, to throw their lives away so easily?

Mistress Ching stood and spread her hands, offering another option. "Shipwreck Cove is a fortress, a well-supplied fortress," she pointed out. "There is no need to fight, if they cannot get to us."

A murmur of agreement rippled across the chamber. That was true. They could hide for a long time here, wait until the *Dutchman* and the East India Trading Company gave up and left them alone.

"There is a third course," Barbossa said. The room fell silent as everyone turned to look at him. He paused, waiting until he had their full attention. "In another age," he began, "at this very spot, the first Brethren Court captured the sea goddess, and bound her in her bones." He leaned forward intently. "That was a mistake. We tamed the seas for ourselves, aye, yet opened the door for Beckett and his ilk. Better were the days when mastery of the seas came not through bargains struck with eldritch creatures, but by the sweat of a man's brow and the strength of his back alone. And you all know this be true!"

Despite himself, Jack found himself nodding along with Barbossa's impassioned speech. The nasty man made a rather good argument and the other pirates were nodding as well.

"Gentlemen," Barbossa continued in ringing tones, "ladies . . . we must free Calypso."

Silence fell. Everyone was too shocked to react.

The Indian Pirate Lord beckoned to his

bodyguard, Akshay. The large man listened and then stepped forward and spoke.

"Sri Sumbhajee says . . ." Akshay pointed to Barbossa. "He has lost his senses! Do not let him speak any further!"

"Shoot him!" Ammand the Corsair chimed in eagerly.

"Cut out his tongue!" Gentleman Jocard agreed.

"Shoot him and then cut out his tongue!" Jack cried enthusiastically. "And trim that scraggly beard!"

Barbossa glared at him.

Elizabeth spoke up. "Sao Feng would have agreed with Barbossa." She remembered Sao Feng's respect for the sea goddess Calypso, and the way he had looked at her when he thought *she* might be the goddess in human form.

"And I would have agreed with Sao Feng," Villanueva said.

Jocard shook his head vehemently. "Calypso was our enemy then, she will be our enemy now."

"And with far better reason," Chevalle agreed.

Villanueva pulled out his pistol and slammed it on the table. "I would *still* agree with Sao Feng," he growled.

"You threaten me?" Chevalle asked.

"I silence you!" Villanueva shouted. He raised the pistol, but before he could aim, Chevalle punched him in the face, sending the Spaniard sprawling into a group of other pirates. As he fell, the pistol went off, and suddenly the room exploded in chaos. All the pirates began shouting and brawling, pushing and shoving. This was sure to lead to bloodshed and death in no time.

Elizabeth was horrified. "This is madness!" she cried.

"This is politics," said Jack.

Elizabeth could not believe the pirates were fighting at a time like this, when the enemy was so close, and it was so important for them all to stand together. Every time they attacked each other, they were doing Lord Beckett's job for him. If they could not find a way to work together . . . the East India Trading Company was sure to kill them off, one by one.

Barbossa banged the cannonball again,

trying to restore order. But the noise was too loud for anyone to hear him, and the pirates were too angry to stop fighting. Finally Barbossa hurled the cannonball at the globe, which toppled over, sending swords clattering in all directions. That got their attention at last.

"It was the *first* court that imprisoned Calypso!" Barbossa cried. "*We* can be the ones to set her free! And, in her gratitude, she will show us her favour!" He spotted Jack Sparrow shaking his head. "If you have a better alternative, out with it!" Barbossa demanded.

"I agree with Captain Swann," said Jack, astonished to hear those words coming out of his mouth. He stood up, and everyone held their breath waiting to hear what he would say.

"We fight," he said simply.

Barbossa rolled his eyes. "You've always run away from a fight!"

"Calumnious lies!" protested Jack. "I have fought hard and often, in order to run away. We all have, else none of us would be here today, and free." He pointed at Mistress Ching. "We can hole up here for years, but we will have become our own jailers." He turned his accusing finger on

Barbossa. "We can release Calypso, but if she's not in a merciful mood, she controls the seas themselves, so there'd be nothing we could run away to. Or on." He raised his fist in the air. "We must embrace the oldest, noblest tradition of piracy. We must fight – to run away."

At last, a plan the pirates could get behind. Cheers rose from the crews lined against the hull.

Mistress Ching thumped her cane. "And what be the target of this fight, eh?" she demanded.

"Beckett," Elizabeth said instantly.

Chevalle shook his head. "Beckett is naught but a cog. Kill him, another takes his place. Like Jones, the East India Trading Company is immortal. No body to kick or soul to damn."

"Ah," said Jack, "but Jones does have a body, doesn't he? Both literal and figurative." He tapped his hat. "And if we kick either hard enough or enough times . . ."

Jocard realized what he was saying. "The *Dutchman* must always have a captain – but if there *is* no *Dutchman* . . . what matters its captain?"

The pirates cheered louder. The decision

was made. They would take on the East India Trading Company, destroy the *Dutchman* and then flee to the safety of the open seas. Barbossa tried to protest, but he was drowned out.

"War," Elizabeth declared.

With whoops of glee, the pirates all began to move out to their ships. Elizabeth led the way with a smile – finally they were working together, as she'd wanted.

Glowering, Barbossa signalled to Pintel and Ragetti, who gathered up the scarf with the Pieces of Eight and followed him out.

Last to leave was Jack, who was looking more serious than usual. His schemes were starting to come together . . . but he still had no idea if they would work out to his benefit. True, he had convinced the Lords to destroy the *Dutchman*, but if the ship were destroyed, so too were his chances for immortality.

This was going to be tricky.

Chapter 19

The *Black Pearl* sailed proudly out of the tunnel, coming up alongside the *Empress*. Jack saluted Elizabeth, one captain to another, and she felt a shiver of apprehension. A real battle lay ahead of them, one that could make a huge difference to the lives of pirates everywhere . . . maybe even save some of them.

Throngs of pirate ships were lined up, all gathered now outside the safety of Shipwreck Island. On every deck, pirates were sharpening swords and readying cannons, preparing for the inevitable action.

An early morning fog lay across the water. At the helm of the *Pearl*, Marty was peering out, searching for shapes in the mist.

Suddenly, a solitary ship appeared through the grey clouds. Marty snapped to attention. It was the *Endeavour*.

"The enemy is here!" Marty yelled at the top of his lungs. "Let's take 'em!"

The other ships responded with bloodcurdling screams of approval as pirates drew their swords and stood forth confidently. One ship against their whole fleet! They would defeat Lord Beckett in no time! Then they'd show him the same mercy he'd shown all those pirates he'd left dying at the end of a hangman's rope.

But then another ship appeared out of the mist. And another. And another. And another.

The cries of the pirates grew less confident, less strong. Their cheers slowly died out as more and more ships came into view. The fog was lifting – and now they could see the full strength of the East India Trading Company's armada. There were hundreds of ships, all manner of sizes, all heavily armed and ready for battle. The fleet of the Pirate Lords looked small beside their vast numbers.

And then the sea began to boil, and a dark ship rose out of the depths to lead Beckett's fleet – the *Flying Dutchman*. The pirates fell silent as its sails broke the surface, and dread plunged into the heart of every pirate as they beheld the gruesome faces of Davy Jones and his men.

Lord Beckett was standing on the deck of the *Endeavour*, pleased to see the reaction from the pirate ships. He lowered his spyglass and smiled. Jack had delivered on his promise to bring the pirates out. "Well played again, Jack," he murmured. "And what's your next move?"

That's what every pirate was wondering. Thousands of angry eyes turned to him, afraid for their lives. He had voted for this battle – now what did he think they should do?

Jack raised his hands in an 'oops' gesture. "Parlay?" he suggested.

Not too far from the fleets of gathered ships, there was a sandbar, a sparkling white strip of sand that formed a perfect neutral meeting ground.

Jack, Elizabeth and Barbossa stepped out of their longboat and walked along the white sand towards the second longboat, from where Lord Beckett, Davy Jones and Will Turner were approaching. The two threesomes met in the middle and regarded each other.

Barbossa scowled at Will before snarling,

"You be the cur that led these wolves to our door."

"Don't blame Turner," Lord Beckett said archly. "He was but the tool of your betrayal." The aristocrat's eyes slid sideways and he smiled with thin lips. "If you wish to see its grand architect – look to your left."

Elizabeth and Barbossa turned to look at Jack. Acting perplexed, Jack turned and looked to his left as well. Nobody else was there. Jack raised his eyebrows and pressed his hand to his chest.

"Me?" he protested. "My hands are clean in this." He took a look at his hands. "Figuratively," he clarified.

Will agreed. "My actions were my own," he said, "to my own purpose. Jack had nothing to do with it."

"There!" said Jack. "Listen to the tool." Will frowned at him.

"Will," Elizabeth said, and her voice was kinder than the last time he had heard it. He looked into her eyes and saw a new forgiveness, perhaps even sympathy. "I've been aboard the *Dutchman*," she said. "I understand the burden you bear. But I fear that cause is lost." She did not think Bootstrap could be brought back to his true self, and she knew that if Will tried, he would be lost to the *Dutchman* forever.

"No cause is lost if there is but one fool left to fight for it," Will said earnestly. His eyes shifted toward Jack, and Elizabeth noticed. Did they have a plan she didn't know about?

Lord Beckett was not interested in playing games, or in lovers' reunions. He held up Jack's Compass, looking directly at Jack. "If Turner was not acting on your behalf, then how did he come to give me this?"

This evidence was enough to convince Barbossa. Jack must have given Will his Compass so that the East India Trading Company could find Shipwreck Island, the Brethren Court and the Pirate Lords. Jack was the true traitor amongst them.

"You made a deal with me, Jack," Beckett continued, "to deliver the pirates – and here they are. Don't be bashful; step up and claim your reward." He tossed the Compass to Jack, who caught it, looking guilty.

"And what reward does such chicanery fetch these days?" Barbossa wanted to know.

Beckett pointed at Elizabeth, knowing

what an impact his statement would make. "Her," he said.

Will was shocked. Was it true? Had Jack been playing him as well, with his offer to kill Davy Jones? Was it all an elaborate ruse . . . so that Jack could steal off with Elizabeth?

Beckett went on, relishing the revelation. "When the cannon smoke clears and the Brethren are slaughtered, off he sails on the *Pearl*, Elizabeth in his arms, and the blame dead square upon his rival." He flicked his fingers toward Will.

Everyone considered this. Will was shaken; he wasn't sure what to believe. Jack was so untrustworthy, it was easy to picture him betraying them all that way. But it was also possible that Jack had been misleading Beckett.

Elizabeth was also confused. What would Jack want with her? The *Pearl* she understood, but to take her as well? It did not make sense.

Barbossa, on the other hand, was far from confused. The scheme Beckett had outlined sounded like vintage Jack Sparrow to him.

Jack sighed, as if displeased that Lord Beckett had blown his cover so thoroughly.

"Even *if* that was my plan," he said, "and I'm

not admitting to anything – there's not a tinker's chance of it coming off any more." He glanced at Elizabeth, then leaned in closer to her. "Is there?" he asked.

She gave him a puzzled look as Beckett said, "There never was."

Davy Jones finally spoke. "Your debt to me must still be satisfied," he said to Jack, his claw snapping. "One hundred years in servitude aboard the *Dutchman* . . . as a start."

Suddenly things clicked into place in Elizabeth's head. The *Dutchman* – Jack's debt – Will's father – the one fool still willing to fight . . . and Jack's determination never to die again. It all made sense. Of course, Jack wouldn't mind killing Davy Jones in exchange for being captain of the *Dutchman*, with immortality into the bargain. And then Will's father would be freed . . . and Will could still be with her.

She looked over at Will, who saw the dawning realization in her eyes. He nodded very slightly. He knew she'd worked out their plan.

Meanwhile, Jack was arguing with Jones.

"That debt was paid," he insisted. He gave a mocking half-bow to Elizabeth. "With some help."

"You escaped," Jones pointed out.

Jack waved his hand airily. "A technicality," he said.

It was time for Elizabeth to speak up, and she knew just what to say. "There's no better end for Jack Sparrow than bilge rat aboard the *Flying Dutchman*," she announced. "I propose an exchange. Will leaves with us . . . and you can have Jack."

"Done," said Will quickly.

"Not done!" Jack objected.

"Done," agreed Beckett.

"Elizabeth, love, you're condemning me," Jack said. "Again."

Elizabeth lifted her hands, palms up.

With a heavy sigh, Jack started forward towards Beckett. Barbossa grabbed his shoulder and pulled him back around, drawing his sword.

"Blaggard!" the old pirate growled.

Jack darted out of reach, but as he moved, his Piece of Eight dropped to the ground. 'Jack' the monkey leaped off Barbossa's shoulder and seized the piece, bringing it back to Barbossa. The two men regarded each other suspiciously.

Then Jack crossed over to the other side of

the sandbar, as Will passed on his way to Elizabeth's side. When Jack reached Beckett and Jones, Jones seized his shoulder and shoved him down to the sand.

"Do you fear death?" he snarled.

"You have no idea," answered Jack.

Beckett stepped back, looking pleased with himself. "Advise your 'Brethren': you can fight, and all of you will die," he said. "Or you can not fight, in which case only *most* of you will die."

"You have chosen your fate," Elizabeth said. "We will fight . . . and surely *you* will die."

"So be it," Beckett said ominously.

Elizabeth and Will turned their backs on their enemies and strode across the sandbar to the longboat. Behind them, 'Jack' the monkey dropped a Piece of Eight into Barbossa's hand, and, with a grim look, Barbossa closed his fingers around it.

The parlay was over. It was time for the fight to begin.

Chapter 20

Elizabeth was all business as they climbed back on board the *Pearl*. Will and Barbossa followed close behind, both scowling, their minds full of Sparrow.

"We'll need the *Black Pearl* to serve as our flagship and lead the attack," she said.

"Will we, now?" Barbossa said. Elizabeth and Will turned to find him holding up Jack's Piece of Eight.

They both realized what he intended to do – release the goddess Calypso from the spell that bound her. Even though the Pirate Lords had not agreed to it, Barbossa had collected their Pieces of Eight after the meeting. That was all he needed. Now he could do it himself, and no one could stop him. There was only one piece missing.

Barbossa signalled, and suddenly Elizabeth

and Will were surrounded by Chinese pirates, who quickly restrained them.

"We've got to give Jack a chance!" Elizabeth protested. If he could break free and kill Davy Jones, then the pirates might have a hope of defeating the East India Trading Company.

"Apologies," Barbossa said, "but 'tis certain the world we know ends today, and I won't be letting the likes of Cutler Beckett say what comes next." He snorted. "And I won't be pinning my hopes on Jack Sparrow, either. Too long has my fate not been in my own hands. No longer!"

Reaching out, he seized Elizabeth's Piece of Eight. Pirates held her back so there was nothing she could do as he added it to the other Pieces of Eight in the scarf-lined bowl that Ragetti held.

As all nine pieces were brought together, the wind suddenly died. Everyone looked up. The sails were flat, and all the ships were dead in the water.

"Is there an incantation?" Elizabeth asked.

"Aye," Barbossa said, holding the bowl reverently. "The items brought together, done. Has to be performed over water; we lucked out there.

Items burned. And some person must speak the words, 'Calypso, I release you from your human bonds.'"

"Is that it?" Pintel asked.

Barbossa grabbed a rum bottle and smashed it over the pile of objects. He lit the pile, now doused in rum, with a firebrand. Smoke rose instantly from the bowl, with orange flames flickering in its depths.

"Calypso," Barbossa called, "I release you from your human bonds!"

The bowl suddenly burst into flames. The fire shot up in a twisting column, and then just as suddenly it vanished, and all that was left of the Pieces of Eight were decaying bits of ashes and metal.

Then, with a shriek of rage, the ancient sea goddess appeared on deck, her eyes glowing with long-suppressed power. She stretched out her hands as the magic returned to her.

"Calypso!" Will cried. She turned her smouldering eyes to him, her expression confused, as if she were waking from a long sleep. Will spoke urgently; there was only one chance to turn her in the right direction. "When the Brethren

Court first imprisoned you," he said, "who was it that told them how? Who was it that betrayed you?"

"Name him," said Calypso in a voice that rang with authority and old magic.

"Davy Jones," Will said.

She whirled to stare at the *Dutchman*, hate and rage building in her eyes. With a howl of fury, she began to grow, transforming right before them into a towering creature that barely seemed human any more. Her hair rippled even though there was no wind; the deck buckled under her weight as she rose up taller and taller and taller.

Barbossa knelt in front of her. "Calypso," he called. "I come before you as a servant, humble and contrite. I now ask your favour. Spare my self, my ship, my crew – but unleash your fury upon those who dare pretend themselves your masters, or mine!"

The sea goddess barely glanced at him. Her voice boomed across the deck, resonating through the fleet. "FOOL!" she howled.

And then, all at once, she collapsed. In an instant, she was gone. The goddess of the sea had vanished completely.

The pirates, struck speechless, gawked for a moment.

Finally, Will said, "Is *that* it?"

"Why, she's no help at all!" said Pintel. "What now?" he asked Barbossa.

The wind stirred again, and the sails began to fill.

"Nothing," said Barbossa. "Our final hope has failed us."

The pirates fell silent again, this time out of despair. If the legendary pirate Barbossa had given up . . . was there any hope for any of them?

The wind grew stronger, and a pirate's hat was lifted off his head. As it spiralled up and around the mast, Elizabeth watched it, feeling something else stirring inside her.

"It's not over," she said.

Will turned to her, his heart lifting at the sound of the courage in her voice. "Hope is not lost," he agreed. "There's still a fight to be had."

The pirates looked at one another, wary. "There's an armada arrayed against us," Gibbs pointed out. "We've got no chance of winnin'."

Elizabeth looked up at the hat again. The wind was blowing even stronger now, and the hat was whipped about in the air. "Only a fool's chance . . ." she murmured. If Jack could free himself . . . and find his way to the chest . . . and stab the heart of Davy Jones . . . it was a long shot, but if anyone could do it, it was Captain Jack Sparrow. And he'd be counting on them to fight as well. He couldn't do this alone. No pirate could survive on his own for long. That was why they had ships and crews; no matter how much they fought, there was still the Pirate Code, and a pirate's life was lived as part of a team . . . part of a crew. They had to work together, or they would each die alone.

She leaped up onto the rail of the ship, looking out at the crewmen around her. Their eyes turned to her, and she could see how much they wanted to believe.

"Listen to me," she called. "The Brethren will still be looking here, to us, to the *Black Pearl*, to lead. What will they see?" Elizabeth cried. "Frightened bilge rats aboard a derelict ship? No. They will see free men. And freedom!" She raised her fist in the air. "And what the enemy will see is the flash of our cannons. They will hear the ring of our swords. And they will know what we can do, by the sweat of our brows and the strength of our backs – and the courage of our hearts."

She met each pirate's eyes, as they looked up to her with dawning hope on their faces. Finally, she turned to Will.

"Hoist the colours," she said.

"Hoist the colours," Will repeated, low and resolved.

"Hoist the colours," said Gibbs, louder and more defiant.

"Hoist the colours!" cried Pintel, and the cry was picked up by the rest of the crew, a murmur passing from man to man as they moved purposefully to their battle stations.

The wind was picking up into a real gale, blowing stronger and stronger, but fortunately in the direction they needed to go. A storm was brewing, and all aboard knew that Calypso's wrath had not yet passed. They just had to hope that it was turned against their enemies instead of them.

"We've got the wind on our side, boys," Gibbs yelled, "and that's all we need!"

Elizabeth cupped her hands around her

mouth and shouted across to Tai Huang on the deck of the *Empress*.

"Hoist the colours!" she cried once more.

The call spread from ship to ship, along the line, to every pirate in their ragtag fleet. Each Pirate Lord stepped to the rail, ready to fight to the death if need be. This was the final stand – their grand chance to defeat the East India Trading Company once and for all. No longer would they flee from danger; no longer would they hide in secret coves and betray each other for the sake of a little short-lived safety. This time they would fight with honour; this time they would stand together, and whatever happened, it would be a glorious moment in the history of piracy – one that would be remembered through the ages.

Elizabeth drew her sword and pointed it towards the *Endeavour*, leading the way forward into battle . . . and whatever the future held.

"Today," she cried, "we are . . . the **Pirates of the Caribbean!**"